THE

LAST

GIRL SCOUT

NATALIE IRONSIDE

This story is dedicated to the memory of Glenn King, a good friend and a good comrade, murdered by capitalism in June of 2019. He lived in a society.

And to Ren Basel, who once looked at me and thought that they saw something worth saving. I love you, sugar.

"You cannot carry out fundamental change without a certain amount of madness. In this case, it comes from nonconformity, the courage to turn your back on the old formulas, the courage to invent the future. It took the madmen of yesterday for us to be able to act with extreme clarity today. I want to be one of those madmen. We must dare to invent the future."

— Thomas Sankara

DISCLAIMER

Dead Dove. Do Not Eat.

The Last Girl Scout is a story about war, and the horrors of war, and it is a story about fascism, and about the banality of evil and the terrible boredom of pain. This is a story about the ways in which our trauma shapes us, especially the trauma of sexist violence, especially the peculiar forms of sexist violence and exploitation to which transgender women are often subjected. It is my hope that I've managed to treat these sensitive subjects with appropriate tact, rather than as salacious spectacle, but racism, transphobia, and violence, including sexual violence, are themes throughout. If you feel that you can't handle that sort of subject matter, please put this book down and choose another one, and come back to mine when or if you feel you're ready. There's already enough pain in the world without you subjecting yourself to more.

[PART 1]
AMERICAN GHOSTS

[1]

OMENS

"The past lies like a nightmare over the world."

- KARL MARX

**[AD 2259, 194 years post-War;
somewhere in West Virginia]**

Night hung over the valley at midday.

The storm had blown in off of the Atlantic on the day every-thing went wrong, and it had followed them every step of the way back to Freeside, howling wind and a sky black with thunderheads rolling out of the east like a warning, and as they travelled through the night it finally caught up with them, so that when the next day dawned they wondered if it had; the sun they'd been depending on,

4 / NATALIE IRONSIDE

had put all of their hopes in, rose unseen behind a veil of inky black anvils, threatening thunder and rain.

Of the six scavengers still alive and scrambling through the laurels up the mountainside, Connor was the most experienced, and between the look of the gathering clouds and the ache in his lower back, he guessed that the sky would burst open and drench them in a real boomer of a summer thunderstorm before evening.

And that was alright by Connor. It had been mid-July when they'd struck out for Baltimore, and it was late July as they made their ponderous way home through the mountains; and even with the sun hidden and the valley cloaked in darkness, its head still hung over all like an oppressive shroud, and the air was so thick that walking felt like swimming. And the group had been in full retreat since Baltimore, moving too quickly to scavenge, and Connor couldn't remember how long ago they'd run out of water. He'd stopped sweating a couple of hours before noon, and as he marched at the rear of the file he could see that the other five scavvers were just as dry. The storm would make for miserable walking and worse camping, but he longed for it, longed for the sky to open up and soak them. It was late July in the mountains, and their canteens were empty, and Connor knew that they couldn't keep up their pace for another day.

And though he'd never been in this part of the wasteland before, he figured that they couldn't be further than another day's march from safety. He slung his long rifle over his shoulder, lit a cigarette, and groaned in frustration. Christ, but wouldn't that be a stupid way to die?

Under normal circumstances, Connor would never smoke on the trail. At night, a good eye can spot a burning cigarette from a mile off, and a good nose can smell it from even farther if the wind is right. But they were well past all that now; the storm wasn't the only thing following them.

From behind and below, from the valley floor and down the mountain's slopes, he could hear the din of hundreds of shuffling feet and an endless chorus of wordless, painful moans coming closer, ever closer, an entire city of shriveled, pickled corpses nipping at their heels, driving the six of them west like a goad. The scavvers had the advantage of knowing the trail, whereas roamers were too stupid for trails and keep trying to scramble up the face of the mountain, through the hawthorns and laurels and azaleas, wasting time; but human beings would need to sleep, eventually, and roamers did not. It was only a matter of time.

Wardog, next in front of Connor in the marching file, had taken off his campaign shirt and wrapped it around his head. Turning back, he pulled the cloth away from his mouth and asked, "Hey, Turlogh, you how many smokes you got left?"

"Enough," Connor grumbled, and tossed him the pack he'd just opened. Wardog caught it with a grateful sigh and slung his shotgun over his shoulder to fish one out and light it. Connor noted that; all of them, himself included, were relaxing their discipline, ignoring the rules, and they were all blooded professionals who knew damned well that following the rules was what kept a scavver alive. The only one of the six who hadn't slung their weapon was Tanya, the short, brown-skinned woman walking near the front of the line, just behind Professor J; but Tanya was a red, and a fanatical one, and she was the only wasteland ranger in the group who'd ever really been a professional soldier, so her stoicism was to be expected. And Tanya was the group's automatic rifleman, and the weapon she kept in front of her at low ready was a hulking black belt-fed machine gun that was as big as her thigh and weighed roundabouts thirty pounds, while even Connor's antique bolt-action rifle with its wooden stock and bayonet only weighed about ten.

When he'd finished his cigarette, he sighed, rolled his eyes, and brought his rifle back to low ready, marveling at how Tanya seemed not at all bothered by such a long march under such terrible conditions. Connor was a feminist, or would've called himself one, like any good anarchist, but he still felt some kind of way about watching his own wife surpass him at his own chosen profession.

The trail up the mountain passed through a break in the trees, giving Connor a good look at the hollow below them and the valley beyond that, and he was reminded that he had no idea where they were. At their last stop, Prof had said they were about thirty clicks from Land's End, which wasn't all that far, and so Connor had figured they must be coming up on familiar ground, but looking out over it he was sure he'd never been here before. And down toward the base of the mountain, only just visible through the tangle of laurel and azalea, he saw their pursuers; hundreds of shriveled, grey things that had once been human and now looked like blasphemous caricatures, scrambling up the slope as their incessant moaning grew ever louder. One would gain a bit of ground, stumble, and roll back down into the seething mass, again and again, and, two steps forward, one step back, they made slow but irresistible progress.

One roamer, who must've had a set of pipes worthy of an opera singer in a former life, chanced to look up and caught sight of them. It stopped, raised its arms up over its head, and did not moan, but it howled, belting out an animal cry of hunger and malice that echoed through the valley.

Professor J, at the front of the file, stopped dead in his tracks. He looked so tense that his shoulders almost touched his ears, and he stood rooted in place like a statue when Tanya bumped into his back. Prof was in his early 50s, with a good two decades on Connor, and Connor thought that if this mad dash to safety was hard on him, it must be brutal on the old man. As if to emphasize the point, he noticed a single, solitary bead of sweat glistening against the dark umber skin on the back of the old man's neck before evaporating as soon as it appeared.

Before anyone could ask why he'd stopped, Prof barked, "Connor, for the love of God, *please* shut him up."

The roamer howled again. Connor shouldered his big rifle, drew a bead on the roamer just between its eyes, and squeezed the trigger; for a moment the moans were drowned out by the deafening rapport, and the roamer's head disappeared in a sickening spray of grey and green. They resumed walking.

"Hey, old man," Connor called out from the rear of the file, "where in the whole hell are we at?"

"Heading west now," Prof called back, "about thirty-five clicks north-northeast of Land's End, or thereabouts."

"How in the entire shit are we further away from home now than we was this morning?"

"Had to take a couple of detours, on account of our fan club back there. Looks like the trail crosses bare rock over a nice spur up ahead; I'll see if I can't raise somebody on the radio."

The six of them—Connor, Wardog, Tanya, Jacky-Boy, Raven Moon, and Prof—broke out of the trees onto the slickrock just as the sky started to mist and heavy fog began to roll up from the valley, which Prof cursed. He took the handheld off of his belt and barked into it, "All call signs, all call signs, this is Ghost One. Commo check, over."

Only static. He repeated the message; static again. He fiddled with the red star pin on his campaign shirt, contemplated taking the time to set up the single-sideband rig in his rucksack and trying to raise Land's End directly; he checked the progress of the roamers down below them and decided to press on.

"Where in the hell are we even going, old man?" Tanya grumbled.

"Top of the ridge, and back down again. There'll be water at the bottom—always is—and we should make it there by nightfall. And if we keep humping, we'll be in Land's End by sunrise."

"If we make it to sunrise. The safe money is we're all deader than Elvis as soon as it gets dark."

They all shuddered just slightly, the shadow of an unspoken fear passing over them, and kept walking in silence.

Walking the switchback up to the top of the ridge took up the rest of their afternoon, a few hours longer than Prof had hoped, and the horde of roamers had gained an uncomfortable amount of ground in the meantime. The mist thickened into a light rain and peals of thunder sounded from the east as the slope flattened out and the tangles of laurel and thorn gave way to scrubby brakes of spruce and fir. The trail led straight ahead over ground that grew ever flatter and rockier, and the group nearly jogged along with the horde's keening close behind them, eager to be over the crest and on their way down the back half of the mountain.

The back half of the mountain was, oddly, a bit farther away than it was supposed to be.

They came to a dead stop on the edge of a cliff that plunged down, down into a gorge with a wide, swift river at the bottom which, if they listened closely, they could just hear over the wind and the incessant moaning, which was getting closer. Their eyes widened, their jaws dropped, but they did not speak, not until Connor blinked a few times and muttered, "Aw, Hell."

"This isn't supposed to be here," Prof said, his voice flat and emotionless.

Connor backed away from the edge. "What the fuck, old man? What the fuck?"

"This isn't on the map. I followed the map here, every step of the way, and there was no goddamn river."

Tanya, who was still standing at the edge of the gorge, asked, "Say, boss, does that map show the trail going in a straight line for a good ways?"

They followed Tanya's gaze to two wooden posts jutting out of the rocky ground, with tattered old ropes hanging off of them and trailing down into the abyss.

"So there was a bridge," Prof observed. "But there's no goddamn river on the map! Fuck!"

"Alright," Connor said, "well, however we got here, we're here now. Let's talk about where we go next."

"Bushwhack along the gorge, get down off the mountain the long way," Wardog suggested.

Prof shook his head. "No way. Brush is too thick. We wouldn't make it half a mile before the roamers were on top of us."

"I got an idea," Connor said, "but it's a real shitty idea."

The moans grew ever louder, and Prof sighed and grumbled, "I'm all ears, buddy."

"Well, we're stuck up here like a cat up a tree, and them's the brakes. Only way I see is we dig in, wait for the storm to pass, and get an assist from the authoritarians over in Land's End. They could be here in under an hour."

"There are two hundred roamers down there at least, Connor. You think six joes can dig in and hold off two hundred? And, Jesus, it could be all night before the storm quits; it hasn't even started yet."

"You got any better ideas, old man?"

Prof stood fuming for a moment, rubbing his temples, then barked, "Tanya, Jacky-Boy, get the single sideband up. Do the rest of you have any pyro left?"

"Just a goddamn minute," Tanya said. "You're going along with this? This is the worst plan Connor has ever come up with something, and that's fucking saying something. We're gonna die doing that."

"Probably. But like he said, we don't have a lot of options. Now, get that radio up and get Land's End on the horn, or we're definitely dead. Rest of you, how about that pyro?"

"Two grenades," Connor grumbled.

"I got one grenade and a nail bomb," Wardog said.

Raven Moon was beaming. "I thought I only had one claymore left, but I've got two! And a nail bomb."

Prof rubbed his temples again. "I've got two nail bombs," he sighed. "It'll do or it won't, I suppose. You three, take all of the pyro and go rig the trail before they get here; I've got string and wire in my rucksack if you need extra. After that, look for hides and get comfortable."

"And what are you gonna do, old man?" Connor asked.

"It'll take Tanya and JB a hot minute to get the single sideband up, so I suppose I'll beating this dead horse." And he took the handheld off of his belt and barked, "All call signs, all call signs, this is Ghost One. Commo check, over."

"All call signs, all call signs, this is Ghost One, my group is holed up thirty-five clicks north-northeast of Land's End, hostiles closing in, this is a mayday, I repeat, this is a mayday, over."

Silence.

"Goddamn shit," he yelled, kicking at the rocks under his feet, "goddamn fucking shit!"

And the radio crackled, and a voice with a Bavarian accent so thick it dripped with butter and cream cheese and beer foam said, *"Mor'n-mor'n."*

Everyone stopped and turn to stare at the radio, their eyes widening in disbelief and growing fear. Prof held it up to his mouth again and asked, "What's your call sign? Over."

The voice chuckled, and, after a contemplative silence, said: *"Nachtjager."*

Everyone took a sudden breath and began to work faster, except for Tanya, who stormed over to Prof, snatched the radio out of his hand, and barked, "Where the hell are you, you son of a bitch? It's the middle of the goddamn day!"

"I am someplace safe, little girl. Ja, someplace safe und warm. But night comes early today, I think, so perhaps my friends and I will pay you a visit soon."

"Come up then, asshole. I'll be real happy to see you again; I got a 240 Bravo and a belt full of dumdums just for you and your friends."

"You try to act strong, little girl, but I can hear that you are afraid—I can hear your heart racing, the tremor in your voice— and you always taste better when you are afraid. I will see you very soon, and I will be paying you special attention, I think. *Tschuss!*"

"Try it, fucker! I'll be waiting for you."

There was silence again. Tanya shoved the handheld back into Prof's hand and went back to setting up the big radio. Prof followed.

Jacky-Boy stared straight ahead for a while before muttering, "Jesus Christ. We're all gonna die." His tone was even, but tears were starting to run down his cheeks.

"Let him come," Tanya barked. "I can't wait to light his ass up."

"If that was who I think it was, I watched him wipe out half of the column by himself. I watched him pick up a tank while the reds were lighting him up. They pumped mags into him and it just pissed him off. As soon as the sun goes down, we're fucked. Some of us literally."

"Not necessarily," Prof said. "We're in a good position here; they'll have to come up a narrow way that we can keep a good watch on."

"The reds thought they were in a good position, too, on a hilltop with all that armor. Look what good it did them."

"Well, they're gone, but we're here. We made it. Hell with all that armor; I told them it was a bad idea. Six disciplined cadres with good rifles they know how to use, well, that's as good as an army."

Jacky-Boy didn't respond, but seemed a bit more hopeful. Tanya, however, sneered and said, "We got out alive, yeah, but we didn't get into the Citadel. The reds sent that whole column because they guessed what was in there. Well, now it's out, and it's followed us here."

"We'll make it," Prof said. "We'll get out of here."

"And what the hell makes you think that?"

"Because we don't have a choice."

They were silent, then, until Jacky-Boy said, "Alright, should be ready to go. Work your magic, old man."

Prof fiddled with the radio a bit until the buzzing from the earpiece quieted down, and he spoke into it, "All call signs, all call signs, this is Ghost One. Commo check; can anybody hear me out there? Over."

At once, a voice came through, saying, "Yeah, Ghost One, this is Land's End East tactical operations command. You are coming across loud and clear, over."

Everyone in earshot cheered.

"TOC, my group is on a mountaintop in the exclusion zone about thirty-five clicks north-northeast of you, hemmed in by roamers, no chance of egress. There are six of us and we have important intel. Requesting earliest possible extraction, over."

"Ghost One, I suggest you seek egress. Thunderstorms and radiation spikes are predicted all night and most of tomorrow. It will not be safe to send any birds out for at least thirty hours. I repeat, you are on your own, seek egress, over."

"Oh god fucking damn shit," Prof pontificated, and he yelled into the radio, "TOC, egress is not possible; we are on a spur at the edge of a cliff, roamers closing in, first contact approximately five minutes. No egress is possible, over."

"Ghost One, it is unsafe to fly in this weather; all birds are grounded for the next thirty hours. I . . . I'm so fucking sorry, comrade. Over and out."

"No, you son of a bitch! You are talking to Professor Jackson McCreedy, call sign Ghost One, leader of Ghost Forward Operating Group! Listen: Six of us survived Bart's column. We have intelligence about the column! We have intelligence about the Citadel!"

A different voice answered him, a woman's voice: "Comrade, I need you to tell me what you know. Over."

"Fuck you! Come get me and I'll tell you to your face!"

"The signalman's right, man; you can't fly a helicopter through this shit. There's . . . there's nothing we can do. I'm sorry. Over and out."

Prof roared a stream of profanity into the handset; he got no answer. Jacky-Boy was crying. Tanya rolled her eyes and asked, "So what now, old man?"

"Guess we'll die."

They were interrupted by the deafening crack of a rifle in the trees over their heads, and Connor shouted, "Contact! They're almost on the wire!"

The rapport of Wardog's shotgun answered, and the others shouldered their battle rifles and rushed to get online. Tanya, with an uncomfortable placidity about her, started checking her big gun and muttered, "About damn time. I could stand to blow off some steam."

The roamers were shuffling up the trail at a fair pace, moaning as they came, and they reeked, like blood and shit and gone-off meat. Their grey skin, their white eyes, and their faces still recognizable as having once been human would've all been horrifying, but the group was used to them; they were a common sight in the exclusion zone. The guns sounded in steady rhythm, and every time a gun went off, a roamer fell, missing part of its head. But there were more than enough, well over thirty visible with at least two hundred more coming up the slope, and the thundering guns did nothing to slow the advance.

At last Tanya got her heavy gun online. She walked calmly up to the killbox and advanced farther ahead than anyone else, knowing they would cover her. She found a rock to rest her bipod on, pointed it downhill, and began firing into the advancing mob in steady, controlled bursts. Most of her shots were center-mass, and a few of the roamers that fell did get back up, but the advance was slowed. After a few minutes, the first wave was gone, without even having reached the traps, though they could see more coming up the trail.

"Ammo check!" Prof yelled. "I've got four magazines left!"

"Green," Tanya cried. "Don't worry about me."

"I got about fifty shells."

"I got ten clips."

"Four mags."

"Alright," Prof said, "Oh Lord, oh Jesus, we might just live through this. Let the next wave walk into the first trap; that'll give us a better idea of how long the ammo will last. You hear me, Turlogh?"

"Yeah," Connor grumbled, lowering his rifle.

"We'll stay alive," Tanya said, "till fuckin sundown. Then our best friend is gonna come finish what he started outside the Citadel."

Nobody responded. The light rain picked up a bit as the sun sank into the west, and Prof barked, "Hey, JB, you think you can pack up the single sideband on your own?"

"Yeah," Jacky-Boy said, slinging his rifle and heading toward the radio.

Connor lit another cigarette. "Hey, old man, I got me a serious question. What exactly are we gonna do when Little Hitler shows up?"

"I'm hoping Tanya can take care of that. If not her, you; that big Russkie antique is the hardest caliber here. No center-mass shots; aim for the head, same as the roamers. It might not kill him, but it'll slow him down long enough to figure something out."

"Shit," Connor pontificated.

The next pack of roamers, about forty in all, approached the first trap. The group held, looking down and away. The foremost roamer hit a tripwire between two trees and fell over pressing all of its weight down on it, yanking the pin out of a grenade. The few seconds' pause brought ten roamers into the zone of effect. The grenade went off with a blinding flash and deafening roar, setting off the pipe bomb attached to it, which went off likewise, and about half of the pack went down. A couple of those got back up, but not many. When the group resumed shooting, it didn't take long to clear the trail again.

"Well hell, this ain't so bad," Wardog observed, relaxing a bit. "We might just pull this off. Just might."

"Don't get complacent on me," Prof said. "That still wasn't even half of them."

"Getting pretty dark now," Tanya said.

"Well damn," Wardog grumbled, "y'all are a couple of rays of fuckin sunshine."

Tanya shrugged. "I'm a materialist. I look reality in the face."

Connor, desperately trying to light another cigarette in the rain, looked down from his chestnut tree and said, "She's right, man."

"Well of fuckin course you'd take her side."

"Yeah."

"Hey!" Prof yelled, "Enough whining. Next wave's coming up, and it's a big one."

It was. At least a hundred roamers, if not more, were coming up the trail. Connor looked them over through his scope and asked, "You want I should hold again, old man?"

"Nah, not anymore. Light the bastards up."

And they did, and though the roamers fell like clockwork, the horde's progress wasn't slowed. They walked into the second mine, which blew out at least twenty, but the gap was soon filled. The sky chose that moment to break, with a deafening thunderclap heralding the change from a light rain to a proper downpour. They could barely see, between the rain and the gathering dark. They heard the third mine go off, meaning that the horde was only thirty meters away, with only one more mine left. And the last line blew, and the horde kept coming. And then, as though someone had flipped a switch, they stopped, standing stock-still less than ten meters from the barrel of Tanya's 240.

"What in the whole shit?" she inquired, struggling to be heard over the growing howl of the wind.

"Keep shooting," Prof hollered. "We can study their fucking habits later."

They kept firing, but stopped again when they heard a new

sound: From down the trail, just barely audible over the rain and the howling wind and their ringing ears, a deep and sonorous voice was singing, and getting louder as the source of the voice came closer.

"Die Fahne hoch! Die Reihen fest geschlossen!
SA marschiert mit ruhig festem Schritt.
Kam'raden, die Rotfront und Reaktion erschossen,
Marschier'n im Geist in unser'n Reihen mit!
"Die Strasse frei den brauen Bataillonen!
Die Strasse frei dem Sturmabteilungsmann!
Er shau'n aufs Hakenkreuz voll
Hoffnung schon millionen!
Der Tag fur Freiheit unde fur Brot nicht an!..."

"This'll be that, then," Connor muttered. "Fuckin bonehead."

All of them felt fear deep in their guts, a primal, animal fear, like sheep before a howling wolf. Connor glassed the crowd, hoping to catch a glimpse of the singer through the rain; he couldn't see him, but he could see the roamers shuffling out of the way, making a path. He was coming.

"Stay sharp," Prof ordered. "Be ready. Remember, if you see him, blow his goddamn head off."

The singing stopped, and a figure stepped into view. He was enormous, at least six feet tall, broad across the shoulders; bald, with a ridiculous blonde handlebar mustache; black eyes with no discernable irises, skin so pale it was almost translucent. He was shirtless, showing off a trunk of knotted, rippling muscles covered in tattoos. Most prominent of those, a big piece stretched all the way across his chest, was an eagle clutching an iron cross.

He seemed to radiate fear, a fear that settled deep in the bones of the seasoned killers and immobilized them. Except for Tanya.

She stood up, held her machine gun to her hip, and screamed, "Alright, bonehead! Here I am!" And she squeezed the trigger.

The gun jammed.

The hunter was on her in a single stride, moving almost too

quickly to see, putting one hand on her jaw and the other on her chest. Between terror and surprise, the group couldn't move, except for Connor, who howled with rage as he fired. The shot went low, the big bullet striking the hunter in the shoulder, punching a ragged hole into him. The hole sealed itself almost instantly.

Still moving with inhuman speed, the hunter pushed with one hand pulled, twisted with the other, and in a moment, with an animal cry of triumph, held Tanya's bloody head in his right hand.

Wardog ran, then, off into the storm, and Raven Moon followed him. Connor almost screamed; almost. He caught it in his throat, swallowed it, and started climbing down from his tree as quiet as he could.

Prof and Jacky-Boy were still on the ground, and Jacky-Boy fired—center-mass, like he'd been trained—through tears, running toward his target. The rounds punched into the hunter's belly and the entry wounds sealed up just as the one in his shoulder had. And when Jacky-Boy was close enough, the hunter struck him, hard, across the face, and he fell to the rocks with his neck at a sickening angle.

Prof pulled the trigger of his battle rifle. The firing pin punched into the primer, which fizzled and did not ignite.

The hunter walked toward him, calm and placid, and said, "Ist the rain, I am afraid. Rain and hand-loads do not mix, ja?"

Prof desperately tried to clear the jam, backpedaling, but he could tell that it was too late. The grinning hunter took another step forward and reached for him.

The tip of a bayonet exploded out of the hunter's chest, just below his heart.

Lanky, quiet Connor Turlogh, silent as a cat in the dark, swung the hunter away from Prof on the end of his rifle and pulled the trigger. The round burst out just above the tip of the bayonet, leaving a hole the size of a fist, and the hunter slumped, twitching, to the ground. The wounds stayed open.

"Saved your ass, old man," Connor said, trying to hide his tears.

Prof blinked a few times. "Connor, we . . . we have to go."

Connor looked around. The hunter was still twitching, and seemed to be trying to stand, or to prop himself up on his elbows. And, with him the ground, the roamers were shuffling toward them again.

"Any more brilliant ideas, old man?"

"Just one. How well can you swim?"

"Pretty good. I—wait, no. Fuckin hell no."

"Could you swim with a broken leg, do you think?"

"Goddammit, come up with a better idea than that, man!"

But Prof was already walking toward the cliff.

[2]

BABES IN THE WOOD

**[AD 2259, 194 years post-War;
somewhere near the Kentucky border]**

MAGNOLIA WASN'T LOOKING FORWARD TO RAIN, ESPECIALLY not a big boomer of a summer thunderstorm like the one turning the evening sky from grey to black. It would make part of their work easier—the boys dug in under concrete on top of the hill would have a better time of it than the men in brown and black shirts trying to storm up the hill—but they'd run out of heating oil two days ago, and Mags wasn't looking forward to losing soldiers to hypothermia in the middle of summer.

Worse still, she thought as she bent her knees to heave up another box of shells, there'd be mud. No good trying to run back and forth carrying 30-kilogram crates in all that wind and rain and mud. It wouldn't be safe.

Hatfield Forward Operating Base, sitting on a mountaintop at the northeast edge of Land's End, almost four hundred kilometers from New Lawrence, was lucky enough to have five field artillery pieces, and they were all seeing use that night, and they were expensive to feed. Mags hauled her box of shells alongside four artillerymen doing the same; the gunner's mate from Charlie Battery had taken a bullet to the face earlier, so Mags had stepped in to cover him and keep the gun fed. It happened like clockwork, but like five different clocks keeping different time, in a maddening way: First, the *ka-chunk!* of a shell loaded into a gun; then, the *boof!* of the gun firing; then, the ominous, high-pitched keening of the flying shell; and, finally, the ground shaking underfoot as the shell found its new home on the mountainside.

A battalion-sized element, almost four times the size of the FOB's garrison, had come knocking around lunchtime, but though the men in black shirts were notorious for their cruelty and cunning, the men in the brown shirts—who made up the greater part of the Blacklanders' forces—were not known for their good sense and had promptly wasted their strength in death-or-glory charges up the mountainside, easily repulsed. After the third or fourth time that that didn't work, the black-shirted stormtroopers must have taken command, because they'd begun bounding up the hill from one piece of cover to another and trenching wherever they could. It still wasn't going well for them, between the FOB's garrison of Ashlander sharpshooters and the five big guns, but they'd managed a few lucky shots. Hence why Mags, political officer, was out schlepping crates instead of cozied up in her hide with her Dragunov rifle.

Holding the crate tight to her chest, Mags ran, booking it across the open ground from the magazine to Charlie's gun pit as fast as she could. She was tall, wiry, used to heavy work, but she'd done this enough times that her entire body ached, from her shoulders down to the soles of her feet. But she wouldn't stop so long as she could put one foot in front of the other; if the guns went quiet, the boneheads down on the slopes would bound and sap their way inside the wire within hours. And even when the stakes were lower, Mags never stopped.

When she reached the gun pit, handed off her box, and spun

around to run back to the magazine, it was getting well dark, and the sky was just beginning to weep, the wind beginning to howl; her great mane of curly red hair whipped behind her as she ran. And she reached the magazine to find two artillerymen in flecktarn Ashlander uniforms staring into the open blast doors, mouths agape.

"Oi," she barked as soon as she caught her breath, "what's with the smoking and joking, huh? We gotta feed those guns!"

"Uh, Mom," one of them said, "there's no more shells."

Mags walked through the blast door, down the stairs, took a look around, and sure enough: There were boxes of explosives, spam cans of 5.45 and 7.62 small arms ammo, all sorts of odds and ends, but not a single one of the white poplar 30-kilogram shell crates she'd come to know so well. The corner set aside for them was empty save for some straw and a few spare nails.

She felt panic rise in her throat, fought it down, and met the two artillerymen with a blank face. "You two, go get your Kalashnikovs and report back to your pits. I'm gonna go see the captain."

Mags ran for the command bunker as fast as she could manage. It was another ugly, sunken concrete hut, distinguishable from the others only by its position at the center of the mountaintop and the field radio antenna sticking out of the top of it. As Mags ran, she heard one gun stop firing, and, as the guard waved her through the blast door, a second.

The interior of the bunker was a mess of desks, papers, radios, and people milling about, and at the placid center of the mess sat Tom, elected captain of Delta Company, studying a stack of reports as Mags ran in.

She came to a stop in front of the desk, clicked her heels together, snapped a crisp salute, and barked, "Comrade Captain!"

"Hi, Mags," Tom said without looking up from his papers. "Bad news?"

"The worst. We're, uh . . . we're out of shells, Tom. The big guns are going quiet."

He dropped his papers. "They're fucking what?"

"*Yiddisher mazel.* Supply never figured on a pissant little communications outpost needing to repel these kinds of numbers. If the boneheads have reinforced, and I'll bet they have, then they could sap us to death or even overrun us in a charge if we can't get those guns back online. Which we can't."

"Hell. All the birds in Land's End are grounded, with the weather and all, and it would take all night for ground forces to get here at a quick march. You don't think we can hold at all, not even another couple days?"

"No way. All five guns are gonna be down soon, and I bet we'll have blackshirts inside the wire by midnight."

"Shit, shit, goddamn shit. God*damn.* I . . . wait. The weather. Mags, I have an idea."

"Oh?"

Tom stood up. "Everyone, I know you heard all that, so you all know what a fix we're in. I have a plan. It's a bad plan, a really bad plan, but it's the only plan I've got. Listen."

The shells ran dry just as the sun set and the sky broke, with wind howling like a hurricane and rain coming down in sheets, so the attackers didn't press their advantage and the hillside went mostly quiet. The garrison liked that. Everyone who wasn't on watch duty huddled together in their blockhouses, where the lit small fires and tried to stay dry.

Mags walked into one of those blockhouses, where she wiped the rain out of her eyes, clapped her hands together, and cried out, "Oi! Everybody up! We've got orders."

"What the hell kinda orders, in all this rain?" one of the soldiers asked as they stood up.

"Bad business. The big guns are out of shells and we're outnumbered four to one. Soon as the rain stops, they'll be inside the wire; hell, there's probably Arditi fire teams crawling up to the wire right now. Orders are we pack up all our kit, and everything else we can carry at a dead run, and muster at the south redoubt in one hour. We're bugging out."

The soldiers rolled their eyes, sighed, grumbled, but they all got up and started checking their gear. All except the one who'd spoken up. And when they saw that, a few of the soldiers stopped and stood behind him.

"Mags," he said, "that's . . . that's fucking stupid. You expect us to march down the hill, in the middle of the damned night, in the middle of a goddamn thunderstorm, and assault through a fixed position? That's suicide!"

"It's a bad business, Chris, but it's what we gotta do. We can't weather an assault. But if we start humping it in one hour, we can eat breakfast in Land's End. Come on, man. I'll be right there, we'll go through wire and fire together, like pals."

"I'm not fuckin doin it, Mags."

"And what the hell else are you gonna do? You gonna sit here and wait for the fascists to come over the wire and ship you off to summer camp in Ohio?"

"Maybe I fucking am. Even that would be better than this dumbass plan. I'm not going . . . and neither is my squad."

Mags started to roll her eyes, until she noticed that a few of the men behind Chris were nodding back and forth in agreement with him. Her frantic expression melted into a blank, emotionless look, and she barked, "Comrade Corporal McKay!"

"Mags, don't--"

"Shut the fuck up. Stand at the position of fucking attention—all of you! And my name ain't Mags anymore, my name is Comrade Political Commissar."

"Mags--"

"Comrade Corporal, did you just stand right here in front of us and express your intention to capitulate? And you're trying to get your fellow soldiers to go along with it? Is that what I'm fucking hearing right now?"

Chris shrank before her for a moment, but only a moment. Steeling himself, he squared up to her, looked up into her eyes, and —with venom in his voice—spat, "Yes, *sir*."

The other soldiers stared at the two of them with wide eyes as soon as the word left his lips. Mags' expression didn't change, but bitter hatred flashed across her eyes, and her Nagant revolver was already out of its holster, in her hand. Without a word, she shot Chris in the chest, and when he sank to his knees, in the head.

"Get packing," she barked at the others. "Muster at the southern redoubt in one hour. Everybody except Chris, I guess."

Mags ran back and forth across the mountaintop, spreading the news, taking care of this and that, oblivious to the rain soaking her uniform. When the muster was underway, she ran into Tom, who, in front of the assembling soldiers, stopped her and asked, "Mags, did you . . . did you shoot a troop?"

"Yeah," she barked. "He refused to muster. Said he planned on defecting, and he tried to make his fire team go along with it."

"Mags, I . . . I'm not sure that that was entirely necessary."

"Yeah, well, I don't care; we need to get off this mountain double-quick. If you don't like my service, write an angry letter to the Commissariat when we get to Land's End." And without waiting for Tom's response, she turned to the mustering troops and shouted, "Oi, step it out! Come on, come on, move like you got someplace to be!" And off she went.

Another officer standing next to Tom shook their head and muttered, "Commissars, man. I don't know what they feed them down at Central Soviet, but we need some."

"I think I will write that letter to the Commissariat," Tom said.

"Most commissars are true believers, but she's . . . something else. She's a fanatic."

"The troops seem to like her well enough, but yeah. Y'know, I don't think I've ever seen that woman sleep."

"She told me once that she sleeps about four hours a night. And I've never seen one person go through as much coffee or as many cigarettes as she does. Like I said, a fanatic."

"Jesus. A person can't live like that, Tom. How old is she?"

"She's 22."

"And she's already a company-grade political officer? Jesus."

"Hey, I never said she's not good at what she does—she is. She's just a fanatic."

Soon, the entire garrison was mustered, formed up into a marching column, and prepared to head out. Everything that could be carried was on someone's back. Everything that couldn't—including, sadly, the field artillery pieces—was mined. Tom and Mags stood on top of the parapet, and Mags, with her long Dragunov slung over her shoulder, pointed south down the mountain and hollered over the wind and rain: "They're down there, but not many; most of the boneheads are dug in on the north face. They'll be hiding, scared of the dark, scared of the rain, and we'll be the last thing they expect. All we have to do is hit their line, assault through, and keep on humping it, and we'll be in Land's End just in time for hot chow. Hot chow!"

The company cheered at that.

"The enemy is cold, wet, scared, and *weak!* Comrades, be bold, be aggressive, hit them hard, and we will come through! *Yrah!*"

She screamed the last word, like the cry of a wild animal, and the troops cheered again. Tom snapped to attention and called out, "*Company!*"

Echoes of "*Platoon!*" and "*Squad!*"

"Ready! *Assault through!*"

And they went over the top.

They marched along in good order and at a fair pace, taking care as they passed through the forest and over the slick and muddy ground. Mags fell into place just behind the first squad and slightly off to the right of the column, and as they went forward she felt fear growing in her, the gnawing fear that knows when fighting and bloodshed are close. She choked it down and kept walking, her Dragunov at low ready.

There came a deafening peel of thunder, and a bolt of lightning smote the top of a nearby mountain and, for a few seconds, bathed the whole valley in terrible light. And to Mags' surprise, she saw, ahead of them, nothing. As far as she could see through the trees and the rain, nobody waited for them. Either they were all further down the hill, or . . .

An explosion from the top of the hill shook the ground under them, followed by another, and screams. And Mags understood: There were no boneheads waiting for them on the south slope because, thinking like fascists, they'd broken the cordon to assault the north slope. And soon they'd realize there was nobody there.

"Pick up the pace," Mags screamed, "they're behind us! Move, move, move!"

The company hit the floor of the valley half an hour later, soaked, freezing, exhausted, their nerves fried from negotiating the woods and steep slopes so quickly. They stopped, huddled together, and made a head count.

They were missing a platoon.

Six squads, one lieutenant, one staff sergeant, the entirety of Fourth Platoon, had gone over the top and not made it to the bottom, without a word, without a sound. Tom and Mags stared back up the hill, mouths agape, confused and afraid.

"I've got a very bad feeling about this, cap," Mags said. "I don't think they just tripped."

Tom nodded. "No resistance, no pursuit; it smells like a trap.

But no shots fired? No sound or sign at all? What in the entire hell?"

Mags stared uphill into the dark, wet forest, as if willing it to give up its secrets, and it seemed to stare back; she felt the hairs on her neck stand up, felt a million eyes watching her. She trembled.

She slung her Dragunov, unsheathed her combat knife, and said, "The company has to keep moving. Get the troops heading south, and I'll grab a couple of joes and go find fourth."

"Mags, are you sure? I should do it; this is my company, my responsibility."

"Yeah, and that means you're the one who can get them to Land's End. I'll worry about the babes in the wood."

And, having made up her mind, she turned away from Tom and yelled, "Oi! I need three volunteers for a crack team!"

Mags got her three, and the team parted ways with the company, heading back up the hill while the others kept moving south towards safety. Mags tried not to think about it.

They moved quiet as cats, trying their best to hear or see anything with all the wind and rain and through the cloying darkness. After about five minutes of walking, one of the soldiers tapped Mags on the shoulder and said, "Hey, Mom, I, uh . . . I found something."

Mags looked to where he pointed; there, on the ground, was a left arm, ending in a ragged stump just above the elbow.

"Fuck," she pontificated.

And at that moment, one of the soldiers swore and staggered backwards as something struck him hard in the chest. They all looked down to where the object had fallen. It was a severed head.

"Oh, fucking hell," Mags barked, "we gotta go. Back, down the hill! Run!"

"But what about 4th?"

"They're dead. Come on, run! Double-quick! We gotta warn the company!"

"The hell's goin on, Mom?"

"Hunters!"

Their faces blanched, and for a moment they stood rooted in fear. Then, they ran.

Gunfire roared up from down the hill as they ran, and at first it was disciplined fire, steady tattoos of hammered pairs; and then it became more random, frantic; and then it was mixed with screams. Mags glanced to her left to shout encouragements at the other three, and found that she was by herself.

Soon she could see muzzle flash through the trees, and, with her knife in her left hand and her revolver in her right, she lept, roaring, into the fray.

It was just as the last gun and the last scream went silent that her boots hit the ground and she stood alone in a clearing full of blood and detritus. She couldn't see much, but she felt like she could sense it, the morass of butchered corpses, torn and strewn about. And she could hear, out of the darkness, over the rain and roaring wind, laughter. Horrible, horrible laughter.

She started backing up, fighting down the urge to vomit, when a voice just behind her growled, *"Ah, you're a lovely one."*

And another, off to her right, hissed, *"Lovely, ja, lovely enough to take our time with, I think."*

She screamed. She ran. Weeping and screaming, she ran off into the darkness of the hills, half-blind from rain, careening off of trees, tripping over rocks, oblivious, with no destination in mind except for "away."

She did, luckily, pick the right direction, because just after sunrise, when her legs and her chest burned and she was sure she couldn't take one more step, she broke out of the trees to stand before a high parapet of red dirt topped by a stout wooden palisade. Three women stood on top of the parapet, staring at her down the sights of their battle rifles. A flag few over their heads, a square of red cloth with a hammer and plow embroidered on it. She looked up at the flag and smiled.

Two of the guards ran toward her and shouted, "Hey, you, stop! Stop! Take one more step and you're dead!"

Mags stopped.

"Identify yourself!"

She snapped to attention and barked, "Political commissar Magnolia Jane Blackadder, warrant officer 2, brevet major. Delta Company, Hatfield Forward Operating Base. Please, take me to your syndicate headquarters. I have intelligence."

"Lady, you look like powdered ass. You sure you don't wanna see a doctor? Come on, I'll take you to the doctor."

"No, no time. Need to see the syndic . . . Gotta make a report . . . Could've been followed . . ."

And Mags collapsed into the grass. The guards thought she was dead, until she started snoring.

[3]
AFTERMATH

**[AD 2261, 196 years post-War;
somewhere near Lexington, Kentucky]**

"Keep it tight, soldiers," Mags barked. "Keep up, and watch for snakes."

The troupe of children behind her all gave sage nods, and a few repeated: "Watch for snakes."

They were a strange bunch, aged eight to fourteen, and two of the 14-year-olds carried battle rifles over their shoulders. Nobody expected any trouble so close to New Lawrence and so far south of the Ohio, but it was an important habit to teach: When you go out into the hills, you go armed.

Mags led them through a forest of oak and hickory and hemlock and chestnut, along the bank of a shallow creek, and signaled for them to stop at the base of a gnarled old oak with its roots trailing into the water. The children bunched around her, and she tapped the trunk with her walking stick and barked, "Can anyone tell me which tree this is?"

"An oak tree?" one of the children offered.

"Very good. But what kind of oak tree?"

Another, a girl of about twelve, cried out: "A white oak!"

"Very, very good. A white oak is one of my favorite trees. Can anyone guess why?"

"Oak is good wood for buildings," one of them offered, "and tool handles and stuff, and it makes good firewood."

"That's all very true. But Miss Lilly would tell you that trees are good to have around without cutting them down; let's talk about that."

One of the younger children cried out: "Acorns! The deer, and the squirrels, and the pigs, they all eat acorns."

"That's it, that's exactly what I wanted to hear. Now, people aren't supposed to eat acorns—they'll make you very sick—but you can eat them if you cook them just right."

All the children made disgusted faces, and Mags went on: "I know you've all heard stories about the Hunger, and your parents and older siblings lived through it. Well, I was twelve years old when the Hunger was at its worst; and when the bread ran out, Mama made us lots of acorn pie. Trees like this one right here saved my life, saved a lot of lives. That's one reason you don't cut down the trees if you don't need to: They're our friends, and they'll be here when we need them."

The children nodded in unison, and Mags glanced up at the sun and announced, "Oi, it's almost lunchtime. Alright, soldiers, let's move out. Back to town."

The group walked on through the forest, following the trail as it circled around the big hill, led over small, rocky streams and through groves of cedar and hickory and laurel and azalea. Mags kept time with her walking stick as they marched, and she drew in a deep breath and began to sing:

"John Brown's body lies a-moldering in the grave
While weep the sons of bondage whom he wagered all to save,
But though he's gone to glory, still we struggle for the slave
And his soul is marching on!"

The children took up the chorus with her:
"Glory, glory, hallelujah!
Glory, glory, hallelujah!
Glory, glory, hallelujah!
His soul is marching on!
"He captured Harper's Ferry with his nineteen men so true,
He frightened Old Virginia till she trembled through and
through,
They hanged him for a traitor, they themselves the traitor-crew,
And his soul is marching on!
"Glory, glory, hallelujah . . ."

The trail wound down out of the hills and dumped them back out onto the New Lawrence farmland, a patchwork quilt of greenhouses, woodlots, beehives, pastures, fields of a hundred different crops, and the residents' cabins lined up in neat little rows here and there. They walked along the winding paths between all the greenery to a big clapboard barn beside a catfish pond. The barn had a broad, handpainted sign over the door that said, "Ashland Farmer-Worker Union Agriculturalist Syndicate – New Lawrence Syndic," and below that, a sandwich board that said, "LIVE MUSIC – BOOK CLUB – SATURDAYS CHURCH."

There was a flatbed cargo truck parked beside the barn, and Mags hopped onto the back of it and came up holding a burlap sack. She took bright green apples out of it and handed them out to the children, and the children took their apples and ran off, with Mags crying after them, "Buddy system! And don't forget to drink water! And watch out for snakes!"

She took two apples for herself and ate them sitting in the sun, humming a tune. She felt happy, at peace, and she wondered why she'd ever left. Bad memories and all, this was home.

She looked up to see a stranger standing at the edge of the pond, watching her. He was young, probably no older than 20, carrying a big green rucksack and wearing crisp new combat fatigues, in stark contrast to her own tank top and flecktarn trousers which were patched and filthy. He looked back and forth, seeming lost. Mags waved at him.

She stood up as he walked over, and he asked, "Excuse me, are you Magnolia Blackadder? One of the commissars for the New Lawrence militia?"

"Call me Mags. So who are you?"

"Central Soviet sent me."

Mags rolled her eyes and sighed. "Alright, then. Let's go inside."

He followed her into the barn, which was full of long tables and benches, and they sat down across from each other. Mags lit a cigarette and asked, "So what does Central want with me now?"

The stranger doffed his rucksack onto the floor, dug around in its pockets, and brought out an accordion folder. "They sent me here with a job. I've got your personnel file here, and you're . . . more than qualified for it."

"The hell does that mean?"

He opened the folder and pulled out a few papers. "It says here you've been involved in civil defense for over a decade, starting with the big militia call-up when the war went hot during the famine. Studied political economy and American history at the university in Ashland, volunteered for the Commissariat, graduated the Academy a year early, served on the frontier with honors, designated marksman . . . And since requesting this posting two years ago, you've had papers published on botany and micology."

"First of all, on that last point; no, I didn't. Lilly Margo, the state ecology director over in Colby, did most of the work; I just contributed. But second of all, are you getting to some kinda point?"

"Well, Mags, I . . . this is an amazing resume. Don't you think your talents should go to something more than watering the grass and handing out apples?"

She fixed him with a dark look and sneered, "Spoken like a true propertarian."

"Huh?"

"Maybe not a propertarian, but you're definitely an egoist. Tell me, stranger—no, really, tell me, I want to hear your answer: What could possibly be more important than our food supply? Or our forests? What is it that's so much more important than teaching children?"

"That's . . . that's a fair criticism."

"Uh-huh, it sure is. Now, you apparently know everything about me, but I don't know jack about you. Who are you, and what's this job about? I won't ask again."

"I'm, ah, political commissar Mark Richards, warrant officer 1, brevet captain. Central Soviet wanted me to, ah, ask you some things about Delta Company."

Mags' face went blank. "I filed a full report when I woke up in Land's End. Go read that, if you aren't carrying a copy in that folder."

"They wanted me to hear it from you, Mags."

"Did they really? Well, let me put it like this: I was born here, in New Lawrence, and I was 11 years old when the Hunger started, when the contamination blew in out of the east and the crops started to die. We ate rattlesnake and acorn pie and boot leather, and lost my dad and my baby sister and all my friends. When I was 12 years old, the Blacklanders moved south across the Ohio and they called up the New Lawrence militia; everybody who could still stand up and hold a gun went north. I didn't get a gun; I had a knife. And I gave myself a present on my 13th birthday. I took my knife and I slit a fascist's throat and I took his Armalite out of his cold, dead hands. That autumn, we finally had a good harvest."

"I, ah, don't understand what that has to do with--"

"Two things. One, I been at this game a lot longer than you have. And two, I ain't exactly got a surplus of happy memories. Think about that when I tell you I'd rather talk about anything,

anything at all, than talk about Delta. Let the dead stay dead, for once."

"Well, Mags, I'll be straight with you--"

"Oh, that's new."

"I'll be straight with you. I came here from DIS—Miss Katie sent me personally—and her eggheads think that what happened to Delta was related to the loss of Bart's column. The theory is that whoever took out the column then moved in to set up an observation cordon around Land's End and Freeside, and your company's position was a target of opportunity."

Mags had prickled at the mention of DIS—the Department of Intelligence and Security—and she muttered, "I can smell where this is going, and I don't like it."

"As the sole survivor of the Delta Company incident, you're the only agent in good standing who has direct experience with those . . . things . . . in the exclusion zone."

"Wait, what do you mean 'in good standing'? There's someone else?"

"I was getting to that next. You know Jackson McCreedy?"

"Professor J? Of course I know Professor J. He taught political economy and American history at the university; I had him for almost every class. What's Professor J got to do with this?"

"McCreedy was one of the people who spoke out against Ken Kilroy back when Ken was general secretary. After he got censured, he resigned his teaching position and moved to Freeside, and at some point he got attached to a gang of scavengers, Ghost Group. Ghost Group was one of the units of wasteland rangers that Bart contracted to scout for his column as they moved toward the Citadel."

Mags' eyes went wide, and she sucked in a deep breath. Mark went on:

"He was presumed dead, but about two weeks after the column went dark, Land's End received a radio transmission from McCreedy, saying he was a day's walk into the mountains and begging for extraction, but all aircraft were grounded due to thunderstorms and rad spikes—the same ones that cut off aid to Delta. He was presumed dead a second time, but about a month later he just sort of showed back up, working at a clinic in Freeside."

"What's all this got to do with me, though?"

"Well, after Kilroy got recalled, Central wanted to rehabilitate all the people he'd purged, but McCreedy didn't want it; he'd rather pull teeth with his anarchist friends. But there is one thing he wants, and it's the same thing every scavver wants."

"No," Mags barked, standing up. "No, no, no way, hell no, we are done here. Go back to Central and tell them you couldn't find me."

"Mags, hold on! Just listen."

"Oh, no. I know exactly what you're gonna tell me next. I know exactly what else is in that folder, and you keep it the hell away from me. There is only one thing on the other side of those mountains, only one thing in . . . in that place, one thing you'll find, and it's exactly what Bart found: Death. Tell Central to come find me if they ever decide to take the war north again, like they ought to. Now, I've got work to do."

And she stormed off, and Mark yelled, "Commissar, the fascists are after it, too!"

She stopped and turned back around. "Alright, well, you shoulda led with that."

"Central is trying to play the war ten steps ahead, to fight a war of positions, and the plan we have right now hinges on that place. We're sure there's a treasure trove of pre-War technology and ordinance we desperately need, and they want to expand the Freeside Special Economic Zone, maybe even renegotiate the Writ of Settlement, start pushing the border into the east and healing the exclusion zone. That would give us the edge we need, militarily and, more importantly, economically."

"I dunno about part of that; those anarchists love their Writ of

Settlement something fierce. But that's . . . that's actually a damned good plan."

"The mission I'm supposed to give you is this: You're to go to Freeside and find the survivors of Ghost Group; that's Professor McCreedy and a designated marksman named Connor Turlogh. Central things that Bart's mistake was in trying to meet force with force without sufficient intelligence; the fact that McCreedy and Turlogh are still alive, and that you're still alive, indicates that a small unit of professionals should be able to cross the wasteland, recon the Citadel, and come back to tell us exactly what is . . . living in that . . . that place."

"Goddamn suicide mission is what that is. But what was all that about the fascists being after it?"

"Freesider scavengers and DIS people are both reporting that small groups of Arditi have been travelling back and forth between Ohio and the exclusion zone, in the direction of the Citadel, for a few weeks now. We haven't figured out what they're doing there, but nothing the blackshirts are up to is ever good."

"Hell. Well, like I said, you shoulda led with that part. I'll do it. I can go home, grab my kit, and be on the road in like fifteen minutes."

"Wait, really? It's that easy?"

"I'm a soldier. Whatever's inside of that hellhole, I'll die before I let Rain and his boot boys get their hands on it. And I probably will die, but I'm a soldier and I take a soldier's risk." She shook her head. "Man . . . I'm gonna have to see Professor J again. That is probably gonna be . . . awkward."

"What makes you say that?"

She gestured at all of herself. "Don't play dumb, man; you've read my file. The last time I saw Professor J was, y'know . . . before."

"Ah, that does sound awkward. I understand."

"I appreciate that, buddy, but trust me, you really don't."

[4]

GUN STREET GIRL

"I'LL BE READY TO GO DOUBLE-QUICK, I JUST GOTTA GRAB THE ol' bag of bones."

Mags led Mark around the side of the barn to a row of poplar cabins butted up against a few acres of soybeans. The cabins were all about the same size—three rooms and a loft—but each was a different shape, along with other irregularities; they'd been built with the tools and materials on hand, rather than to a set plan, but had been built to last. Each cabin had a patch of vegetables or a brake of fruit trees out front and a bank of solar panels and heaters on its roof. Most had chickens as well, and a few had beehives. Mags walked up to the first cabin, the one built up against the side of the barn, where a woman sat in a rocking chair on the front porch with a book in her lap. The woman looked to be in her late 40s, her face creased with lines of stress and worry, her kinky red hair pulled back into a bun. As they approached, Mark caught a better look at the book she was holding; Lenin, *What Is To Be Done?*.

"Hey, Mama," Mags said with a wave.

The older woman looked up from her book and gave the

vaguest hint of a smile. "Hey there, Magnolia Jane. Who's the foreigner?"

"This here's Mark. Central Soviet sent him to fetch me."

"Oi. What do they want now?"

"Job. Came here to grab my kit and then we're rolling out. Don't know when I'll be back."

"Feh. Well, you be careful out there, Magnolia Jane. You better come back to me in one piece this time."

"I will. I love you, Mama."

"I love you too, darlin."

Mags headed inside. Before Mark could follow her, her mother stopped him and asked, "So what's your name, stranger?"

"Uh, I'm Mark, Mark Barton. Political commissar."

"Noted. Now, you listen: If my girl don't come back, neither will you." And she went back to her book.

He followed Mags inside, into the front room and kitchen. The little house was cluttered with all the odds and ends of life, but it was immaculately clean and smelled of citrus and spice, with candles in the windows and a dried orange studded with cloves hung above the door. As they entered, he said, "Well, she seemed to, ah, take that really well."

"Yeah," Mags said, heading toward one of the two interior doors. "Mama's used to me coming and going by now. Plus she's an old-school party worker, real serious about it; she understands."

"The apple doesn't fall too far from the tree, I see."

Mags laughed at that. "Yeah, I do take after her, don't I? By the way, don't let her scare you—she ain't as mean as she looks. She's just like that."

Thick smells of cigarette smoke, coffee, and cosmoline wafted into the kitchen the instant Mags opened her bedroom door. It was sparse and spartan, the only furniture a set of drawers, a bare cot, a bookshelf, and a secretary desk, but it was plainly a lived-in space, with stacks of books and notebooks in every corner, clothes strewn around—all of them Ashlander combat fatigues; flecktarn trousers and blouses and blue-and-white striped tanktop undershirts—and full ashtrays and old coffee cups here and there.

The only hint of decoration was on the walls. A gun rack holding a long Dragunov marksman's rifle took pride of place over the cot, and next to it hung the flag of the Ashland Confederated Republic, a square of red cloth with a hammer and plow. Five portraits were stretched across the far wall: Marx, Lenin, and Trotsky, and two women. The one had a light brown complexion and long black hair and looked forward with an almost mischievous half-smile, and under the portrait was a plaque that read, *"Laurelei Bluecrow – Cherokee Nation – Subcommandant, Free Appalachian Army – Founder, ACR, 2191."* The other had buzzed black hair and a scar across her face and glowered forward as though having the portrait done was an annoyance; her plaque read, *"Maxine Reyez – Commandant, Free Appalachian Army – Co-founder, ACR, 2191."*

Looking over the portraits, it occurred to Mark that they were displayed so prominently that he could feel them watching him no matter where he stood in the room.

A mostly-packed rucksack sat on the floor beside the desk. Mags opened it, snatched a notebook and a few pens and the odds and ends of a rifle cleaning kit off of the desk, and stuffed them inside. She lifted the top of her secretary desk, took out two cartons of cigarettes, and packed them as well. And she took her Dragunov down from the wall, tied it across the top of the rucksack, and announced, "Alright, that ought to do it."

"That's it? Really?"

"Well, yeah. I'm a soldier, honey; I'm never not ready to go."

He nodded, impressed. "Okay, McCreedy's clinic is in a settlement all the way over Freeside, near the edge of the habitable zone. I can give you a ride. If we leave now, we should get there before dark."

"Well, what are we standing around kvetching for?"

Mags gave her mother a quick peck on the cheek as they left

and headed over to the truck Mark had arrived in, a big diesel flatbed rock-crawler. She nestled her rucksack in between the two seats, hopped inside, and settled in, reclining back to make enough room to kick her boots up on the dashboard. Mark maneuvered into the driver's seat, slithering around the stock of Mags' rifle, and off they went. As they rolled along the red dirt road out of New Lawrence, past the big fields of corn and soybeans and potatoes, smaller fields of herbs and wildflowers and various vegetables, the woodlots of fruit and nut trees carefully blended in with the local flora, and the cabins, outbuildings, and machine shops scattered throughout, Mags sighed, lit a cigarette, and started humming *John Brown's Body*.

"So," Mark said, breaking the silence.

"So."

"I, uh, wanted to ask you about some stuff."

"Uh-huh."

"So your personnel file lists your rank as chief warrant officer 3, brevet major."

"Last time I checked."

"Well, uh, I'm still new to this whole thing. I'm W-1, brevet captain. This is my first assignment, actually; I just graduated the Academy a couple of months ago."

"You looking for advice?"

"Ah, yes, if you don't mind."

Mags perked up at that. She took a long drag from her cigarette and said, "Tell me, comrade political commissar: What is the Commissariat, and what's it for?"

Mark rattled off a definition from memory: "The Commissariat is a special branch of the ACR military that's independent from military command, reporting directly to the Central Soviet General Assembly. Its purpose is to ensure direct civilian control of the military at all levels. When embedded in a unit, the duties of a political commissar are to observe and report on the unit's activities, to assist the unit commander, and to facilitate the political education and development of rank-and-file soldiers; a commissar's primary responsibility is to act as a soldiers' deputy and shop steward and make sure they're familiar with the party program and the Soldiers' Bill of Rights. Political commissars are appointed by warrant, rather than commission, and given brevet commissioned ranks because they have the authority to overrule the unit commander during field operations."

"Straight from the book. Now, here's the real question: Why are you and I out here doing wetwork that has nothing to do with any of those responsibilities? Why am I being pulled out of my unit, and why are you here doing the pulling instead of getting embedded in your own unit?"

He puzzled on that one for a moment. "Well, because our commitment isn't in any doubt. We volunteered for this job and had to struggle to make it through the Academy, and we report directly to Central, so that means we can be Central's eyes, ears, and hands out in the field."

"Exactly right. Now, if you want to be an effective political officer, you need to remember that and learn how to trust your own judgment. You're a brevet captain, which means you'll have the authority to overrule a lieutenant—and that's not hard, lieutenant don't know jack shit about shit, lieutenant's even greener than you are. But pretty soon you'll be a brevet major, with authority to overrule a captain, and that can be a hard thing to do. But that warrant in your pocket, where does that come from?"

"Well, from Central. From the General Assembly."

"Damn right. You, comrade political commissar, are the eyes, ears, and hands of the General Assembly, the sword and shield of Ashland. The better you can believe that, the better you'll be at your job. And it's not just about kicking the bigwigs around and making sure officers know their place; if your unit goes into combat, you're gonna have to be the unit's backbone, because the enlisted soldiers will know to look to you for guidance, and if you run, they run. Don't be a dick about it, remember that you're there to serve and not lead, but also don't forget that you're six times taller than God."

Mark chewed on that for a while. After a few more minutes' driving, he said, "So . . . combat."

"Yeah?"

"Well, I know the border's hot, and I know about bandits and roamers east of Freeside, but I hear different things about what things are like this far south. Just how rough is it?"

"Oh, life can get pretty interesting." And Mags looked around and took note of where they were, and a sardonic half-smile crossed her face. "Take the next right. Faster way to get on the main road anyways."

"Uh . . . okay. What's that way?"

"You'll see, kid. You'll see."

The right fork led onto a paved road and past another agricultural settlement, and at the far edge of the settlement was a crossroads, and on the far side of the crossroads was a tree, a great old white oak with a broad crown of gnarled and twisting branches. Twelve dead men swung from those branches.

Mark stood on the brakes. "Oh, Jesus! What . . . what the fuck?"

Mags pinched her cigarette out between two fingers and tossed the butt away. "Take a closer look."

He did, and he noticed that each corpse had a bullet hole in its head, and each corpse was wearing brown cargo pants and a black button-up campaign shirt with silver eagles embroidered on the collar.

"Are . . . are those . . ."

"Yup, sure are. Arditi. Blackshirts. Roland's own special boys."

"Good Lord. I didn't know they came this far south."

"Well, that's what special forces are for; that's what makes 'em special. Nine times out of ten, those skirmishes back and forth across the river are just fireworks to keep us busy while these rats sneak across to make trouble, poisoning wells and burning barns and whatnot. They never get very far, but it does keep things interesting. Hey, you see that one up there swinging on the far right?"

"Yeah."

"That was one of mine. Got him with my Dragunov at 600 meters."

"Jesus. But what's the point of stringing them up like that?"

"It puts the fear into their comrades and gives our people a bit of hope."

"Ugh. That's barbaric."

Mags shrugged, lit another cigarette, and quoted: "'I will early destroy all the wicked of the land, that I may cut off all wicked doers from the city of the Lord.'"

"Psalm 101; the Sniper's Psalm. You very religious, then?"

"I'm a materialist and an atheist."

"I thought you were Jewish."

"That, too."

East from the crossroads, the cracked and pitted blacktop widened out as the land flattened and the settlements they passed grew less slapdash, more intentional. The land around them was a patchwork quilt of fields, ponds, orchards, and woodlots, broken up here and there by circles of buildings. The air was thick with the buzzing of bees.

After a while, they came to the canton border, a bridge over a wide, deep river where the road was narrowed to two lanes by a funnel of sandbags. There was a guard shack at the funnel's mouth staffed by a woman wearing the same outfit as Mags, flecktarn cargo pants and a blue-and-white striped tank top, with aviator sunglasses and a Kalashnikov slung over her shoulder. Mark slowed down as they approached, and the guard took one look at the truck and its occupants and waved them by.

"Stop," Mags barked before Mark could drive on. He did, and

she sat up, lifted herself halfway out of the passenger side window, slapped the roof of the truck, and shouted, "Hey! Hey, staff sergeant! We're fascists!"

"Mags, what the fuck are you doing?" Mark demanded.

"I killed a troop and stole her pants! We're on our way to blow up the Huntington battery!"

The guard stormed over, glaring at them down the sights of her battle rifle, and growled, "Lady, what the fuck are you trying to pull?"

"I'm trying to pull that the Ohio fucking River is right over there and maybe you ought to be checking folks' papers, comrade staff sergeant."

"Alright, weirdo, have it the fuck your way. Papers. Now."

Mark and Mags each fished a billfold out of their pockets and handed them over. The guard snatched them in a huff, opened the one Mags had given her, lifted her sunglasses, looked it over a second time, and stammered, "W-w-what brings you to Land's End, comrade major?"

"Good try, but nope. I'm only a major if you're a captain, and I can see that you work for a living."

"Oh, uh, of course, comrade commissar."

"Call me Mags. This here is Mark."

"W-what's your business in Land's End, Mags?"

"On assignment from Central. Spooky shit, wetwork, usual need-to-know rules apply."

"Of course. You, uh . . . you can pass."

"Thank you. You have a nice day, sweetheart."

After they drove off, Mark cocked an eyebrow at Mags and asked, "Was that . . . was that really necessary?"

"Absolutely. We're a couple days' walk from a very, very hot border and those checkpoints are here for a reason. Say, Mark, you smoke?"

"No."

"More for me."

They rode together in silence as the hills rose up again in front of them, the road taking them over ridges and up switchbacks and through valleys, and the road grew steadily worse, with Mark having to maneuver the truck over gaping potholes and wide rock-slides before, at last, the pavement disappeared entirely. And as they country grew rougher, the settlements they passed changed as well, with less agriculture and more biomass plants and machine shops, fewer barns and more ugly concrete Quonset huts, and even from the road Mark could see that a lot of the huts bore placards with warnings like: "DANGER: EXPLOSIVE ORDINANCE." The ubiquitous vegetation looked stunted, sickly, and far too intentional.

"Yeah," he muttered, "we're in Land's End, alright."

"That we are," Mags said. "And don't it just suck ass?"

"It's so . . . grim."

"Tell me about it. I spent a month convalescing in Land's End after the Delta incident. Most God-forsaken place on Earth, besides Ohio."

"Why is it . . . well, why is it so shitty?"

"Ecological devastation. Before the War, this was all coal mines and coal processing. They ripped up the mountains, poisoned the dirt and the water, and it's still getting better from it. It's not going too bad—a lot of the work we did revitalizing New Lawrence after the Hunger was based on models developed here—but there's still a long ways to go. They got hydroponics, but most of the soil agriculture is devoted to hyperaccumulators and native flora. Don't worry; it gets less shitty the closer you get to Freeside."

"Have you spent a lot of time in Freeside? I've never been."

"A bit. It's a weird as hell place. The people are nice enough, but they can be mighty suspicious of folks from west of the fence, and it's pretty chaotic as a general rule."

"Violent?"

"Nah. Well, a bit—they have to deal with Arditi coming over the river, same as us, plus bandits and roamers from the exclusion zone—but it's disorganized as all hell. You can't rely on infrastructure or supply, and the roads are shit. Speaking of; you sure you know where we're going?"

"McCreedy's clinic is in a settlement called Parson's Hollow; they told me you'd have heard of it."

"Oh, yeah. I mean, I've never been there, but I could find it on a map."

"Good, because like I said, I've never been across the fence myself."

"Well, you're in for a . . . You're definitely in for something. A close look at one of humanity's most fascinating social experiments."

The next checkpoint was more robust, more permanent than the one between New Lawrence and Land's End, but it was also far more casual. There was a cyclone fence running north to south, twelve feet high and topped with razor wire, but it had fallen down in several places and looked like it hadn't seen repairs for decades. Footpaths ran across the fallen sections, and as they drove up to the guard shack they saw a man in a long black duster coat with a rucksack and a hunting rifle on his back walk over one of them, heading west. He stopped and waved at the guard, who waved back and made a mark in a notebook. A sandwich board above the guard shack read, "YOU ARE NOW ENTERING THE FREESIDE SPECIAL ECONOMIC ZONE," and below that someone had tacked on a scrap of plywood sporting a jolly roger and the words, "Mama Anarchy Loves Her Sons."

Mark was expecting Mags to dress this guard down as well, but she didn't; when asked for papers, she handed hers over and asked, "Any word on what the roads look like?"

"Depends," the guard said. "Where y'all headed?"

"Parson's Hollow."

"Ought to be fine, then. I hear tell the locals were running all over the place doing maintenance projects up thataway a few days back. What brings y'all to Freeside?"

"On assignment from Central. Secret squirrel type shit."

"Cool. Well, y'all have fun over there."

And they drove off. Just around the bend from the fence, they passed a massive signboard made from old doors and sheets of plywood. It was painted black, emblazoned with a red jolly roger and the words, "YOU ARE NOW ENTERING FREE TERRI-TORY – WELCOME HOME."

They made good time, for just as the guard had said, the roads were newly repaired. It was simple work, earth and hempcrete and garbage compacted into a roadbed, but it was serviceable. The settlements they passed through were fascinating jumbles of restored pre-War buildings, log cabins, and rammed-earth beehive huts, and seemed to grow up organically out of the various cross-roads. Every time they passed through a settlement, a crowd of people would come out to watch them drive past. Most smiled and waved. A few watched them with suspicious eyes and blank expressions. Once or twice, children would run out toward the road and throw rocks.

After a few hours' driving, with the sun just starting to dip below the mountains in the west, they came to another settlement, this one marked by its own signboard, also painted black and sporting a jolly roger, and its text read: "WELCOME TO PARSON'S HOLLOW – DEATH TO ALL THOSE WHO STAND IN THE WAY OF FREEDOM FOR THE WORKING CLASS!"

After passing the sign, they saw an old woman in a gingham dress walking down the road, a basket of ginseng strapped to her back. Mark slowed to a stop and called out, "Excuse me, do you know how to get to the clinic?"

"What one?" the old woman asked.

"Ah . . . the one where Jackson McCreedy works. We're trying to find him."

"What's it to you, red?"

"Professor J is an old friend of mine," Mags said. "I'm wanting to see him."

"Ahhh, suck my cock. Turn around and go on back to where you come from. Goddamn reds."

As the old woman walked away, Mags rolled her eyes and said, "Goddamn anarchists. Y'know what, just let me out here."

"Are you sure? I could drive you to--"

"Nah, bud, you really couldn't."

"Um . . . okay. Oh, here, you'll be wanting this." He handed over his accordion folder, containing the mission dossier.

"Thanks. You have a safe drive back, alright?"

"Uh . . . thanks. You, ah, how are you planning on getting back?"

"To tell you the truth, kid, I ain't."

[5]

BLOOD ON MY NAME

THE CLINIC WAS EASY TO FIND. IT WAS ONE OF THE LARGER buildings in Parson's Hollow, a two-story house still standing from before the War, with a big sheet of tin with a bright red cross painted on it propped up amongst the bush beans in the front yard. And leaning against the wall next to the front door was a tall, broad Black man in his mid-50s with a long beard, wearing a set of clothes that seemed just a bit too nice for his surroundings, puffing a cigar. Mags knew him on sight; this was Professor Jackson McCreedy, who'd once taught political economy and American history at the university in Ashland. He eyed Mags with suspicion as she walked up, his gaze lingering on her uniform and on the marksman's rifle tied across her rucksack. She smiled, waved, and cried out, "Hey, Professor J! Been a while, ain't it?"

The big man cocked an eyebrow. "Do I . . . know you?"

"You don't recognize me. I took your classes for two years, you're the one who wrote my recommendation letter to the Commissariat, and you don't recognize me."

Prof blinked at that. The words sounded like a rebuke, but the strange woman in front of him was grinning from ear to ear as though he'd just paid her a high complement. He studied her up and down a moment, and at last something clicked in his mind and he smiled back and asked, "Good God, Mike, is that you?"

"It's Mags, actually. Magnolia Jane Blackadder, political commissar."

Mags was expecting him to return the sentiment, to ask why she'd come, but instead his eyes lit up and he asked, "So it's Magnolia now, you say?"

"Call me Mags."

"And you're a commissar? Well, Mags, I'm glad you're here. Hell, nobody better could've showed up. Come inside."

Before she could ask what he meant, he opened the door and disappeared into the house. She followed him in with a shrug. The interior was dim, but it was clean—spotless—and reeked of soap and bleach and whiskey. The old man kept walking, and she followed him through a foyer converted into a reception area and down a hallway to a room with a big wooden dining table and a few chairs. The room, like everything else, was spotless, though the table's finish was marred by dark brown stains.

Prof shut the door behind them and asked, in a harsh whisper, "So you're here on business from Central? You report to Central, and to the Commissariat?"

"Well, yeah. Listen, Prof, the reason I'm here is--"

"Later, later. Right now . . . Aw, hell, Mags, I'm sorry for running you over like this, but this has been eating at me for ages now. I'm dealing with a . . . with a sensitive situation here in Freeside, and Central needs to know about this, but I've been hesitant to call it in; hell, I've been putting that off for a year. As I said, it's a sensitive situation, needs a delicate touch. I'd rather been hoping that someone from the Republic would pass through town, and here you are, and good God I don't think it could've worked out better."

The words "sensitive situation" and "Central needs to know" caught Mags' attention. She set her confusion aside and said, "Alright, Prof, lay it on me. What is it you need?"

"I'm so sorry for dumping this on you when you've only been here a minute, but, well, you'll see. I'm hosting a Blacklander; a defector. She fled here seeking asylum about a year ago. She was in a terrible state, physically and mentally, so I sort of took her under my wing, and she's been staying here with us, working as our gardener while she convalesces. But she . . . well, she knows some things about what's going on up there, and this is intelligence—important intelligence--that I'm sure DIS doesn't know anything about. She needs to be debriefed, and someone needs to make a report to Central."

"Well, that all sounds pretty routine. DIS has people who specialize in processing defectors. Hell, Prof, you came here from Central, you know that. Why not just grab a radio and call it in?"

"As I said, it's a uniquely sensitive situation. She . . . well, she's from the Arditi."

"She's from the fucking what now? Prof, that don't track. They don't let women into the blackshirts. They don't let women fight at all."

"Well, it's . . . ah, you'll see. Hold on."

Prof opened the door, looked around the hallway for a moment, and shouted, "Julia! Julia, could you come here for a second? There's someone here I'd like you to meet."

From somewhere out in the hall, a voice dripping with annoyance spat back, "Yeah, yeah, alright," and a moment later a woman walked in. She was small, only just over five feet tall, with long, black hair pulled back into a ponytail, wearing jeans, a long-sleeved plaid shirt, and a leather vest. She walked with her head down, staring at the floor, her face contorted in a perpetual scowl. Mags couldn't have explained why, but in some subtle way the woman gave off tells that set off her instincts as a soldier; something about the way Julia walked, something about the scowl on her face, made her feel like a threat.

Prof shut the door behind her and said, "Mags, this is Julia. Julia, this is Magnolia."

"You can call me Jules," Jules grumbled, not looking up.

"And you can call me Mags," Mags said, and offered a handshake.

Jules stared at the hand for a moment, sighed, and asked, "So what's this all about?"

Prof pulled out three chairs and motioned for them to sit. As they took their seats around the table, Mags took a pack of cigarettes and a zippo out of her pocket and lit one. Jules stared at her for moment with sad, brown eyes before whispering, "Hey, can I . . . can I have one of those?"

"Of course," Mags said, and slid the pack and lighter over. Jules seemed to relax a bit.

"Jules," Prof said, "Mags is an agent from Central Soviet. She'd like to talk to you."

Jules tensed up again, turned to him, and barked, "Leave."

"Huh?"

"Get out."

The old man gave a silent nod, stood up, and left the room. When he was gone, Jules leaned back in her chair and kicked her feet up on the table, and Mags noticed her shoes: Heavy, high-topped, steel-toed black combat boots. She unbuttoned her sleeves, started to roll them up, and said, "So I guess the old man probably gave you the short version already."

"Well, not really. He told me you used to be Arditi."

"Used to be," she said, and presented her newly bared forearms. They were covered in crude stick-and-poke tattoos, each one a symbol, all of them symbols that Mags knew entirely too well; she sucked in a quick breath and, on instinct, reached under the table and rested a hand on the hilt of her combat knife. Jules rolled her eyes, turned her head to the side, and lifted up her ponytail, displaying a soaring eagle and an iron cross tattooed at the base of her neck.

"Holy fuck," Mags whispered, "you . . . you are. You're a goddamn blackshirt."

"Well, not no more. But I used to be."

"I . . . I feel like I'm missing something here. The boneheads let women fight now?"

Jules met her eyes then, and her scowl curled up into a smile, a warm smile full of relief and gratitude. She gave a soft laugh and asked, "You really can't tell? Sugar, I guessed about you the second I saw you; you look great, but can't we smell our own?"

Recognition flashed across Mags' eyes, and she muttered, "Oh, fuck. Oh, good Lord. I thought . . . I thought that they just merc'd people like us."

"Yeah, that's what I thought, too. That's what I thought. I . . . I wish it was that easy."

And Jules began to cry.

Prof came to check on them after an hour of waiting, but as he approached the door, he could hear Jules quietly sobbing while Mags whispered, "It's okay now, it's okay. It's all over. You're here now." And he thought better about interrupting.

He returned to the hallway after another hour, late into the evening, and the door swung open and the two women walked out. Jules looked exhausted, her eyes red and swollen from crying, and she leaned against Mags as though she could barely stand; Mags, by contrast, stood up ramrod-straight and her face showed no emotion.

"She told you, then," Prof said.

Mags nodded. "Everything. All the gory details. Y'all have a radio that can at least reach Land's End here, right?"

"Ah . . . yes, of course."

"Good. Tomorrow morning, I'm gonna submit a report, and once I'm done with my mission here I'm gonna go north and burn Ohio to the fucking ground."

Prof nodded and chewed his lower lip. He turned to Jules and said, "Julia, dear, I . . . I'm sorry."

"No," she said, wiping her eyes, "nah, you didn't do nuthin, old man. This . . . this was okay, I think. She . . . she understands."

"Good, good. That's, ah, that's what I'd hoped."

Mags fixed him with her blank, icy soldier's stare. "I'm taking Jules up to her room now. We'll see you in the morning, Professor J."

"Would you, ah, would you like me to find you a place to sleep for the night?"

"I'm taking Jules to her room. She should not be left alone right now."

And the two women walked off down the hall together before he could speak again.

As he watched them leave, he wondered about Mags. The serious attitude and sardonic wit tempered by a need to please people, that much he recognized from his old student, but the way she'd gone all business coming out of that room, that cold and empty way she'd looked at him . . . Even back when he'd known her, as young as she'd been, Mags was already a killer, but this person wasn't a cowgirl, wasn't a bushwhacker. No, this was a professional. And a shiver ran up and down his spine as he wondered what mission Central Soviet could've possibly given this professional that sent her right to him.

Jules' bedroom was tucked away in a corner on the second floor. It was small, containing a bed, a chair, a dresser, a little bookshelf, and a window that looked out over the back garden. A black candle and a little silver Madonna sat on top of the bookshelf, which held three volumes: An old leatherbound Bible and two books of poetry, one by Yeats and the other by Wilfred Owen. Clothes lay strewn about on the floor, all of them jeans and long-sleeved button-up shirts. Jules locked the door behind them as they walked in, and they sat on the bed together in silence for a moment until Mags said, "Hey, that was a hell of a thing, y'know."

"Oh, yeah," Jules sighed, "that's one way to put it."

"No, I mean it was a hell of a thing to relive all of that. To tell anyone that story. Thank you."

Jules looked up at her with confusion that melted into gratitude, and she muttered, "Yeah. Thanks for listening."

"Of course. Is there anything you need right now?"

"Just this, I think."

"Well, I'm not going anywhere. I did want to ask you something, though."

"Yeah?"

"Tomorrow, I'm gonna have to call up my people and tell them about all this. You got that, right?"

"Yeah. The old man said that this would happen sooner or later. I . . . I wanna help."

"I figured you'd say that."

"Yeah?"

Mags took her hand and traced her thumb across her wrist, which was covered in a layered mat of scar tissue. "I can't imagine what you've been through. Even after hearing all about it, hearing all the gory details, I still can't even imagine it. And punishment isn't the same as justice, not by a long shot, but even so, if you were still half the person you used to be, I'd be goddamn surprised."

Jules chewed her bottom lip and examined her lap without speaking. She leaned over and rested her head on Mags' shoulder, and Mags said, "I mean it. You don't have to be that person anymore. I don't know if the anarchists have explained restorative justice to you, but here's all you gotta do: Make up your mind to do the next right thing, and then do it. And it sounds like you've already started."

"Alright. I . . . I do want that. And, hell, when I hear you say it, I can almost believe it. Thank you."

"Well, this is kinda my job."

"No, I mean . . . I can't explain it, but there's something about you. I've known you for, like, three hours, but I . . . I feel like I trust you."

And Mags leaned over, resting her cheek on the top of Jules' head, and after a beat she muttered, "Oh, god*dammit.*"

"Huh?"

"I think I trust you, too."

Jules stayed in good spirits for most of the night. But afterwards, as Mags lay sprawled across the bed trying to catch her breath, she rolled away and faced the wall, her arms wrapped tight around herself.

"Hey," Mags said, propping herself up on her elbows, "are you alright?"

"Yeah," she lied.

"Was that too much? Did I do something?"

"Nah. Nah, you didn't do anything."

"Can I touch you?"

Jules sighed. "I guess."

And Mags stroked her hair and said, "Talk to me, lady. What's on your mind?"

Jules was quiet for a long moment. At last, she sighed again and asked, "Why the hell are you bein so nice to me, huh?"

"Huh?"

"You. Everybody. Why is everybody bein so nice to me?"

"You finally found some good people, Jules."

"*Merda.* Maybe y'all are, but I fuckin ain't."

"Ain't what?"

"Good people. I don't . . . I don't fuckin deserve any of this. And I don't wanna assume shit about nobody, but let's be honest here: I sure as fuck don't deserve it from you of all people."

Mags digested her words for a moment, shook her head, and said: "Goddamn anarchists sure do love skipping steps. Yeah, I think I see where you're coming from."

"Huh?"

"You feel a lot of guilt about where you came from and who you used to be, awful and debilitating guilt. And you *should* feel guilty, and you know that. And yeah, you're right; you don't deserve all this grace. But you can't square up to that or process it because trauma and guilt are wound up too tightly together."

Jules turned over slowly and studied Mags with her big, brown eyes for a while before muttering, "Jesus, am I really that much of an open book?"

"Not so much; reading people is sorta my job. But, really, has nobody here ever told you about yourself?"

"One guy did, the guy who found me in the woods and brought me here. Everybody else is so nice they treat me like a china plate they're afraid to drop. They wanna help me move on from the past, but they don't wanna acknowledge it; and like you said, can't really move on from trauma when it's tied up with guilt."

"Sounds about right. Listen, is that what you're asking for? You want me to tell you about yourself?"

"Honestly? Yeah. Fuck me up. It'll be about damn time somebody told me the truth around here."

"Well, I mentioned restorative justice a bit ago; where I come from, we grow up learning that nobody's beneath redemption and that anybody can move on and be better if they're willing to do the work—and it sounds like you're willing to do the work. I wouldn't be lying here with my dick out if I didn't think that. And nobody, not nobody, not the lowest rotten bastard on Earth, deserves to go through one little bit of what those bastards put you through; no matter what you did or what kind of person you used to be, nobody deserves that. Like I said, punishment is not the same thing as justice."

Jules nodded. "But."

"But your ledger is pretty deep in the red. You played a stupid game, and you won a stupid prize."

"Yeah."

"Nah, nah, that's not quite right. I just . . ." She sat up, found her cigarettes and lighter, and lit a smoke before continuing: "Listen. I grew up in the New Lawrence township, just a couple days' march south of the river. Men in black shirts shot my friends. After I grew up and went to school, the Army posted me along the Ohio Valley. Men in black shirts shot my friends. And sometimes the men in black shirts would take our friends away alive, and we never found out what happened to them, and after hearing about what they put you through, well, I'm glad we never found out. And I've never worked with DIS personally, but I have a couple of friends who escaped from the BNR, and anyways all Ashlanders grow up hearing the stories. You were complicit in that, and you're going to have to square with that."

Jules rolled over and put her arms behind her head, staring up at the ceiling. "Sugar, can I steal another smoke?"

Mags handed her the cigarette she'd been smoking. She took it, took a long drag, and said, "Yeah, that's right. That's what the truth sounds like. I . . . I knew what I was and what I was doing way before I ever wound up on the wrong end of it; I'm not about to even try and act like I didn't. When I got caught, I'd already died a hundred deaths before they came for me, because I knew exactly what we do to people. Nobody deserves to go through what I did, and fuckin thank you for not trying to put that on me, but . . . it's like the scorpion and the frog, I guess."

"Uh-huh. I knew you knew that, but it's good to hear you say it out loud."

"Yeah. I could say I was sorry, and I sure am, but what the fuck was 'sorry' ever good for? And I . . . I . . . I need to *do* something. Not just 'cause it's right, but 'cause if I spend one more goddamn day hiding here pruning the roses and feeling sorry for myself, I'm gonna crack. You talked about doing the next right thing. Sugar, what's the next right thing look like?"

"Well, all that intelligence I'm gonna call into Central in the morning is a real big step. And whatever else you might know, that'd be helpful for us to know. Also . . . Hey, what did you say your old job was, before all the shit went down?"

"Heavy assault specialist. Head idiot in charge of door-kicking."

"You remember earlier, before shit got all intimate, I said I feel like I trust you?"

"Yeah."

"Well, I'm not just here for a friendly visit. I'm on a mission from Central. I don't know exactly what I'm walking into, but I know it's gonna be pretty hairy. I think I could use a door-kicker."

Jules laughed. "*Merda.* Sugar, you remember what I said about I don't deserve any of this? The most beautiful woman I've ever seen comes to my house, gives me an ear and a shoulder to cry on, and comes to bed with me, and now she's offering me a job. This ain't real. I'm still locked up and this is all an escapist daydream."

"It'll be good for me to have another pro, I'll feel better about whatever I just got myself into, and I think it'll be good for you to get out and do the right thing. Also, if I can be real for a minute, Prof was probably right that it's a good idea to keep you away from the DIS spooks for a little while; they'd end up coming to the same conclusions about you that I did, I'm sure, but they might not be very nice at first."

She shuddered. "Before I say yes, I wanna ask: What happens if I say no?"

"If you say no, then that means I was wrong, and we're done here. I'll get up, put my clothes back on, call in my intelligence report, and pretend I never saw you. Central will send a spook to come drag you back to Ashland for a full debriefing, and everything that that entails. But I think I already know what you're gonna say."

"Bet. I'm all in. Wherever you go, I'll go."

They sat together in silence for a little while, before Jules lit another cigarette and said, "Sugar, tell me something."

"Tell you what?"

"Your story, sister. I spilled everything about me; I'd like to know something about you. You've been in the shit, too, same as me. I can see it in your eyes. Those are a killer's eyes." She laughed. "I showed you mine, now you show me yours."

"I . . . I really don't like talking about myself, Jules."

"You ain't got to. But if you want to, I can listen."

Mags sighed. "You know where the New Lawrence township is?"

"Yeah. We operated out of Cincinnati."

"I was born in New Lawrence, lived there till I was about 16. But when I was 11 . . . when I was 11, there was a famine. A bad hurricane season kicked up a lot of contamination out in the exclusion zone and dropped it right on top of us. The crops failed. People got sick. People went hungry. My baby sister got sick, and she didn't get better. Same with my dad and most of my friends. We call it the Hunger. And then . . . When I was 12, the war got hot again. There were groups of Arditi moving south across the river, killing everyone they found, burning everything, and there were companies of brownshirts trying to capture and hold territory. So they called up the militia, and everybody went north. Including me."

"Christ," Jules muttered. "And you were twelve years old . . ."

"Oh, it gets better. See, less food surplus meant less hands available to work in the arsenals, which meant not enough guns to go around. I had a knife. It was on my 13th birthday that we made contact with the enemy, and I'll tell you what I did. While our unit had them pinned down, I snuck closer through the woods, and I saw a blackshirt off by himself, and he didn't see me. So I ran my knife across his throat, and I took his Armalite out of his hands. Hell of a birthday present, huh?"

"Shit."

"I relive that moment every time I close my eyes. I can still hear the sound of steel cutting into flesh, I can feel the hot blood all over my hands, I can hear that sick choking noise he made just before he flopped to the ground like a sack of meat. But if you want the truth, do you know what I feel every time I relive that moment? I feel proud. Satisfied. I've got my demons, that's for sure; I've done a lot of shit I ain't proud of, and I've buried family and friends. But all the shit that haunts me is from seeing human beings suffer. And fascists ain't people."

After a long silence, Mags heard Jules grumble, ". . . the fuckin truth."

"Whatcha say, hon?"

"I said if that ain't the fuckin truth. That they ain't people." She clenched her fists until her knuckles turned white. "I'm going with you, wherever you go. I'm gonna confront this, and I'm gonna keep going, too. I dunno if I'm a red or an anarchist now, or what—I never been real political; hell, I couldn't even tell you what the Falange actually is—but I know one thing. I know who my enemy is. And goddamn, Mags, I . . . I'm so fucking angry."

"You have every right to be angry, Jules. You have every right to feel whatever you feel. And that anger is righteous."

Jules sprang up from the bed and began to pace around the room, clenching and unclenching her fists, and as she grumbled her voice, previously a luscious mezzo-soprano, grew gruffer, and deeper, until it fairly dripped with cordite fumes and cigarette smoke. And as she paced, Mags noticed something she'd overlooked before. Just like her arms, most of Jules' torso was covered in stick-and-poke tattoos, but one on the top of her buttocks stood out: A pair of cats' eyes, and unlike the others it was rough, jagged, obviously done under duress. And just above that, at the small of her back, were more scars where three crude letters had been carved into her skin with a dull knife, spelling out a word: "*FAG.*"

"I hate them," she growled, her voice thick with malice. "God, but I fucking hate them . . I'll fuckin kill 'em all, every last one of those goddamn animals . . . I . . . *Fuck!*"

And she screamed, her entire body shaking with rage, and threw herself back onto the bed.

"Y'know," she said after a while, "that was the first time in like two years that I've let myself feel angry. After everything, I . . . I learned how to just go numb to keep myself alive, and that's all it's been. If I wasn't crying, I was just numb."

"Sounds about right," Mags said. "But that can be good, being angry, letting yourself have those emotions. You're right to feel however you feel, and goddamn if you ain't right be angry."

And she looked over the naked, prone form lying facedown on the bed in front of her, and she met Jules' second set of eyes again and repeated, "Yeah, you have every right to be angry, and sometimes it's not so bad to hate. But for now, we should get some rest. I reckon we'll have a long day ahead of us tomorrow."

Mags woke up early, before sunrise, same as she always did, and she slipped out of bed and threw her fatigue trousers and tank top back on and crept out into the clinic. As soon as she was downstairs she ran into one of the nurses walking the halls, waved at him, and asked, "Hey, uh, do y'all got a radio around here?"

The nurse cocked an eyebrow at her. "What's it to you if we do, red?"

"I'm with the professor."

He still looked dubious, but he led her down the hall to a utility room containing a desk and a big, clunky shortwave, a pre-War military model with the usual encryption. She sat down in front of the rig, powered it up, selected a channel, and broadcast, "This is Crow 12 calling Land's End command, repeat, Crow 12 calling Land's End command. Anybody copy? Over."

A response came back at once, crisp in the early morning air: "Yeah, this is Land's End east. You're coming through loud and clear, Crow 12. What do you got? Over."

"Land's End east, I'm a field agent calling in from east Freeside and I've got some important intel, need to make a report. If you've got a political officer or a DIS agent lying around, be a pal and put 'em on the horn for me. Over."

"Will do, Crow 12. Just a minute. Over."

After a pause, a new voice came over the wire: "Crow 12, this is the Land's End east political officer. Now, who are you—I don't know that call sign, Crow 12—and what goodies have you got for me? Over."

"Yeah, yeah. The name's Magnolia Blackadder, political commissar, chief warrant officer 3, New Lawrence Militia. I'm out in Freeside doing some wetwork for Central, details are need-to-know. Over."

"Alright, that tracks. I'm ready to receive your report, commissar. Over."

"Call me Mags. Well, I met my contact in east Freeside, but before I could continue my mission he told me that the anarchists were hosting a defector from over the river. Female, about five-four, black hair, slight build, and get this: She used to be Arditi."

The man on the other end of the wire interrupted: "Wait, wait, hold up a sec. This defector was a blackshirt, and . . . female? That would be some new shit. Uh, over."

"Yeah, yeah, that's about the shape of it. She, ah . . . she . . ." Mags shillied over how tactful she ought to be, decided to be blunt: "Subject is a transsexual. As she tells it, she was outed and arrested for degenerate sexual deviance while in active service. And that was roughly a year and a half before she made it to Freeside."

"Oh my fucking God. How did . . . how did she . . ."

"Survive? Yeah, that's why I wanted to get this report out right away; I only just got here yesterday evening. Buddy, I hope you've got a strong stomach and I hope I didn't interrupt breakfast, because you are about to hear a real goddamn horror story. You got a pen and paper ready? Over."

[6]
DEBRIEFING

M AGS SHUT OFF THE RADIO AND SAT ALONE IN THE EARLY morning stillness, trying to relax. She lit her first cigarette of the day and kicked her feet up on the comms desk and thought about Jules, found that she couldn't stop thinking about Jules. The woman's story had touched a personal nerve and rekindled a sense of pity and compassion that had long lain dormant. And she had such a nice smile, and such big, expressive brown eyes . . .

The blue light of pre-dawn began to creep in through the window, and she thought that it wouldn't be right to let Jules wake up alone. After finishing her cigarette, she crept back out into the empty hallway and tiptoed up the stairs to Jules' bedroom.

The door was locked.

When she tried the knob again, a voice from within whispered, "Mags? That you?"

"Yeah, honey, it's me. Can I come in?"

The lock clicked, and Jules whispered, "Yeah. Yeah, you can come in."

Mags opened the door to find Jules standing a few feet back from it, naked and visibly shaking, clutching her Nagant in a trembling right hand. Mags took a step back on instinct, then strode forward, threw her arms around Jules, eased the revolver out of her hand, and whispered, "I'm here, honey. What's up?"

Jules melted into her arms, buried her face in her shoulder, and muttered, "I'm sorry. I'm sorry, I'm sorry, I'm sorry, I . . . I panicked."

"Talk to me, hon."

"I . . . I had a nightmare, and, and some of the stuff you said last night kinda got to me, and then I woke up and you weren't there, and I . . . I panicked. I'm sorry."

"Some of the stuff I said? What did . . . Wait. Fuck. You woke up and you thought someone was coming to take you away again, didn't you?"

"Yeah. I . . . It's stupid, I know it's stupid, but I . . . I'm sorry."

"No, honey, I'm sorry. I fucked up. I should never have brought that up. Hell, if anybody knows what a trauma response looks like, I ought to. C'mere."

And she walked Jules over to the bed, where they sat down together, and she whispered, "You're safe here, hon. Nobody is coming for you. Nobody's going to hurt you again. I promise."

Jules leaned into her embrace, and they sat together in silence for a while until she muttered, "It was about . . . him."

"What was about who?"

"My nightmare. It was about Tomassi. They're always about Tomassi, if they're not about the corpsman. And then I woke up, and I was all alone in the dark, and I thought, 'Fuck, this is it, she's gone and John is gonna come through that door for me any minute now.' So I grabbed your strap off of your bag and . . . waited."

"Hell. You . . . you go through this a lot, don't you?"

"Oh, yeah. Sometimes it feels like every little thing sets me off—if people say the wrong words, or if somebody walks up behind me, or dumb shit like that. And I'll run up here and lock the door and sit here like I'm waiting for someone to come after me until I chill out. Y'know this is the only interior door in this place with a deadbolt? When I got here a year ago, the old man brought me up here and told me this was my room, and the first thing I did was lock the door. And then I cried like a little baby, I was so happy. So the next day they put an exterior lock on it, and me and the old man are the only ones with keys."

As she spoke, she began to rock back and forth, rubbing her thumbs against her index fingers. Mags held her tighter, and she muttered, "I'm sorry. I'm sorry. I don't know why I'm telling you all this."

"It's fine, hon. It's healthy to talk about it, and I like listening to you talk."

"Fuck. You really mean that, huh?"

Mags cocked an eyebrow. "Of course I do. Why wouldn't I?"

"Hell. I . . . I . . ." She pinched the bridge of her nose. "I started to say 'emasculating', but nah, that'd be about as wrong as it gets. It's fuckin *humiliating* when I get like this, especially in front of anybody, but . . . Like I said last night, I feel like I trust you."

"You can trust me, hon. And I promise there's no shame in any of this."

"Huh. If you really mean that, you can do me a favor. Reach under my pillow over there and find Carmilla and give her to me."

Mags reached over and fumbled around beneath the pillow until she found something and brought up a handmade sock doll in the shape of a black cat. Jules took it, clutched it to her chest, and seemed to relax a bit.

Mags let out a laugh, stopped herself, and stammered, "Fuck, I'm sorry, I'm sorry, I wasn't laughing at you. It's just . . . you named your comfort object Carmilla."

"Yeah, and what about it?"

"Remind me, what did you say your last name was?"

"Binachi. I'm Jules Carlotta Binachi."

She laughed again. "It's just so . . . well, it's just so appropriate."

"Ahh, *brutta figlia di puttana bastarda*," Jules sneered. But she was laughing, too.

And Mags watched her, finding it hard to reconcile that this small, frightened, shaking woman rocking back and forth and clutching a doll to her chest was a soldier, a blooded killer, was very likely a murderer. As if to underline the contradiction, she noticed that the inside of Jules' left elbow—the arm clutching the sock cat—sported a very recognizable tattoo: A grinning skull with a dagger clutched between its teeth, wreathed in the words, "*Non mi interessa davvero.*" *I really don't care.*

"How old did you say you are?" she asked.

"Ah, I just turned 25 a couple of months ago."

Mags did some quick mental math—one year convalescing in Freeside, eighteen months' internment, long enough in service before that to have become a corporal—and she thought to herself, *Good God, you must have been a* child *when they got their hands on you.* Out loud, she said, "Y'know, *partigiana*, I definitely did not mean to let you wake up alone, but I didn't expect anybody to be up this early. The sun's not even up yet."

"Normally I like to sleep in, but it's Wednesday. I cook breakfast on Wednesdays."

"Breakfast sounds nice. Am I invited?"

"Of course, sugar. Everybody's invited around here. We don't have any longterm patients staying right now, so it'll just be me and you and the old man and the two other nurses, plus anybody from town who wanders in."

"I'd love to help. What are we having?"

"Eggs. Probably won't be any meat—Kat and Keith won't touch meat—but if you want I could pull you out a slab of bacon or . . . Ah, *merda*, I'd have to see what else we have. How do you take your eggs?"

"Sunny-side-up, fried all the way through."

"Fried all the w-- . . . You goddamn degenerate."

"What? I don't like runny eggs."

". . . I'm making you an omelet."

They laughed together for a while, and as Jules got up to get dressed, Mags asked, "So what else do you usually do around here?"

"I do a little nursing sometimes—well, really I just hand out pills and go fetch stuff for those other three; I'm an okay field medic, but I ain't no nurse. Mostly, I'm the gardener."

"Oh, please tell me all about that. What kinds of stuff do y'all grow?"

"Oh, all kinds. We got a regular market garden in the backyard over there; herbs, spinach, tomatoes, beans, peppers, couple of peach trees, all the good things in life. But my very favorite are the roses. It's *our* garden, but they're *my* roses."

"Jules, will you show me your roses later?"

"Didn't I already last night, sugar?"

They laughed together at that as they made their way down the stairs and through the hall into the kitchen. It was a breezy summer kitchen that reminded Mags of home, with polished oak cabinets and countertops and big wood stove and shop sink, a rack of iron and copper cookery hanging over it, a big oak table in the center, all illuminated by the light of the rising sun filtering in through a picture window. The picturesque stillness was broken only by the low, quiet hum of electricity, the building's solar battery bank powering the big, clunky refrigerator in the corner.

"I love it," Mags muttered as they walked in.

Jules beamed with pride. "Yeah, it's pretty nice, ain't it?"

"It reminds me of my mama's house, back in New Lawrence."

"I'd love to hear about it. Now, you get the stove started—there's a woodpile right outside that door—and let's keep talking.

Jules chopped onions while Mags lit the stove and recounted, "We lived in a cabin next to the library and schoolhouse—Mama was a librarian and a schoolteacher when we weren't busy on the farm—out on one of the big collective projects where they grow potatoes and soybeans. We kept chickens and a couple of goats and worked part of the neighborhood's vegetable patch, too. It wasn't a big place, but after the famine it was just me and Mama, so we had plenty of room. Before that, and after, there was plenty to eat, and me and Mama loved to cook, especially when the whole town came together. It was Mama taught me to read, along with all the neighbor kids, and really it's all her fault I am the way I am 'cause she was always shoving this or that book into my hands. It was her idea that I should go to the university in Ashland; that was when I was about 16. Didn't see much of her or the home place for, oh, damn near six years, but then a couple years ago I transferred from the regular army to the militia and wound up right back home." She shook her head. "And here I am, leaving again."

"If you don't mind me asking, sugar, how did your people take the, uh . . . well, the whole girl thing?"

"Oh, easy as can be. Gender identity is a protected category in the Republic, has been for as long as there's been a Republic. Lauri saw to that right at the start."

"Who's Lauri?"

"Y'know, Lauri. Wait, you mean to tell me you've lived in Free-side for a year and you don't know who Laurelei Bluecrow is? Lauri Bluecrow and Maxine Reyez founded the Ashland Confederated Republic in 2191 after the Free Appalachian Army secured the Ohio Valley. That's a whole other story, but yeah, Lauri was a girl like us." She cocked an eyebrow. "It seems . . . odd that you wouldn't know that. When I was at the Academy, we had classes all about the Blackland New Republic's history and structure; Father Murphy Covington and Commander Ragnar Rockwell signing the Writ of Union in Columbus back in 2195, all that crap. Hell, I could tell you the size of Roland Rain's jackboot."

Jules shrugged. "Well, you're a political officer; I was just a grunt. Maybe war clerics know about Lauri Bluecrow and communism and shit, but they always told us that the only thing you need to know about Bolshevists is where to shoot 'em. Probably they know that if more people knew what this place is like, more people would get real eager to go south of the river."

"Sounds about right. But like I was saying: I think a part of me knew early on, but I was always too chickenshit to deal with it. But right after I turned 18, I'd just passed selection for the Commissariat and started my first year at the Academy—my only year, actually; I graduated early—and we had this training instructor, a real hard-nosed bitch, a real battleaxe of a woman. The kind of person you'd follow through wire and fire, but just as soon piss in their coffee. You know the type. Anyway, she was a girl like us, and it kinda got me to thinking about my life and where I wanted to be and what was gonna make me happy. So one day I go up to her in private and I says, 'Comrade training instructor! Permission to speak?' And she says, 'Go ahead, Blackadder.' And I says, 'Comrade training instructor, permission to speak freely?' And she says, 'Go ahead.' And I just started bawling my fucking eyes out."

"And what happened then?"

"I'll tell you. She gave me a great big bear hug and she called me 'sister', and that night she walked me down to the Academy records office and showed me how to get my name changed. I've been Magnolia Jane ever since."

"That easy, huh?"

"Yep. The Republic is pretty great like that. I'm not sure how they do things here in Freeside, but it's probably similar. Hell, with no central records office keeping track of people's names and whatnot, it might be even easier here."

Jules was quiet for a while as she moved from chopping onions to buttering a skillet and pulling out eggs while Mags fumbled around for cheese. After a few minutes, Jules said, "Me, I . . . I pretty much always knew, y'know?"

"Honey, are you sure you wanna talk about that? You don't have to if you don't want to."

"No, sugar, I want to. Maybe not with anybody else, but you . . . you get it. As far as I knew growing up, we just didn't have trans people in Ohio or, hell, anywhere; I never even heard words like *transsexual* or *transgender* until after I'd already broke bad. But I always knew, from as far back as I can remember, I always knew that something was . . . wrong. That I was supposed to be different, y'know? When I got to be old enough to understand how girls and boys are different, I started being able to put words to it: *What's wrong with me is everybody thinks I'm a boy even though I'm a girl. Mama Maria,* but my old man would beat the living shit outta me the one or two times I tried to talk about it."

Mags laid a comforting hand on her shoulder and nodded without speaking. Jules went on:

"I took those beatings to heart, I guess. I been . . . running away from myself my whole life, I think. When I was in my teens and my number came up for conscription, I threw myself into the army like I'd been born for it. Volunteered for the Arditi. I thought that if I could be the meanest, hardest man around, then I could finally, well, be a man. Like being hard and mean would fix me." She gave a cold laugh. "Well, you can see how good that worked out. Wound up getting fixed but good in the other direction."

"Honey, are you sure that--"

"Let me talk, goddammit. I . . . I've got started, and now I don't think I should stop. Did I tell you about the night it happened? I don't think I did, nah, just about what happened after that. Well, as a corporal in the blackshirts, I was deemed to have a big enough dick that I got my own room in the barracks instead of just a bunk and a locker. A while before, I'd gotten my hands on this dress, a long black evening dress. Fit like a fuckin glove and I looked great in it—first time in my life I ever felt comfortable. I kept it stashed up inside the drop ceiling over my bed, and whenever I had some time alone I'd lock my door and put it on and just relax for a little while, y'know? One night, though, I came back from chow and my room had been tossed and the ceiling panel had been moved. I knew I was fucked, so I started throwin shit in my ruck, wondering if I should run off east to the exclusion zone or west to the desert. Then the door swung open and there they were, couple of MPs and my old pal Captain Tomassi. He was holding the dress. Fucker looked right at me and he said, 'Always had you figured for a faggot, Binachi.'"

Jules' hands shook as she cracked eggs into the skillet, and Mags put her arms around her waist and whispered, "I'm so fucking sorry, hon."

"Ahh, it ain't like it was your fault. I just . . . I . . . Sugar, I've already told you everything else; can I tell you one more thing? Get it off my chest?"

"Of course, honey. Always."

"John made me wear that dress the next time I saw him."

Mags felt bile rising in her throat. Jules sighed and said, "Enough. Enough about the past. Let's . . . let's have us a nice breakfast together, alright? You go put on some coffee."

"That sounds like just the thing. And while I'm doing that . . . Jules, tell me about your roses."

Jules' sour expression curled up into a smile, and she did, telling of when she'd first been brought to the clinic, finding work to do, tending the garden, finding a thick tangle of brier roses growing through the rusted wreckage of a Ford Ranger while helping to clear a new patch; replanting them, feeding, tending, and pruning them until they gave her big, beautiful flowers – mostly red, a few a gorgeous black. Her smile grew warmer with every word.

Mags listened as she rinsed some of Jules' eggsheslls, crushed them, mixed the fragments with some of the coarse, brown coffee grounds she'd found in the cabinet, added the concoction to the big tin kettle warming on the stove. And with their pot of cowboy coffee brewing, she rested her elbows on the countertop and just listened; Jules had by then stopped talking about her roses in particular and launched into a more general spiel about different varieties of roses, plant parasites, nutrient requirements, and soil pH. When she finally stopped—which took a while; she seemed to know everything there was to know—Mags whispered, "God, hon, you're so smart."

Jules blushed. Mags smirked and added, "Hey, honey?"

"Yeah, sugar?"

"You're so goddamn cute. You know that, right? Now come over here and kiss me."

She did, and Mags got up and threw her arms around her, and they stood there in the kitchen, staring into each others' eyes, until a voice off to their left barked, "Oh, shit—I'm not interrupting, am I?"

They turned to see the nurse that Mags had met in the hall earlier standing in the doorway. Jules gave him a warm smile and said, "Naw, naw, come ahead in. The omelets are done and we're just waiting on coffee."

He gave Mags that same suspicious look as he walked in and scrounged around for a plate and fork. Walking over to his side, Jules said, "Keith, I'd like for you to meet my, uh . . . my new friend. This here's Magnolia."

"You can call me Mags," Mags said. "We, ah, we met before. Briefly."

Keith's expression softened. "Well, red, any friend of Jules here is a friend of mine, I guess."

"The others up yet?" Jules asked.

"Dunno. I got up early to make sure there was nobody waiting outside; there weren't. The old man should be awake by now, though, and you know Kat's gonna come running as soon as they smell food."

She chuckled at that. Mags took the kettle off of the stove, poured a bit of cold water into it to settle the grounds, and announced, "Coffee's on. Y'all want some? First cup's the least bitter."

"You go on ahead, red," Keith said. "You did the work, and you're our guest."

"Much obliged. My name's Mags, by the way."

"Yeah, red, I know."

"Asshole."

"Soulless authoritarian."

"Liberal. Reactionary idealist."

Jules cut between them and growled, "Would you two cut it the hell out? You're my friend, and Mags is my . . . uh . . . good friend, and I want us to have a nice breakfast."

"I'm sorry," Mags said. "I just . . . I have a name, my name is Magnolia Jane Blackadder, and it's my name and I'm kind of attached to it. I picked it out myself."

"I'm gonna have to take her side on that one, bud," Jules said.

Keith nodded. "I'm sorry, Mags. I just . . . it's rare enough to see any reds this far east of the fence, let alone a commissar. What brings you to Freeside?"

"Came to see Professor J," Mags said, which was not, strictly speaking, a lie. "He's an old friend from way, way back."

"Oh, yeah? You knew him back when he used to teach school over there in the big city?"

"Sure did! He was kind of a mentor for me, back in my wilder days."

The two fell into talking over their coffee, which pleased Jules well enough, and she slid in beside Mags and leaned against her. A minute later, a person about Jules' size wearing a black tank top and ragged blue jeans stumbled into the kitchen, walked up to the coffee pot, and yawned, "G'morning, fuckers. So who's the red?"

Mags sighed.

"Morning, Kat," Jules said. "Kat, this here is Mags, my, uh . . . new friend."

"'Friend', huh? The two of you 'very good friends', then?"

Jules looked uncomfortable. Mags grabbed her hand and said, "I'm her girlfriend."

"Ooh, cute! But I know I've never seen you around here before."

"I just got in yesterday."

Kat stifled a laugh. "Of course you did. Well, long as you're here, you better take good care of our girl, alright, red?"

Mags grinned and gave a mock salute. "She's in good hands, I promise."

"Better be. So—Mags, is it?"

"Yep. Short for Magnolia, but everybody calls me Mags."

"Cool. I'm Kat, by the way. So what brings you to our neck of the woods?"

Mags spun the same not-quite-a-lie about visiting her old teacher, and the four of them chatted over their coffee until Prof at last walked in, his hair and beard and clothes still bedraggled, and went to fix himself a plate of eggs, saying, "Good morning, Kat, Keith, ladies."

The four welcomed him as he sat down. With the table full, Mags started to dig her fork into her eggs; Kat reached out a hand to stop her and shook their head. She glanced to her left and saw Jules cross herself and quickly whisper, *"Bless us o Lord and these Thy gifts which we are about to receive from Thy bounty through Christ our Lord amen."*

She started to lift her fork but stopped when she noticed Jules looking at her expectantly, as though waiting for her to say something. She smiled from ear to ear, held her forkful of eggs up, and said, "Alright, then. *Baruch atah adonai elokeinu melech haolam, Shehakol Nihyah bidvaro.* Anybody else, before I show my ass again?"

"Nah," Kat said, "I think we're all atheists."

"Well so am I."

Prof threw back a cup of coffee and asked, "So, Magnolia, are you enjoying your stay?"

"Yep. The company's real cordial."

Kat and Keith snickered. Jules blushed, elbowed Mags in the stomach, and hissed, "Cut it out, alright?"

"Fuck, I'm sorry, honey."

"Yeah," Kat echoed, "we were just making fun. We'll cut it out."

Prof got up to fetch more coffee and added, "Mags, I wanted to ask if you had any thoughts about our little operation here."

"It seems, well, awfully quiet. This is a fairly sizable settlement, there must be at least three or four hundred people here; I figured that the medical services center would be a lot busier."

"Oh, we used to be up until about six months ago, before we franchised."

"Franchised?"

"There are three other clinics in Parson's Hollow, and this is actually one of the smaller ones. Outside of cold and flu season, we don't see too much work beyond regular checkups, routine dental work, and the occasional accident. A year ago, though, we were the only clinic in this entire settlement, and to say the least it wasn't easy. That's part of the reason I came back here and stuck around."

Mags was listening intently, taking mental notes. "What do y'all do about pharmaceuticals? Is there a fablab here?"

"That there is. The best engineers in Freeside have got a little shop running just on the other side of the mountains, and we keep their reactors and wet-printers busy. There's never much of a surplus, and sometimes we get bottlenecked by a lack of precursors, but we do get by. Every year is easier than the last."

"All the comforts of home, then?"

"With a few ups and downs. Manufacturing in the ACR is more efficient, more productive, more reliable, but the way things are done in Freeside has a certain . . . flexibility. A black fablab can respond to changing conditions and come up with innovative solutions to a new problem much faster than a red fablab can. It's an odd trade-off; nobody dies of cancer here, but occasionally someone might die from stepping on a rusty nail because of an interruption in the penicillin supply."

"Yeah, that tracks. Also, you guys probably have a much easier time tackling the computer problem than we do, so close to the exclusion zone."

Jules, who'd been leaning against Mags and listening, broke in: "Wait, what's a computer problem?"

Mags shook her head. "Jeez, they have not told you diddly shit, have they?"

"Not really."

"Well, one of the biggest issues we're dealing with back in the Republic, and to a lesser extent here in Freeside, is that we're just about at the end of our ability to optimize production. All the optimization in the next set of five-year plans is still just moving the same old pieces around the same old chessboard; it all still comes down to human eyes watching the machines and human hands lifting the tools. Making things better will mean automation, and automation means computers, and we just . . . can't. The raw materials needed to manufacture new tech on a big enough scale are, for the most part, on the other side of the planet, across an ocean and God-knows-how many roamers and God-knows-how many other exclusion zones. Might as well be on the fuckin moon. Other than the little we can do restoring or repurposing pre-War tech that the scavengers bring back, we're stuck in analogue. But the Freeside settlements are in an advantageous position, being so close to the wasteland and all those pre-War ruins; there's more scrap to be restored or repurposed, and it's easier to get to. Nobody is better at doing more with less than a Freeside engineer, and you can take that to the bank. Really, that's what's at the heart and soul of the relationship between Freeside and the ACR, the agreement struck in the Writ of Settlement seventy years ago; we give them guns and corn and don't interfere with their political economy, and in return they keep us in semiconductors and lithium."

Kat and Keith beamed with pride at those words and looked just a bit smug. Mags let them have it; it was earned praise. Enjoying this newfound harmony, she addressed the table, saying, "Now, y'all didn't hear this from me, but back in Central there's been some talk about renegotiating the Writ of Settlement, making things more open and less frosty. Bluecrow and Reyez thought that Freeside was an inherently unstable political unit and that it wouldn't last another generation; but that was seventy years ago. Y'all are alright for a bunch of liberals, and there's a lot more for us to learn out here than just how to get a smartphone turned back on."

The two anarchists nodded sagely, and the conversation continued along political lines until all the omelets were eaten and dishes done. Pulling Prof and Jules aside, Mags said, "I need to get a couple things out of my rucksack, up in Jules' room. You two should, ah, come with me."

Upstairs, Jules and Prof sat down together on Jules' bed while Mags rooted around in her rucksack until she came up holding an accordion folder. She held it away from herself, like a snake, and Prof shook his head and said, "Magnolia, you do not even know how badly I hoped I'd never see one of those damned things again."

Mags was ice-cold, all business, the blooded professional, with the happy sparkling in her eyes gone and replaced by nothing at all. "Professor J," she said, "let me start by saying that you and I share a very special bond, one that most people are lucky enough not to know anything about."

"How's that?"

"When I graduated from the Academy, I was assigned to the Land's End border division of the regular Army. When I made chief, I got embedded in the division's Delta Company, the garrison of a communications outpost at the north end of the border between Land's End, Freeside, and the exclusion zone, just on our side of the Ohio. One day, out of nowhere—we had no warning, none at all—the outpost was attacked by a battalion-sized element of Roland's boys. We managed to hold our position, but it was a tricky business and we were getting critically low on ordinance. We raised baseplate on the radio and begged for some help, but no dice; all aircraft were grounded by the thunderstorms and radiation spikes. So we bugged out. Packed everything we could carry, mined everything else, and took off south as soon as the coast was clear.

When we hit the bottom of the mountain, we were short one platoon. I backtracked to look for them and I found . . . I found what was left of them." Her hands started to shake. "I went back to the rest of the unit, and I . . . I found what was left of them, too. I started to freak, but then I heard . . . voices coming out of the rain and darkness. Hard, cold voices with funny accents. So I really freaked, and I ran. Ran all the way to Land's End."

Prof pinched the bridge of his nose and sucked in a deep breath. "Mags, I can already tell you that I want absolutely nothing to do with whatever else is in that folder."

"Funny; that's exactly what I said."

"Before you go on with your sales pitch—which, by the way, I am absolutely going to say no to—I have to ask. Why are you dragging Julia into this?"

"I go where she goes," Jules snapped.

"Jules, take my word for it, you do not want to go where she's going."

"And what are my other choices, old man? Should I just sit here forever and pretend like nothing's wrong? Or should I go back over the river?"

"I know where this conversation is going, and I need you to understand that this . . . this is suicide. It's worse than suicide, because the thing that Mags is talking about is worse than death."

Jules sighed and shook her head. "You're a good man, Professor J, and you've got so much love and compassion in that big old heart of yours, but you're letting it get you into trouble. The thing that . . . the thing that keeps me awake at night, keeps me staring at my shoes and crying in the shower, it's not just trauma. It's guilt. You're a good man, and I can't tell you how much I appreciate all the help you've given me, but that's the whole thing: I don't deserve it. You're such a good man that when you look at me, all you see is a lost, hurt woman who needs a home and a therapist. But that ain't me, man." She pulled her sleeves up to her elbows, showing off the stick-and-poke map of hate that ended at her scarred wrists. "I am a bad person, professor J. I haven't just suffered unspeakable things, I have *done* unspeakable things. I hurt people, man. A lot of people. And no matter how sweet you and everybody else are to me, I'm never gonna get any better until I deal with that. Hanging around here watering the plants and handing out aspirins while everybody tries to be so nice to me, I ain't been healing. I just been hiding."

"I promise you that you're a better person than you think you are, Julia, but alright. Mags, you might as well tell her the whole story."

Mags took a sheaf of photographs out of the folder and handed them to Jules. They were in black and white and had been taken from a far distance, and at first it was hard to make out what she was looking at, but it gradually came into focus: A wide, flat cove; the ruins of what had once been a sprawling residential suburb; and, at the center of it all, rings of 20-foot-high concrete blast walls with an office tower, a radio antenna, and a cooling tower peeking up over them. A flag flew from the roof of the office tower, an American flag, a pre-War ghost fluttering in the poison wind. The very last photograph had been taken at night, the outline of the office tower made starkly visible by the electric lights flickering in some of the windows.

"What the fuck," was all she could say. Prof turned ashen grey and said nothing.

"They call it the Citadel," Mags said. "About 200 miles due east of here, not too far from the ocean, someplace in between the one plane of poison glass that used to be Washington DC and the other plane of poison glass that used to be the New York metropol, is the Citadel. We don't know much about it other than it has the profile of a pre-War military facility, it is intact, and it is functional, inhabited. And that's all we know, first of all because it's so deep in the exclusion zone, and second of all because nobody's ever been inside of it that we know of. Only a handful of people have ever even seen it and lived to talk about it."

"But what makes it so special?"

"From a practical standpoint, it's special because of the computer problem. Pre-War military and other government installations always have the best scrap, but it's been almost two centuries since most of it was powered on, and a lot of it was never properly shielded, so it's always a bit of a gamble if dealing with the hostile environment and fighting off monsters to get into these places is even worth it. But this? An intact, maintained, state-of-the-art facility . . . God, there must be so much tech in there. WE could automate the arsenals. Automate the machine works and the biomass plants. Set up wireless digital comms from the Ohio Valley to the Georgia line. Put a fully-equipped fablab in every single settlement. And that would cut through so many labor hours, free up so many pairs of hands . . . we could finally start building it. Finally start sowing the seeds of the post-scarcity economy."

She looked off into the middle distance, visions of 3d printers and fabrication vats dancing in her head, and when she tried to talk about the Citadel from a less practical standpoint, she stumbled over her words; as well-read and as experienced as she was, she was no scavver.

Prof took it up then, his eyes locked on the photograph in Jules' lap. "That damned thing," he muttered, "that goddamned thing . . . That, that's a burning candle on a dark night, and we're the moths. Wasteland scrapping is rough, dangerous work, you see, unpleasant, leads you far from home and deep into ruined environments where humans can't live. But there's . . . something about it. Once you start scavving, it awakens something deep in your mind, something primal. It's hell out there, but it's also fascinating and darkly beautiful. You see plants and animals learning how to live in those environments, sprawling cities standing empty as nature slowly reclaims them, and an entire world of secrets just lying there to be picked up. And when you come back home, it gnaws at you to start getting the next expedition ready, to go see what wonders and horrors you can uncover. And the Citadel . . . the Citadel has become something of a legend in Freeside. What is that place?

What's happening in there? What secrets is it guarding? The fact that no-one who comes near it ever comes back makes it that much more alluring." He shook his head. "I feel like an addict jonesing for a fix, but that's how it is. I . . . I still have dreams about that place, and not all of them are nightmares."

"Couple years ago," Mags said, "a bunch of people got close, and two came back."

Prof sighed. "Bart."

Mags nodded. "Bart."

"And who the fuck is Bart?" Jules asked.

Mags took another photograph out of her dossier. It was of a tall, brown-skinned man with long, billowy hair, a ridiculous handlebar mustache, and piercing black eyes. He wore a crisp military uniform under a long black trenchcoat.

"Comrade Field Marshall Bartholomew Reyez," she said. "Mechanized infantry commander."

"Fucking tankers," Jules muttered.

"Yes, exactly. A fucking tanker. You know the type. Well, couple years ago, Bart got the ear of our then general secretary and convinced Central to approve an expedition into the wasteland, to crack open the Citadel. Two entire companies, tanks and trucks and APCs and all that, with a whole company-sized element of Freeside scrappers hired on as wasteland rangers, went into the shit. Two men came out."

"I'll take it from here," Prof broke in. "Whatever you've got in that file, there's no way it can capture the horror of it all. Some of those Freeside scavengers were my group, we called ourselves Ghost Group, and I was . . . I was there. I was our spook; picking apart the sins of the old world was my academic speciality, and I picked up the hands-on approach easily enough. There was also Connor Turlogh, designated marksman; Tanya Firelake, heavy weapons specialist; Jacky-Boy, medical corpsman; Wardog, mechanic; and Raven Moon, explosives specialist. We moved out a day ahead of Bart's column, and we found the way but didn't find resistance. There were bridges collapsed, debris blocking the roads, mundane things like that, but there were no bandits, no hunters, and the roamers were few and far between. That . . . that should've been our first warning that something was wrong. Covering all 200 miles only took a week. And then . . . and then . . ." Prof's hands shook. "The column rolled into the city in the afternoon and set up on top of a hill overlooking the Citadel at evening. The plan was to observe it through the night and make our terminal approach at sunrise. Once then sun went down, though . . . We'd walked right into a trap. First, one of the scouting teams radioed in that there was a horde of roamers coming up from the south. Then, another radioed in about roamers coming down from the north. We made ready to break camp and retreat to a more defensible position, but that was when lights started coming on inside the Citadel and we saw . . . them . . . flitting up the hill, a hundred shadowy human-shapes, barely visible. You, ah . . . Jules, you were in their special forces. You know about hunters, right?"

Jules crossed herself and gave a silent nod.

"Hunters. A hundred of them. Most of the soldiers had never seen a hunter, a lot of them thought that they were just a ghost story, but there they were, as real as anything. The Republic never bothered with specific training on how to engage hunters because nobody'd ever seen more than two or three in a group before, so only the old hands and the wasteland rangers really knew what was happening. We managed to blow a few of them away—I certainly hope so, with all of that armor we'd brought—but they just . . . they just soaked up bullets like they couldn't even feel them. They tore our front line apart, and then . . . then I saw him. He was enormous, like a carnival strongman, and I watched bullets tearing into his flesh and the wounds just closing up. I watched him stand there, under fire the whole time, and he put his hands on the front of one the tanks, and he . . . he crawled underneath it, and he lifted it up over his head, and he threw it into one of the APCs. It was pure panic after that, and I couldn't tell you how we got away, I just remember running, running, and the rest of my group running behind me, running west until the sun came up, and then rucking 200 miles back. It was . . . it was hard traveling. Most of the group didn't, ah, well, they didn't make it. As far as I know, Connor Turlogh and I are the only ones who survived Bart's column."

"Goddamn," Jules observed.

"Back home, it was an unprecedented disaster," Mags said. "The column was two full companies, two-thirds of our mechanized infantry. All that ordinance just walked into the wasteland and . . . didn't come back. It's put a severe strain on the war effort, to say the least."

"And now we come to the heart of the matter," Prof said, his hands still shaking. "Mags, what in the hell kind of hair-brained scheme has Central cooked up now, and what has it got to do with me?"

Mags rubbed her hands together. "The Citadel is an absolutely unprecedented pile of untapped resources, we know that much; resources we desperately need. And here's the kicker, here's what sold me on this wild idea: The blackshirts are after it, too. Intelligence has reports on teams of Arditi, squad-sized elements, heading into the wasteland and following Bart's trail toward the Citadel at regular intervals. They're going there, and then they're coming back."

That got Prof's attention. Mags went on:

"My mission is this: I'm to come to Parson's Hollow and meet up with the only two people we have on hand who've seen the Citadel with their own eyes and lived to talk about it; that's you and your designated marksman, Connor Turlogh. Once I've done that, I'm to put together a crack team of at least the three of us but no more than six, head east, recon the Citadel as thoroughly as we can, and then return to Central and report back. The thinking is that Bart, on account of he was a tanker and therefore an idiot, tried to pull off a force-on-force assault without sufficient planning or observation, but the fact that you, me, and Turlogh are still alive indicates that a small unit of professionals should be able to get close, have a look around, and get the hell out without running into too-too much trouble."

Prof was silent for a long time, staring off into the middle distance, the look on his face like that of a man who'd just been politely asked if he wouldn't mind walking off of a cliff. "I don't want to do that," he said after a while, his voice far away. "Every bone in my body is screaming at me to throw you out and pretend I never saw you. But."

"But."

"You say the blackshirts are checking it out?"

"Yup."

"And you say they're coming back?"

"Yup."

"That's . . . I suppose I don't have much of a choice, then, do I?"

Mags' all-business look broke into a soft, sad smile. "That's how they got me, too, old man."

"There is one hang-up, though, and that's Connor. Talking Connor into this will be . . . difficult."

"Central told me that you two were old war buddies."

"We used to be, before Bart and the column and the Citadel. Connor, he . . . he blames me for what happened. One of the people we lost, Tanya, our heavy weapons specialist, she was Connor's wife. He blames me for getting her killed. After we made it back, he didn't speak to me for almost two years. The last time he and I had words was, oh, about a year ago, when he . . . Well, he . . ."

Jules laid a comforting hand on Prof's knee and said, "The last time them two spoke was when Connor dropped me off here."

[7]

A MURDER OF CROWS

[AD 2261, somewhere in Pennsylvania]

THE GROUP STUMBLED INTO THE GHOST TOWN JUST NEAR TO sundown, and it was a lucky thing because it had been looking like rain since noon. They found a standing house in serviceable condition, which would save them bivouacking in the rain, and so the five men were in high spirits as they swept the building for roamers and then settled in for the night—all except for John, who hadn't been in high spirits for close to a year.

Discipline broke down at once. Rucksacks opened, and out came decks of cards and jugs of wine. Rocko, the signalman, dug around in his and came up with a pipe and a bag of crank, filthy and yellow-brown like stale piss. John sighed and pinched the bridge of his nose.

"Rolf," he barked, pointing at a hulking giant of a man with a wild mop of blonde hair who'd just started on a jug of wine, "put that shit away. You got first watch."

"I just fuckin sat down," Rolf grumbled.

"Ask me do I give a fuck. Put the booze away and go get on that window."

"It's fuckin raining, man. Nobody's out there. Reds don't come this far north anyways."

"Rolf, quit whining and go stand your post before I fuckin drag you there."

Grumbling, the big man stood up, picked up his Armalite, and walked to the big picture window next to the front door. John sat down in Rolf's place in the card game that was about to start, but he kept his big black boots on and his rifle over his shoulder; he, at least, would never be caught with his pants down. He was a captain, after all.

"Bullshit's the name of the game, boys!" Rocko roared as he dealt out cards, his pupils dilated, his face split in a trickster's grin. "Who wants to go first?"

John had already taken up his hand, and before anyone else could speak he threw a single card facedown in the center of the circle and spat, "Ace."

Rocko laughed at that. "My man don't waste no time!"

Sitting to John's left was Haraldson, a small man with buzzed blonde hair and a perpetual smile on his face. He threw down three cards and spat, "Three twos."

"Bullshit," John said with a smirk.

"Aw, fuck you, Tomassi!"

"Pick 'em up, dipshit."

Haraldson picked up the four cards, John's ace as well as the jumble of numbers he'd thrown down, and the game continued. It moved around the circle as the men passed around their wine and Rocko's pipe, and the pile grew higher and higher, and as it grew the players grew ever more reluctant to call one another's bluff. After a few rounds, it came to John's turn again, with the previous player—Peterson, the oldest of the five—having thrown down two jacks. He had two cards left in his hand. He took another slug of wine.

"Jesus fucking wept," he growled, "but this shit is rank. Y'all brew this in a fucking toilet?"

"Probably," Peterson said, with an obvious edge in his voice. "Make a man out of you. Puts hair on your chest."

"Make you fuckin go blind, more like."

"If you don't like it, don't drink it. You gonna fuckin play cards or what, Tomassi?"

John grinned as he held his last two cards between his thumb and index finger and flicked them onto the pile. "Two queens. And that is the game, boys."

"Bullshit," Haraldson spat.

John flipped the cards over, revealing the queen of hearts and the queen of diamonds. "That is the game, kid."

Haraldson fumed as they threw their hands onto the pile and Rocko scooped them up. As he began to shuffle them to deal again, Haraldson grumbled, "Well, Tomassi, if anybody here knows a thing or two about queens, it'd be you, after all."

Everyone burst into laughter at that, even Rolf over at the window. All except for Peterson, who rolled his eyes, and John, who stood up and made a perfect left-face to stand facing Haraldson. The laughter stopped at once.

"Jeez, Johnny," Haraldson said, "it was just a--"

John grabbed Haraldson by the collar of his black button-up campaign shirt, lifted him up, and threw him back down onto the floor. Before Haraldson could get his bearings, he felt John's boot pressing down on his neck.

"The fuck you said about me, you little faggot?" John growled.

"Not shit! Not shit! I ain't said shit!"

"Goddamn right. Little bitch."

He gave Haraldson a hard kick in the kidneys before storming off to another part of the house.

"The fuck you wanted to say that for, man?" Peterson asked as soon as he was gone.

Haraldson sat up, rubbing his side. "It was a fuckin joke. Ain't my fault if he can't take a joke. Besides, every one of y'all thought it was funny enough."

"It was pretty funny, Peterson," Rocko said.

"Yeah, well, now you done pissed him off. Look, the map says we're at least a week out from the objective, and over some rough goddamn country too. Unless you wanna make this trek go real goddamn slow, you best learn to watch that smart mouth."

"It was just a fuckin joke," Haraldson repeated. "Besides, it's true. He ain't got no right to be sore about it like that. The hell did he expect?"

At that, Rolf turned away from the window and moved toward the circle. "Wait, hold up," he said, "what's true? I thought y'all was just talkin shit."

Rocko rubbed his hands together. "Oh, that's right! New guy here never did get to meet the captain's little black angel."

"Another fuckin time, Rock," Peterson grumbled. "He's right the fuck over there."

Rocko ignored him. Thunder clapped over their heads and wind shook the building. "Well, just shy of three years ago--"

"Fuckin don't, man. Tomassi's gonna rip your balls off if he hears any of this. And I don't wanna hear it any more than he does. Binachi was my friend. She was my friend."

"Well, now y'all done piqued my curiosity," Rolf said.

Peterson stood up, rolling his eyes. "Alright, have it the fuck your way. I'll go keep Johnny Tomato busy."

He left, and as the rotting house rattled and shook under the booming thunderstorm, Rocko began the story:

"It was just shy of three years ago, we had this other guy with us. He was a top-tier weirdo--"

"He sure beat your ass, Rock," Haraldson broke in.

"And I'll fuckin whip yours if you interrupt me again. Anyways, this guy was a real weirdo, a faggy long-haired lisping little sissy, but at the same time he was a stone-cold killer, a door-kicker. Bloodthirsty, never lost a fight. He was our heavy

assault specialist. Corporal, he was; Corporal Julian Binachi . .
."

John Tomassi stood alone, just out of a side door, sheltered from the rain by the eaves of the old house, chain-smoking. He knew someone—probably Rocko—was telling Rolf the new guy the story behind Haraldson's little "knowing anything about queens" joke, and he desperately wanted to storm back in there and beat their asses, but he knew he needed to decompress or he'd probably kill the kid. Not that Haraldson didn't deserve it, but they still had two hundred miles of rough country and poison wind between them and their destination, so priority one was keeping the unit together. Haraldson, and probably Rocko, could have convenient accidents once they were safe in Baltimore, or maybe the long-timers down in Baltimore could find something to do with them. But for now, they were useful.

He rolled up the sleeve of his black campaign shirt and took a long, deep drag on his latest cigarette until the cherry glowed bright orange, almost yellow. In one swift motion, he snatched it out of his mouth and dug the burning cherry into his bare arm, into one of the few spots that hadn't been tattooed yet, and held it there. Gritting his teeth and trying not to scream, he felt his mind clear at once.

Pain . . . Righteous, purifying pain . . . The sweet, aromatic bouquet of smoldering flesh . . .

As soon as John had pulled his sleeve back down and lit a fresh smoke, the door swung open and Peterson stepped out into the wind, gave a jaunty wave, and said, "Hey there, Johnny Tomato. Whatcha doin out here in the cold?"

"Get fucked, Peterson."

Peterson leaned against the wall next to him and held out his right hand, palm up. John handed him a smoke. They stood together in silence for a little while before John asked, "Rocko in there telling jack-tales?"

"Yessir."

"Ought to go in there and stomp his fuckin teeth in."

"Yeah, y'ought to. But you won't."

"He's useful. I'll fix him once we're over the mountains."

"And what about the way back?"

"This is the big one, Peterson. The way back is in a straight line down the 81 into Ashland. I ain't worried about a tweaker and a faggot; if we need to replace 'em, they'll probably have some spare tweakers and faggots in Baltimore."

They were quiet for a while longer, and Peterson said, "Y'know, man, they're never gonna stop telling that story."

"Fuck you, Peterson."

"Look, man, I tried to tell you: You shoulda just let her go, forgot the whole thing. And the boss tried to tell, you, and, hell, that creepy-ass doctor tried to tell you, too. Forget about her, man."

John cocked an eyebrow at him. "So you call her 'her', huh?"

Panic flashed across Peterson's eyes for an instant, but John didn't notice. John wasn't a man known for noticing things. Taking another drag off of his cigarette, and thinking quickly, Peterson shrugged and said, "Hey, don't ask me why, but I liked that little freak. But she's gone like yesterday, Johnny, and if I was you I'd put in for a transfer to another unit. That, or kill Rocko and Haraldson, and now Rolf too I guess."

"Eh, suck my cock, old man. I'm gonna go back in there and shut Rocko up."

As Tomassi headed back toward the door, Peterson watched him go, his eyes lingering on the spot on Tomassi's back just below the left shoulder, just behind the heart, and he thought about how good it would feel to slip a knife into that spot.

But no, not here, not now, Peterson thought. And, sardonically, echoing the captain's words: There'll be plenty of time for that once we're over the mountains.

Rocko was getting to the end of the story as John crept in, quiet as a cat.

"Wait, so what happened to him?" Rolf asked.

"Hell all we know, brother; just gone like yesterday. I heard tell that they had him working as a courier up there in Columbus, and the rumor is that he saw a shot and took it, and they found his bike all busted up a few miles down the 70. And that's all she wrote. Gone like a fart in the wind."

"Goddamn. Where you think he was running to?"

"The reds, I bet. I hear tell the reds let degenerate faggots like him run shit down south. But he didn't make it; nobody coulda made it, not that way."

Rolf nodded. Rocko laughed and added, "Oh boy, but Tomassi was mad as hell. You never saw a man pitch a fit if you ain't saw the captain when they told him his favorite piece was gone. You shoulda seen it, man."

Stepping out of the shadows, Tomassi barked, "Oh, yeah, you shoulda seen it."

Everyone jumped. Rocko squawked. Tomassi walked behind him, rested his hands on the sitting man's shoulders, and looked Rolf in the eyes, saying, "Well, lance corporal, now you know all about Third SOG's little . . . incident. You got anything you wanna say?"

Rolf was stone-faced. "No, sir."

"You sure?" John was grinning like a wolf. "We're all brothers-in-arms here. You can tell me anything."

"No, sir."

"*Good.* Anybody else got anything? How about you, Rocko? Any more stories?"

"N . . . no, sir."

"Haraldson? You got any more jokes?"

"N . . . n . . . no, sir."

"That's what I fucking thought. Now, listen: Now that y'all have got the lance corporal up to speed on all the latest gossip, I've got a new standing order. From here on out, anybody in this unit who says or so much as thinks the name of Julian C. Binachi, I'm gonna slice your belly open and fuck the hole. Understood?"

Everyone nodded. Tomassi, still grinning, gave Rolf a pat on the shoulder and said, "You go right on ahead and have fun with the boys, new guy. I'll take your watch."

"Yes, sir."

From the shadows near the side door, Peterson watched the whole exchange with a smile on his face. Tomassi thought that he'd won something, but Peterson could see the truth plain as day, and the other men had an inkling of it, too: Captain John Tomassi was losing control.

Peterson suppressed a chuckle. Just like the man had said himself, they had a long, hard march ahead of them, and out there in the wasteland, well, anything could happen.

[*That same evening, somewhere north of Harrisburg*]

The truck lurched over yet another pothole in the ruined, disappearing blacktop, its electric motor whirring in protest; Barns' knuckles where white as he gripped the steering wheel, trying his damndest to keep control in the dim cone of vision that the headlights pierced through the darkness.

From the passenger seat, Becky popped her gum again and kept talking, kept rambling on about the things she remembered. She did this every night. She had been doing this every night, through all the hours of darkness, every night since they'd left Kingston. Barns mostly just tuned her out.

"So then," Becky said, pantomiming with her hands, "Silent Bob looks at Dante, and he says, 'Y'know, there's a million fine-looking women in the world, dude, but they don't bring you lasagna at work. Most of 'em just cheat on you.' So then Dante runs off, and-- You're not listening to me, are you?"

"Uh-huh," Barns muttered. "Fascinating. And then what happened?"

"Honestly, Steve, I work so hard to keep you entertained on these long drives, and what do I get from you? Nothing."

"Uh-huh."

She reached out and laid her hand on the side of his neck. He jumped and cursed, and the truck swerved off of the road before straightening out again, and he barked, "Jesus fucking Christ, Becky! Don't do that!"

"What's the matter, bloodbag? Do I have cold hands?"

"You goddamn know you do! What are you trying to pull?"

"I'm bored."

He rolled his eyes. "Well so am I, Becky. I'm bored out of my skull, and my nerves are frayed like an old rope, because it's been nothing but fucking night-driving since Ontario and we still have two fucking hundred miles to go. Go, I dunno, sit in the back and review the dossier or something; I'm tryna drive. Unless you wanna take over for a few miles and let me have a fucking break for once."

"Nah," Becky said, popping her gum, "that's a no-go. Every-body knows draculas can't drive."

"Oh, bullshit. Why am I the only one who ever does any goddamn work around here?"

"Pfft. You, do the work around here? Fat chance, bloodbag."

"I done told you, I don't like it when you call me that."

"Well, it's true. This is my mission; you're just my chauffeur and my canteen."

"Oh yeah, and the navigator, and the point man, and the one who remembers what city we're fucking going to. Could you even find Baltimore on a map?"

"That's beside the point."

"Honestly, you've got a lot of fuckin nerve talking to me like that when your ass can't even eat real food or go outside half the time."

She smiled at him, dancing her tongue playfully around her canines. "You know you love me, Steve."

"Yeah. Against my better judgment, but yeah."

"Relax, dude. Two hundred miles is, what, another couple of nights if we're lucky? We'll be there in no time, and then the fun starts."

"Alright. So you wanna make yourself useful and drive, or what?"

"I told you already, draculas can't drive. Everybody knows that."

"Jesus Christ."

"Don't you cuss me, Steve Barns."

They rode together in silence for a while, and then in near-silence as Becky started dancing in place in the passenger seat and humming Mindless Self Indulgence songs to herself, until the road came to a narrow stretch between two hills and Becky perked up like a bird-dog and whispered, "Steve, stop. Kill the lights, pull over."

He complied, whispering, "Shit, what is it? Roamers?"

"Nope, they're alive, I can smell it." She sniffed the air again. "Seven of them. I don't know if they saw us, but they're close enough they probably did. No . . . no, they definitely saw us. There's three coming toward us and four hanging back."

"Could they be friendly?"

"This far north? Hell no. You stay here, keep low, keep quiet."

And Becky stepped out of the truck, pranced out into the middle of the road, and waited, her hands behind her head. After a beat, three men stepped out of the darkness, men wearing black button-up campaign shirts, carrying Armalite battle rifles.

"Lady," one of them said, "what in the whole hell are you doing out here?"

"Hi!" she said, waving. "I'm looking for a friend of mine."

"I could be your friend, mama," one of the blackshirts sneered.

"You probably couldn't afford it. Anyway, like I said, I'm looking for a friend of mine. Well, he's not my 'friend', really, kind of the exact opposite, but we've got history. Do you know him? You guys look like people he'd know."

The blackshirt who'd spoken first turned to one of the others and said, "Okay, so this one's nuts."

"His name's Otto," Becky went on. "He's really tall, and really big, and he has a stupid handlebar mustache, and let's see, what are some of his other distinguishing traits? Oh, yeah! He can do this."

She rocked back onto her heels and then, moving too fast for sight to follow, sprang onto the first blackshirt, sinking her teeth into his neck, ripping his throat out in a fountain of gore. Then she moved onto the next. The third man had time to fire his rifle; a burst of three rounds punched through Becky's stomach, slowing her just for an instant, but the wounds closed up just as suddenly as they'd appeared.

The four men who'd stayed hidden in the darkness had more warning than their companions, but all that meant was that they had time to scream.

Barns watched the entire grim spectacle from the driver's seat of the truck. "Goddamn," he muttered, with a smile on his face, "but I do love that woman."

[8]

FOR AN OLD KENTUCKY ANARCHIST

ON THE OUTSKIRTS OF THE SETTLEMENT STOOD A THREE-ROOM poplar cabin that, if not for the eggbeater windmill and bank of solar panels atop its tin roof, could've passed for something ancient, a cabin standing from before the War. Its windows were black with soot, and its front porch and rusted roof bowed inward from age and disrepair, and the door to a storm cellar peeked up from beside the front porch steps.

As the three of them approached, Prof said, "This probably isn't going to go well. Even when we were friends, Connor was . . . a tedious person to be around. When he says he doesn't want to speak again, well, he means it. That's the worst thing about him; he always tells the truth."

Mags was unfazed. "Well, we have to try."

Jules, was walking off to Mags' left, examined her boots and said, "The old man's right, sugar. Last thing Connor said to me after Prof took me in was he never wanted to see me again. And, like . . . I respect that."

"Alright, so we're here to either recruit him or whup his ass."

At that, Jules stepped in front of Mags, stopping their approach to the cabin. "Mags," she said, with a tremor in her voice, "please cut that out."

"Cut what out, hon?"

"I don't . . . I don't wanna be protected, Mags. Are you trying to be my girlfriend or my mom?"

Mags started to protest, but caught the words in her mouth before they could escape and gave a silent nod, signaling for Jules to keep talking. Jules chewed her bottom lip and continued: "Yeah, I'm not . . . I'm not . . . I'm not doin great, and yeah, I appreciate everything you've said to me, but I'm 25 goddamn years old, Mags. I'm a grown-ass adult woman. I'm a soldier. I can take care of myself. And you remember what I was telling the old man earlier, about the difference between healing and hiding?"

"Yeah."

"Well, the shit that Connor said to me, the reason it hurt me so much was because he was telling the truth and I knew it."

Mags chewed on those words for a while, sighed, and said, "You're right, hon, and I'm sorry, and yeah, I'll cut it out. Can I say one more thing, though?"

"Of course."

"You remember the part where I'm a Jew? And I don't know if it was the way I talk or this amazing hair or what that gave it away, but you already knew that last night."

"Yeah?"

"Well, *schmeckla*, I think I've got enough sense in my head to know a Nazi when I see one, and I think I would have enough self-respect not to fuck one when I did. I'm not gonna say to cut yourself any slack, but you could give me a little credit."

Jules gave the slightest hint of a smile, and they resumed their walk up the hill toward the cabin.

A small person of indeterminate gender sat in a rocking chair on the front porch, nursing a jug of whiskey. They wore a long pleated maxi skirt and a leather jacket, and they watched the three approaching interlopers with suspicious eyes.

"Um, hey there, Millie," Prof said with a wave. "Is your brother home?"

Millie gave them a quick nod. "McCreedy. Miz Binachi. Stranger."

"Ah, everyone, this is Millie Firelake, Connor's in-law."

"A pleasure, I'm sure."

"And Millie, the, ah, stranger is Magnolia Blackadder, an old student of mine."

"You can call me Mags," Mags said.

"Magnolia," Millie repeated, chewing on the name. "You got a back-west accent. Kentucky?"

"Got it in one. New Lawrence township, New Lawrence canton."

"You a red?"

"Last time I checked."

Millie rolled their eyes, turned to Prof, and said, "McCreedy, you got some nerve comin up here. Yeah, Connor's inside, but he ain't gonna be happy to see you."

"I know, Millie. Believe me, I know. But we've got, ah, well, we've got some important business to discuss with him."

"Oh, I bet." And they leaned over and pounded on the front door, shouting, "Turlogh! Hey, Turlogh! Get your scraggly ass out here! You got visitors!"

A blue streak of curses erupted from the cabin, and the door swung open, and Connor Turlogh walked out onto the porch. He was a man fascinating to look at, well over six feet tall—even taller than Mags—and as scrawny as a broom handle, his face just a pair of burning eyes glaring out of a wild, wiry beard and unkempt shock of brown hair. He looked over the three visitors, spat on the porch, and growled, "Well, wouldya look what the dogs drug up. We got us an old has-been, a bonehead, and a girl scout."

"Don't be rude, Connor," Millie said.

He ignored them and pointed to Jules. "I believe I told you I didn't wanna look at your sorry ass no more. Till I see different, I says you're just a bonehead who didn't have no problem with bein one till it became her problem."

Jules nodded and examined her boots.

"And you," Connor growled, turning his attention towards Mags. "I dunno what in the hell a girl scout like you wants with me, but I don't wanna have shit to do with you. Did the old has-been tell you what happened the last time one of you busy-bodies showed up at my door?"

"It's my door, Connor," Millie said, "you just live here."

"Even so." And Connor Turlogh turned around and went back inside. Millie got up to follow him, stopped in the doorway, turned around, and said, "Well? Y'all comin in, or what?"

The three of them looked back and forth at each other for a beat before following Millie inside. The interior of the cabin reminded Mags of her childhood home, with its front kitchen and dining room packed floor to ceiling with all the accoutrements of life, all centered around a big cast-iron stove and a rough wooden dining table. Millie limped over to the table where Connor was already seated, took a seat next to him, and slid him their jug of whiskey.

"Sorry the place is such a mess," they said. "My joints been giving me trouble, and my brother-in-law here is plumb useless. Been meaning to get some folks from the union hall to come help me fix the place up, but, well, I don't want to." They stared across the table at the three visitors for a moment before barking, "Well, what are y'all waitin for? Sit."

They sat, and Connor grumbled something unintelligible and took a long drink from the jug, and Millie said, "So I take it you ladies done heard the story about why McCreedy and this asshole is on the outs?"

Mags and Jules nodded.

"Well, McCreedy, believe it or not, Connor's got somethin he'd like to say to you."

Connor grumbled again. Millie socked him hard on the shoulder and said, "Speak up so the man can hear you, Turlogh."

Connor took a long, slow drink of whiskey, looked Prof in the eyes, and said, "I'm sorry, man."

"There. Now, don't you feel better?"

"Nah, Millie. Feel like shit."

"Well, that'd be on account of you're an asshole."

Connor went back to grumbling, and Millie looked at Prof and said, "Two year ago, that man come here and told me you killed my sister. So I says at him, 'Then how come you let his ass come back alive?' So he tells me you got her killed. So I says at him, 'Then how come you let his ass come back alive?' So he told me the real story, then, and I called him a fuckin idiot—which is God's honest truth—and been tryna get him to go talk to you ever since."

There was an awkward silence that dragged on into a couple of minutes. Prof gestured at the jug and asked, "May I . . ."

Millie slid it over to him and he took a long drink. "Connor," he said, "I just . . . I just wanted to say that I've never been upset with you for being sore with me."

"I see her face every time I think about you," Connor said at last.

"I know you do. So do I. She and I weren't close in the way that you two were close, but I loved her in my own way; she was like a sister to me. Same with the others. We . . . we lost family that day."

"I fucking hate you, McCreedy."

"I know, Connor. I fucking hate you, too."

"But."

"But."

"It weren't your fault. It weren't mine, neither. We both know who we ought to be hating."

"That we do. And, about that--"

Millie interrupted before he could finish. "There, now, don't we all feel better about ourselves and the world and all that shit? I hope the two of y'all are finally fuckin done using my fuckin sister as a plot contrivance for yins little spat."

"I'm sorry, Millie," Connor grumbled.

"Uh-huh, you sure are. Now, is there perchance anything else you might wanna say to anybody else at this here table?"

Connor glared daggers at Jules and said, "No. No, there ain't."

Millie reared back to sock him in the shoulder again, but Jules held up a hand to stop them and said, "Mx. Firelake, please don't. It's fine."

Millie cocked an eyebrow. "You think it's fine, all the untoward horseshit this man has said at you, after everything you been through?"

"Yeah, Millie, it's fucking fine." And she snatched the jug from Prof, took a long drink, stood up, and barked, "Jesus fucking Christ, can people quit mollycoddling me for like two goddamn minutes? Yeah, I been through it, and yeah, I'm pretty fucked up about it, but I'm a goddamn adult woman, I ain't a fuckin china plate. Yeah, Millie, it's fucking fine that Connor don't like me; I don't like me! All Connor ever did was tell me the truth, and y'know what? I'm grateful to him for that. It's about goddamn time somebody around here told me the truth instead of pretending like the past just didn't happen. Shit."

She took a step back from the table and unbuttoned the top of her lavender plaid shirt, enough to reveal the top of a chestpiece tattoo, a cross and wheel; it had been inscribed before her breasts had begun to grow, giving the symbol a warped and otherworldly look. And she sighed and said, "Y'all know what this shit is. I . . . I . . . I'm a bad person, Millie. I've hurt people. I've done terrible things. And yeah, I've paid for it, I've paid for it with fucking interest, but Connor's right; I didn't have a problem with being who I was until it got to be my problem." She sat down with a huff and held her hand out towards Mags, palm up. Mags handed her her lighter and pack of cigarettes. She lit one and kept talking: "You see, y'all, there's trauma, and then there's guilt. You can deal with trauma and learn to live with it, but guilt? Guilt without action is fucking point-less. And that . . . that's what's got me all fucked up, y'know? I can't get on any of that living and healing type shit until I can pick apart the one from the other, the trauma from the guilt. And that's why I came here today, man, and why I'm following this girl scout around. Because I gotta balance the ledger."

Connor had been watching the entire blow-up, and when Jules stopped he gave her an approving nod and said, "Y'know, Jules, I think I might hate you just a little bit less."

"That means a whole goddamn hell of a lot coming from you, man. But we still got a long ways to go, figurative-like and literal."

Mags put an arm across her shoulders and said, "Y'know, if you don't mind me asking, I'd like to hear what happened between you two. I never got that part of the story."

"Yeah," Jules said, leaning into the embrace. "When I got out, I . . . I didn't really plan for it, I just saw a chance and took it. I managed to keep my head down and play nice for long enough that they fucked up and started to trust me, so sometimes I got to leave the compound to go pass letters and stuff between the general officers. This one day, I got handed three deliveries, and they were all over the place, and the girl working pickup that day warned me that there'd been some new staff officers posted at the Oberkommando the night before. We knew at least one or two of 'em would be after entertainment that night, and I couldn't go back. I couldn't go back. I couldn't go back. I couldn't go back. I--" She shook herself, then continued: "At my second delivery, I managed to get the drop on a guard and I merc'd his ass. Got his Armalite—*my* fuckin Armalite now—and some food and whatnot into my courier bag, took off east, and just . . . went. When I ate shit on the highway between Columbus and Zanesville, I got up, dusted off, turned south, just kept going. And that, that was hard fuckin traveling, let me tell ya. I couldn't even tell you how long it took, or where I crossed the Ohio. After I crossed the Ohio, though . . . Well, I only had the one set of clothes, and I was too scared to light a fire and dry off, so I got sick. Real fuckin sick. I kept going as long as I could, but I was exhausted, dehydrated, sick, off my fuckin meds, and eventually I couldn't go no further and I just laid down on the ground and waited to die. Lucky for me, a team of scavvers that had been out picked up my trail on their way back, and they were right on top of me. One of 'em was this fine gentleman."

Connor snorted.

"I don't really remember the next part," Jules said, "on account of I was basically dead, but they cut me outta my clothes so they could check me for injuries and stick an IV in me, and I guess they noticed, well, my whole situation. When I woke up, I was bare-ass naked and I had my hands tied behind my back, and I may have panicked a little bit and had me just a little bit of an episode."

"You stood up on your shoulders like a fuckin acrobat and you kicked me right in the fuckin teeth," Connor grumbled.

"I don't really remember, but yeah, that sounds like somethin I'd do. After I calmed down, I gave 'em the short version of how I wound up where they found me, and they untied my hands and gave me some food and then Connor, well, he explained that they all felt real bad for me but even so didn't see why they should trust me. And that lifted my spirits, see, 'cause I was so goddamn sure anybody I met was gonna just shoot me on sight. Soon as I could walk again, the scavvers took me back to town with 'em and handed me off to the old man. And Connor repeated about how they wanted me safe and I was gonna be safe now, but it would be a good long while before he could look at me and see anything but another bonehead. Which, like I said already: Fair." She took another slug of whiskey. "But that's why I'm here, man. It's time to face up to shit and balance that ledger. From here on out, either my life's books are gonna get into the black, or I'm gonna be dead, and either way I'll be better off."

Connor gave her another nod, then looked to Mags and said, "But that there just brings up another question, namely this here one: What in the hell are *you* doin here, and what's it got to do with me?"

Mags took the accordion folder out of her rucksack, lit one of her cigarettes, and said, "I'm glad you asked. Connor Turlogh, I'm here as a representative of the Ashland Central Soviet General Assembly, and its affiliate Department of Intelligence and Security. We would like to offer you a job."

"I took a job from the reds once. Didn't turn out too good."

"Yeah, about that."

Connor was speechless when Mags finished her spiel, staring at her with his mouth agape and disbelief flashing in his eyes. Millie, however, was not. They looked him dead in the eyes and said, "Well, if you don't wanna go with 'em, I guess my busted ass is gonna have to."

"The hell you on about, Firelake?"

"I'm on about how my sister was murdered and the fuckin creature what did it is still walkin around. This girl scout walks in here and offers us the best shot we ever gonna get to do somethin about that, well, I reckon somebody ought to take that shot."

"Millie, you ain't seen what's out there. This here is suicide. Hell, it's worse than suicide, 'cause what's waitin out there is worse than dyin."

"I don't give a rat's ass, Connor Turlogh. I wanna see justice done for my baby sister I never got to bury. And Tanya was your wife, too, allegedly, but it sounds like you only remember that when it's convenient for you."

Connor glared at them as though he were about to rip their head off, but instead, cooly, he said, "Millie, listen to me. This is a bad idea. I slipped the noose one time already; fate ain't gonna let me slip it again. I ain't goin."

"Oh, you're goin fuckin somewhere, alright, 'cause Millie

108 / NATALIE IRONSIDE

goddamn Firelake sure as shit ain't got no coward for a brother, and I sure as shit ain't gonna let no coward sleep under my roof. If you ain't gonna help these fine people, then I says my sister was too goddamn good for you."

Connor stared at the table in silence for several minute. At last, he looked up at Jules, sighed, and asked, "Miz Binachi, would you be so kind as to spare me some of them smokes?"

"A'course, man," Jules said, sliding them across the table. "'All is for all', right? Ain't that what y'all say?"

"But those are my smokes," Mags said.

Jules smiled a shit-eating grin. "I thought us reds was supposed to share everything in common."

"Well yeah, *private* property is abolished, but private property is like a town, or farmland, or a factory. My smokes are *personal* property. It ain't like we all share the same goddamn toothbrush."

Jules pecked her on the cheek. "I know that, sugar. Call that revenge for breakfast."

Mags rolled her eyes. "Go ahead and help yourself, Connor. All is for all."

Connor grunted in acknowledgement, lit a cigarette, and said, "Well . . . in light of my sibling's unmatched rhetorical skill, it sounds like I ain't got no choice but to go along with this horseshit."

"Glad to hear it. Now, you two are the experts here, so--"

"I'll take you. I'll take you over the mountains and get you right up inside the asshole of that place, but listen: There's gonna be a toll to pay. I got a feeling we ain't gonna make it back."

"I'm prepared to pay that toll," Mags said, her face blank and emotionless. "I'm a soldier, and I take a soldier's risk."

Jules nodded in solemn agreement.

"Well alright then!" Millie said, clapping their hands. They struggled to their feet and added, "Job like this, y'all gonna need some serious kit."

"I know you anarchists have got arsenals and magazines," Mags said. "Figured either me or Professor J could sweet-talk a way into one."

"Oh, it's a lot easier than that, sweetheart. You're lookin at 'em."

"Looking at what?"

"The black arsenal! Follow me. And put out them damn cigarettes."

And Millie limped back out the front door without another word. Mags and Jules watched them go in confusion, but the other two seemed to have expected it.

"Millie is a gunsmith," Prof said. "They used to be this settlement's master machinist, before their back started to give out."

Jules snorted.

"What's funny?"

"Well, it's just . . . They're a machinist. And their name's Millie."

It took a moment for the joke to register, but when it did, everyone groaned. Jules laughed.

The four of them followed Millie out the door and down the front steps to the storm cellar's entrance. They yanked the doors open, turned to Mags and Jules, and said, "Would one of you ladies mind givin me a hand down these here steps?"

Jules helped Millie hobble down the stairs into the cellar, and at the bottom they idly flicked their hand out and flipped a light switch, bathing the room in a flickering fluorescent glow.

"Well," they said, "here's the better part of what's on offer. Help yerselves; I'll sort the paperwork later. If'n y'all want extra, you'll have to go see the militia post in town; they'll have more, but the paperwork'll take longer."

The cellar was a square room slightly bigger than the cabin above it, filled from floor to ceiling with shelves, and the shelves were stacked with equipment of various sorts: Tools, bags, boxes, parts, and, of course, weapons and ammunition.

"Jesus fucking wept," Jules said, her eyes roaming about the cellar. "What . . . what the hell is all this? Where'd it come from?"

"Here and there," Millie said, "over a whole lotta years. We made some of it, scavved some of it, traded some from the reds for e-waste. Y'all go buck wild."

Mags looked to Prof and Connor. "You two are the scavengers," she said, "so I'll follow your lead here. I've got the basic bag of bones and a marksman's rifle with me."

Jules shrugged. "I got an Armalite. That's about it."

"Alright," Connor said, as he and Prof each grabbed an empty duffel bag, "what kinda ammo are we lookin for?"

"Rifle's .303 Winchester," Jules said. "Ain't got a sidearm, but I'd like one."

"Long gun's 7.62x54R," Mags said. "Sidearm's 7.62x38R."

Connor cocked an eyebrow. "That weird-ass revolver ammo that looks like it's uncircumcised?"

"7.62 Nagant, yeah."

"Why the hell do y'all carry around them piece-of-shit antiques?"

"Because back in the Free Appalachian Army days we found thousands of them in storage and they still work. And you're one to talk about antiques, nugget boy."

Connor laughed. "Alright, then. Binachi, do you got a preference on sidearms?"

"Something automatic," Jules said. "No antiques for me."

Mags gave her a playful sock in the shoulder. Looking back at the two men, she added, "Oh yeah, and I don't have any pyro. If you can find any, I imagine I'll want a belt of grenades, and something for demo, and some det cord."

"You worried about weight?" Connor asked.

"Nah. Right now my ruck plus the Dragunov is thirty kilos, and I can hump sixty kilos at a dead run."

Connor looked at her dubiously. She shrugged and said, "What can I say? I'm a farm girl. So are you two gonna fill those bags, or what?"

Prof and Connor went to do just that, leaving the two of them standing by the stairs with Millie. Millie cracked their back and asked, "So, you two are . . . sweet on one another?"

Mags grabbed Jules' hand. Jules blushed and said, "Uh, yeah, you might could say that."

"Y'all known each other long?"

"Uh . . ." Jules felt her usual reticence rising, but she fought it back, tried to hide it behind bravado. "Well, we met about 24 hours ago, and I told Mags here my life story and gave her an itemized list of my trauma, and then I put my dick in her mouth, and then we had breakfast, and then I swore I'd follow her through wire and fire, and now we're here."

Millie gave them a wide, warm smile and clapped Jules on the shoulder. "Y'all two are adorable. So, any big plans for this here whirlwind romance?"

"Uh . . . do we, sugar?"

"Well, to tell you the truth," Mags said, "there's a pretty good chance we're not gonna come back from this. But if we do . . . If we do, I want you to come back to New Lawrence with me. You can stay with me, meet my mama; she'll love you. Fuck, I'm gonna have to get a bigger bed . . . probably some more chairs, too . . ."

Jules drank in the words like wine, and she stared at Mags for a long moment and muttered, "I have a future."

"What was that, honey?"

"I have a future."

And Jules started to cry. Mags threw an arm around her and asked, "Hey, honey, what's the matter? Are you okay?"

"I'm okay. Sugar, this is the first moment in my entire life that I've ever been okay."

Mags pulled her closer, pecked her on the cheek, and said, "Well goddammit, woman, now we have to survive."

Millie laughed long and hard at that, and said, "Oh, if that ain't just the way! But, listen: How old are you girls?"

"I'm 24," Mags said.

"And I'm 25," Jules said.

"Coupla youngsters, y'all are. Coupla pups. Well, take it from me, you two: No matter how rough it gets, there's always a future."

Jules gave them a pat on the shoulder. "Thanks, Millie. I . . . I need to hear that."

"Oh, I know you do, girl. And here's somethin else you might need to hear even more'n other folks: That future is whatever you want it to be."

And Jules smiled, and held Mags closer, and said, "Y'know what, Millie? I think I might just believe you."

———

Prof and Connor emerged from the menagerie with full bags, and Connor tossed Jules a rucksack and said, "Here, Binachi, this is yours. Put most of a kit in it."

Jules threw it over her shoulders with a nod and asked, "So what's the plan?"

"Reckon this should be all the kit we'll need. Travel on foot's gonna be at least a week in good conditions, prob'ly closer to two or maybe three in real life. We'll finish getting everything together today, get some rest, then hit the trail just before dawn."

"Why not leave this afternoon?" Mags asked.

"This close to the edge of the exclusion zone, you don't travel after dark. I think you know why."

Mags gulped, then nodded.

"Connor," Prof said, "you get the rest of your gear together and meet us back at the clinic. We'll pack some food, go over the maps, all that stuff."

Connor grunted his assent. After the group had left the cellar and come back around to the front porch, Millie said, "Hold on, y'all, wait right here." And they disappeared inside, returning a minute later with a combat knife in a black canvas sheath. They handed it to Jules and said, "Take this, girlie. You might just need it."

Jules took the knife out of its sheath and examined its twelve-inch straight blade ending in a needle-sharp tip. It was handmade, but only the honed edge had the dark and colorful sheen of damasked steel; the rest was a bright metallic white.

"Millie," she said, "this is . . . it's beautiful."

"Glad you like it. Made it myself, couple years back."

"What's goin on with the blade here?"

"Electroplated silver. For one it's pretty to look at, and for two . . . might come in handy."

"Holy shit, thank you so much. This is wonderful."

"It ain't nuthin, girlie. Now y'all go on and finish getting ready; I reckon I won't see none of y'all for quite a while."

* * *

Back at the clinic, Mags, Jules, and Prof dodged questions from Kat and Keith and went to Prof's room, a small space almost as spartan as Mags' but with a bigger desk and more bookshelves. They laid out the bags of gear and waited on Connor, who arrived a few minutes behind them a packed rucksack and a big bolt-action rifle. They divvied up the gear until everyone's ruck was suitably furnished: Weapons; ammunition; cold- and wet-weather gear; a few changes of clothes; water filtration system; and food, dehydrated and concentrated plant proteins that came in two-kilogram sacks of white powder; along with various odds and ends. And Prof laid out a topographical map across his desk, marked Parson's Hollow, marked the Citadel, and marked out various approaches over the mountains, based on the lore of other scavengers and on his and Connor's memories. At the end of it all, Connor said, "Well, folks, I reckon we're as prepared as we're ever gonna get, for all the good it'll do us. We're all agreed to set out at 05 tomorrow?"

The group nodded. Prof sighed and said, "It's almost dinnertime. Not sure how I'll explain this to Kat and Keith."

"You could try tellin 'em the truth, dude. We're going on a run, doin a job for the reds. Just don't mention where to."

"Yeah, that's true. I was never a very good liar, anyway. I'll go ask Keith to set an extra place."

Before Prof could get up, Jules grabbed Mags' hand, squeezed it, and said, "Don't worry about it. We're gonna skip dinner."

"We are?" Mags asked, cocking an eyebrow.

Prof nodded. "Of course. We'll save you two some leftovers."

Jules got up and motioned for Mags to follow, leading her up the stairs and back to her room. When they were inside with the door locked, Jules threw her against the wall, hard, and planted a kiss on her lips.

"Not that I'm complaining, honey," Mags said, "but what's up?"

Jules kissed her again. "We going on a mission tomorrow? Real deep down in the shit, no assistance, not much chance we'll come back?"

"Yeah, that's about the shape of it."

"Then I wanna spend one last night, in a real bed, with my girl."

They made their way to the bed, ripping at each other's clothes, and when they fell upon it, Jules said, "Mags, sugar, I want you to fuck me."

"Are you . . . sure about that? I mean, I'm not complaining, but-_"

"Yes, Mags, I'm sure. Last night . . . last night was amazing, you were so sweet, and that was exactly what I needed then. But right now, I don't wanna make love. I want you to fuck me until I forget who I am, before we march off to die tomorrow."

"If you're sure. I just--"

Jules grabbed a fistful of her hair, kissed her earlobe, and whispered, "Mags, sugar, listen."

"Yeah?"

"I trust you."

[9]

NO ROADS HERE

Jules Binachi drifted right off to sleep in her lover's arms, with a satisfied smile on her face, but it was not a dreamless sleep.

She found herself in the shower, a place she often returned to, sitting on the floor next to the drain while the water cascaded over her. The hot water had run out a while ago, and she was freezing cold, and she knew she'd probably get her ass crawled for wasting so much water, but getting up to turn it off seemed like so much work. Even the cold was nice, because the constant sensation meant that she didn't have to think, and the water washing over her body almost made her feel clean. She wondered if she would ever really feel clean again.

Her eyes wandered to her left forearm just below the elbow, to the tattoo she'd gotten on first being inducted into the blackshirts as a lance corporal: A grinning death's-head with a dagger clenched in its teeth. And, staring at it, a thought wandered unbidden into her brain: *Remember when you used to be somebody? Remember what it felt like to feel strong?*

She did not.

Off in the distance, a door swung open—they had their own rooms, but of course none of the doors had locks—followed by the sniper's crack of sensible heels tapping across the tile floor and a sickening, sing-song voice calling out, "Julia? *Juliaaaaaa?* Oh, where on Earth have you gotten off to, darling?"

Jules pulled her knees tighter into her chest and wished that she could disappear.

The bathroom door swung open and Corpsman-Major Wenden strode in, turned off the shower, and all six feet and ten inches of her stood towering over Jules. She wore a pressed black campaign shirt decorated with a major's palms and the rod of Asclepius, a long black skirt, and, of course, sensible heels. Her blonde hair was styled into a perfect pageboy, and she looked down at Jules with a terrifying, empty smile splitting her face. The corpsman-major was always smiling. The signs of another life peeked out from the edges of her clothes, with an Orthodox cross tattooed on the back of her right hand and a cross and rosary on the back of her left.

"Oh, there you are, dear," she cooed. "What on Earth are you doing in here? You look like a drowned rat, and you must be freezing."

Jules stared up at her, the gleam in her sad brown eyes fluctuating as smoldering hatred competed with sweet, merciful nothingness, and said nothing.

"I have wonderful news, darling! I just spoke with your friend the captain on his way out, and he had nothing but nice things to say. That's all I need to approve you for the next stage of treatment. Isn't that marvelous?"

Jules' lip quivered, and she started to speak, but all that came out was a whispered, " . . . Tasha . . ."

Corpsman-Major Natasha Wenden bent forward and asked, "What was that, dear? Do speak up."

"Tasha, why . . . why . . . why didn't you tell me? Why the fuck didn't you tell me?"

The doll-like smile on her face widened into a rictus grin, and something sparkled in her crystal blue eyes. She slapped Jules across the face, hard, sending her flying into the shower wall, and she fixed her with a burning glare and growled, "Oh, you knew. Don't pretend that you didn't; you can't even fool yourself, and you certainly can't fool me. I know you're not that stupid, Julia."

"But why ... why ..."

"Because we are women, Julia. We are women, and so we have certain expectations we must meet, and certain God-given duties we must perform. That is the natural way of things, darling; men fight, and women serve."

Jules groaned. The corpsman-major knelt down so that their faces were level, and she hissed, "You know that this is a voluntary program. All completely voluntary. If you're not woman enough to handle it, that's fine. Just say so. I'll write 'Subject did not respond to treatment' in my little book, and you'll get an official pardon and be declared fit-for-duty immediately. You'll be on your way back to your unit tomorrow morning. You and your friend the captain would see so much more of each other that way. Is that what you want, darling?"

"N ... no ..."

"I didn't think so. Of course, if you continue to be obstinate, then you'll be ejected from the program anyway. But that route doesn't come with a pardon. Is *that* what you want, Julia? I could take away all of these wonderful gifts you're enjoying so much, no more pills, no more skirts, no more Julia, and toss you right back into that hole I found you in. Perhaps they'll finally get around to hanging you. Or perhaps they won't."

Jules started to speak, bit her tongue, and looked down at the tiles, cowed. The struggle inside of her concluded as nothingness won out over hatred. Natasha stood up, and her expression softened a bit. She shook her head, rested her right hand on the inside of her left elbow, and said, "You must get your shit together, Julia.

They tell me you know a little Italian; do you know what *Arditi* means?"

"*Those who dare,*" Jules muttered, like a whisper from far away.

"*Those who dare.* Do you think it was by chance you slipped the noose? Or by chance that I heard about you, and drew you up from perdition? You must get your shit together, because I have great expectations for you, my sister." And she turned to leave.

Once she was out of the corpsman's withering gaze, Jules found enough of herself to bark, "You're a fucking kapo, Wenden. You know that, right? A fucking kapo."

Tasha stopped in the doorway and slowly turned around. "Kapo," she repeated, her voice ice cold and dropping to a low basso register. "Kapo. *Kameradschaft-Polizei.* Why yes, darling, that's exactly what I am. You would do well to remember that. I'll tell your friend the captain that you said hello."

The sound of the bathroom door slamming hit Jules like an elbow in the stomach, and she shot awake, pulled out of her memories, to find that she was in fact taking elbows to the stomach; Mags was rolling and thrashing in her own fitful sleep, the snoring that Jules had fallen asleep to replaced with small, pitiful whimpers.

"Mama," Mags mumbled into the darkness, "where's Maggie? Where's Maggie, Mama?"

The dark spell that the flashback had cast over Jules was broken at once. She almost wanted to laugh, and with a yawn she muttered, "Well goddamn if you and I ain't just two birds of a feather, eh, sugar?"

She wrapped her arms around Mags, held her tight, and whispered, "It's alright, sugar, it's alright. I gotcha. I'm here. I gotcha."

Mags grew still after a few minutes, settling into the embrace and purring like a cat. Jules kissed the top of her head and attempted to settle back down herself, but sleep wouldn't come. Not wanting to disturb Mags tossing and turning, she sighed in resignation and sat up in the darkness.

She felt the shadows creeping into her mind, as often happened when she was in a dark room alone. As her eyes adjusted, she looked down to the spot just above the elbow of her bare left arm, the grinning death's-head, the sign and seal of the Arditi. Once upon a time, it had meant so much to her . . . And it still did, in another sort of way.

At the beginning, the night after selection, there'd been a ceremony. A bonfire in the woods, red meat, whiskey, strange and decidedly unchristian oaths sworn over stones and trees and the blades of their knives. Initiation. "Initiation" meant that each man in the operating group slit their right palm and they took turns shaking hands, mingling their blood. Reaffirming their brotherhood, inducting their new lance corporal. "That's the blood of the race, new kid," Tomassi had said, solemnly marking a cross and wheel in red across her forehead. "The blood of heroes. The last pure blood in the world that's not polluted with degenerate mud and slime. A birthright of ten thousand years. Stand up, white man!"

And Jules had stood up, and Tomassi had given her a great big bear hug, hoisting the short and scrawny 17-year-old up into the air, and called her a brother. In her bedroom, Jules found herself picking the moment apart, interrogating the memory. Had that embrace lingered just a moment too long? Had she felt breath on her neck, a hand on her ass, or was she imagining it now? That night was three (or was it four? Five?) years removed from the night it all broke bad, but she had already begun shaving her beard, growing her hair out, walking and talking "like a faggy little fairy," as Rocko had said, once, when she was new, right before she broke three of his teeth for it. Had John always known? It made sense, she thought; a wolf can smell a sheep in wolf's clothing.

And one of the other blackshirts had shoved another jug of shine into her hand, and when they were all good and drunk, then the gunpowder and the needles came out. Tomassi had quite the steady hand for a man too drunk to walk straight, managing to free-hand the skull with impressive speed. As he started to color it in, he'd laughed and asked, "So how you like that, brother?"

And Jules, through clenched teeth, her arm pouring blood like a wound, had smiled back and groaned, "I really don't care."

That was their phrase, the corps' unofficial motto. Through long marches, snow and rain, war and death, blood and barn-burnings and murder, the trooper was to grin like a naked skull and laugh: "I really don't care."

"I really don't care," Jules muttered into the darkness, lighting a cigarette. She felt herself stand up, walk across the room, open her dresser, root around in her things, looking for something, though she didn't know quite what, wasn't quite sure what her hands were even doing. When she came back to herself, she was sitting cross-legged on the floor in the little square of moonlight streaming in through her bedroom window. Beside her on the floor lay a bottle of whiskey, a couple of ballpoint pens, a knife, a sewing kit.

"My name is Julia Carlotta Binachi," she whispered into the darkness. "I'm a woman, somebody's girlfriend, somebody's daughter, and I'm . . . I'm alive. The past is done, and the future is whatever the fuck I want it to be, and y'know what? I care a whole hell of a lot."

It hurt like a motherfucker, and it bled a lot more than she liked —they always had—but it didn't take very long. She even managed to work in a little artistry; when she got up and crawled back into bed beside Mags, the fresh bandage wrapped around her left elbow covered a new tattoo, a crescent moon. It was a bit rough, but that could be touched up later, and anyway, she really didn't care.

When they woke up, Mags didn't mention the bandage. As she stretched and groaned she muttered, "Bad dreams last night."

"Yeah," Jules yawned, sitting up. "You woke me up tossing and turning."

"Oh, shit. I'm sorry, babe."

"Nah, sugar, you did me a favor. You woke me up outta my own dreams."

And Mags laughed, and said, "Lord, we were just made for each other, huh?"

"That's exactly what I said."

They laughed together as they got up and started getting dressed, until Jules said, "Sugar, can I ask you something?"

"Of course. Anything."

"Who's Maggie?"

Mags sighed. "I been talking in my sleep again, huh?"

"Yup."

"She was my baby sister. Margaret Bronstein Blackadder. We lost her when she was 6 and I was 11. Malnutrition, wasting sickness."

"Fuck. I'm sorry, sugar."

"Nah, don't be. I should say her name, and you should know it." She ran a hand through her long red hair. "Maggie Blackadder – that was my baby sister. We lost my dad the same way; he was Abe O'Donnell Blackadder. May their memory be a blessing."

"Fuck. I'm sorry, sug, but . . . thanks for telling me."

"'Course. Thanks for asking, honestly. And as long as we're naming names, my mama's Emma. But she's too damn mean to die, and God willing I'm gonna introduce you to her someday."

"Well, that sounds just nice as hell."

"Oh, it will be. She'll love you." And Mags put an arm across her shoulders and asked, "So . . . last night was nice?"

Jules yelped and took three quick steps backward toward the door. "No! I mean . . . fuck . . . it was wonderful, just what I needed then, but I . . . I don't wanna talk about sex right now, Mags."

"Fuck. I'm sorry, hon."

"Nah, nah, you didn't do nuthin. It's just . . . some days are easier than others, y'know?"

"Yeah. That I know."

They finished getting dressed and throwing their gear together, and in the early-morning stillness, Jules muttered, "It was about her."

"What was about who?"

"My nightmare you saved me from. It was about her. The corpsman."

"Shit."

"Yeah. Y'know, after everything broke bad, one of the ways I kept myself sane was I remembered everybody's name, every single one of 'em, and I used to whisper that list to myself every night before bed; I told myself it was a list of people I'm gonna kill. She was always at the top. In front of all the others, even in front of Johnny, she was always at the top."

"Oh, I'll bet. Listen, I sure don't know exactly where this thing is headed, but I have a feeling that when we get back from this job, things back west are going to pop off in a big, bad way. Whatever happens, I can guarantee that all those people are gonna find themselves staring down the wrong end of some good old-fashioned prompt, severe, and inflexible justice."

As they talked, Jules walked over to her chest of drawers on the far side of the room, and she opened the top drawer and took out a sleek, black Armalite AR-10 battle rifle. At first she held it away from herself, like a snake, but as Mags finished she began to inspect its action and said, in a half-whisper, "Sure."

"What's up, honey?"

Jules looked into the rifle's star chamber like a farmer inspecting a blighted crop. After checking the bolt's lubrication, she sighed and muttered, "I'm tired, sugar. I'm just so fucking tired."

And she slung the rifle and turned away from the chest of drawers, then stopped and turned back, looking to the little bookshelf beside it. She reached out, and for a moment her hand lingered over the Bible, then moved one to the right and snatched up the volume of Wilfred Owen poetry. She clutched it tight to her chest, just as she'd clutched Carmilla the previous morning.

"That's a good one," Mags said, softly. "Yeats is good, too. You very into poetry?"

"I guess, yeah. A year ago I barely knew how to fuckin read, but when I was settling in here the old man gave me these books and said he thought I might get something out of them. He was right."

She opened the book, and it near to fell open on its own to a well-read and often visited page, the lines of verse underlined, the page wrinkled and ink smudged with tears. And she ran her index finger across the lines as she read aloud in a slow, halting, careful voice:

"What passing-bells for these who die as cattle?
--Only the monstrous anger of the guns.
Only the stuttering rifles' rapid rattle
Can patter out their hasty orisons.
Nor any voice of mourning save the choirs--
The shrill demented choir of wailing shells;
And bugles calling for them from sad shires."

Mags digested the moment in silence for a while, then gave a solemn nod and said, "Yeah. Yeah, that's a vibe."

Connor and Prof were waiting for them in the kitchen, a pot of coffee already simmering on the stove. Prof handed them each a tin cup as they walked in, and Connor grumbled, "Y'all lovebirds ready to go?"

"Born ready," Mags said, slamming back her coffee and filling a second cup. "Y'all?"

"Yup. If'n we leave now, we'll hit the exclusion zone before dark. There's a safehouse in old Winchester, pretty secure, we should be able to get to. Might even be occupied. You ever gone on a scavengin run, red?"

"Nah. Been to Ohio a few times, but that's hardly the same. I defer to your expertise."

"That's wise of you. Like I said, I'll getcha there, but this ain't gonna be fun. Shit's gonna get rough out there."

"And like I said, I'm okay with that. I'm a soldier, and I take a soldier's risk."

Connor met her eyes for a moment, then nodded, satisfied. "I'll take it. Now, let's have us some breakfast—somethin light, lotsa carbs—and get to it. We got a whole hell of a lot of walking in our future."

"If it's close enough that we can hump it there in a day, it can't be more than, what, about thirty clicks? How come we can't catch a ride, at least to the edge of the zone?"

"Nah. No vehicles. Sets off the roamers."

"Jeez. Everybody pack plenty of socks?"

"Ain't nobody said this was gonna be easy, red."

"Yeah, I got that much. The name's Mags, by the way."

Connor grumbled something—all Mags could make out was "goddamn girl scout"--and Prof said, "Just ignore him. He's grumpy in the mornings."

"I get the feeling it's always morning around here."

Everyone else laughed. Connor's mouth twitched in a slight smile and he said, "Alright, Mags. You see much action, up there in Ohio?"

"A fair piece. I've drilled a few fascists in my time."

"Sniper?"

"Designated marksman."

"How you like that Dragunov?"

"She's a little sensitive, but she gets the job done. Better than that antique you're carrying around."

"Alright, alright," Prof broke in. "If you two get started like that, we'll never leave. There'll be plenty of time to discuss windage and trigger pulls on the road." And he went to the fridge, and out of it he handed each of them two green apples.

Mags tried not to laugh.

The path east out of town followed a clear and well-trod trail at first, taking them past vegetable and flower gardens, fields, wood-lots, and groups of log cabins and rammed-earth beehive houses, and though signs of habitation grew fewer and farther between as they walked further east, gradually fading into the spruce and maple and oak and laurel, it was still plainly habited land, and here and there they would pass intersecting trails and people going this way or that. Most of them seemed to recognize Prof, and they all waved and smiled, but they took note of the guns in the four travelers' hands and didn't stop to make small talk, instead going about their business with a "Good luck!" or a "Happy hunting."

The day broke blue and clear around them, the bright morning sun bathing them in a soft green glow as it filtered through the canopy of trees overhead, and by then they'd left the signs of habitation behind them; all about was deep woods, broken only here and there by an abandoned shack, or a bare foundation where a building had once stood. They started down the eastern face of a high ridge, granting them a view of the wooded valley below and the next ridge looming blue in the distance. Mags lit another cigarette and said, "Wow . . . it's fucking beautiful out here."

"Don't get used to it," Connor grumbled.

"Wuzzat?"

Prof pointed toward the looming mountains and said, "That over there, at the top of the ridge, is where the habitable zone ends. The transition is . . . well, it's dramatic. It's difficult to describe—you'll have to see it for yourself—but as Connor said, don't get used tot his; we'll be on our way down the other side of that ridge before suppertime."

"Reckon we'll be safe on this side of the valley so long as it's broad daylight," Connor grumbled, "but once we hit topside over there, we'll be in the heart of the shit. No more nature walk then;

noise discipline, light, discipline, all that good shit. All that dead country is et up with roamers and hunters."

The sun was getting high, and the day growing sickeningly hot, as they approached the floor of the valley. A wind picked up from the north and they reveled in it, luxuriating in the cool mountain air ruffling their clothes dampened with sweat and humidity. At the valley floor, the wind shifted, coming toward them from the east, bringing with it a low, sad sound, as of many voices keening far away.

Prof had been right; the transition was dramatic.

Just as the sun started to drop behind their backs, the group crested the far ridge and found themselves staring across another valley, this one wider than the last. They could only just make out the next ridge looming blue like a bank of clouds in the distance, and between it and them was a broad, flat floor with a river coursing through it. And the valley was filled with life and death.

The living foliage appeared stunted and juvenile, stubbornly clinging to life in a hostile environment. The scenery was dominated by a forest of ghosts, by the mummified carcasses of trees looming leafless and barren over all.

"Shit," Jules observed.

Connor nodded. "Uh-huh, you said it, sister. You see them ruins down there on our side of the river? That's where we're headed. We gonna wanna get there as ASAP as possible, and keep our eyes and ears open along the way; it'll be dark soon, and shit gets interesting after dark. Y'all got yer Geiger counters and pro-masks loose?"

Everyone nodded.

"Alright. Well, let's get to it."

And the group started down the mountain. It was still and quiet in the oppressive shadows of the trees, the sounds of birds and other animals growing fainter and farther away. They passed by ruined buildings overgrown with tenacious foliage, the buildings growing thicker and closer together as they came nearer to the valley floor, and as they passed them they thought they could feel eyes drilling into the backs of their heads, but they saw and heard no sign of recent humanity, only the wind whistling through the trees and windows.

Toward evening, when the shadows were long and the sun had disappeared behind the ridge at their backs, the trail broke out of the woods to run along the remains of a highway choked with the rusting wrecks of a thousand cars, all pointed west. The ruins of a town loomed ahead in the distance.

"That there'd be Winchester," Connor said. "The safehouse is real close, just down the road here, but don't get complacent; it's getting dark quick, and if anything fucked is gonna happen, it'll happen now."

They moved into the town, into the shadows of its crumbling, vine-choked buildings, keeping their weapons up and glancing all about as they walked along its cracked and pitted streets. After a few minutes of this, Connor stopped, held up his left fist, and whispered, "Dead ahead. Looks like five or six of 'em."

Mags looked down the scope of her Dragunov and saw, about two hundred yards out, six human figures milling around on the street.

"Yeah, that's roamers," she said. "Take 'em out? That's an easy shot."

"Nah, not in the dark; if there's more, it would just bring 'em right to us. This way."

He led them down another street, around the side of a three-story brick building, but as soon as they were around the corner they heard cracks of gunfire coming from farther down the road, and as soon as the gunfire died down the air filled with pained, keening moans from all directions and the sound of shuffling feet.

"Hell," Connor observed.

Mags took a quick look around, threw her Dragunov over her shoulder, and started climbing hand-over-hand up the brick building's fire escape, barking, "Y'all, follow me. I've got an idea."

They did, in single file, and Jules called out, "So what's the big idea, sugar?"

"I'm gonna go do that thing that I do."

Upon hitting the roof, Mags brought her Dragunov up and ran to the roof's far edge, where she dropped down prone and began glassing the street. Sure enough, the streets were filling with shambling, moaning human figures pouring out of the ruined buildings, two or three dozen in all, but she could also see the source of the gunshots; there were people gathering on the rooftops, firing into the crowd of roamers, hooting in triumph every time one of the shriveled grey heads burst in a spray of green.

The others had come alongside by then, and they all joined in the festivities, the horde of roamers shrinking in time with the steady tattoo of gunfire. Mags was over it all; the world around her faded to nothing save for the tiny slice of it she could see through her scope, hideous grey heads filling it and bursting in a spray of bone chips and pickled brain matter in a mechanical, passionless sort of way, one after another. Until someone cried out, "Oh, holy shit!" followed by a terrible roar, and for an instant that tiny circle of vision was filled with blinding red and orange light.

Mags looked up to see that a circle of roamers in the center of the pack were enveloped in fire. The people on the rooftops were cheering, and one of them lobbed another glass jug full of clear liquid with a burning wick tied around its neck. The projectile sailed down to the pavement and shattered in a ball of fire. The cheers grew louder, and when the fire died down there were no roamers left. The people began climbing down from their rooftops, and a few looked toward Mags and the others, gave animated waves, and pointed down the street before heading that way themselves.

As the group climbed back down from their roof, they spotted one of the scavengers, a small person with brown skin and indeterminate gender with a battle rifle slung over their shoulder, hanging back from the group and waving at them. When they came close, the scavver laughed and cried out, "Is that Connor motherfucking Turlogh I see? What the fuck is up? You finally find yourself some friends?"

Connor laughed, turned back to the group, and said, "Folks, this here's TJ. Friend of mine. Damn good scavver."

TJ surveyed the four of them and asked, "And is that Jack McCreedy I see? How'd they drag your ass outta retirement?"

Prof gave a slight wave. "Good evening, TJ."

"Small fuckin world. But I see me a couple of new faces, too. Who are these lovely ladies?"

Mags took a step forward and gave them a friendly smile; Jules took a step back and stood behind her. "I'm Magnolia," she said, "but you can call me Mags. This here's Julia."

"You a red, Mags?"

Mags gestured at her tank top and flecktarn pants. "What gave it away?"

"Alright. What about you in the back there? Whatcha hidin from?"

"You," Jules said, meeting their eyes. "I don't like people."

"Valid. So where are you assholes headed?"

"B&B for now," Connor said. "Gonna crash for the night and figure it out from there."

"Hell yeah. That's where I was headed, too; just a little day trip, see if anybody's up to anything. What say we get moving before it gets any darker?"

And as they followed the crowd deeper into the ruined city, Mags asked, "So what is a B&B?"

"The safehouse I had told y'all about," Connor said. "There's people there damn near all the time, so there's some amenities and such. We call it the Boot and Braces."

"Best place in the wasteland," TJ said. "Booze, boys, chems, and warm beds all waiting for you. Y'all gonna love it there. Well, probably; you straight, red?"

Jules stifled a giggle. Mags shrugged, said, "Depends on what 'straight' means."

"You like to party?"

"Not on a job."

"Well in that case you're probably gonna hate it. What if 'straight' meant somethin else?"

"If that were the case, I'm about as straight as a recoil spring."

"Heh. Word."

Further down the road, the town was full of signs of human habitation; not permanent habitation, but the trash and markings of a million comings and goings. The walls of the buildings were covered in graffiti, with tags of black cats, red stars, and jolly rogers the most common. One entire wall was devoted to a mural of a dead blackshirt and the words "ZONA ANTIFA."

A set of train tracks cut across the street at a diagonal, and the trail led them down the tracks, and they saw their destination: A hill rose up in front of them, and the tracks led into a tunnel in the hill's face. The surrounding buildings were decked out in solar panels and eggbeater windmills, and the tunnel's mouth was guarded by sandbag redoubts. A sign hung over the tunnel's mouth, emblazoned with a pair of suspenders and a big black jackboot and the words "WELCOME TO THE BOOT & BRACES."

TJ gestured to the tunnel, grinned at Mags and Jules, and said, "Here she is, ladies. Our home away from home."

"Before we go in," Prof said, "let's agree to meet back up at the bar tomorrow morning. It might not be a bad idea to spend another day here, gathering information, and things inside can get rather . . . well, anarchic."

TJ sneered. "Yeah, I sure hope they do."

As they approached, one of the door guards—a middle-aged man with spiked hair, holding a shotgun—gave TJ a friendly wave and said, "Hey there! You brought some friends this time?"

"I handled them and now the mother won't take them back," TJ said. "The ugly one's Connor, and that there's Professor J, and them two are Mags and Jules. The ladies ain't never been here before."

"Oh, is that so?" He turned to Mags and Jules. "Well, we're real glad to have y'all. There's food, booze, and beds inside, and y'all are welcome to it. Say, are you a red?"

Mags shrugged. "Last time I checked."

"Well, it might do you good to finally see what real communism looks like."

She sighed and rolled her eyes as they walked inside.

The tunnel was illuminated by flickering fluorescent lights and led straight into the hill a ways until it opened up into a wide caldera hollowed out into the rock. Numerous side passages branched away from it, and in the center of it all stood a collection of tables, chairs, and crates serving as a makeshift bar. A crowd milled about eating, drinking, talking and smoking—the air was thick with the smell and haze of marijuana—and a few had instruments and were playing and singing. The bar was staffed by a man in a cocktail dress, who noticed Mags and Jules watching the whole affair from the edge of the crowd and called out, "Hey, come in! Don't just stand there!"

Jules smirked. "Y'know, sugar," she said, "you look like I need a drink."

"I don't drink on the job."

"The old man says we're gonna be here for the rest of the night at least. We're off the clock."

"I . . . aw, fuck it. I can't tell you no for anything."

They walked up to the bar and found two seats together, and the bartender pranced up to them and said, "Evening, sisters. What'll y'all have?"

"Y'all got wine?" Jules asked.

"Hell yeah we do."

He brought up a jug of dark purple liquid from behind the bar and put it down in front of them. Jules nodded her approval at it and asked, "What do y'all take in brass?"

The bartender laughed, until he realized Jules was serious. "Oh, sweetheart, it's just yours. Around here, all is for all."

"Hell yeah. Say, could we get a couple of glasses?"

"Sure thing, sweetheart. I'll be right back."

Somewhere off behind them, someone strummed a guitar and sang, *"People of every color are marching side-by-side . . . Marching o'er the fields where a million fascists died . . . You're bound to lose, all you fascists bound to lose . . ."*

The bartender returned a moment later with two tin cups and asked, "So who are you strangers, if y'all don't mind me asking?"

"I'm Magnolia," Mags said, "but you can call me Mags. This here's Jules."

"Pleasure. My name's Knives, and I'm prob'ly the only one you'll meet here who stays at the B&B full-time. Most folks are just passing through, but this here's home to me. Where y'all hail from?"

"New Lawrence, way back over the fence."

"Damn, honey, you come a ways. What about you?"

Jules made prolonged eye contact with him and muttered, "Nowhere."

"I didn't mean no offense, sweetheart. Hell, most folks around here are from nowhere." Knives looked up and saw that someone else had sat down further down the bar, and he disappeared with a quick apology.

When they were alone, Jules filled the tin cups with wine and asked, "Mags, sugar, how long have we known each other?"

"We've known each other for exactly 48 hours, honey."

"Well, I just wanted to say . . . I've loved every single one of them." She handed Mags one of the cups. "How's about a toast?"

"Sure. What to?"

"To second chances. To a future that's whatever the fuck we want it to be."

"I'll drink to that." She held her cup up towards Jules. "To a future worth fighting for."

"Hell yeah. to a future worth fighting for."

After a while, when the jug was mostly empty, the two women sneaked away from the bar and down one of the side passages until they found a small defile far away from anyone else, and there they laid out a bedroll and clumsily laid down together. Mags held Jules close and mumbled, "You . . . you're really pretty."

"You're sweet. And drunk."

"No, you're drunk."

"Maybe so, but that don't change the truth, and the truth is that you're pretty."

"Jules, that's gay."

They laughed, and Jules nuzzled her chest and said, "Sugar, I think you mighta fucked up and made me fall in love with you."

"Well yeah, I fucking hope so."

"Yeah, well, you . . . You feel safe, Mags. I . . . feel safe, in your arms like this. This feels like home."

"Fuck, are you trying to make me cry?"

"I love you, you big dyke."

"Yeah, well, I love you, too. So there."

"Mags, that's gay."

And they fell asleep together, giggling, their lips sweet and heads silly with wine.

Something was wrong. Frank didn't know what, but he knew that something was hinky, and that it had something to do with the girl with the long sleeves.

Frank Russo had been sitting off by himself at the bar, watching people come and go, taking stock of them, and for the most part they didn't register as too much of anything. By his estimation, the B&B was full of degenerates, druggies, bums, and faggots, an undisciplined rabble, no threat to him or to his mission. He'd been able to just sit right in the heart of them, carrying on a perfectly pleasant conversation with the disgusting trap serving drinks, and not a one even suspected that he didn't belong. The captain would be over the moon about that, once they rendezvoused.

But those two . . .

When the two women had walked in, they'd caught his eye immediately because he could tell right away that these weren't scavengers, these were soldiers. Seasoned killers. The tall one, the red-headed Jew in the combat fatigues, she was obviously an Ashlander, a red, and quite out of place in the anarchist bar. But the other one, the short one with the black hair and the long flannel shirt and the leather vest with the scowl frozen onto her face . . . there was something about her.

He'd watched them out of the corner of his eye while they sat and drank and talked, and he'd watched them stumble off together when they were done, and he wracked his brain for why the dark-haired woman's presence bothered him so much, but kept coming up with nothing.

After they were gone, though, something clicked: He had seen that woman before.

He couldn't remember when or where, and he couldn't put a name to the face, but Frank Russo was sure of one thing: He and the scowling, dark-haired woman with the killer's eyes had met somewhere before.

[10]

A MURDER OF CROWS

MAGS AWOKE FROM A PEACEFUL, DREAMLESS SLEEP TO THE sounds of people moving around further down the passage, and to the smell of food. Stirring, she found that Jules lay wrapped all around her, clinging like a koala, and she couldn't get up.

"Honey, it's morning," she groaned, trying to roll the sleeping woman off of her.

"Hrrmphhmm," Jules pontificated. "Fuckin . . . don't wanna."

"Get up, babe. I smell breakfast."

"I'll tell you where you can put breakfast, you Raggedy Anne-lookin bitch."

At that, Mags burst into a peal of laughter, which shocked Jules awake, and she sat up and mumbled, "Fuck . . . fuckin . . . what time is it? Did we miss formation?"

"Get up, dummy. Let's go see what's cooking."

They got up, rubbed the sleep from their eyes, shouldered their rucksacks, and headed back down the passage. As they walked, Mags turned to Jules and said, "So . . . last night."

"What about it?"

"You told me you loved me."

"I was drunk."

"You weren't that drunk."

"Nah, I wasn't that drunk." She gave her a sheepish grin. "It's true, sugar; ya got me. But, as I recall, I weren't the only one throwing the L word around."

Mags stopped, grabbed her shoulders, and planted a long, slow kiss on her lips. "Guilty as charged, honey."

Jules couldn't find her words, only took Mags' hand and leaned against her as they walked down the tunnel towards the bar and the source of the sounds and smells.

The B&B was full of scavengers bustling about, the bar having been repurposed to dish out coffee and soup, and Mags and Jules saw the crew they'd come in with sitting at the bar, nursing bowls, and made to head that way. Mags hadn't taken two steps into the chamber before Jules grabbed the back of her rucksack and pulled her back into the tunnel.

"Hey, what gives?" she demanded, and then, a bit softer: "Is something wrong? Shit, something's wrong, ain't it?"

Jules' sad brown eyes were the size of plates and all the color was gone from her face. "That guy," she hissed, "far side of the bar from our people, long brown hair, flannel shirt, black backpack."

"Yeah, I see him. What about him?"

"I . . . sugar, I know that guy. That's a fucking stormtrooper."

"Oh, *Hell*. You think he'd recognize you?"

"Doubt it. I ain't seen that face in years and years; he wasn't an officer and he wasn't in my group, so I doubt he'd have kept up with all the comings and goings."

"That's good, at least. Alright, I've got an idea."

———

The two women walked up to the bar and took seats next to their companions as if nothing was wrong, but as soon as they were seated Mags slipped Prof a scrap of paper, which he unfolded and read, and after turning as grey as an angry sky he passed it to Connor. When Connor had read the note, Mags took an offered bowl of soup from one of the people tending bar and asked, "So have y'all heard anything? We pretty much went straight to bed last night."

"Nothing special," Prof answered. "Mostly just complaints that the valley's been cleaned out and that people have to move deeper into the wasteland to find decent salvage—but that's an old complaint. The closest thing to news is talk of groups of blackshirts moving around, but that's all much farther north than we are, and in any event we already knew about that."

Jules twitched and gave Mags' hand a squeeze, the shadow of an unspoken fear passing over her. Mags squeezed back and pulled her closer. Prof went on:

"Personally, I think we should go ahead and keep moving east as soon as the sun's up. As much as I do enjoy this place, I don't think that we're going to hear anything interesting, and it's probably best not to waste time."

Mags nodded her assent. Taking another glance around the bar, she saw that Frank had gotten up and was moving toward them, moving at an easy pace and with a friendly smile. Mags signaled this to the others, and the four of them tried their best not to look suspicious as he came up to the empty seat between Connor and TJ and said, "Well hey there! I don't believe I've seen y'all around here before."

"Oh, you wouldn't have," Mags said. "We're new in town. Now, if you don't mind, buddy, we're kinda in the middle of--"

"Well, see," and Frank leaned over the bar and looked toward Jules, "the reason I came over here is that I'm absolutely sure I've seen you someplace before. Don't we know each other?"

"I doubt it," Jules said.

"Oh, I like your accent. What's your name, sweetheart?"

"Jane," Jules said, meeting his eyes.

"Where do you come from, Jane?"

"I'm from nowhere."

Frank's friendly smile became a trickster's grin. "Oh, what a coincidence," he said, and winked. "I'm from nowhere, too."

Before anyone else could speak, TJ reached over, plucked Frank on the back of the head, and growled, "Hey, dipshit, can't you tell that the lady don't wanna talk to you? Piss off. Go bother somebody else."

Frank ignored them, and he gave Jules a knowing look and asked, "I'm not bothering you, am I, sweetheart?"

TJ grabbed him by the hair and slammed his face into the bar, then did it again. Frank got up and staggered backwards with blood streaming from his nose. He started to reach for the combat knife hanging from his belt, but thought better of it when he saw that every pair of eyes in the bar was fixed on him, and that a few of the scavvers had stood up and started moving in his direction. He backed away and headed toward the tunnel's entrance.

"Christ," TJ said, taking a long drink of coffee, "but what the hell was that guy's problem?"

No-one else spoke until Frank was out of sight. Once he'd disappeared into the shadows, Mags, Jules, Prof, and Connor all stood up and went to follow him.

"I can't tell you how," Jules said, "but I do know that guy. And I can't tell you why, but we cannot let that guy get outta town."

———

Frank was content; he'd gotten what he'd wanted.

He managed to make his way out of the squat ahead of the news about his little altercation, and the morning's door guards didn't bother asking questions about the bloody nose, so he was able to make a quick and quiet exit. In addition to the information he'd gleaned observing the squat and its occupants, he'd confirmed that the dark-haired woman was certainly from Ohio, and he saw in her eyes that she'd recognized him. He'd have liked to bait her into a conversation, or at least get a real name, but he'd gotten more than enough to scratch the itch of curiosity. As for who this woman was and what she was doing there, he was sure that one of the operating groups would have some idea.

As soon as he was out of sight of the tunnel's entrance, he brought his Armalite to low ready and turned east, picking a careful path through the ruined streets, avoiding the scavengers. When he was near the outskirts of town and could see no-one else around, he stopped, turned around, and said, "I know you're all following me."

Silence.

"Come on out, sweetheart, and let's talk. I know you just like you know me, and don't we both serve the Commander?"

Frank heard something then, the sound of running footsteps, but to his surprise they weren't coming from the way he'd come; they were coming from behind. Before he had time to turn around, something struck him in the small of his back, hard enough to put him on his knees, and struck him again between the shoulders, dropping him in a heap on the ground. He rolled over to find himself staring down the wrong end of a marksman's rifle.

Mags smirked. "I thought you guys were supposed to be operators or something."

Frank's face didn't show an ounce of fear, or even surprise. He gave Mags a sad smile and said, "So it's gonna be like this, then. Say, where's our mutual friend?"

"Oh, I'm right here," Jules said, walking up to Mags' side. "Hey there, Frank. Long time, no see."

"I suppose we're through pretending. Jane, was it? Miss Plain Jane? Well, Jane, I'm flattered you remember me from when and wherever it was we met, but I'm afraid I still only know you as a familiar face. Jane."

"Holy shit, you are tellin the goddamn truth, ain'tcha? Frank, you probably wouldn't understand, but that is the nicest thing anyone has ever said to me. Look at me, Frank, and think about it for two seconds. It was four, five years ago now, back when you were still just an egghead, not a spook yet. You remember Sunrise? The last big Huntington blitz?"

Something clicked in Frank's mind, but the pieces didn't quite fall into place. He cocked an eyebrow. "I'm afraid I'm still not quite following, Jane. Why don't we start with your real name?"

Mags sighed, and she growled, "Hon, is this really necessary? I could just shoot him."

"Nah. I wanna know what this piece of shit is doin here, and who he's with."

"I'm with the Arditi, obviously," Frank said, "and I'm here to do the work of the New Republic. But, of course, you know all of that. I may be having a time putting a name to that face, but I do remember Huntington. I'm fascinated to discover where your true loyalties lie, Jane."

Jules doffed her vest, unbuttoned her shirt, and threw it to the ground next to Frank's head. As Frank's face—and TJ's--contorted in confusion, surveying the map of hatred carved into her skin in pinpricks and gunpowder, Jules smirked, and met Frank's eyes, and said, "Stand up, white man, and do your duty. The blood in your veins cries out with ten thousand years of purpose. Stand up, white man, and take up the sword."

Though uncomprehending, Frank finished the catechism: "Stand up, white man, and claim your birthright. Stand up, white man, and take back what's yours."

"Life sure do take us to some wild places, don't it, Frankie?"

"Woman, who—or what—the fuck are you?"

By way of answer, Jules turned around and gave Frank her back, letting him survey the symbols inked there, and she lowered her jeans just enough to flash him her scar and her second set of eyes.

"Wait a fucking minute," he stammered, "there is no goddamn way. You're . . . you *must* be . . . that corporal they disappeared. Binachi? Jules fucking Binachi? How the fuck are you alive?"

"Because I'm too goddamn mean to die, Frank. Julia Carlotta

Binachi is made out of sin and spite and the world ain't hard enough to do me in. And now that we've got the introductions outta the way, I got a couple of questions."

Frank's look of confusion contorted into a sneer of pure, smoldering hatred, and he spat, "You're a faggot and a traitor, Binachi."

"Yep, yessir, I sure am." Jules drew her knife, the silvered knife that Millie had given her, and said, "Now, like I said, I got questions, and we can do this the easy way or we can do it the fun way."

Frank laughed. "Oh, this is fucking rich! This is something else! I'm about to be done the fuck in by a red, a couple of muds, a yid, and Julian fucking Binachi. God must have a sense of humor after all."

"You're about to find out about my sense of humor, Frank. Reckon I'll start with the toes and work my way up."

"You . . . you have no goddamn clue what's coming, do you? None of you have any idea about what's coming! This is fucking gold. Jules, I just hope that before we come back through and burn all this red shit to the fucking ground, I just hope that John has a chance to hear about this. Goddamn, but I wish I could be there to see his face!"

Jules' eyes widened, and she hissed, "What do you know about John?"

"Oh, you really haven't got a goddamn clue, do you? Johnny must be halfway to Owings Mills by now! Oh, good Lord, but I wish I could be there to see that reunion. Why are you so worried about him, traitor?" And he looked her up and down again, and something clicked in his mind; he burst into horrible, mocking laughter and wheezed, "Oh, no goddamn way! It was *you? You're* where all those jokes came from? Oh, this is rich. Why you ask about him, faggot? You miss your boyfriend?"

Jules held her knife in both hands as she plunged it into Frank's chest, and again, and again, and over again until he stopped moving. She knelt beside the mangled corpse, and Mags knelt next to her and said, "Well . . . I think we got everything we needed to know."

From to the left, they heard TJ growl, "Oh, not even fucking close."

Jules looked left and found herself staring into the barrel of TJ's battle rifle. She put out a hand to stop Mags from getting up and said, her voice flat and emotionless, "I reckon you've got some questions."

"Oh, you're goddamn right I do!"

"Ask away. I'm an open book."

"You a fucking fascist, Jules?"

"Not anymore. But I was once."

"What the fuck is going on?"

"You gonna shoot me, TJ?"

"I sure am thinking about it!"

Jules leaned forward, pressing her forehead into the rifle's barrel. "I won't try to stop you. I deserve it."

"Give me one good reason why I shouldn't blow your goddamn head off right now."

A glance down at Frank's cooling body, then back up into TJ's eyes. "I'm not gonna give you one. I want you to do it."

TJ considered her for a moment, sighed, lowered their rifle, and spat, "Alright, somebody here had better start fucking talking."

When Mags and Jules finished speaking, TJ pinched the bridge of their nose and muttered, "I swear to God, you're all as stupid as a box of rocks."

"I ain't never denied it," Jules said, wiping her eyes.

"First of all: Jules, you have my deepest sympathies for all the shit they did to you, and I respect your growth and all the work you're putting in and all that mushy shit, but . . . please put a fucking shirt on."

Jules grabbed her flannel and pulled it back on. TJ turned to Mags and said, "And you. You fuckin suicidal or something? You think you're just gonna waltz into the place that kills everybody who waltzes into it? Is this what they teach y'all at that goddamn school across the fence? Jesus Christ. And if it wasn't bad enough that there are boneheads in my wasteland, now we've got boneheads in my fucking bar. Shit. Y'all . . . we have to go back to the B&B."

"I was hoping to get on the road," Mags said, "but yeah. The people need to know about this. You, ah . . . you think they'll mind that we merc'd a dude right outside their back porch?"

"You kidding, sister? You saw the mural on the way in. Hell, if anything, they'll probably be jealous Jules got to him before they could."

Mags looked over at Jules. She was sitting on the ground, staring at her shoes with her knees tucked up under her chin, the bloody knife cast aside like something venomous. "Hey, honey," she said, "you, ah . . . well, I was gonna ask if you were alright, but I can tell the answer's no."

"You'd be right about that, sugar."

"You need anything, babe?"

Jules drew in a long, ragged breath. "He's out there, Mags. He's out there. I can't fucking get away."

"Yeah, he is. But listen: So are we. He's not the predator anymore; today, he's the prey."

"Mags, sugar, I know you mean well, but fuck all that. This . . . this didn't feel good, didn't feel cathartic. I . . . I don't wanna go on some grand quest for vengeance; I don't wanna give him that much credit. I just . . . I just want this shit to be over."

"Word. Well, honey . . . the best way to make sure the past stays over with is to get out in front of it. If you don't wanna be the angel of death, be a soldier. Be a soldier with a mission."

Jules stood up and stretched. Her eyes were still red and puffy with tears, but she smirked and said, "Now, that . . . That I can do."

[*Later that evening, Maryland, somewhere near Hagerstown*]

Crossing the highway cloverleaf was slow, tedious work, the north- and westbound lanes choked with countless rusting cars, all locked bumper-to-bumper in an eternal, futile retreat. Peterson wished they could've just gone around all this ironmongery, but this was the rendezvous point with the head spook, and it was a rendezvous that nobody dared to miss, much as Peterson might like to. They were too far south now, into land that was just as much anarchist country as it was bandit country, and whatever the head spook had to say would be more than worth hearing.

The sun had started setting an hour before and now was almost hidden behind their backs, and the play of the long shadows and fading light across the graveyard of rusting steel felt sickening, unnatural, and in Peterson's mind it only further drove home the point that this was a rendezvous he would really prefer to avoid. Nobody else seemed troubled; Rolf, and the other lance corporal they'd picked up at the last rendezvous, looked excited, even downright eager to see who they were about to meet, while Rocko and Haraldson, old hands, looked out over the cloverleaf and the sea of wreckage and seemed unimpressed if anything. And John? Well . . .

The group had made remarkable time across the valley, easily breaking 35 clicks per day, and all because they'd been beating feet to match John's pace. Tomassi was eating up miles like he had someplace to be, sleeping little, speaking less, spending every spare moment staring into the east and cleaning his rifle or sharpening his knife. Peterson would've been worried about him, if he weren't so eagerly awaiting the captain's inevitable breakdown.

It was full dark when they finally stopped for the night, making camp beneath an overpass at the center of the cloverleaf. As they set up their bivouacs and got supper together, Tomassi growled, "Our guy should be along any minute now. We take his report, then we're back on the road bright and early tomorrow morning." And he walked off to sit by himself and brood, staring into the east.

Peterson watched him walk off and decided to go lean into it. He followed Tomassi to the far side of a decaying old minivan, where the captain sat down, lit a cigarette, and sighed, staring off into the darkness.

"Hey there, Johnny Tomato," Peterson said, sitting down next to him. "Somethin on your mind?"

"Fuck off, Peterson."

"Dude, I been with this outfit long enough that I can tell when somethin ain't right. You are goin through it, Johnny; I can see it, and so can everybody else."

"Suck my cock."

"I'd really rather not, if it's all the same to you, boss."

They sat in silence for a while, until Tomassi cracked his neck and asked, "You say the others are picking up on it?"

"You're about as subtle as a sledgehammer, man."

"Shit." A long drag on his cigarette, a long, sad sigh, and Tomassi asked, "You got a woman back home, Peterson?"

"Nah. I'm on the road too much to keep a woman. Never was much of a family man, anyways."

"Then what is it you're fighting for?"

Peterson shrugged. "What else am I supposed to do? Men fight; it's what we're for."

"Yeah." Another long sigh. "Y'know, I thought I had me a woman back home, once."

It took Peterson a long minute to come up with a response, because that was the last thing he'd been expecting to hear. Possessiveness, anger, those were to be expected, but from the look on Tomassi's face and the cadence of his voice, he could see . . . pining. The bastard was *pining*, and almost sounded tender. *Oh sweet Lord Jesus Christ*, Peterson thought, *he ain't just a monster, he's also a complete goddamn fucking idiot.*

"She still on your mind, boss?"

"Yeah. Never met anyone like her. And she just . . . left."

That's real fuckin rich coming from the piece of shit who sold her out in the first place. Gonna be doin the whole world a favor when I get rid of you.

"Well, boss, you know that you can't trust no woman. Already can't even trust no normal woman. If she ain't wanna stick around, well, that just means she don't know what's good for her."

"Yeah. Yeah, Peterson, you're right." Tomassi stood up. "Enough of this touchy-feely horseshit. And listen, if you speak one word of this to the rest of 'em--"

"Yeah, yeah, you'll kill me. I got it." *Not if I get you first, you backstabbing rapist son of a bitch.*

As Tomassi headed back to the group, the air around them began to grow cold, and in the still, silent night air they could hear the sound of boots clapping against pavement on the overpass over their heads.

"That'd be our guy," Tomassi said with a hungry grin.

The footsteps stopped, and a human figure fell from the overpass and stuck the landing on the pavement in front of them. The figure spun on its heels and walked toward the group, a tall man with buzzed blonde hair, wearing a black dress uniform. The soldiers shrank back with mingled terror and excitement, save for Peterson, who pretended not to see the man, and Tomassi, who just kept grinning.

As he strode up, they saw that his skin was sickeningly pallid, almost translucent, and his eyes were solid black.

"Sir," Tomassi said with a curt nod.

"Good evening, *Hauptsturmfuhrer*," the man said. "Are you ready to receive the report?"

"Yes, sir. Uh . . . *Herr Sturmbanfuhrer*."

"Very good. Now, I do come with some bad news: The intelligence officer embedded in Winchester did not make his evening check-in. Other agents in that sector have reported significant

Bolshevist activity in the past few days, so we must assume that he has been compromised."

"Goddamn," Rocko muttered, "they got Frank? He was a good dude. Damn good spook."

"Indeed, *Unterfeldwebel*. Now, from there—and it is very likely that these two developments are related—intelligence agents have reported that, in addition to the increased scavenger activity the Bolshevists have also assembled a team of specialists for another mission to the Eagles' Nest; I suppose they never learn, do they? We do not have much for certain, but we know that the team numbers between three and seven professionals, and three of them are of great interest to *Herr Feldmarschall* von Hochulf and the high command personally."

"We got names?"

"Connor Turlogh, designated marksman. Jackson McCreedy, call sign Ghost One, intelligence specialist. And Magnolia Blackadder, call sign Crow 12, political officer."

The other two could've been anyone, but the last name meant something to Tomassi. "I've heard about that bitch. They say she's bad trouble."

"Indeed, *Hauptmann*. So now we come to the final piece of business: Your updated orders."

"Lay 'em on me, boss."

"You are to take a small detour in your journey east. From this spot, you are to lead your group south, toward the confluence of the Potomac and Shenendoah rivers, and resume your eastern march past Sandy Hook. If our conjectures are correct, this should put you on a path to intercept the Bolshevist agents, with a bit of luck. You are to travel with all speed, and if you encounter any scavengers or any enemy agents, they are to be . . . dealt with. Quickly. Do you understand?"

"Yes, sir. Understood, sir."

"We are at the eve of our greatest victory, *Hauptmann*. Do not disappoint us; it will not go well for you if you disappoint us. Now,

I must be on my way—dawn comes all too quickly, ja?--but we will see each other again soon. Happy hunting."

The dark man took a few steps backward, then turned and sprinted off into the darkness too quickly for their eyes to follow. All the men shivered, save for Tomassi, who kept grinning, and Peterson, who wore a sickly look like h'ed just swallowed something foul.

The strange men from Baltimore with the funny accents, the men who moved wrong and never came out in the daytime, had always given Peterson the creeps, made him feel the way a laying hen must feel when the fox is close by, but this exchange felt even darker than the others. The updated orders filled Peterson with a sense of dread that he couldn't explain, left him with the thought that he might not have as much time as he'd thought.

He watched the men settle down to their nightly card game, watched Tomassi—still grinning like a shark scenting blood in the water—pick up a jug of wine and sit down to join them, and he thought: *Any day now, you son of a bitch. Any day now.*

[11]
JOHN BROWN'S BODY

JUST AS TJ HAD SAID, THE SCAVENGERS AT THE BOOT & BRACES were overjoyed at the news of a dead fascist, and even the guards neglected to ask too many questions. Concern over the fact that Frank Russo had been there at all seemed subdued, until one of the guards explained to Mags that this sort of thing happened from time to time, the squat's open nature making it difficult to prevent, and the long-timers had turned "spot the bonehead" into something of a game. Frank Russo had been smoother than most; the typical spook wouldn't last longer than a couple of hours.

And when the eyes of the several dozen scavvers in the B&B were turned toward the group, TJ took it upon themself to announce why they were there and where they were headed, which turned them into instant celebrities; Connor and Prof seemed to accept this as the price of doing business in the waste-land, but Mags and Jules tried their best to slink around the outskirts of the crowd and avoid being seen. As the day dragged on, TJ joined them, and the three sat off in a corner, sharing a jug of wine since they'd accepted that their early start would have to wait for the next morning. Jules and TJ couldn't stop staring at Connor and Prof moving about the crowd like social butterflies.

"Y'know," Jules said, "I've known that old man for better than a year now, and I have never seen him be smooth or talkative before. He's always been real squirrely, never wanted to hold a conversation unless it was about something, y'know?"

"It's social engineering," Mags said. "What you've seen of him, that's the real Professor J—I knew him for a lot of years before you did, and yeah, he's just like that. What he's doing now is putting on a face, like an actor in a play, so he can pump all these people for information. Watch the way he carries himself, what he does with his hands; you can tell he hates every second of this. Connor, though . . . I think he's the genuine article, actually. I think he's just finally loosening up now that he's around more of his own people."

"Yeah," TJ broke in. "I wouldn't say I 'know' Connor, but I've seen him around for years and we've done a couple of jobs together. He knows anarchy and he knows scavenging, and if you know both of those things too then he'll talk your ear off about it. Now, don't get me wrong, the guy is definitely an asshole, but he's our kind of asshole, y'know?"

Mags laughed. "Yeah, I'll drink to that."

"Say, red, I been wanting to ask you: What do you think of the space here?"

"It's pretty neat. A textbook example of spontaneous organizing. I'd love to stick around and study it. Why do you ask me?"

"Well, 'cause you're a red. We don't see too many reds this far east, especially not political officers. I'm curious to hear what you think of non-hierarchical organizing now that you've seen it up close."

Mags took a long drink of wine. "Well, see, my whole take on it is that there's no such thing. All human society under the present mode of production necessarily degenerates into hierarchy, because our social relationships reproduce production relationships. Just sitting here and watching people run the bar and pick up the trash and stuff, I can already see that some people and groups take charge of certain tasks faster and more frequently than others, and are listened to when they do. Just because there's no formal democratic structure or political roles doesn't mean there's not a hierarchy. Say, that pretty boy who tends bar, what's his name again?"

"That's Knives."

"Right. You can tell me that nobody's in charge here, but looking at it as an outsider, I think it's pretty obvious that Knives is in charge."

"Knives gets a lot of respect, yeah—this is basically his house—but nobody commands anybody to do anything. It just happens organically."

"No, no, that's exactly my point. These hierarchies generate organically because they're a superstructural reflection of the mode of production. See, if you read Lenin--"

This went on for several hours.

As the time wound down to afternoon and then evening, and the crowd grew more intoxicated, a pickup music show started up at the corner of the bar closest to their table, with instruments being passed around and scavvers taking turns playing and singing. At first the three paid attention because it drowned out their conversation and was too loud to ignore, but as time ticked on they started to enjoy the festivities, even singing along when one of them knew the words to a song.

At the end of one set, Knives helped a singer stumble drunkenly down from where he'd been standing on the bar, looked at Mags, and called out, "Oh, hey! Hey, red!"

Mags blinked. "Wuh . . . uh . . . me?"

"No, the other authoritarian. Yes, you! You play?"

"Um . . . I play a little. I'm a bit out of practice."

Everyone cheered at that. "So whatcha play?"

"Uh . . . I pick a little banjo."

Applause. Cries of, "Somebody get this lady a banjo!"

Mags took a very long, very deep drink of wine, and didn't

bother resisting as she was hoisted up onto the table and a banjo was shoved into her hand. Surveying the crowd, she asked, "So, uh . . . y'all know *John Brown's Body?*"

"Of fucking course we do!" someone shouted. "We've all heard that one a million times. Come on, fresh cut, give us somethin we ain't heard before!"

"Um . . . how 'bout *There's Power In A Union?*"

"Everybody knows that one!"

"*The Red Army is the Strongest?*"

"Fuck outta here!"

"Shit. Alright, uh . . . Oh, yeah, I've got one. Sing along if you know the words."

And Mags began to pick, and after a few false starts she began to sing in a soft, sad voice:

"We will meet, but we will miss her
There will be one vacant chair
We shall linger to caress her
While we breathe our evening prayers
When one year ago we gathered
Joy was in her fair blue eye
But now the golden cord is severed
And our hopes in ruins lie
We will meet, but we will miss her
There will be one vacant chair
We shall linger to caress her
While we breathe our evening prayers . . ."

Though Mags was glad the exchange had happened, exhilarated by the sight and sound of all the people cheering her on and clapping along, she was a pile of frayed nerves by the last verse and gratefully handed the banjo back into the anonymous crowd, ignoring demands for another song. Before she could climb down from the table, though, Jules climbed up to join her, planted a long, slow kiss on her hips, and declared, "Damn, sugar, I didn't know you could sing like that."

Mags returned the kiss, laughed, and asked, "Honey, what's got into you? Not that I'm complaining, but you never do shit like this in public."

"I'm drunk as fuck."

The crowd roared with laughter and applause at that, and a few people rushed forward to help them down from the table and back into their seats. The next musician started up, the crowd turned their attention toward them, and Mags and Jules slipped away to the alcove where they'd spent the previous night and laid down together again.

"Honey," Mags whispered as she stroked Jules' hair, "I wanted to ask: Are you holding up okay? You've, ah . . . well, you've had a day."

"Well," Jules slurred, her voice sweet and heavy with wine, "I merc'd a dude, and I found out that you-know-who is slinking around out there someplace, and I found out some other things I'd rather not have known, so that's, y'know, not great. But after that I got to listen to my girlfriend sing, and I gave her a great big wet kiss in front of God and everybody, and that . . . that was nice." She yawned. "God, I'm fuckin smashed. I'm gonna be mad as hell at myself in the morning, sugar. I don't usually drink this much. Never liked it. Let's not go making a habit of this, alright?"

"Yeah, that's . . . that's probably a good idea."

"Oh, yeah. See, some people drink to forget, but me . . . Jeez, everything feels so fuckin real right now; this would be un-fucking-bearable if you weren't here with me, y'know? Shit. I'm rambling. I'm sorry."

"Nah, honey, I like it when you ramble. I like the sound of your voice."

"You fuckin mean that? On God?"

"Of course."

"Bitch. You're too fuckin nice to me. And y'know what? I like *your* voice. You sound so pretty, sugar. You should sing more often. And I . . . fuck, dammit, I love you."

"I love you, too."

"Good. I . . . I . . ." And with one last great yawn, Jules was gone, her slurred words of affection replaced almost at once by obnoxious snoring. Mags settled into sleep, luxuriating in the warmth of Jules' body against hers, and within a few minutes she had almost drifted off herself, until Jules began to shake, and her snoring turned into sad, quiet whimpers.

Mags squeezed her tight, stroked her hair, and whispered, "It's alright, honey, it's alright. I'm here. I've got you."

The shaking eased up a bit, but only a bit, and Mags held her tighter as she drifted off into her own restless sleep.

The facility's proper name was the Institute for Integration Through Applied Sexology, but nobody called it that. The Arditi staff officers at the Columbus Oberkommando next door had taken to calling it names like "the officers' club" or "the trap house," and tried not to be seen coming or going from it. The clergy were given handsome bonuses in brass and finery for pretending it didn't exist, though some of the Ecclesiarchs—Father Elias and his friends— were happy to pretend such on their own. Most people knew nothing about it, never linking the name on top of occasional research papers with the little parcel service center next to the capitol building. And the women who ended up there were so grateful for what they'd been told was a second chance at life that they pretended not to notice the bars on the windows, or the spirals of razor wire on top of the fence, or the fact that the corpsman-major appeared to be the only occupant older than 30.

And like so many others, Jules Binachi had been so overcome with desperate relief that not even her seasoned killer's instincts quite registered the bedroom door with no lock, or the bars across the windows, or the fixtures that required frequent repair because they'd all been designed not to hold an adult woman's full weight.

She'd been there, undergoing treatment, luxuriating in this new existence where she wore a skirt and someone called her Julia, just starting to register that all of this was far too good to be true and that something was rotten not too deep under the surface, for just over a month when the corpsman-major called her in for their weekly session and spat out a bunch of official-sounding jargon; it was difficult to follow—she had already gathered that Natasha was the world's greatest bullshit artist and could write a novel about soap—but words like "autogynophilia" and "confirmation of hetero-sexuality" and the corpsman-major's very favorite word, "duty," came up a lot, enough to raise suspicions. At the end of all that, she announced that Jules had a visitor. Her former commanding officer would be stopping by.

That night was a rough night, but in a strange way Jules was able to distance herself from it in her mind, like a bad dream – it wasn't any more rough than the stockade, she kept telling herself. And over the next month there were two others, but those were Oberkommando officers she'd never seen before and would prob-ably never see again. Bad dreams. Ghosts and shadows.

The next time John showed up, it was worse, precisely because he tried to make it better.

He didn't leave immediately, but stayed lounging on the bed as if it was his room, smoking a cigar and talking, talking, talking endlessly. Jules didn't catch most of what he said, though in the brief moments when her mind flitted back to the present, she was cognizant of a stream of complements. She turned her head to look at him for the first time, his long blonde hair spread out across the pillow like a halo, his body knotted with iron muscles, every inch of it below the neck covered in tattoos and scars, a smoldering cigar hanging out of his satisfied smile, and he said, "I never thought I'd say this, but you are so fuckin beautiful, babe. You look just like a real woman."

That snapped Jules fully into the moment, and she barked, "Get out."

"What was that, baby?"

"*Get the fuck outta my room, you backstabbing piece of shit!* The fuck makes you think I wanna listen to all this horseshit? You already fuckin ruined my life once; wasn't that enough? Get out! Get out!"

"Jeez, the hell is your problem?"

That threw her for a loop, and she had no idea how to answer such a monumentally stupid question, until she met Tomassi's eyes and found a word for the thing she saw written across his face: Entitlement.

"The fuck do you think my problem is, you stupid son of a bitch? You're a fucking traitor and I wish I'd never fucking met you! Get the fuck out or we'll find out if I'm still fast enough to throw you."

They both knew that she wasn't. She'd tried that on his first visit.

Casually, effortlessly, as though he were scratching an itch, Tomassi threw an elbow into the small of Jules' back. Something moved which was not supposed to move, and she rolled off of the bed and onto the floor in a heap. He did get up, then, and he laughed, and said, "Heh, still the same old Binachi; I guess some shit don't ever change. Don't worry, baby; I'll come visit my little black angel next time I'm up this way."

She lay there, sensation just beginning to return to her limbs, when he left, slamming the door behind him, and Jules snapped out of her dreams and sat up in the darkness of the tunnel, expelling a blue streak of curses into the passage. She started to panic, started to get to her feet, started to run, when she was struck all at once by the cloying closeness of the walls, the smells of human habitation, the warmth of the bedroll, and Mags, just inches from her, snoring. When the panic passed, she laughed.

"Wuh . . . wuzzat?" Mags inquired, sitting up.

Jules, her breath heavy and her heart racing as though she'd just run a mile, dove back into the bedroll, threw her arms around

Mags, and held her close. "Di...didn't mean to wake you," she stammered.

"Fuck," Mags muttered, returning the embrace. "What's going on, hon?"

"I had another nightmare, sugar. It was . . . bad. Real bad. Worse than usual. But at the end of it, something amazing happened."

"What happened?"

"I woke up next to you."

[*That evening, somewhere in Maryland*]

A few hours after the operating group received its updated orders, around the time Jules was waking up in the dark, someone hailed Becky on the radio. She threw on the headset, treating Barns to a one-sided conversation, which he hated, and which she knew he hated, which was why she did it.

"Uh-huh," she said, kicking her boots up on the dash, popping in a fresh stick of gum. "Yeah, you're talking to her. Uh-huh. Wait, I'm sorry, *who*? Yeah, yeah, put him on!"

"So who is it?" Barns asked.

She ignored him. "What the fuck is up, boss? How the hell are you doing? . . . What? . . . Shit, for real? Alright."

The word "boss" got Barns' attention.

"Already? No fuckin way! . . . Yeah, yeah, understood, loud and clear . . . Yeah, I'll let him know right now . . . You too, boss . . . Yeah, love you, too. See you soon. . . . Yeah. Over and out."

"So what was that about?" Barns asked.

"You are not gonna fucking believe it, bloodbag. Guess who just called me on the radio. Guess."

"There ain't exactly a lot of people you'd call 'boss'."

"Steve, sweetheart, that was the lad himself. That was Lukash."

"Holy shit. What did he want?"

"Couple things. First of all, apparently he's making way better time than he thought he would, even better time than we did; he's only a couple days behind us."

"Christ."

"Don't you cuss me, Steve Barns. Second of all, apparently our guys managed to squeeze a little information out of one of Otto's cronies before they bugged out, and it looks like things are coming to a head way, way ahead of schedule. So, change of plans for our little fact-finding expedition. We're not going south anymore. We're going west."

"West?"

"Yeah. Lukash is on his way to go chat with his old war buddy personally; we'll meet up with him somewhere on the road, but you and me, bloodbag, we're needed in Harper's Ferry, West Virginia fucking yesterday."

"Uh . . . shit. Alright. What's in Harper's Ferry?"

"If we get there in time? Backup. If we're too late? Bodies to bury."

The group got up before dawn and assembled in a quiet corner of the bar after talking Knives out of a few pots of coffee. TJ joined them right away, as though they'd been along from the beginning.

"You coming along?" Connor asked.

"Yeah, that's the plan," they said, rubbing the sleep from their eyes. "I mean, I definitely don't want to, and you're probably gonna all get killed, but . . . I can't not. It's the fucking Citadel."

Connor and Prof nodded their understanding, and Connor pointed to the map of the valley he'd laid out on the table: "Next leg of the trip's a little bit of a detour; we gonna spend today headed north. You do not wanna head dead east outta the valley, 'cause Old DC is that way and it'll put you right up the ass of the worst stretch of country you ever saw in your life, nuthin but roamers and poison glass. We gotta get over the rivers afore we can pick up the road east again, and the bast place to get over the rivers is the railroad bridge up here in Harper's Ferry."

At that, Mags' eyes lit up, and a giant grin split her face, and she rocked back and forth in her chair and asked, "Harper's Ferry? As in Harper's Ferry, West Virginia? We're going to Harper's fucking Ferry?"

Connor and TJ rolled their eyes. Jules asked, "What's in Harper's Ferry?"

"Harper's Ferry was where Captain John Brown had his last stand, way back in 1859."

"Who the hell is John Brown?"

Mags' grin became a slack-jawed gape of disbelief. "You . . . you don't know who Captain John Brown is? Okay, back in the 1850s, in Kansas--"

Prof laid a hand on her shoulder. "Magnolia, if we start giving history lectures now, we'll never get on the road."

"Okay, yeah, you're right. But . . . but we'll get to see the engine house, right? We're gonna see the engine house?"

Connor groaned. "Yes, Mags, we'll get to see the goddamn fucking engine house. You goddamn girl scouts and your dead white men."

"Hey," Mags said, "John Brown went to war."

———

The road north was much easier than the road east had been, running the length of the broad, flat valley, and they made excellent time, leaving as soon as the first rays of sunlight peeked over the furthest ridge. Connor and Prof picked an easy route through the rolling meadows and eerie, half-dead forests, and they passed only occasional roads and even fewer buildings, with here and there a crumbling grain silo or wild hedgerow standing in silent testament that this had once been farmland, long ago. They passed a few packs of roamers, groups of hunched human figures shambling through the brush, but spotted them from far off and were able to avoid confrontation, though here and there they passed signs of what confrontation might mean: On the trail at intervals, usually near some dilapidated building or other dark place hidden from the sun, they saw discarded gear and, in some spots, discarded bones cracked open for their marrow and bleaching in the sun. A much rarer sight, but a sight far more chilling, were neat, intentional little piles of discarded gear and bleaching bones, the remains of scavengers who'd been not merely devoured, but hunted.

Around dinnertime, Connor led them east in a detour around the ruins of what had once been a sizeable town, and once they were back on the trail north he told them, "We're only a couple clicks away from the crossing; we'll get there afore dark if we hurry. But, listen: Once that sun goes down, we stop and we hunker down wherever we're at. East of Winchester is hunter country, and I'd rather not fuck with no hunters if we ain't got to."

Everyone gave a solemn nod and picked up their pace, against the protests of their burning legs and aching feet. As they walked, the roads grew more choked with the rusting wrecks of cars, the decaying buildings closer together, until near to dark when the road took a sharp turn east and brought them within sight of the broad, green river flowing over its rocky bed. The foliage around the river's banks seemed greener, healthier, more wholesome than in the surrounding wilderness, even seeming pleasant. Connor pointed them toward a narrow side street running northeast along the river's course, between a creek and a high, stony ridge. It led them into a ruined town of old brick, marble, and stucco buildings, and, just as dark came on, to the point where two rivers met: The Shenendoah flowing north, the Potomac flowing east.

"Well," Connor said, "looks like we made it after all."

Mags' attention was fixed on a tiny, crumbling building of red brick, close by the embankment overlooking the rivers. Her eyes were wide with reverence, and she walked up to it with slow, deliberate steps. She put her hands on the building's decaying brickwork next to a marble plaque with an inscription faded near to illegibility with age and neglect. Though it was almost impossible to read, Mags knew what had once been written there, and she recited the words from memory as though she were in a church, reciting a catechism:

"That this nation might have a new birth of freedom, that slavery should be removed forever from American soil, Captain John Brown and his 21 men gave their lives. To commemorate their heroism, this tablet has been placed on this building, which has since become known as John Brown's Fort."

"Alright, girl scout," Connor grumbled, "let's get a move on. We're gonna camp out on the Point; hunters get nervous around running water."

Mags did not get a move on. Still resting her hands on the building, she turned her head upward and sang a whispered verse, almost a chant:

"The stars above in Heaven are a-looking kindly down,
The stars above in Heaven are a-looking kindly down,
The stars above in Heaven are a-looking kindly down
On the grave of old John Brown . . ."

And she turned away from the building slowly, reluctantly, and before leaving to catch up with the others she snatched up a piece of crumbling red brick from the ground and dropped it into her pocket.

The group made their camp for the night on an open cement pad on top of the promontory where the two rivers met, looking out toward a standing railroad bridge. Connor pointed north over the bridge, saying, "That there, that's the Potomac. Tomorrow morning, we's gonna cross that bridge, and when we do, we are gonna be right up inside the Devil's asshole. Get some good sleep tonight, 'cause from tomorrow on this trip is probably gonna turn into a running fight."

They drew lots for watch shifts, and Mags got last, so, as the last dying rays of the sun disappeared behind the mountains to the west, she bedded down beside Jules, hoping to get a head start on sleep.

"Sugar," Jules whispered, nuzzling her chest, "you forgot somethin."

"What's that, hon?"

"You forgot to tell me all about this John Brown guy."

Mags chuckled. "Oh hell, honey, you must want me to keep you up all night. Alright. Way, way back, back in 1855, there was this place called Kansas. Back then, the United States—may it rot in piss—still had slavery, but Kansas wasn't a state yet and the capitalists still hadn't decided if owning men would be legal there or not. And in Kansas, there was this town, a town called Lawrence . . ."

Mags' watch was almost done. The blue light of pre-dawn was just starting to creep in across the Shenandoah, and she guessed it wouldn't be more than another half-hour before it was time to start waking up the others. She paced back and forth around the cement pad, weaving around the sleeping forms sprawled out on their bedrolls and she willed the sun to come up faster, her boredom tempered by a sense of being terribly alone in the darkness.

As she made another pass around the edge of their camp, she heard a twig snap somewhere out in the darkness, shattering the early morning silence. She dropped to one knee, trained her Dragunov on the source of the sound, and shuffled over to where Connor slept. Still glassing the high brush at the edge of the pad, she nudged him awake and hissed, "Get up. There's somebody out there."

Connor shot awake and reached for his rifle, but not fast enough. Through her scope, Mags saw the shadow of a human figure bounding from one patch of brush and shadow to another; on instinct, like she'd done so many times before, she squeezed the trigger.

The figure went down, illuminated for half a moment in the rifle's flash, and she was rewarded with a cry of shock and anguish and a human voice shouting, "Fuck! She fucking shot me! The big yid fucking shot me!"

Another voice called out, "We're burned! *Go loud, boys!*"

Only just visible in the darkness, Mags saw two objects about the size of baseballs arching out of the brush and through the air towards them.

"Aw, shit!" she cried out, diving to the ground and throwing her arms over her head. "Incoming! Incoming!"

And the two flashbangs went off.

For a horrible moment, Mags couldn't see or hear anything around her as all awareness was replaced with a bright light and deafening roar that lingered in her eyes and ears. She tried to get to her feet, but her head swam with vertigo as the roaring in her ears became silence and the silence became a horrible, ear-splitting squeal, and she rolled over onto her back, groaning. As her vision started to clear, she felt strong hands grab her and pull her up to her knees, felt something cold press against her throat.

She blinked until her vision cleared, and she took in the scene around her. There were men, four of them, men in brown cargo pants and black button-up shirts, one behind each member of the group, holding them fast with a knife to each throat. She tried to look around, and a voice just behind her—barely audible over the ringing in her ears—hissed, "Don't fuckin move, sweetheart, or you're gonna get a real close shave."

In front of her she saw Jules, on her feet, her Armalite at her shoulder, her face contorted in a sneer of terrible, bestial rage. In front of her stood a blackshirt, a scarred and golden-haired giant, staring at her down the sights of his own battle rifle. He was grinning like a shark, and laughing.

"Well if it ain't a small goddamn world after all!" John Tomassi roared. "Get a load of this, boys! It's a goddamn family reunion!"

The blackshirts laughed.

"What's the matter, Binachi? Ain't you happy to see us?"

Jules' entire body shook with hatred, and she spat, "Ahh, fuck you! *Fuck you!* Fuck all y'all!"

"Is that a proposition?"

Another round of laughter.

In the midst of the laughter, the blackshirt holding Connor, just off to Mags' left, put his mouth to Connor's ear and whispered, "Hey. Hey, buddy, can you hear me? Keep quiet; tap my leg if you can hear me."

Tap.

"Okay, good. That big guy's a real clever sumbitch, so whatever trick he's about to play on Binachi is probably gonna work. That's good. That means he's gonna lower his rifle. You follow me?"

Tap.

"Don't matter what you say, Binachi," Tomassi laughed, "I know you missed me. I can tell you're happy to see me."

"Fuck you!"

"I see that fire in your belly ain't gone anywhere. That's what I always loved about my little black angel."

"*Fuck you!*"

"Sweetheart, why don't you put the rifle down and come over here where you belong?"

"*Fuck! You!*"

With their free hands, the blackshirts began patting down their captives for weapons, to the sound of knives and sidearms being tossed into the center of the circle. Peterson patted the long hunting knife on Connor's belt, left it where it was, and whispered, "As soon as Johnny Tomato lowers his rifle, I'm gonna let you go, rush right, and take out the guy holding the redhead. You rush left. We're only gonna have one shot at this, so get ready to move like you got someplace to be. You follow?"

Tap.

From off to Jules' right, she heard Rocko burst into a peal of laughter and call out, "Hey, boss! This lady's packin' a real big weapon!"

She and Tomassi both turned to look at Rocko, his right hand holding a knife to Mags' throat, his left hand cupping the crotch of her pants.

"You get the fuck away from her!" Jules growled, fixing her sights on Rocko's forehead.

"Who do we got here, Jules?" Tomassi asked. "Is he your brother?"

"Fuck you!"

"Rocko, stick the redhead."

"No! Don't you fucking touch her!"

"Then tell me who he is to you, if you're so worried about him."

Concern for Mags started to break the spell of senseless rage, and she stammered, "She's . . . she's my girlfriend."

Tomassi laughed long and hard at that. "Of fuckin course he is. Heh, traps of a feather, right? Say, red, how you like my leftovers?"

Mags met his eyes, glaring up at him with silent, icy, and patient hatred. Tomassi studied her for a moment, laughed again, and asked, "Holy shit, are you for real, Binachi? Is this how far you've fallen? Say, does your mama know that her little boy grew up to be faggot, *and* a bitch, *and* a traitor, *and* a good little *shabbas-goy?*"

Mags sucked in a quick breath through her nose and spat a long, viscous stream of phlegm onto Tomassi's left boot. Rocko grabbed a fistful of her hair and pulled her head back, about to cut her throat, but Tomassi put up a hand to stop him and said, "Julia, sweetheart, I just got a great idea. If we keep up this here Mexican standoff, you and all your new friends are dead. Maybe you'll get the drop on me, and maybe you won't, but either way all these freaks are done for. We can let it go down like that . . . or we can make us a deal."

"Fuck you!"

"Put the rifle down and come over here, and we let the redhead go."

"You're a lying sack of shit, Tomassi."

"Maybe I am. I am a world-class bullshitter, after all. But here's the real question, baby: What are you willing to bet on it?"

Jules kept her aim on him, but her shoulders slumped just slightly. Mags noticed.

"Take the deal, sweetheart. You put the strap down and come over here, and the merchant walks."

"I know a trick when I fucking see one, Tomassi."

"Do you, Julia? Do you really? I think there's evidence to the contrary."

"Fuck you!"

"Maybe it is a trick. But it's a sure thing that she's deader than Elvis if you don't."

Jules' sneer of hatred melted into a sad, resigned expression. She lowered her rifle.

"Yeah, that's my girl. That's my little black angel. Now come here."

"No!" Mags screamed, her frosty expression melting at last. "Jules, I'm not worth it! I'm not fucking worth it!"

Jules turned to her and gave her a sad smile. "Don't . . . don't worry about me, sugar. I'll . . . I'll be okay. I know how this goes."

"No! I'm not fucking worth it! He's fucking lying anyways! You know he's lying!"

Jules dropped her rifle and took a slow, halting step forward. "Mags? I love you, sugar."

Mags' shouts had turned to sobs, and she stammered, "I . . . I love you, too, honey . . ."

Jules took another step forward.

Tomassi lowered his rifle.

And then a lot of things happened at once.

Peterson let go of Connor, rushed right, and buried his knife in

Rocko's back, expertly sinking it into the sweet spot just below the signalman's left shoulder. Rocko went limp, spilling Mags into a heap on the ground in front of him. Connor went left, stabbing Prof's captor. Tomassi brought his rifle back up, and, at the moment of truth, hesitated, his aim swinging back and forth between Jules and Mags and Peterson, unsure which of the three he hated more. And before he could make the choice, his eyes locked on something out in the shadows, and went wide as plates, and he screamed, threw down his rifle, and turned, and ran.

In all the chaos, someone else had appeared in their midst, a young woman with blood-red lips and long, dark hair. She stood just behind Rolf, pulled his arm away from TJ's throat with no apparent effort, and sank her teeth into his trachea, ripping his throat out in a fountain of gore.

Peterson ran after Tomassi, swinging his battle rifle around to his shoulder and dropping into a crouch at the edge of the pad, drawing down on his target as Tomassi's blind panic took him in a mad scramble up and onto the railway bridge. Peterson took aim, exhaled, and squeezed the trigger. As soon as the rifle bucked into his shoulder, he knew that it hadn't been his best shot, knew it would go low, and he almost panicked, but stopped when Tomassi howled in pain and dropped, clutching his leg. Before Peterson could fire again, John Tomassi lost his balance and tumbled off of the bridge, into the Potomac.

The survivors of the conflagration got to their feet and looked back and forth at one another, their minds still catching up to where their bodies had been. All except for Becky, who sat down next to Rolf's corpse and patiently waited to be noticed, and Peterson, who dropped his Armalite and ran toward Jules.

"P . . . Peterson?" she muttered.

He threw his arms around her, buried his head in her shoulder, and wept. "You're alive," he wheezed, "oh my fucking God, you're alive! Jesus fucking Christ, you're alive!"

Jules pushed him away and took a step back. He sank to his

knees and sobbed, "I'm so fuckin sorry, buddy, I'm so goddamn sorry, I thought you were lost, I thought you were dead, and . . . and . . ."

Mags walked up to Jules, then, putting an arm across her shoulders, and Jules melted into the embrace. Peterson looked up at her and stammered, "Um, ma'am, you're one of them political officers, right?"

Mags nodded.

"I, ah, I'd like to defect, please. I just fragged my signalman and my commanding officer, and I've, uh, I've got intelligence."

She ignored him, looked into Jules' eyes, and sobbed, "You're a goddamn idiot, you know that, right?"

"I ain't never denied it, sugar."

"I fucking love you."

"I fucking love you, too, sug."

"Don't you ever—fucking ever—do shit like that again, alright?"

"Well, if you don't let us get bushwhacked again, I won't have to."

And she buried her face in Mags' chest, and wept.

Connor walked up, put a hand on Mags' shoulder, and gestured to Peterson. "Not to interrupt yin's emotional moment or nuthin," he said, "but that guy did just save all our lives."

Jules stood up straight and looked down at him. "Is that right, Pete?"

"Well, I like to think I helped. I . . . I been plotting on that motherfucker for a while. I was the one talked him into trying to take y'all alive; figured it'd be my best chance to get the drop on him. I thought it was just gonna be revenge, but . . ."

She bent down, picked up her battle rifle, and drew down on him. She met his eyes and growled, "How much did you know?"

"Not enough. They . . . they told us you were safe. I heard they sprung you out of the lock-up, but that was all they'd tell me; 'she's safe'. And on account of I'm a fuckin idiot, I believed 'em. I . . . I didn't know why Tomassi was spendin so much time in Columbus, he wouldn't tell us, and we only got him to tell us 'cause he pitched a fit when you got away. And we . . . everybody thought you were dead, man. We thought there was no fuckin way anybody could make it out there alone. So I . . . I decided that if I couldn't make things right with you, the least I could do was kill that mother-fucker, merc the piece of shit who hurt my little buddy." He wiped his eyes and laughed. "Goddamn two-for-one special tonight, huh?"

Panting, Jules put the rifle down and offered him her hand. He took it, and she hauled him up to his feet and threw her arms around him, burying her face in his chest and sobbing a spirited stream of Italian profanity. And she looked up into his eyes, smiled, and said, "Don't fuckin call me 'little', old man."

"I'll call you whatever the fuck I want to, shortstack."

She kissed his cheeks and sobbed, "You . . . you hurt the most, man. John was always a fuckin asshole, and hell, we were all a buncha assholes, but it hurt so fuckin much when I thought you'd thrown me away. I love you, you stupid, ugly piece of shit."

Peterson held her close, and she shook her head and said, "Y'know, man . . . I think you're a better person than me."

"How's that, buddy?"

"I'm only here because bein a piece of shit got to be my prob-lem. You're here for somebody else's sake."

"You're my best friend, Binachi. Now, I'm not gonna lie, I ain't exactly sure what to make of you, but nobody—not fuckin nobody—hurts my best friend and gets away with it."

From off to the side, Mags sighed, pinched the bridge of her nose, and muttered, "Oh my God, I am gonna have to fill out so much fucking paperwork when I get back to Central."

Peterson met her eyes, gave a solemn nod, and said, "Don't worry about all that, ma'am. I'll be on my way as soon as the sun's up."

"On your way where?"

"West. I know Freeside ain't that far. For one thing . . . well, if y'all ain't figured it out already, y'all been burned. They know what this little expedition is about and where it's headed. Fragging my signalman probably bought y'all a couple days, but bringin anybody else along is just gonna drop y'all's chances from slim down to none. And for two, well . . ." He plucked at the silver eagles embroidered on the collar of his black shirt. "I ain't askin nobody for shit. I'm . . . I'm gonna go face the music. Gonna go do the right thing for the first—or, well, I guess for the second time in my life."

The scavvers looked back and forth at each other in a chorus of nods, and Mags said, "Yeah, that's . . . that's probably the best thing for you to do. Listen: When you get there, if you can make it to Land's End, drop my name and tell them what you did here tonight. It'll mean something."

"There is one thing, though. I wanna know what the hell it was Tomassi saw that spooked him so bad."

At that, Becky hopped to her feet, pranced toward them out of the darkness, and said, "Hi! That would be me."

Everyone turned and stared at her in surprise, and, staring, noticed the blood drying around her mouth, her sallow, almost transluscent skin, and her black, empty eyes.

"That's a fucking hunter!" Connor shouted, stepping back and reaching for his rifle.

"Sure am! And first of all, you're fucking welcome. But, listen, the sun is gonna be up in like 15 minutes, so can we try and make the introductions quick? It's past my bedtime."

Connor drew down on her, aiming at the middle of her forehead. She rolled her eyes, then locked those eyes with his and took a step forward. At once, everyone felt a cold shiver of fear run down their spine, and Connor's face contorted in an expression of exquisite terror. He lowered his rifle and backed away, trembling.

"That's what happened to the blonde guy, if you were wondering. That's a thing some of us can do. Pretty neat, huh? Anyways," and she took a stick of gum out of her pocket and popped it into her mouth, "I'm Rebecca Gladstone, but you guys can call me Becky.

You, ah, well, I have some stuff I need to tell you guys. You're kind of, ah, well, you're all kind of walking right into a trap a little bit."

No-one spoke.

She grinned, dancing her tongue across her canines, and popped her gum. "Well jeez, you guys sure are a talkative bunch. You act like you've never seen a dracula before."

[12]
LUCKY BREAKS

STILL REELING FROM DISBELIEF, THE GROUP FOLLOWED BECKY off of the pad and back into tow, past the engine house, and toward one of the crumbling brick buildings where a short, round man with a scruffy beard stood by the entrance, smoking a cigarette and tapping his foot. He sun was beginning to rise by then, so Becky didn't stop to make introductions, but pranced inside, gesturing for the others to follow. The man by the door said nothing, but followed her in with a sigh and an eyeroll.

They stood outside looking back and forth at each other for a beat before going in, following Becky and the stranger to a dusty, sunken room tucked away from exterior doors or windows. She gestured at the man and said, "This is my associate, Steve Barns. Say hi, Steve."

Steve gave them an awkward wave and sat down on the floor at her feet, throwing up a cloud of dust. The others, one by one, did the same, and Steve looked up at Becky and grumbled, "It fuckin took you long enough."

"Hey, it's not my fault if people are racist against draculas."

"I told you you shoulda just let me do it."

"It was a very sensitive situation, bloodbag. Speed and precision were called for."

"Is somebody gonna explain what in the entire goddamn hell is goin on here?" Connor growled.

"Yeah, yeah," Becky said, sitting down. "This is gonna be . . . complicated, so I'll start with the important stuff and you guys can pick up the details later. The place you guys are headed to . . . what is it you call it again? The Fortress?"

"The Citadel," Prof offered.

"Right. Good name for it. Do you actually, like, know anything about it? When it was established, what it was used for, what it's doing now?"

"A lot of speculation, wasteland legends, but nothing concrete."

"That's what I thought. What if I told you that I can tell you exactly what that place is, and exactly what's going on behind its walls?"

Everyone stared at her, and Prof stammered, "Well, I . . . I have to know. Please, by all means."

"Alright! Well, maybe not *exactly*, but I got the cliffnotes. Does the name Harry Truman mean anything to you? The year 1946? Operation Paperclip?"

Prof and Mags both gave solemn nods. TJ shook their head and said, "Well, maybe that means something to you nerds, but I got no clue what this lady's on about."

"You know the Second World War?" Prof asked.

"Oh yeah, that one I know. When the reds whipped ass on the Nazis the first time around."

"Precisely. Well, toward the end of the war in Europe, the United States grew covetous of the fascists' technical knowledge, particularly in aerospace engineering, whereas it was known to all that the Russians had no interest in granting the criminals clemency and were eager to deal out justice. The United States military made it a priority to round up as many fascist technical experts as they could and funnel them to safety in the west, and many were relocated here, to Old America, and assigned to work on military projects. They called it Operation Paperclip. The missiles that carried thermonuclear warheads around the world two hundred years ago were, in no small part, the children of fascist engineers."

Mags gave a solemn nod and quoted, "The past lies like a nightmare over the world."

"Got it in one," Becky said. "But it wasn't just brain genius rocket surgeons who got a trip on the ratlines. It was all sorts. Including a lot of doctors, biologists, biochemists. Chemical and biological warfare specialists. The people who'd worked on Operation Nachtjager."

That word made Prof and Connor both jump. Becky went on: "This facility, its proper name is Marion Proving Ground, was where a lot of those guys wound up, and quite a few of 'those guys' included what little of Operation Nachtjager had survived Stalingrad. Nachtjager was a supersoldier program, an attempt to build a corps of perfect killing machines, based on some . . . um . . . information that the Wehrmacht had uncovered in eastern Europe. And Nachtjager was one of the few things the Nazis tried that actually sort of worked; it only failed in as much as the whole Wehrmacht failed, and the Americans, well, they got pretty horny over the idea of supersoldiers. Anybody wanna venture a guess what *Nachtjager* means in English?"

Prof nodded, his face a mix of terror and excitement. "Yes, it . . . it means 'night hunter'."

"Exactamundo."

"Wait, wait, wait, hold up a sec," Mags said. "How have I never heard any of this before? American history is a core part of the curriculum at every school in the Republic from as soon as kids can read, and the anarchists have been fucking around in the exclusion zone since before the apocalypse. Somebody had to have found or heard something."

"Same reason it's still standing while everything around it got turned to glass; it was a very well-kept secret. As far as our people have been able to figure out, there were no external records kept of it at all; the only people who knew what was happening behind those walls were the people who worked or lived there. To the rest of the world, Marion Proving Ground was just a boring old National Guard armory. I guess they learned what happens when you maintain records of your war crimes the first time around."

Mags winced. "Yeah, that's . . . a way to put it. So what's the move? Why are you so free with all this intel?"

"Couple things. Y'know the two things that are the biggest roadblocks to human reclamation in the exclusion zone? Even more than the radiation or the crazy weather?"

"Well, yeah. Roamers and hunters."

"Exactly! Zombies and draculas. But I bet you don't know where the roamers came from."

"Oh, everybody knows that. It was a project by the American military to economically and socially destabilize target nations by making their populations maximally violent. Roamer physiology hinges on tiny, self-replicating machines that mimic the bheavior of white blood cells so that--"

"No, no, no, I didn't say *why*, I said *where*. As in, from what point in space?"

Mags blinked a few times. "So you're saying . . . it came from the Citadel?"

"Bingo. Marion Proving Ground, your one-stop shop for CBRN ordinance and crimes against humanity. It all started right where you're wanting to go, and it has not stopped. But, you and I . . . we share a common interest."

"And what's that?"

"That facility is still operating, as I know you know. And a facility in operation needs an overseer, don't it? You two," she gestured at Prof and Connor, "you two, I know have run into him before. A certain *Oberst-Gruppenfuhrer* Otto von Hochulf. Formerly Waffen-SS, formerly United States Army, currently . . .

well, God knows what he's calling his little crew nowadays. Point is, there is a man in the high castle, and he's planning something. We're not sure what, but it's gonna be big, and it's gonna be soon."

To everyone's surprise, Peterson broke in, clearing his throat and saying, "She's right, y'all. Or, anyways, that jives with what I been hearing."

All eyes were on him, and he continued: "That place, we know about it. There's some kind of connection between whatever the hell's in there and the Oberkommando. Nobody I've met knew exactly what, but we've got notions, and ma'am, you've confirmed a lot of 'em. For the past year or so, the Oberkommando's been sending operating groups into the east, one every few weeks, like clockwork. They always come back, but they come back short most of their men, and the few who do come back don't got nuthin to say about what they found out there. But there have been rumors. Rumors of some big secret under the Eagles' Nest—that's what we call it—that's gonna turn the war hot and win it for the BNR once and for all. And those men who don't come back . . . folks say that they stay to receive a great honor, to claim their birthright. That's the mission I was on, and my CO was real fuckin excited about it, lemme tell ya."

Becky nodded. "Bingo. I mean, from my own personal experience, I think that that's dumb as hell; yeah, I'm stronger and faster than any of you, but I'm allergic to vegetables and I can't go outside half the time and if I wasn't traveling with my boyfriend I'd starve to death. Does that sound like any master race you ever heard of? But, point is, Daniel Day Lewis over there is right on the money. Our old pal Otto is building an army, and your pal Roland is going to use it. I'm here to help make sure that that doesn't happen."

"How do you know all this?" Mags demanded.

"Us draculas tend to be equal parts cliquish and nosy; word gets around." She fished around in her pocket, came up empty, sighed, and asked, "You got any smokes?"

Steve shook his head. "Becky . . ."

"Oh, come on. As if I can even get cancer."

Mags tossed her a pack of cigarettes. She lit one, gave a happy sigh, said, "Thanks, sister. I've been trying to quit since 2009, but gum gets harder and harder to come by. Anyways, as I was saying, my, ah . . . let's call him my employer, Mr. Lukash, really doesn't want to see that happen. In addition to the fact that it's politically unpalatable and just generally unacceptable, Lukash also has a personal grudge against our pal Otto. See, they knew each other before the War. Well, before the war before the war before the War, if you see what I mean. From the first one, before the second one. Steve and me, we'd been sent out on basically the same mission as you guys: Go down and scope the place out, to prepare for a bigger cleanup later. But Lukash had some people embedded in with Otto's boneheads, so we got advance warning about . . . well, about that whole three-right shit circus that I walked into earlier."

TJ cocked an eyebrow. "2009, you say. How old are you?"

"I'm 20."

". . . How long have you been 20?"

Becky cackled, as though that were the funniest thing she'd ever heard, and Steve rolled his eyes. Regaining her composure, she said, "So here's my plan: We'll be you guys's advance scouts. We hang here the rest of the day and head out as soon as it's dark, then you guys roll out tomorrow morning and we'll meet back up tomorrow afternoon." She yawned and added, "I hope that's that on that, because it is past my bedtime."

"How do we know we can trust you?" Mags asked.

She yawned again. "Well, you can call it a show of good faith that I'm about to go curl up in a little ball in the corner someplace and be all vulnerable all day. But didn't I already save that person's life earlier, and spook the daylights outta that big blonde fucker?"

"She does got us there, sug," Jules offered.

"What was that asshole's deal, anyways? I came in on the tail end of it, but that didn't feel like army stuff, nah, that felt personal."

A tense silence settled over the room, and everyone stared at

Becky with wide eyes for a long, awkward moment, and she knew that she'd asked exactly the wrong question. She was about to apologize, but before she could, Jules' lips twitched in a humorless smirk, and she met Becky's cold, black eyes and deadpanned, "Oh, he was my rapist."

"Oh. *Fuck.*"

"Uh-huh. Right now, if he ain't dead, then he's probably mad as hell that he didn't get spend his morning balls-deep in ladyboy pussy."

"Fuck. I am *so* sorry."

"You sure are. That little scrap you walked into was him trying to leverage my girlfriend's life to make me come back to him. It's a good thing you showed up when you did, 'cause it worked."

"Fuck, fuck, I am so sorry, I shouldn't have--"

"Uh-huh, you shouldn't have. Now, have we learned a little lesson about minding our fucking business?"

Becky examined the floor. "Yeah. Yeah, we have. I'm sorry."

"Oh, no, it's *fine*; I love telling this story. There's nothing I'd rather be doing in the whole fucking world than reliving all this shit in front of God and everybody. You got any more questions? You want a fucking blow-by-blow?"

Becky kept studying the floor. Mags looked over at Jules and said, "Honey, are you--"

"*No, I'm not fucking okay, Mags!* I might be a *tiny* bit keyed up right now. Just a little stressed out."

Wanting to break the tension, Connor looked toward Prof and barked, "Hey, old man, guess what."

"What is it, buddy?"

"We got a name."

It took Prof a moment to register what Connor was saying, but when he did he gave a sad smile and said, "Yeah, buddy, that we do. We've got the bastard's name."

Becky got to her feet then and said, "Okay, well, if the, uh, if the plan's figured out, I'm gonna go catch a nap. We'll see you guys around sundown." And, yawning, she loped off deeper into the building's interior, with Steve following at her heels.

The group looked back and forth at each other in silence for a while, until TJ spoke up, saying, "Well, uh . . . it's been a hell of a morning, ain't it?"

Mags stole a quick glance at Jules. "Yeah, it's been something. Honestly, y'all . . . as eager as I am to get on the road, I think we should take a day. It sure has been one hell of a morning."

One-by-one, the group nodded their agreement, and Mags made eye contact with Jules and nodded to the door. They got up and left together, and as soon as they were away from the others, Mags threw her arms around her and held her tight, saying nothing.

Jules returned the embrace, whispering, "You okay, sug?"

"I just . . . I just wanted to be close to you. I'm shook, honey. I finally found the one thing I'm afraid of."

Jules met her eyes and nodded, and she went on:

"I'm not afraid to die. I'm not afraid of anything they might do to me. Like I've said, I'm a soldier, and I take a soldier's risk. Apparently I am afraid of one thing, though."

"Yeah. Me, I . . . I'm not gonna lie, I'm afraid of a whole lotta shit. But I guess I'm afraid of one thing more than I'm afraid of the others."

They sat down together in the dust of the dim hallway, sharing a cigarette as Jules sat in Mags' lap, and Mags looked down into her eyes and whispered, "You didn't even hesitate."

"I didn't even think about it. I'd jump right into Hell, I'd go through anything and do it all again, if it meant giving you a chance."

Mags held her closer and muttered, "I just . . . I just feel so shitty."

"Yeah, I'll bet you do. It's a hell of a thing, being powerless, having somebody else take control. Being helpless. It fucks a person up. And don't I know it."

"Yeah. I'm less worried about me, though. How are you holding up, honey?"

Jules shrank into her arms. "I'm pretty fucked up, I'm not gonna lie. A lot of bad memories, a lot of shit I'd rather not be thinkin about, and oh my fucking God but we came so close. But at the same time, it feels like something's been settled. I wouldn't call it 'closure,' exactly, but it feels like a start. I'm all mixed up. I feel okay, after seeing all that, but at the same time I feel so fucking low."

"Hell, I'll drink to that."

"I feel bad for you, sugar, that you had to wind up with me and I didn't even come with an instruction manual. Like how to take care of your very own pet ladyboy." She laughed.

Mags didn't laugh, but gave her a serious look and said, "Don't say shit like that, babe."

"Ah, c'mon. I was only goofing."

"I know. But if you tell yourself shit like that often enough, you'll start to believe it. Ask me how I know."

Jules didn't speak, only smiled. Mags stroked her hair and looked down into her eyes and said, "I'll tell you what you are. You're a woman. You're the most beautiful woman I've ever seen. Honey, you know what it is I always notice about a girl first?"

"What, sugar?"

"Her eyes. And I could get lost in those big, brown eyes of yours forever."

"Sugar, you remember when we first met, and I gave you a hard time about not clocking me?"

"Yeah?"

"Well, I'll tell you how I clocked you. I saw it in your eyes. All that yearning and fire and deep, deep sadness behind those eyes. It's exactly what I see every time I look in the mirror."

"Kiss me, you dumb bitch."

"Mags, that's gay."

After they'd sat together a while, they returned to the group, who were sitting in a circle alternately laughing and swearing at each other. As they came closer, they saw that they were playing cards.

"Oh, goddammit," Jules said, shaking her head. "Come on, Peterson, you gonna just corrupt everybody you meet?"

Peterson grinned. "Hey, lady, I intend to spend my last day as a free man doing the one thing I'm good at. You want me to deal you in?"

"Nah. We'll sit this one out."

And Peterson tossed two cards onto the pile and announced, "Two aces."

"Bullshit!" TJ spat.

"Flip 'em, then."

They did, revealing that Peterson had been telling the truth, and through a stream of curses they picked up the pile and added it to their hand. And the game went on.

After a while, Jules turned to Mags and asked, "So, you figured it out yet?"

"Yeah, and it's fascinating. It's about deception and calculated risk; the goal is to run out of cards, but they have to be discarded in numerical order, so if your turn and the order don't line up you have to weigh the benefit of getting rid of some cards against the risk of having your bluff called and getting the whole pile."

"Got it in one, sug. You wanna get in next?"

"Oh, hell no. I can't tell a lie to save my life. Watching this, it's like they invented a game specifically for me to lose."

"If you win, you can top tonight."

". . . . You're on."

[*Later that evening*]

John Tomassi had spent a lifetime chasing death . . . but not like this.

He couldn't feel his leg, which had turned blue under the tourniquet, and that was just as well, because it couldn't take a bit of weight and he knew that his kneecap must be shattered. He tried not to think about it, tried to focus on the ground in front of him, tried to keep crawling, still moving east an inch at a time. East. If he could make it before roamers or dogs or something worse found him, make it before gangrene set in, make it while he still had any blood left, he just might be okay. He kept crawling.

As he tried not to think about his situation, his thoughts kept wandering back to the morning, to seeing his girl still alive, knowing he could talk sense into her again, watching her take those few steps forward . . . before it all went wrong again.

"Ungrateful bitch," he growled through a mouthful of leaves and gravel, and he dug his hands into the earth and pulled himself a few inches further east. East . . .

All he had to do was make it—and he would make it; if anyone was strong enough, worthy enough, it was him—and then things would go right. He would claim his birthright, become the hero he was born to be, and when he marched west again in the ranks of an army of the damned, then no-one would be able to stop him. Then she would see. Then she would see that she was his girl, his little black angel, that she belonged with him. Belonged *to* him.

"Ungrateful . . . bitch . . ."

It was after sunset when he finally made it to the top of the ridge, his hands raw and aching, his numb leg throbbing, and the cool night air brought something else with it: A delicious and all-too-familiar pall of fear. He heard a twig snap nearby.

"I believe I told you not to disappoint us, *Hauptsturmfuhrer*," an icy and all-too-familiar voice hissed, and *Sturmbanfuhrer* von Ulfkessel stepped into view.

Tomassi's eyes wandered from the hunter's jackboots up to his coal-black eyes, and he muttered, "Oh, thank fucking God."

Ulfkessel shook his head. "No, I am afraid He is busy at the moment, and tonight there is only me. Did I not warn you not to disappoint us?"

"Help me, goddamn it . . ."

"No. We help warriors. We help heroes. We do not help pitiful little men who fail at simple tasks. It is a pity; destiny was sitting right in the palm of your hand, *Hauptsturmfuhrer*, but it seems you did not have the strength to grasp it. *So-wie-so.*"

Ulfkessel reached down and grabbed Tomassi by his mangled knee, lifting him onto his shoulders like a sack of flour. Tomassi was too weak to fight back, and almost too weak to scream, and the hunter's touch was cold, so horribly cold . . .

"We will still find some use for you, though; some small use, suited to your station. You see,, *Hauptsturmfuhrer*, we are all of us so very, very hungry . . ."

[13]

DOWNTOWN

Steve Barns luxuriated in the last rays of sunshine as Becky, who'd just woken up, talked and talked in the other room. Well, she didn't do much of the talking; right now, she was mostly listening. The conversation was grim, and being able to overhear it made him feel like a voyeur, but he was relieved to know it was happening. He'd been afraid that her big mouth had absolutely fucked their chances that morning, but if Becky was good at anything, she was good at keeping a group together, at least whenever she shut up and actually put her mind to it. He wondered how much better she must've been at that back when she was alive . . . but he didn't like to think about that. It reminded him of just how old she actually was.

". . . so I spent a few weeks in the stockade," Jules said, her voice tinged with sadness alongside a defiant hope, and even a bit of warmth now that the story was being given freely. "You ever done any time, Becky?"

"Here and there. But it was only ever little shit, never more than a week or a month, and that was way, way back in the day. Nothing like this."

"Yeah, the stockade was hard time. Hard fuckin time. I gave as good as I got, busted plenty of skulls, but, well, you can only keep up that fight for so long."

"Yikes."

"Yeah, yikes is right. That was where I got marked."

". . . marked?"

Barns decided that it was long past time to move to another part of the building, hassle though it was, when Jules said, "Ehh, I don't wanna talk about this no more. Let's pick it up tomorrow night; then it'll be your turn to start."

"Sure thing, sister. Me and the boytoy need to be moving out soon, anyways. And hey, I'm . . . I'm sorry, again, about earlier."

"Eh, forget about it. Just use your goddamn brain next time, alright?"

"I will. Thanks."

"Yeah. Thanks for listening." A pregnant pause. "You really do listen. Everybody wants to pull all the gory details outta me, but you and my girl are the only ones who've really listened."

"Hey, don't go mushy on me now. It'll be your turn tomorrow, and I've got my own horror stories."

"Bitch, you are a horror story."

Laughter, the easy laughter of two friends, and Becky sauntered out of the room, saw Steve sitting in the dying light before the window, and asked, "You ready to get moving, bloodbag?"

"Yeah, yeah," he grumbled, standing up. "We taking the truck?"

"Nah, not with these warmies trailing after us. It'd piss off the walking-deads."

"Hell. We'll make terrible time."

"I dunno, we're only about sixty, seventy miles out. We could get there in two or three nights if we really book it."

Barns shivered. "This far from home, any time out there without cover is too much time. Especially considering where we're going."

"Ah, don't even worry about it; you've got me! Nothing out there could be spookier than me."

And she stepped into the view of the window just as the last rays of sunlight faded away, and spread her arms, and said, in a horrible accent, "Listen to them! My children of the night! What sweet music they make!"

Barns rolled his eyes. They walked out into the building's foyer, where the others were moving around, and Becky announced, "Alright, losers, we're gonna get on the road. We've got a two-way, so I'll have my manservant here raise one of you if we see anything nasty."

"What route y'all taking?" Connor asked.

"Cut dead east toward Damascus. After that, northeast to the 70."

"Yeah, that's the best way. Y'all be careful out there."

"Oh, don't worry about us, my dude; we'll be fine. You guys be careful. We'll see you tomorrow."

And the door swung open, and the two strangers disappeared into the night. Prof and Connor took out a map and deliberated a moment before reaffirming that Becky had chosen the best route and that it was still a good idea to follow. The group huddled together to fix a quick dinner and to draw straws for the night's watch; Jules came up last.

When she and Mags announced that they were going to bed early, Peterson pulled her aside and asked, "Hey, buddy, you think you could wake me up when you get up?"

She gave him a solemn nod. "Yeah, Pete. Early start?"

"Yeah. May as well get it all over with."

They shared an awkward hug before she and Mags disappeared deeper into the building.

———

Later, after, as she lay sprawled out across their bedroll, trying to catch her breath, the thought crossed Jules' mind that the others had probably heard them through the soft, crumbling walls. To her surprise, she found that she didn't care.

"Fuckin Hell," she panted, "*mama Maria*, but I needed that."

Mags lit a cigarette, took a drag, and passed it to her. "Yeah," she panted, "so did I."

"Sugar, how is it you always know exactly what I need?"

"Magic. But, as I recall, turning this into a bet was your idea."

"Only 'cause I knew you could win."

They laughed, and Jules slid closer to Mags, pressing her body against hers, and said, "Nah, but that really was just what I needed. It's . . . it's hard sometimes, y'know?"

"I know, honey. Listen, I'm in no hurry for anything; I wanna do whatever you wanna do."

"You're a saint, sugar." She sat up, looked down at her own nakedness, and went on: "I've already spent a good 25 years hating my body. Feeling like it's not really mine. And after everything . . . Goddamn, after everything, it made me sick to think of you touching all the places where all those other people had been. Not to be too vulgar, but I definitely felt some kind of a way about letting you stick your tongue in the same hole where John liked to stick his cock."

Mags winced. She put an arm across Jules' shoulders and said nothing. Jules leaned into the embrace and went on:

"But you . . . Sugar, you're something else. You . . . you love every part of me that I don't. You're . . . you're tender where I've been hurt. And y'know what? This is my body, and maybe it ain't the best, but it's mine and I get to choose what I do with it. And I choose to share it with you."

Mags sat staring into Jules' eyes without speaking for a long moment. At last, she smiled, and whispered, "Julia . . ."

Jules smirked. "Yes, Magnolia?"

"Julia, I love you so goddamn much. I . . . Fuck, I can't even begin to tell you how much that means to me. And for what it's worth, I think your body's pretty great; you're the most beautiful woman I've ever seen, and I will love every part of it that you don't, 'cause I'll worship every inch of it you're willing to give me."

"Aw, hell, sugar, you tryin to make me cry? Fuck . . . When I hear you say it, I can almost believe it."

"Well, that's 'cause it's true. And I don't think I've ever told you this, but you are so fucking strong, babe. I know it probably doesn't feel like, but it's true; you've walked through six kinds of Hell that I can't even imagine, but here you are, this brassy, sarcastic, goddamn beautiful woman. That's . . . that's a lot."

Jules gave her a funny look. "Sugar, it ain't the same, a'course, but you were a child soldier who buried half her family in a famine and been at war for 12 straight years."

"Yeah. What about it?"

"We spend so much time fawning over me, sometimes I worry we ain't saved any for you. How old are you, again?"

Jules could feel Mags' entire body tense up at being the subject of conversation. "I'm 24," she muttered.

"I know it's one of them shared tragedies that we never got to be girls, but damn, sugar, you never got to be a kid at all. I know you've got some demons floating around in that stupid red head of yours."

"I . . .I really don't like talking about myself, Jules."

"Oh, I'll drink to that. I just wanna make sure that you know that I know you're my girlfriend and not my fuckin therapist. If you ever do wanna talk, sugar, I'm here."

Mags relaxed. "Thanks, hon. That . . . that means a hell of a lot."

Jules lit another cigarette and reclined back onto the bedroll. "If I'm too close to home, you might try talking to that hunter, Becky, when we see her again. She's a hell of a good listener, and goddamn but that woman has been through some shit."

She tensed up again, and Jules looked up at her and asked, "Uh-oh, what's wrong?"

"Nothing."

"Bullshit."

"Yeah. I . . . it's nothing to do with you. I'm just being a bitch."

"You're jealous, aren't you?"

"It's irrational, it's stupid, it's selfish, but . . . yeah."

Jules read the I-know-I've-fucked-up look written across Mags' face, and her growing anger melted away. She smirked and asked, "So you need me to tell you about yourself?"

"That . . . sounds like it would help, actually."

"Every little thing you do, sugar, you turn it into your pet project, and that includes us. Most of the time it's sweet, but . . . Mags, that part of my life belongs to me. And yeah, I'm glad that working on it has helped us get close, but it ain't a plot contrivance for our little romantic comedy. It's a disease. It's killing me. I can see in your eyes you understand."

"You're right, hon, and I'm sorry. I just . . . I've been alone for so long, it feels like every little thing we share is so precious I have to cling to it or it'll slip away. I know that that's not how it works, though, and it's not fair to you."

Jules laughed. "Sugar, never before in my life have I ever seen anyone take an L with more grace than you. Where did you even come from?"

"Kentucky."

"Is everybody in Kentucky a fuckin diplomat?"

She shrugged. "You can't solve a problem without taking a look at it, and feeling sorry for myself never solved shit. Maybe I'll feel like garbage—and I sure do—but I'll feel all warm and fuzzy about myself quicker the quicker the problem's fixed."

"Christ, you really are a professional. But one thing you said, how you've been alone for so long . . . That's what it is, that sadness I see behind your eyes. You're pretty fuckin lonely, ain't you, sugar?"

"Oi. Spending all this time with you, it's been . . . bittersweet. Like, it wasn't until I'd already met somebody that I realized just how badly I needed to." She flopped down onto the bedroll and lit another smoke. "I was single for four years, Jules. And I don't have any friends; I just have colleagues. And it wasn't until meeting you that I even realized I'd been so miserable. I threw myself into the work so much that I didn't even know I was alone until I wasn't."

"I get the feeling that every little thing you do is work. You work too much."

"What else am I supposed to do?"

"Sugar, what do you ever do for fun, other than fuck me?"

"I practice rifle drills, and I read Marx and Lenin, and work out, and tend the vegetables, and teach kids to read, and volunteer on work details, and facilitate political education, and get in arguments." She sighed. "I go through three packs of smokes and three pots of coffee a day, I sleep four or five hours a night, and I have no friends. I never go to parties or music shows or festivals unless somebody drags me. I've taken two furloughs in my entire career and both of those were to go to funerals."

"Sugar, you are gonna burn yourself out like a match if you don't learn how to unwind. Jesus Christ."

"Feh. Eventually, yeah, but right now there's work to be done. There's a revolution on. I can't just stop. What if Lenin had just stopped?" Another long sigh. "Lenin dropped dead from four strokes in a row when he was 53. Jules, I'm a goddamn mess."

"Yeah, looks that way. Roll over, you dumb bitch."

"Do what, now?"

"Roll over. Just trust me."

Mags rolled over, and Jules sat up and straddled her and began rubbing her shoulders. Mags groaned with relief as Jules worked the knots out of her muscles and whispered, "When we're done with all this bullshit and you take me back home, I'm gonna work on you like this every night. And you don't gotta tell me about the shit that's bothering you, but I'm gonna ask. And I'm gonna cook for you—I make a badass minestra—and drag you to all the May Day parades and poetry slams or whatever the hell it is that reds do for fun."

"That sounds so fucking nice," Mags yawned, and groaned again as Jules moved down to her back.

"It will be. Y'know, I keep thinking about how I heard you sing the other day . . . There's this one song, my grandma used to sing it to me all the time. My old man used to beat the fuck outta me if he heard me singing it, and one day Nana got arrested and I never saw her again. I didn't put two and two together until a long time afterwards."

And Jules cleared her throat, and started to sing in a high, sad voice:

"Una mattina me son svegliato
Oh, bella ciao, bella ciao, bella ciao, ciao, ciao
Una mattina me son svegliato
E ho travato il fascista . . ."

Mags didn't understand the words, but she recognized the tune at once, and she sang the verse back in English:

"One fine morning, I woke up early
Oh, goodbye, goodbye, goodbye, beautiful
One fine morning, I woke up early
To find the fascist at my door . . ."

"Oh, partigiana, portami via
Oh, bella ciao, bella ciao, bella ciao, ciao, ciao . . ."

"Bella," Mags echoed with a yawn, and started to snore.

A few hours before sunrise, Connor went to look for Jules and found her there entangled in Mags' arms, both of the women as naked as the day they were born. He shook his head and grumbled; with discipline like this, it would be a miracle if they made it to the Citadel alive, let alone making it home.

"Hey, Binachi," he barked, "you're up."

Neither of them stirred. He nudged Jules with the toe of his boot. She rolled over, spouted a blue streak of Italian vulgarity, and resumed snoring. He knelt down and gave her a hard shove in the shoulder.

Jules' eyes snapped open, then, and as quick as thinking he felt deceptively strong hands clamp around his forearm and bicep; before he quite knew what was happening, he found himself on the floor, on his back, with Jules sitting on top of him, those strong hands wrapped around his throat.

"Jesus fucking Christ," he wheezed, "it's just me!"

For a horrible moment, Jules' eyes shone with pure, burning malice, and staring into them made Connor feel like a mouse under a cat's paw, but the moment passed, and she released his throat and muttered, "Oh, shit! Are you alright, man?"

"No thanks to you! Now get the fuck offa me!"

She lept up off of him and rushed to throw her clothes on, stammering, "Dude, you . . . you can't wake me up like that, man."

"How the hell I'm supposed to wake you up, then?"

"Fuckin . . . kick me or something. Just not like that."

"I did!"

"Well then do it harder next time. Honestly, man, what the hell did you expect to happen?"

Connor started to object, then blinked a few times and said, "Y'know, that's a fair point."

Next to them, Mags had begun to stir, and she sat up and grumbled, "Wuh . . . wuzzat? What's goin on?"

"Nothing, sugar," Jules said. "Connor shook me awake and I tried to kill him."

"Oh, okay." A long, dramatic yawn. "You can't wake her up like that, man."

He rolled his eyes. "Oh, I figured that one out pretty quick. The sun's gonna be up in a couple hours; I'm goin the fuck back to bed."

When they were alone, Mags got up, stretched, and began pulling on her clothes, saying, "I'm wide awake now; I can take this watch."

"Thanks, sugar. I . . . I wasn't gonna ask."

Mags squeezed her shoulder and smiled. "Tell him I said thanks."

Peterson was already awake when Jules made it to where the rest of the group had bedded down. He was wearing blue jeans and a flannel shirt, both a bit too long for him; she recognized the outfit as one of Connor's spare sets of clothes. His brown cargo pants and black button-up shirt with the silver eagles and sergeant's chevrons lay roughly in a pile at his feet.

"Hey, Pete," Jules said, walking up.

"Hey, buddy. Where's your ladyfriend?"

"Up and about; she offered to take my watch for me. Listen, we've still got a while before sunrise, do you wanna . . . you wanna step outside for a minute?"

"Yeah."

They walked out to the front of the building and sat down side-by-side on the curb. Jules lit a cigarette and passed the pack to him, and they sat in silence a while until Peterson said, "Y'know, buddy, there's somethin I want to tell you, but I dunno if it'd be weird to say."

"Lay it on me."

"You look great."

Jules smiled and examined her boots. "Thanks, man."

"You look . . . happy. Shit, you were my best friend for all them years, and I've never seen you look happy before. I guess bein a lady suits you."

"I am happy, man. I'm who I'm supposed to be, and I'm where I'm supposed to be, fucking finally. It took a minute to get here, but I'm happy, and for the first time in my whole sorry-ass life."

"That's good. So what's 'Jules' short for nowadays?"

"Julia. The name's Julia Carlotta Binachi."

"*Julia.* Where'd Carlotta come from?"

"Carlotta was my nana, my mom's mom. Carlotta Moreno. She taught me how to cook, taught me Italian . . . God, but my old man hated her guts." A long sigh. "She got black-bagged when I was 13."

"Jesus Christ! What for?"

"Hell all I know, brother. But whatever she did to piss off the marshals, we never saw her again. I think about her a lot. I think about Mom, too. Mom never wanted me to leave home, y'know; she told me she'd say a prayer for me every day. I wonder if she's still praying for me, wondering if her little boy is ever gonna come home."

Peterson put an awkward hand on her shoulder. She sighed again and asked, "Pete, buddy, why the fuck did it take us so long to get out?"

"Well, man . . . I didn't think there was such a thing as getting out until yesterday. When I found out what had happened to you, I decided I'd rather die than keep going on with it, and that's what I went on this mission to do. To die."

"'Get out' wasn't quite what I meant. More like . . . checking out. That moment when you realize you can't take anymore and still face yourself in the mirror." She lit another cigarette. "I could tell you exactly when I checked out."

"Tell me."

"You sure about that, brother? It ain't no fairytale."

"I . . . I think I need to hear it."

"Alright. It was on my third day in the stockade, and the first time in my life I ever lost a fight. I'll . . . spare you the finer points, I think you get the general idea, but it was . . . it was the first time for some other shit, too. And one of 'em . . . Pete, one of 'em was one of us. He made sure to show me the death's-head on his elbow before they got to work on me. And . . . Y'know them moments in life where you hit rock bottom and can't really do nuthin but sit there and think about the series of choices that led you to this? Well, afterwards, while this dude's buddies held me down and tattooed cat-eyes on my ass, I kept staring at my own elbow. And in that moment, I realized that I'd grown up to be the exact same piece of shit who took my nana away from me."

They were quiet for a while, until Peterson spoke up, saying, "I could tell you what checked me out. I believed in it, the whole thing about honor and loyalty and sacred brotherhood and all that horseshit, and you . . . Jules, you were my best friend. And when you were gone, I learned that you were my only friend."

"Y'know, I kinda wondered how that whole song and dance went over with Third SOG. I guess I got my answer yesterday morning."

"I could tell you, if you really wanted to know."

"Yeah. Yeah, Peterson, I do. I already know the answer, but hearing it sounds . . . vindicating."

"Not one of 'em gave a single solitary shit, man. After you got sold out, I tried asking Rocko how he felt about our guy getting busted for being a weirdo, and the fucker just laughed. And after you ran for it, and we found out what Tomassi was doing in Columbus, it . . . it turned into a joke they all told behind his back. There was this one time, we were playin cards, and John dropped two queens, and Haraldson tried to call him on it and had to eat shit, so Haraldson says, 'Well, if anybody here knows a thing or two about queens, it'd be you.' That type of shit."

In spite of herself, Jules snorted. "No way," she said, "I don't believe Haraldson's dumb ass ever said anything that funny. Where'd he go, anyways? I didn't spot him in the lineup."

"He was the one your lady got. Drilled him right through the thigh; he had just enough time to bitch about it before he bled out."

"Hell yeah. That's my girl." She lit another cigarette, sighed, and said, "Y'know, brother, as far as questions I shouldn't ask and that I probably already know the answer to goes, I got one more."

"Shoot."

"What happened to my bike?"

Peterson sucked in a quick breath through his teeth, examined his boots, and said nothing. Jules gawked at him for a moment before growling, "Oh, you gotta be fucking kidding me."

"I'm afraid so, buddy."

"That . . . that was a goddamn Triumph Bonneville T120! No fuckin way that piece of shit even knew what he had. You have any idea what I had to go through to get that thing running again? Hell."

"I'm so fuckin sorry, man. We all knew how much you loved that thing."

"Yeah. That motherfucker took everything from me, huh?" And she drew in a long, ragged breath, and sighed, "He fucking took everything from me."

Peterson draped an arm across her shoulders. She melted into the embrace, buried her face in his chest, and sobbed, "*He fucking took everything from me . . .*"

He held her while she wept, and when her sobs began to quiet, he said, "Y'know, buddy . . . I dunno what all it's worth, but I think you're a bigger badass than I'll ever be."

"Wuh . . ."

"You got some salt in you, Binachi. I know I couldn't survive half of what you been through; hell, I can't even think about it. You're a survivor, man."

And Jules gritted her teeth and held her arms out, palms up, displaying the layered mats of scar tissue on her wrists, and she hissed, "Well, man, it fuckin wasn't for a lack of trying, I'll tell ya that."

And she lay there in his arms, and after a brief silence she muttered, "He . . . he kept coming back."

"What's that, buddy?"

"The first time, in a weird way, it wasn't so bad; he almost killed me, and that made it easier to pretend it was all a bad dream. But he just . . . *kept . . . coming . . . back*. He called me horrible things, y'know; every horrible name in the book. Faggot, nelly, sissy, tranny, trap, ladyboy -- I heard 'em all. But you know what the worst one was? You know what the worst thing he ever called me was?"

Peterson nodded for her to continue.

"*My fucking name.* When he called me my fucking name. It's . . . it's Hell to feel violated, to feel used, but it's a whole new circle of Hell when somebody makes you feel *owned*."

"I'm . . . I'm so fuckin sorry, buddy."

"Thanks, brother. You . . . I'm so fuckin glad you're here." And, wiping her eyes, she let out a cold, humorless laugh, and said, "So I just thought of somethin. Y'know what I've got to say about all that? About all this? I got four words."

"Whatcha got, Jules?"

"I really don't care."

They laughed together, bitterly, and Peterson smiled and said, "Y'know, buddy, it turns out that brotherhood may be a crock of shit, but also turns out I found somehin better than brotherhood."

"And what's that?"

"I got me a little sister."

Jules gave him a wide, warm smile and socked him in the shoulder. "Don't you fuckin call me 'little', old man."

"I'll call you whatever the hell I want to, shortstack."

"Ahh, fuck you."

"So how does it work if you're goin with Olive Oyl back there? She carry you around in a backpack?"

"Ahh, *stronzo!*"

More laughter, and Jules said, "Y'know, buddy, I guess I'm dancing around what I really wanna say, on account of I'm pretty fuckin sick of talkin about it, but . . . thanks."

"Of course, sister. There was nuthin else I coulda done."

"No, really. Thank you. You . . . you saved my ass. More importantly, you saved her."

Peterson turned to face her, giving her a serious look. "Listen, Jules: You're my best friend, and nobody, not fuckin nobody, hurts my friends and gets away with it."

She threw herself back into his arms. "No, you don't understand, man. I thought I was fuckin done for. I thought he had me. I thought . . . I thought he'd finally found the one thing he could still take away from me. But I'm here, and he's dead, and she's okay. Fuck. She's okay."

"I just wish I coulda been here sooner."

"Don't do that to yourself, Pete. You ain't a fuckin psychic, and anyways, if you thought I was dead, that's 'cause that's what I wanted everybody to think. You were there in the end. You were there when she needed you."

"You're really taken with this girl, huh?"

"Brother, she is everything. She's the entire fucking world. I see those big, green eyes every time I close mine." A quick pause, then, "I'm gonna see you again."

"I mean, God willing."

"Nah. Fuck God. *I* will it. We're gonna live through this whole dumbass adventure, and we're gonna come back, back west, to where Mags grew up, and me and her are gonna get settled and build a life there. I know we will."

"I'm happy for you, bud. After everything, you deserve that."

"No, I don't."

"I'm happy for you, but . . . I dunno where I'm gonna land."

"Honestly, man? The fact that we ain't been shot on sight makes me pretty hopeful. I think, whatever the reds plan on putting us through can't be any worse than the shit we've already seen. Mags has talked a lot about making amends and proving which side you're on, and I'm working on that right now, but you? Brother, you showed that off in spades yesterday morning."

"Well hell, it's just been one piece of good news after another, ain't it?"

"Aw, hell, that reminds me, I wanted to show you something." And she started rolling up her sleeve.

"Whatcha got?"

"Fresh ink."

And she tapped the inside of her elbow, where the crescent moon was.

"Alright," Peterson said, nodding his approval. "Good on you. That musta hurt like a motherfucker."

"Yeah, but I really didn't care."

They laughed at that, and Jules glanced up to check the position of the fading moon and said, "Oh, hell, that gives me an idea. We still got some time before we can head out. You mind doing me one more favor?"

"Shit, hell, of course. Anything for my little sister. Whatcha need?"

"Wait here. I'll be right back."

And Jules sprang up and ran inside, returning a few minutes later with a bottle of clear whiskey, a sewing kit, a ballpoint pen, and two loose rounds of ammo. "I'd like to employ that steady hand of yours," she said. "Got a spot I can't reach."

"Oh, hell yeah. Just tell me where and what."

She sat down in front of him, leaned forward a bit, and lifted her hair, showing off the back of her neck. "Let's get this outta here. I don't like to think about my girl having to look at it."

"Well, buddy, when y'all are together I reckon she's lookin over into the next county. Whatcha want over it? We ain't got time for anything too fancy."

"Well, I've got a bit of a motif goin on here. I was thinkin a star."

Peterson cut open the pen, wiggled the bullets out of their casings, started mixing. "This is gonna hurt like hell, though, and you were always a bleeder."

Jules pulled the belt out of her jeans, bent it in half, and set it between her teeth. She gave Peterson a thumbs-up over her shoulder.

And he got to work.

———

As the moon sank into the west and the air turned blue with gloomy predawn light, Mags came out of the door to find Peterson sitting on the curb and Jules lying facedown on the sidewalk, a bloody strip of cloth wrapped around her neck. She looked back and forth between the two of them and asked, "Everything, uh . . . everything okay out here?"

"Oh, yeah," Jules said, sitting up. "Just a couple of old war buddies catching up. Nuthin to write home about. This old has-been here was just givin me a hand with somethin I'd been meaning to take care of."

And she stood up and, wincing, lifted up the bandage, showing Mags the black, 5-pointed star on the back of her neck.

"Good job, hon. That looks nice as hell."

"I fuckin hope so; we got blood all down the back of my second-favorite shirt."

"Listen, I . . . I woke everybody else up and got breakfast started. It's gonna be time to roll out soon."

At that, Peterson stood up, stretched, and said, "Yeah. Reckon I'll finish getting my kit together and hit the trail. I'll see you lovely ladies on the other side. You take good care of my little sister, alright, red?"

He and Jules shared a long, warm hug and went to head inside. Mags held Peterson back, telling him, "Just a minute. We should talk."

"Yeah, I reckon we should."

"You're not going to be hanged or shot or anything like that. Well, actually, I can't speak for what the anarchists might or might not do, but the Republic isn't going to merc a guy who saved an entire away team. Speaking of that . . . thanks. I don't even want to think about what would've happened if you hadn't found religion."

He shrugged. "I did the only thing I could do. The only thing any decent person coulda done."

"And for exactly how long have the men in black shirts been decent people?"

"Yeah. You got me on that one."

"I know I do. As I was saying, there's not going to be any summary execution, but walking back from where you used to be is a hell of a journey, and you and I both know that there's a hell of a lot a person can go through without dying. How smooth and how quick the debriefing and processing will go depends on a few factors. All of that derring-do yesterday is going to count for a whole hell of a lot already—I can't think of a better place to start than fragging your CO—but the rest hinges on one more thing: Information."

"Oh, that won't be a problem. Whatever I've got, y'all are welcome to it. That's . . . that's the least I can do." He smiled and gave her a pat on the shoulder. "Part of me wants to give you some macho protective-older-brother shit about how you'd better do right by her, but I can tell I ain't gotta worry about that."

"Yeah. Your friend's in good hands. And not just my hands, either; she's well on her way to becoming one of us, and we look out for each other."

"How long y'all know each other, anyways?"

"Couple days."

Peterson cocked an eyebrow. Mags smiled and added, "Hey, these things tend to play out like that. We've got a lot in common, after all."

"Wait, so you're . . ."

"I'm a transsexual, yes. I know you probably don't know anything about that—you should start learning, though, for her sake if nothing else—but we make up something like two percent of the population. Which, if my math is right, accounts for somewhere around eighty to a hundred thousand Ashlanders. And how many more people live in the BNR? Few million, at least?"

Peterson's eyes widened and he let out a whistling sound as horror compounded with a sense of scale. Shaking his head he said, "Learning, yeah. That's what I'm gonna do; I'm gonna learn. Like . . . I'm gonna be honest with you, I don't get it. I can't fathom what would possess a man to be a woman; that just sounds wild to me. But I do know a couple of things. I know I love that kid; she's family to me. I know we've been friends for a whole lot of years and this is the first time I've ever seen her happy. And I know I'm never gonna forget the way her eyes lit up when I called her my sister."

Mags squeezed his shoulder and said, "You've got a long road ahead of you, but I think you'll get there. If you head south out of town and then southwest when you reach the highway, you'll be in populated territory by evening. West of Freeside, you'll find Land's End canton and the hard border; there'll be a guard shack in radio contact with Central, and probably a political officer or a DIS agent you can talk to in person. When you meet that person, drop my name and mention what happened here yesterday. If I make it through to the end of this little camping trip, we'll see each other again in Central in a few weeks."

"Oh, you'll make it. Our girl's betting on it."

———

The only thing Barns hated more than driving at night was walking at night.

It was safe enough, with Becky able to see and hear like a cat in the dark and smell like a bloodhound, and she picked a careful path around groups of roamers and packs of dogs that he never saw, like a bat flitting through a dark forest, and the closest they came to danger was when she warned of a pair of hunters a ways off, moving east, and they hunkered down behind a rusting old car until the coast was clear. And Barns never saw any of it.

Even so, trudging through the wasteland in the dark gave him the creeps. The rusting, derelict cars choking so much of the cracked pavement as it disappeared under a carpet of wildflowers and prairie grass; the leafless, unnaturally cured hulks of old dead trees and the canopies of their young, hale children and grandchildren hiding the stars overhead; and the regular rows of ancient, rotting buildings falling into themselves all seemed to loom over him in the darkness, like the silent idols of some forgotten cult, and every little sound made him jump. Becky moved through it all with an easy, catlike grace, well at home in the dark, but Barns kept a white-knuckle grip on his rifle and couldn't stop looking all around them, trying to discern movement in the shadows, so that his nerves were good and frayed by the time they came to the heart of what had once been a town and Becky announced that dawn would be coming soon and they should look for a place to spend the day.

"Let me take care of that," she said, in that direct way which told she'd hear no argument. "I'm looking for something."

"For what?"

But she was already moving.

After gliding through the streets and around a few blocks, she at last came to a stop outside the decaying hulk of what had once been a boutique shop, its roof and walls still intact enough to keep out the sunlight and weather. They entered, and she took a quick look around, pronounced it safe, and while Barns got to work making camp in one of the back rooms, she began tearing through the stacks of decaying merchandise, boxes that had sat untouched for just shy of two centuries, most of which collapsed into clouds of dust at the slightest touch. But a few were mostly intact, or at least their contents were.

"So what are you looking for?" Barns grumbled.

"I'll know it when I see it."

"Alright. One of these days, I'm gonna learn to quit asking you questions."

"I hope not. Y'know, here's pretty much the only good thing about full synthetics: If you keep 'em safe from the sunlight and the damp, sometimes they last."

"So did you find what you were looking for?"

"No. Maybe. I think I might—ah, here it is ! Needs a bit of patching, but it'll do."

She pulled something out of the pile of dust and rotting scraps and held it up in triumph: A small black evening dress, dusty but mostly intact.

"That's what you were looking for?"

"Yup, just the one. It's perfect."

"What's it for?"

She smiled as she began to fold it up. "I just felt like doing something nice. For a friend."

[14]

DUALITY

EAST OF THE SHENENDOAH, THE MOUNTAINS SOFTENED INTO rolling hills and the coves and hollows grew into broad, flat basins and meadows. The blanket of forest over the landscape thinned just enough for the group to see what lay ahead of them, and when they stopped for lunch in the lee of a low ridge, they could just see a highway viaduct and, beyond that, a town looming in the near distance, about a half-mile in front of them. As they passed around portions of food—dehydrated fruit and protein concentrates mixed with water to make a sort of pudding—Mags kept her eyes on the top of the ridge and muttered, "I don't like that. No, I don't like that one little bit."

"What don't we like?" Connor asked.

"That bridge in front of us. With how sparse the tree cover is, somebody on top of it could spot us from miles away, and we're well inside the distance for a clean shot. Don't like that."

"Yeah. When we go, we're gonna go low, go fast, bound from cover to cover. There probably ain't nobody up there—this far east, bandits are mostly up north or down south—but there might be."

Mags licked her finger and held it up to check the wind. Satisfied that they were leeward and behind the ridge, she reclined on the grass and lit a cigarette. The others followed suit, and TJ said, "Y'know, red, you talk and act just like a pro. Are you sure this ain't your first rodeo?"

She shrugged. "I'm not wasteland ranger, but I did grow up right by the Ohio Valley. I've been at war my whole life. And you ain't gotta be Lyudmila Pavlichenko to know it's a bad idea to waltz across open ground right past a crow's nest."

"Alright, girl scout. You got any suggestions?"

"I'd like to stay here in cover and glass that bridge for a minute or two before we move out. After that, just what Connor says: Move low, move quick, bound from cover to cover. Not really anything else we can do. If there are any people up there, well, under normal circumstances counter-sniper operations without aircraft or artillery would call for a company-sized element. If anybody is up there, I could *probably* outdo them, but I really don't wanna try."

"No shit? A company-sized element is, like, a hundred dudes."

"No shit. That's why the Republic trains so many sharpshooters; we're force multipliers. Speaking of . . ."

She snuffed out her cigarette and crept up to the top of the ridge, bringing her Dragunov to her shoulder and scanning the viaduct. It looked just as much an inert part of the landscape as anything else, cracked and tumbling down in places, all choked with moss and vines, but it still gave her a bad feeling, a prickling in the spot just between her shoulderblades, like being watched.

She saw something move on top of the viaduct and started to focus in on it when her eye caught a bright flash of sunlight reflecting off of glass. Instinctively, quicker than thinking, she threw herself to the ground; a slug of lead thumped into the tree where her head had been a moment ago, followed by a rifle's crack splitting the still air a split-second later.

"Well," Mags hissed, crawling backwards toward the others, "I guess that answers that."

"Mmhmm," Connor grumbled.

"I just caught their sunburst, and I guess they caught mine too. And they're real fuckin fast."

"Hell. Well, that might be a problem, on account of that goddamn bridge is gonna have visibility over this whole damn valley, and if whoever's up there knows we're here, well, that could be trouble, especially if there's a group of 'em. Unless we wanna backtrack far enough to lose a whole fuckin day."

Mags sighed. "Do we got a spare handheld?"

"Of course," Prof whispered, creeping up beside them. "I brought four. I'd never leave home without the wireless."

Connor smiled and clapped him on the shoulder. Mags shrugged off her rucksack, started digging around in its pockets, and said, "Let me borrow one of them. Also, who here is the best at, like, math and stuff?"

"Probably me, red," TJ said. "But what's the plan?"

"Alright. You, stick with me. The rest of y'all, get moving on my signal, and stick to the trees as much as you can. Me and TJ here are gonna cover you."

"The hell does that have to do with math?"

"Well, it—ah, here they are!" She pulled out a pair of binoculars. "Targets are damn near a kilometer out. I could use a spotter."

"Word."

As the rest of the group got ready to move out, Jules grabbed Mags' shoulder and said, "Listen: Fuckin be careful, alright? If you die, I'm gonna kill you."

"I will. You be careful too, alright?"

"Pfft. Like I haven't been shot before."

"Enough," Connor barked. "We need to get this show on the road. One way or t'other, gunshots are gonna attract some attention."

As if on queue, they heard a chorus of low, sad moaning carried on the wind from far away.

Mags and TJ crept along the tree line for about fifty meters and cozied up inside a thick brake of azaleas with a clear view of the viaduct. TJ looked it up and down through their binoculars and whispered, "Okay, I think I got it."

"Hell yeah. Gimme the numbers."

"Alright, I'm looking at I think eight hundred yards . . ."

"Seven three zero meters," Mags whispered to herself.

"Whatever. Top of the span's about, uh, twenty feet off the ground . . ."

"Six point one meters."

"Fuckin nerd. And you've got a light north wind."

Mags fiddled with her scope a moment, said, "Alright, got it. This should be easy." She brought the radio to her mouth and hissed, "Ghost One, this here's Crow 12. You there? Over."

"Yes, Mags, we're here," Prof sighed.

"Copy that, Ghost One. We are in position to cover, and y'all are clear to bound whenever you're ready. Crow 12 out."

"Time to party?" TJ asked.

"Will be any minute now."

Mags glassed the overpass, letting the whole world fade away until nothing existed for her but the weight of the rifle in her hands and the circle of vision through her scope. A few seconds that felt like days had passed when TJ hissed, "Up top and to the right."

Mags shifted right and saw a human figure peeking over the guard rail, holding a hunting rifle. She fired, and the figure fell back out of sight.

"Shift left. Two of 'em."

She shifted, fired twice, and the two men went down. After that, all was quiet for about thirty seconds, and she whispered, "We ought to get moving soon. Ask the others if they're in cover yet."

TJ picked up the radio and did that, but Mags wasn't listening. Her attention was fixed on a four-inch crack in the concrete guard rail, right in front of them. Something about it felt . . . off, triggering the prickly sensation between her shoulders. She took slow, deep breaths and teased her finger across the Dragunov's trigger.

She saw it first, then: The flash of sunlight playing off of glass. She took the shot, and as the rifle's crack faded into the trees, she kept her sights on the crack, letting the shadows behind it come into focus. She saw the outline of a scoped hunting rifle lying dropped on its side and, behind it, a human figure, not moving.

"Mags," TJ hissed, "come on. They're back in the trees, and we need to get there and get back on the road before company shows up."

And as Mags stood up and stretched, she heard it again: The chorus of low, pained moaning. It had grown closer, and added more voices.

When they made it back to the group, TJ clapped Mags on the shoulder and announced, "So it turns out that the big dumb gun ain't just for show after all."

Connor gave her an approving nod. "How many?"

"Four," Mags said. "And that was all we saw. Y'all have any trouble?"

"Good shootin. Nah, we didn't see or hear shit; reckon you kept 'em busy enough. But, look, we need to get movin, and get movin quick, and get movin now; we drawn a whole lot of attention to ourselves, and I'd sure as hell like to make our rendezvous before dark."

"Any more death traps like that back there we gotta worry about?"

"Nah, shouldn't do. Trees should be a lot thicker near the 270. It ain't human beings that I'm really concerned about."

Mags nodded, and made sure her revolver was loose in its holster. They took off at a quick march, almost a jog, and though they made excellent time through the fields and half-dead forests, the chorus of moans seemed to stay just behind them. Mags thought about where they must be, forced the map of Old America that she remembered from school to appear in her mind, and figured that a day's march southeast might be enough to take them hard by the urban sprawl of the old capitol, right to the edge of the poison crater that had once been Old DC. She shivered, chewed the insides of her cheeks, wished for a cigarette.

They'd been on the move for a little over an hour when they came to a four-lane highway, its northbound side choked with the rusting wrecks of a thousand cars frozen bumper-to-bumper like a wall. Connor signaled for them to stop, took a look around, and called Prof over to deliberate. After a beat, he announced, "Alright, I got some good news for once. We would up a bit further north than I thought we would, and that means two things. One, we're only about three hours out from the rendezvous, and two, if we remember right, there ain't dick between it and us but woods, and pretty thick woods, too, least as thick as woods get in the east. Goin through there, shouldn't be too hard to wag our tail."

"How come they're still followin us all this time?" Jules asked. "No way they can see us, and we ain't made a sound since lunchtime."

"Well, they ain't followed us; they're followin each other, all that godawful yellin and racket they make. Normally we'd have lost 'em already, but this close to the big cities we are right up inside the Devil's asshole and there's gonna be multiple hordes all settin each other off. Long as we stay quiet and under the radar, though, we should be alright."

He took another look around, checked the wind, and knelt down low to the ground in the shadow of a rusting box truck and lit a cigarette. Mags and Jules joined him, and he shook his head and said, "We're close, y'all. We're real close."

"How close?" Mags asked. "I ain't exactly familiar with the area."

"If we leave from the rendezvous tomorrow morning and don't run into no delays . . . we're about two days out from there."

"Shit. I . . . fuck, I can't believe we're that close."

Connor and Jules both nodded. Connor's hands were trembling just slightly, and his face was as pale as a sheet, but Jules seemed unimpressed. Ever since leaving Harper's Ferry that morning, she'd been moving through the day with a sort of easy grace, unbothered by the distance or the pace or the weight of her gear, unimpressed with the scenery, speaking very little. Mags laid a hand on her knee and asked, "You holding up okay, hon?"

Jules shook her head. "I dunno, sugar. On the one hand, I feel pretty good. I feel like a soldier with a mission, doing the one thing I've ever been any good at. But on the other hand, well . . ."

She let the statement hang in the air as she stood up, stretched, and said, "Oi, y'all ready to roll out, or what?"

Connor crushed out his cigarette. "Yeah. Yeah, let's get moving."

Connor had been right about the woods. The sound of pursuing roamers followed them a while into the trees, but not far, and they crossed no roads and saw no buildings for several miles. Just as it began to get dark, they passed by a row of ruined houses tumbling down in the shade of the half-living forest, and crossed a road, and passed another row of decaying houses, and Connor announced, "We must be right on top of it now. Old man, give our advance scouts a holler and see where the hell they're at."

As Prof brought up his radio, Jules gave Mags an excited tap on the shoulder and pointed down the road, deeper into the overgrown town. A herd of whitetail deer, four bucks and eight does and their fawns, all of them looking fat and healthy, trotted from the shelter of one crumbling house to another. One of the bucks stopped in the middle of the road and considered them for a moment, then continued on his way, unimpressed.

"Yeah, they're waiting for us," Prof said, putting the radio away. "It's not far. This way, I think."

They followed him further into the town and the forest that covered it. After they'd gone a ways, Mags turned around to check their rear and saw a group of low, sleek shapes darting out to sniff around where the deer had gone past a moment before. At first she thought it was a pack of wild dogs and started to alert the others, but then saw that they were in fact coyotes. The pack stopped to consider the humans for a moment before loping off into the trees and out of sight.

They found the department store easily enough, and as they approached they saw Barns standing outside, waiting for them. He didn't say anything, but gestured for them to follow as he turned and headed inside. Once they were out of the dying sunlight, Becky came bouncing toward them out of the shadows, looking happy to see them. With one hand tucked behind her back, she gave a friendly wave and asked, "So how was you guys's trip?"

"Touch and go for a minute there," Connor grumbled. "Ran into some bandits, but we shook 'em. The girl scout's a real deadeye."

"Uh-huh," she said, giving Connor the vaguest nod of acknowledgment, and she walked up to Jules and said, "So we've still got like an hour and a half, maybe two before me and the bloodbag can head out."

"That sounds like enough time for a story."

"Yeah. But first, I . . . Well, I found this."

And, turning her face away, she held out the thing she'd been carrying behind her back: A folded bundle of black fabric. Jules took it and began to unfold it, and as she did, the placid, determined expression she'd been wearing for most of the day slowly melted so that, when she held up the black evening dress, she was on the verge of tears.

Becky was still looking away. "Oh, fuck, you hate it, don't you? This was a bad idea, I should've known this was a bad idea, I'm so fucking stupid . . ."

Jules threw her arms around Becky and wept into her shoulder. Mags, smiling, patted her other shoulder and said, "Yeah, I think she likes it. That was . . . that was very thoughtful, Becky."

"*Tu stupida, bella puttana,*" Jules muttered, "who the fuck do you think you are, being so nice to me, huh?"

"So you don't hate it?"

"Of fucking course I don't hate it! I . . . I . . . God, this is fucking perfect." And she released Becky and took a quick step back, shivered, and added, "Jesus Christ, you're so . . . cold."

"Well, I mean, I am kinda, like, dead a little bit. But what are you waiting for? Go try it on!"

"Please do," Mags added. "You're going to look great, hon, I just know it."

Jules nodded, darting off into the shadows with a laugh, and when she was gone Mags looked down at Becky and repeated, "That was . . . that was really thoughtful of you. Thank you."

"It's the least I can do, honestly. I feel like I'm still making up for my little fuck-up from yesterday, and besides that, that girl deserves something nice." She gave Mags a light sock in the arm. "I'm glad she's got you. You're good for her, I can tell."

"Uh . . . thanks."

"You and me, though, maybe we should talk. I can tell you're jealous."

Mags sighed. "Is it that obvious?"

"It's really not, actually. Well, not to like a normal alive human person. But I can smell the acetone in your sweat."

Mags shivered at the thought, but regained her composure and said, "She and I already talked this over last night, and I don't want either of you to start doing anything different on my account, but . . . yeah."

"You wanna talk about it?"

"No. I just . . . That woman has been to places I've never had to go to, lived through things I've never had to see, and that means she's going to need things I can't give her. And that scares the living shit out of me. Like, I want to give her the whole world, but what if I'm not enough?" Another sigh. "This is the first real relationship I've had in, like, four years. I love her so goddamn much it hurts, and I can't bear the thought of doing wrong by her any more than I can bear the thought of being alone again."

"Well, I think you're fine. Would it help if I told you that she's absolutely crazy about you? Like, for real; she never shuts up. You're all she ever thinks about."

Mags laughed. "Yeah, that does help. And, like I said . . . please don't pay me any mind. I'm just being a bitch. I can tell it's gonna be good for her, having a friend who understands."

"Yeah, well, on that same note, the two of you have got stuff in common that I know I'll never understand the way you do. For one, I'm straight, and for two, I don't have a dick."

She tried to stifle a laugh, failed, and doubled over giggling. Wiping her eyes, she said, "Wow, you . . . you just say shit, don't you?"

"I do! It's one of my many endearing qualities."

Jules came walking up out of the darkness, then, and the dress fit her perfectly, hugging her curves and flowing down to her boots, which she stared at as she muttered, "So, uh . . . how's it look?"

Mags gawked at her, her eyes widening and her jaw sinking to the floor. When Jules looked up, she met her eyes and muttered, "Oh my God, I . . . Honey, I'm fucking gay."

"So you, uh . . . you like it, then?"

Mags ran up to her and threw her arms around her. "You look amazing, honey. You're the most beautiful woman I've ever fucking seen. How do you feel?"

"I . . . I feel good, Mags. I feel really good. It . . . it feels like me."

"Hon, it looks it. You're absolutely owning this."

And Jules leaned in close and whispered, "Maybe later you can help me take it off."

"Ah, *shikse*, I should be so lucky."

"Oh, you are so lucky, sugar. You even get to take me to dinner and show me off."

"I can't wait. But first . . . well, we're wasting daylight, and I think you've got an appointment to keep."

They kissed as they broke off their embrace, and Jules blew her another as she walked towards Becky. Mags forced a smile.

As the two of them walked off together into the shadows to find somewhere private, Becky said, "Well, my good bitch, it might be a two-for-one special this evening. The thing I feel like getting off my chest dovetails right into who Lukash is and this whole 'Becky's a dracula' situation, so that might be, like, I dunno, convenient." A long, sad sigh. "Let's talk about my dad."

"Ooh," Jules winced, "yikes."

"Yeah, 'yikes' is right. Like I said, horror stories."

And they disappeared into the dark. When they were gone, Barns walked up to Mags' side and grumbled, "Yeah, she has that effect on people."

Mags wasn't sure what to say, since this was the first time that the silent, grumpy little man had directly spoken to her. Barns went on: "Lemme guess. At first you hated her, but now you think she might be alright."

"Well, 'hate' isn't the word I'd use, but yeah, I had my reservations."

"She is alright. She's just not very good at the whole 'people' thing. But hey, neither am I; that's probably why we get along."

Mags didn't say anything, a bit puzzled that this man who'd been so silent and seemed to take an instant dislike to everyone had come up to her and started talking as though they were already friends. Barns seemed to pick up on it, and he continued: "I've never been too good at the whole 'making new friends' thing, so I figured, fuck it, might as well jump in."

She noticed, then, that he was chewing on his lower lip, and tapping his right thumb against his fist, imitating the motion of clicking a pen. Barns was terrified.

"Yeah," she said, "I feel that. So like . . . not to be too blunt, but who the hell are you? Where did you two come from? Who's this Lukash?"

"All that stuff might have to wait till Becky gets back; it's, uh, kind of a lot. But the short version is we're from Ontario and she's my girlfriend." And Barns smiled, staring off into the middle distance and idly rubbing the side of his neck, which Mags then noticed sported two fresh wounds, like twin pinpricks, or a snakebite. "She can be a bit much, but goddamn do I love that woman."

John's mind swam in a sea of confused and disjointed memories, and when he finally woke up he wasn't sure if he had. He was conscious of a dull, throbbing ache in his leg, but other than that he had trouble making heads or tails of himself. With time, sensation crept back into his fingertips, up his arms, and he tried to move and found that he was restrained to something. He opened his eyes and saw a low concrete ceiling in a dimly-lit room. Looking around, he saw that he was handcuffed to a bed in a small room not much bigger than a utility closet, and that he wasn't alone. On the far side of the room, a small man sat at a desk, his feet propped up, a book resting in his lap. John tried to yell for him, but only a wordless, bestial groan came out.

The man at the desk looked up from his book and said, "Oh, wow, you awake already? You must be even tougher than you look."

Tomassi groaned again. The other man got up and walked toward him, saying, "Hey, hey, take it easy there, big guy. I shot you up with enough ketamine to kill a horse; you are tripping absolute balls right now."

Tomassi wrestled with his disobedient mind, trying to remember how language worked, and he managed to ask, ". . . leg?"

"Oh, yeah, that. Well, big guy, I've got some good news and some bad news. The bad news is that you're pretty fucked up; your right patella is basically just gone and there's tissue damage, siginificant nerve damage, and some infection. Rough stuff. But the good news is that your ol' buddy Todd got you patched right up. You're gonna have to deal with a whole lot of reduced mobility, but the leg stays on. That's good news, right?"

He groaned again, starting to fade back into the sea of dissociated memories. He tried to ask where he was, what was going on, but all that came out was the question that had been at the front of his mind for the past two days: "Where . . . where is she?"

Todd shrugged. "Don't know, man. They brought you down here alone. Listen, you should really try and rest, you're still in rough shape."

John tried to sit up, found that his body wouldn't obey him even if his hands weren't shackled. "Where . . . is . . . Julia?"

"Don't know any Julia, my man. Like I said, the boss dropped you off here alone. You can try asking him when he gets back. For now, really, dude, you need to rest. That's doctor's orders."

Todd's casual and insolent attitude made him angry, and being angry made him almost lucid, and he growled, "Where the fuck is that little faggot? Where the fuck is that ungrateful, backstabbing whore? You bring her here right now! You tell her I am gonna fix her good this time!"

Todd sighed, reached under his desk, and brought out another syringe of ketamine. "Alright, buddy, I think it might be time for another cat-nap."

The dissociation won out, then, and John muttered, "Where . . . where's my little black angel?"

"Probably waiting up in Heaven, I guess. Are you gonna chill the fuck out now?"

The lucid part of John's mind forced him to close his eyes, to lay back relax, take deep breaths, try to calm down. When he felt more in control, he asked, "Hey, uh . . . Todd, was it?"

"Uh-huh. The one and only."

"Where the hell am I?"

"The Eagles' Nest, baby! Or, well, we're under it, anyways. One of the bigshots dropped you off down here and was all like 'Zee if you can keep zis one alive, he may still be useful.' So I did, and here we are."

Tomassi smiled, and laughed, and he said, "Oh, thank fucking God. He had me going for a minute there, he really did, but I knew they wouldn't really do me dirty like that. I knew it was just a nightmare."

And Todd walked up closer to the side of the bed, and as he drew closer his easygoing smile stiffened into a rictus grin, an empty and soulless grin like one painted on a doll's face, and Tomassi recognized it as the same expression that was always fixed on the face of another doctor he knew, one who'd once done him a favor. "Oh, you've got it all backwards, lunchbox," Todd said, leering over him, and John Tomassi at last noticed the mosaic of tiny round scars that covered each side of the doctor's neck.

"Your nightmare hasn't even started yet."

[15]
WELTKRIEG

[September 1918; somewhere in western Russia]

THE BLOODSTAINS WERE PROVING HARD TO SCRUB OUT.

It had been a month since the operation, since the changes had begun, and Lukash was finally starting to feel whole again, to get used to himself, but he still vomited after every meal. Eating was still an ordeal that turned his stomach and brought up pints of blood, most of it his own, and left him feeling even weaker than before. And now there were ugly rust-colored stains on his fine green overcoat.

Not that he needed an overcoat anymore. Even with the endless autumn rain pissing down and turning everything to impassible mud, bringing with it the promise of a terrible winter, the cold didn't bother him. His rain-soaked uniform and mud-filled boots almost felt warm, compared to the brick of ice that had settled in his chest over the past month, though it did serve as another reminder of his miserable existence, posted here on a front in the war that had been won long ago, with nothing better to do than sit in the rain and shoot at the occasional Bolshevik and worry over the latest dispatches from France and the endless bad news they brought. Every little thing smacked of futility, and he wanted to throw the overcoat down and walk away in disgust . . . but no, no, he was still an officer, still *Rittmeister* Wolfgang Kristops von Lukash, a captain of the Pomeranian *Jagerkorps*, and a captain must have a clean coat.

He did, however, need a break. It had stopped raining for the moment, so he would set down his coat and his brushes and go outside and have a smoke, and perhaps the sky would be clear and he could look up at the stars. That, at least, was a joy that had not been taken from him.

He stepped out of his tent and lit a cigarette that was as dry and harsh as a desert. The changes had made him far more sensitive to taste and smell, but even before that he had already noticed the cigarettes becoming progressively worse as they became progressively fewer, along with the food rations, and the ammunition, and the new boots and uniforms. Even so, the night sky had cleared a bit, and standing under the stars made him feel almost human. Almost.

Across the field, about one hundred feet in front of him, Otto was pacing. Otto was always pacing.

Otto had always been a man of bottomless energy who never knew what to do with himself when there wasn't enough work, and he'd taken to the changes with far more ease than Lukash, so that life in the camp was hard on him and he often spent entire nights pacing a great circle, like a bear in a cage. Lukash shrank into the shadows beside his tent and hoped that Otto wouldn't notice him; they had been the closest of companions once, dearer than brothers, but over the past few months he'd noticed Otto . . . changing, in ways that scared him. He'd begun to feel that the big, blonde Bavarian was walking down a path he could not follow, and the past month had certainly not helped.

Otto did, of course, notice him, and came right over. They looked like perfect opposites, the tall, fair Bavarian cannoneer with his great knotted muscles and his big, soft belly that shook when he laughed, against the dark little Pomeranian ranger with his black hair and lean, wiry frame; once upon a time, Lukash had enjoyed the contrast, back before Otto had begun to frighten him.

"Ah, my little wolf crawls out of his den at last," Otto said as he walked up. "Where have you been, brother?"

Hearing the nickname—*mein Wolfchen*—lifted and stirred Lukash's spirits just a bit, and he smiled and said, "Hello, *mein Knuddelbar*."

A dark look crossed over Otto's face, and he growled, "You do not say such things here, Lukash. Not in public."

They were, of course, alone, and Otto had been the first to use one of the names they'd once called each other in private, and Lukash felt something die inside of himself. Rolling his eyes, he said, "Yes, yes, of course. What do you want, Otto?"

"Only to see how you're getting on. We haven't talked in several nights."

"If you must know, quite poorly. I feel tired and ill always, and I can't keep a bit of blood down. I . . . good God, Otto, I'm so fucking hungry, I swear I'd trade my cock for a slab of roast beef right now."

Otto grinned an eager, hungry grin, like a snarling bear, and said, "Myself, I've never felt better. I'm so strong now, brother!"

"You were already strong."

"But now I am stronger still! And faster, and fiercer. I can't wait to go to battle again, Lukash; I can't wait to see what the new corps can do."

"You'd need to go to France for that, I think."

"And what is that supposed to mean, little wolf?"

Lukash puzzled over how to answer such a monumentally stupid question, and as he puzzled he felt all the frustration and resentment that had been building within him over several years of war, ever since Tannenburg, come bubbling to the surface, and he growled, "Because that is where the war is being lost, Otto. Because there is no reason for us to be here at all! Russia is beaten and broken; it has been a year since the Tsar was overthrown, and months since Brest-Litovsk; and the Russians are too busy fighting one another to be bothered about us. Why on Earth are we still here, Otto? What is the point of any of this?"

"That I can tell you, little wolf. We are here because there's a cancer in Russia, a foul disease that cannot be allowed to spread. If it infects any more lands, it could upend the natural order of the entire world."

"Well, perhaps that would not be so bad!"

"And what on Earth do you mean by that?"

"Take a look around and tell me where the natural order of things has gotten us. Millions are dead. Our empire is bankrupt and starving and been brought to the very brink of disaster. Perhaps we could do with a bit of upending; the Russians, at least, have backed down from the war with some little shred of honor intact, rather than being merely beaten. I don't want to think about what horror might spring up from a Germany beaten and disgraced."

"But that is nothing to fear, Lukash! We are winning this war, and we will end it crowned in glory, glory we have earned with our iron and blood. Of that, I am sure."

"Well then you're a damned idiot! You've read the same dispatches that I have. You heard what happened in Belleau Wood, at Amiens, on the Lys, and just again on the Somme; I know you remember Tanneburg as I do, but we will never have another Tannenburg. The *Siegfriedstellung* has fallen, Otto, and there is nothing but open country between the Entente and Westphalia. The Fatherland cannot feed or clothe what men are left, let alone replenish the losses. The war is as good as over. I give us, at most— at most—a hundred days."

"This is cowardice, Lukash, and it's nonsense. All of the blood that's been shed for the honor of the Fatherland will not be so idly discounted. We will win this war, because victory is the destiny we have earned with our iron and blood. Indeed, it is *in* our blood; ours is a race of heroes. Look at us, brother, and the other men who are now like us. We are a living testament to the fact of it!"

"You sound like a mystic, Otto; like a damned Theosophist, or a Romantic druid singing about Votan and Siegfried. And what of us? 'Living testament,' my ass; we're abominations is what we are. Freaks! You think I can just go home to Rostock like this? You think I can just knock on my sister's door and she'll take me right in and forget that her brother is a monster from a fairytale? Hell. But—but perhaps I will go, but not home. Perhaps I'll go to Berlin, for when the Kaiser and Ludendorf fall-and they will fall—someone will have to be there to help build a new Germany."

"Yes," Otto said, with a faraway look in his eyes, "a new Germany. A new Germany, for true Germans. Lukash, I think that you are a coward, and I think that you are a fool, but now I wonder if you are not even less than that. Perhaps we could lose this war . . . if we are stabbed in the bag. Perhaps Russia is not the only place languishing under infection, full of rats, backstabbing rats, scheming rats, money-grubbing rats."

Lukash felt a familiar old fear form an icy fist around his spine, and he gulped, and he hoped that Otto didn't notice. The big cannoneer's empty black eyes bore down into Lukash's own as he went on: "Perhaps I was wrong about you, and there is more rat in that dark, inscrutable little face than I thought."

That did it. Lukash's fear melted away, then, and a rage just as cold and just as ancient replaced it. His hand shot to the bayonet sheathed at his belt, and he growled, "You will not speak to me like that!"

"Do I strike to close to home, my little wolf?"

The bayonet came out, then, and in a flash its tip was resting just under Otto's chin, and Lukash growled, "No, Otto, I am not your fucking dog. Whatever path it is that you're walking down, you'll be taking it alone, for I'm through with you. Now, you get the hell out of my sight this instant or by God we are going to learn exactly how much it takes to kill one of us."

Otto took a step back. For an instant, the big man looked hurt, but only for an instant. And rather than meet the challenge, he only gave Lukash a pitying look, and shook his head, and walked away.

Lukash, with tears in his eyes, did not stay to watch Otto go. Otto's words were setting off a thousand alarm bells in his mind, and he knew that, whether he was a monster now or not, it would not be safe to stay in the army camp.

It proved to be a small thing, running away. He'd been toying with the idea a while anyway, and as a captain in the *Jagerkorps* he knew how to cover more ground, and faster, and more silently than any other man in the camp. As he threw his coat back on, and got his gear together, and slung his Mauser, he was faced with two burning questions. The first, of cours,e was how far he could get in the few hours he had left before daylight; but he was satisfied that it would be many more miles than Otto would be able to track in a night anyway.

The second question was which direction to go.

He needed to go south and west, of course; out of Russia, away from the front, to the big cities where all of those socialists and trade-unionists he'd read about in the newspapers might be found. But, then, that was exactly the way anyone who might be coming after him would expect him to go.

And so Lukash struck out east, just as it began to rain again.

Lukash covered many miles of forest and swamp that night, moving with the unnatural speed he was at last getting used to, and it wasn't until nearly morning, when he'd stopped to consider where he might shelter through the coming day, that he heard and smelled people nearby. He stood there in the darkness, having a long, hard think about whether or not to approach, when someone shot him.

The bullet punched into his chest, and he heard the rifle's crack even before it had exploded out of his back, and he knew that the shooter must be terribly close. He laid his Mauser on the ground, raised his hands up over his head, and called out, "Hello? I'm alive, and, ah, I suppose I would like to surrender."

There was furious shouting in Russian, and a moment later five armed men emerged from the darkness, one of them wearing a great fur hat with a red star pinned to the front of it. Lukash gave that man a curt nod and said, in his best Russian, "I knew someone was out there, but you must be very skilled to have gotten so close to me. I'm impressed."

The Russian shook his head. "Give me your name, rank, and how many are with you. Now."

"Lukash. Captain, Pomeranian *Jagerkorps*. And no-one is with me; I'm a deserter. They may be looking for me, but they're more likely to have gone south or west."

"So you are a coward, as well as an imperialist dog and an aristocrat?"

Lukash rolled his eyes. "Yes, yes, and I'm a homosexual and a Jew and I cheat at cards and I never write home to my mother. Now, if it's all the same to you gentlemen, I would like very much to be taken prisoner somewhere inside and out of the sun before daybreak comes; sunlight disagrees with my constitution."

The five Russians looked back and forth at each other, unsure of what to make of the man they'd just found, and the one in the big hat cocked an eyebrow and asked, "You . . . wish for us to hide you from the sun?"

"Yes, of course, if you'd be so kind." And he gave them a wide, toothy grin, and he danced his tongue across the long, sharp canines that overlapped his bottom teeth. As they recoiled in horror, he laughed and said, "Oh, come now! You men act as if you've never been in a fairytale before."

[16]

HUNTED

THERE WAS A LONG SILENCE AFTER BECKY FINISHED
speaking, her words lingering in the darkness like smoke. She
sighed and stared at the floor, a veil of unpleasant memories
clouding her mind, when Jules finally broke the silence.

"Hey."

Becky looked up. Jules tossed her their pack of cigarettes and
said, "You know that none of that was your fault, right?"

"Yeah." She lit a cigarette. "That . . . took a lot more out of me
than I thought it woud."

"Oh, I'll bet it did. That was a hell of a thing, sharing that story
with anybody. Thanks for telling me."

"Of course." She ventured a sad smile. "Thanks for listening."

"Always. That's what this little game is about, right?"

"Yeah, that's right. You . . . you really listen. Steve and the
others, they listen, but they don't . . . they don't get it. They really
don't get it."

"Oh, if that ain't the truth. Like, talking to Mags . . . she listens,
and she's so goddamn sweet, and God bless her she's trying, but she
doesn't . . . she doesn't get it." Jules gave a humorless chuckle. "How

do I even explain what the problem is to somebody who's never spent six hours sitting under the shower wondering if she'll ever feel clean again? It's a one-of-a-kind experience."

"Fuckin word, sister." Becky stood up in the darkness in the same unsettling way she always moved, as smooth and quiet as a cat. "And with that, I declare this meeting of the Sad Bitch Society officially adjourned."

"Hold up. Not quite."

"What's up?"

"You were gonna tell me about that guy you mentioned. Louis?"

"Lukash. Oh yeah, well, that story does have a happy ending. You, ah . . . you ever meet a person who just feels like a friend? It's like, 'I've never seen you before in my life and I know nothing about you but I want to hang out with you and share all my deepest secrets'?"

"Yeah, I have. She's back there in the other room."

"Oh, right. Well, this was about two years after I ran away. That was . . . hard. I'd been sleeping rough, eating out of dumpsters, turning tricks, wondering if I wouldn't be better off going back home; honestly, I don't know how I made it as long as I did. This one night, it was about two o'clock in the morning, and I'd . . . I'd had a really bad time that night, and I was sitting on my favorite bench in the park having a good cry and wondering where I was gonna sleep, when I heard someone singing. Someone was walking through the park drunk off his ass and just singing at the top of his lungs in German, like, '*Auf, auf, zum Kampf, zum Kampf . . .*' I looked around and I saw this guy who was dressed like a fucking actor from a Renaissance faire, wearing slacks and a waistcoat and these big black boots and a fucking tophat, carrying a bottle of peppermint schnapps and singing to himself."

"Huh."

"Yeah, exactly. And he had this ridiculous mustache that made him look like a dastardly villain on his way to go commit some train

228 / NATALIE IRONSIDE

crimes. So this guy finally notices me staring at him, and he stops and looks me over and goes, 'Oh, madam, do you need help?' Fucking 'madam'. I asked him if he had any money, and he reaches into his pocket and just hands me a hundred dollars. A hundred dollars!"

"Yeah, I don't know what that means."

"Oh, right. It's . . . I can't think of what it would be in the weird pretend money you people use, but it's enough to rent a room for a couple of nights, or enough to eat for a week. And he just hands it to me like it's nothing. I figured he must be a john, so I stood up and started asking him what he wanted, and he goes, 'Oh no, no, no, young lady, I need nothing. This is a gift.' Then he asked if I needed a place to sleep. Now, you do not just go home with strange men, especially fucking not with strange men who get drunk and wander around the ghetto in the middle of the night dressed like Willy Wonka, and every survival instinct in my body was telling me to get the hell away from him, but . . . well, he just oozes this wholesome dad energy. When you see him, you'll understand. And that is how I met Lukash."

"Well, that's . . . not what I was expecting."

"Yeah, and how do you think I felt? So this guy lived in a crummy, ground-floor apartment a couple of blocks away, and it was . . . well, it looked like him if he was an apartment. There was all this ratty, ancient furniture, and there were paintings and maps and flags and a bunch of guns and a sword hung up on the wall. He goes, 'You may sleep in the bedroom, and I will take the sofa, as a gentleman should. I'm afraid I don't have any food, but we could order something.' So I ask him how long he's gonna let me stay and he shrugs and goes, 'As long as you'd like, Miss.'

"He ordered me a pizza, and we talked while I ate. Right off, I noticed that he was, like, super evasive about who he was and his whole situation; I gathered he was Jewish, German, and super duper gay, and he'd moved to America after fighting in a war and was living off of his richy-rich family's money. But, like, a lot of stuff didn't add up. About then was when I started to notice that his skin was all pale and weird, and that he wasn't breathing.

"I told him my story—same as I told you, but a bit lighter on the details—and he was quiet for a long time and looked like he was thinking real hard about something. After a while he sighed and said, 'Rebecca, look into my eyes.' I did, and I finally noticed the other thing that was wrong with him. The eyes. And he says, 'This is probably a mistake, but . . . what if I told you that I can give you something so that no-one will ever be able to hurt you like that again?' I, uh . . . well, let's just say I took some convincing, but yeah, a few short nights later I was a little baby dracula with a weird gay dad."

Jules stared up at her in silence for a long while before she finally asked, "Becky?"

"Yeah?"

"What the fuck?"

She shrugged. "What can I say; life takes us places. Now, come on, they've got dinner started out there and they've probably got some questions for me and I don't wanna waste moonlight. And you've got a hot date with a tall sexy redhead."

And she helped Jules to her feet, and Jules shuddered at taking the ice-cold hand, and as they walked back toward the others, Jules said, "Tomorrow . . . tomorrow, I'll finish telling you about why this dress is such a big deal."

"Oh, shit, did you not already?"

"Only part of it. The saga of the black evening dress has a thrilling second act. And now, I guess, a conclusion." She smiled. "Tonight, I'm gonna lie down in my girlfriend's arms, and it's gonna feel just as good as if I was pissing on John's grave."

Nearer the front of the building, the others were already circled up and passing around bowls of food, and to her surprise Becky saw that

Barns was sitting and talking with them rather than waiting for her by himself. She sat down next to him, pecked his bearded cheek, and said, "So what's got into you, nerd? Making new friends and shit."

He shrugged. "Hey, you found one. I felt left out."

She smirked and put an arm across his shoulders. TJ, their mouth full of dinner, gestured toward Barns and said with approval, "This dude . . . this dude is a trip and a half."

"Uh-huh," Becky nodded, "he sure is. Say, what the hell is that stuff you guys eat? We in the Matrix or something? It'd suit y'all if we were."

"Concentrated plant proteins," Prof said. "Beans, mostly."

"Not to be rude or anything, but it looks like baby shit."

He shrugged. "It doesn't taste like much of anything, really, but it can be seasoned to taste. This that Mags fixed has fruit in it, so it's more or less the same as a bowl of oatmeal. Personally, I find the texture practically unbearable, but it weighs almost nothing and it keeps forever, so here we are."

Mags, who was starting on a third bowl, laughed and said, "You just don't know what's good, old man. See, this is basically the same stuff as the Republic's field rations; I grew up on this shit. You can fix it straight, like this, but it also makes a great base for stews, and you can mix it with cornmeal and make some real badass cornbread. This here's the kind of chow that wars are won on."

Prof gave her a look that was somewhere between pity and horror. Mags was too focused on her bowl to notice. Finishing another spoonful, she asked, "So what's a Matrix?"

Becky gawked at her with growing horror. "Wait, you've never heard of *The Matrix*? I figured that that must have survived, at least with so many of y'all around."

"Doesn't ring a bell."

"It's an Old American film, pre-War," Prof said. "You might like it, actually. Strong anticapitalist themes. Your mother could probably help you find a copy."

"Ooooh, a film. Yeah, I've seen one or two films. Weird art form."

Becky blinked a few times. "Good Lord, the future really is a godless place."

"Sweetie, I've read enough about Old America to know I like this a lot better, films or no films. And it's not like we don't have films; I just never saw the appeal."

"Okay, that's valid. But in any case, you . . . you gotta watch *The Matrix*. It's, like, important."

"How come?"

Becky chewed her bottom lip. Prof snickered and said, "She's trying, I believe, to say it's important because it was made by two trans women. At least, I think that's right; art history was never my forte."

"Alright, you've convinced me. Still, betcha it's not as good as *Battleship Potemkin*. Now *that's* a film."

The hunter shook her head. Prof, laughing, reached out and patted her shoulder and said, "You may be fighting a losing battle, Becky. I spent two years trying to give this woman a sense of culture, and you can see how far I got."

"Hey, what's that supposed to mean?" Mags said.

"Mags, what's your favorite song?"

"Uh . . . Probably *John Brown's Body*. Maybe *The Red Army Is The Strongest*."

The entire group rolled their eyes in unison. Barns made a throat-clearing noise and grumbled, "So the sun's good and down already."

"Oh, hell," Becky replied, "it sure is. But I can afford to waste a few more minutes—the 70 is, like, right there—and I figured you guys would have a couple of questions."

"Yeah, a couple," Mags said. "We agreed to trust y'all because you helped us out of a tight spot and then gave us your back, but we still don't, like, know anything about you. Where did you two come from? And this guy you said you work for, Lukash; who's he, and what the hell's the move with that?"

"Okay, so you've probably gathered—or at least I hope so—that not all the draculas are racist murder hobos, some of us are just idiots trying to get by, same as you. Well, up north near the Great Lakes, there's a settlement where a lot of us live and try to do normal-people stuff along with the warmies. We try to keep a low profile, but we like to keep an eye on what's going on around us, so we know about the Nazis in Ohio and we know about you guys's little intentional-community hippie situation, and we knew about your friend Bart and his little derring-do expedition. When that happened, well, it kinda caused a stir. One of our people, Lukash, he's like you, he's a commie; and he'd been saying for a while that we need to get out of our homey little Letterkenney bubble and try to do some good in the world. And that whole Bart fiasco really lit a fire under his ass, on account of when word got back to us, he knew right away what was going on because, like I said yesterday, he and Otto—the big fucker—have got some history. Nobody back home really listened to him, but they didn't try to stop him either, so a few of us packed up and headed south. And here we are."

"How many are y'all bringing?"

"Honestly? Don't know. We had a crew together, but there was a big change of plans when we found out about you guys, and it's been radio silence since then. It might just be me, the bloodbag, and Lukash."

"I hope that's it. We're here for a scouting mission, not an assault, and my team's already as big as it needs to be."

Becky winced. "Yeah, about that. If the boss is coming down personally, I can almost guarantee that he's planning some kind of assault."

Prof and Connor winced, and Mags pinched the bridge of her nose. Becky went on: "But we're probably going to run into him sometime in the next couple days, and you can just, like, talk to him about whatever the plan's gonna be. I promise he's not gonna be a dick about it; the dude is like 300 years old, so if he's anything he's patient. Shit, speaking of, me and my manservant here had better get moving."

"How far y'all plan on humping it?" Connor asked.

"We were gonna shoot for Albeth, but we probably won't make it that far."

"Nah, you'll make it. That's right down the 70, and the eastbound side is mostly clear."

"How do you know that?"

"'Cause that's how we approached last time. From Albeth, you're gonna head southeast to the river and then be right up that place's asshole in about a day, maybe half. And trust me, you'll know it when you see it."

"You really can't miss it," Prof concurred. "You'll see the cooling tower and the blast walls from a good while away. When you get to a soccer field surrounded by broken Abrams tanks, well, that's as far as anyone's gotten."

Becky gave a solemn nod. "Okay. We'll rendezvous in Albeth tomorrow night, and from there . . . from there, we'll start plotting our terminal approach."

Connor was right about the 70.

Picking their way through the brush and the remains of buildings that it grew over as Becky and Barns struck out north took a bit of time, especially in the dark, but when they reached the interstate they found a clear path into the east. Like most roads in the area, the westbound lanes were choked with an endless line of derelict vehicles rusting bumper-to-bumper beneath the ghostly trees, a snapshot of an abortive evacuation cut short, but the eastbound side was mostly unencumbered. And the 70 was even more clear than most such roads, for all the trees that had grown up through the cracked pavement and all the rusting wrecks of cars that had been scattered on it here and there had been pushed rudely to either side, evidence of the passage of an armored column sometime in the recent past.

"Huh," Barns said, peering eastward as far as he could into the darkness, "well this seems too good to be true."

"Yeah," Becky agreed. "On the one hand, we're definitely gonna make Albeth before morning, but on the other hand, jeez, just looking at this makes me feel naked."

"Plan?"

"I'll take point, and if I hear anything nasty . . . well, let's hope I don't."

They'd been walking along the crumbling highway for a little over an hour when Becky stopped dead in her tracks and, rather than signal for Barns to take cover, she grabbed him and pulled him off of the road and into the trees.

"People up ahead," she hissed. "Five of them, coming this way."

"Fuck. What kinda people?"

"The spooky kind."

They stayed crouching in the brush for several minutes, and sure enough Barns soon heard the metronome of boot-heels clapping across the crumbling pavement, moving at a sprint, and he watched as five tall, dark shadows passed in front of them, barely visible in the dim light of the moon. The five hunters moved too quickly to take any notice of them. Moved like they had somewhere to be.

"Well, hell," Barns whispered as soon as they were alone again.

"Yeah. This isn't good."

Becky pulled the two-way radio off of her belt and whispered into it, "Hey, nerds, it's ya'girl. You guys up?"

A moment's silence, followed by a long, dramatic yawn and TJ's voice saying, "Yeah, I'm here. What's up? You losers in trouble?"

"No, but you might be. An assault group just went past us. Five men, hunters, running like they were trying to win the big race. Looked like they were headed your way."

"Oh, motherfucker. You fucking serious?"

"Afraid so. At the pace they were going, they'll probably be on top of you in about an hour."

"Goddamn Jesus Christ shit piss fuck . . . Okay. What are y'all gonna do?"

"I could be back there in an hour, but not my nerd; he doesn't have cross-country running magic yet."

"Hell. Okay, you two . . . you two just keep going, I guess. I'll go wake up the others. If I don't call you back by morning, well, you know."

"Yeah. Good luck."

Becky and Barns stood staring at each other in the dark until Barns said, "Y'know, if you think it'd help, you can go. I can hole up here 'till they come through in the morning."

"Hell no. I'm not leaving you alone in the dark for a fucking second, Steve. They're cool and all, but you're my dude, my guy, my main hoe. We stick together."

"Alright. What do we do, then?"

"I guess . . . I guess we keep going to Albeth. And if we don't hear back from them in the morning, well, we'll burn that bridge when we come to it."

The department store was the tallest building around, so the group made their way up onto the roof, the silence only broken by the occasional yawn as they tried to shake off their sleep. Once on the roof, they huddled together in silence until TJ said, "Maybe . . . maybe they're headed somewhere else."

"We're the only target out here," Connor grumbled. "This is it."

"Five," Prof said, a faraway look in his eyes. "Five hunters.

Christ, that's as good as a company. I'd hoped we wouldn't have to deal with more than two or three in a group."

"You hope too much, old man."

As the conversation went on, Jules kept her eyes on Mags, watching a change come over her. At first Mags looked just as terrified as the others, but her face gradually hardened until she wore a flat, neutral expression that betrayed no emotion at all. During a lull in the talk, she cracked her knuckles and said, "Alright, I've got a plan."

Connor snorted. "What the hell you gonna do, girl scout? Sell 'em some cookies?"

"If Becky was still alive to call us, that means they don't know about her. They'll be expecting to find one or two of us on watch and the rest asleep. That gives us an edge."

"Some fuckin edge that is. Hell, we shouldn't even be up here; we should be beating hell back east, try to keep dodging till sunrise. No way in hell we can win this as a stand-up fight. This is it; we're done."

Mags turned her head to look into his eyes, boring into him with her own, and she said, flatly, with no emotion in her voice: "Coward."

"The fuck did you just call me, red?"

"No discipline, either. If you don't want me to call you a coward, you should soldier the fuck up and stop acting like one. I have no use for cowards. Yes, we're probably going to die; but I'm going to die on my feet, feeding the fascists iron and lead, like a fucking soldier."

Everyone stared, waiting to see how the confrontation would play out, but Mags didn't give it the chance. "I'll take the northeast corner," she said. "Connor, you get on the southeast. Jules and TJ, you've got northwest and southwest, respectively. Professor J, you watch the door."

"Hold the fuck up," Connor barked. "I ain't agreed to none of this."

Mags kept her eyes locked with his and said, "Contact is esti-mated at 45 minutes. When the train you're on is hurtling towards a cliff, you don't have time to wait for all the passengers to reach consensus on whether or not to pull the brake."

As she spoke, her right hand was already reaching towards her revolver. Prof jumped between the two of them and stammered, "No, no, no, you two cut this out. Connor . . . Connor, it's a good plan."

"I think I know entirely too goddamn well what you think sounds like a good plan, old man."

TJ shrugged, said, "The egghead's right, my man. Yeah, the red bitch is out of line and can go eat a whole carton of dicks, but a good plan's a good plan. Well, I mean, it's actually a pretty bad plan, but it's still one more plan than I've got, so."

Connor looked around at the group, reading their faces, and grumbled, "Alright, fine, we'll do it the dumbass way."

Mags nodded, her face still expressionless. "We've got approxi-mately forty minutes."

"Yeah. When they come . . . when they come, take the shot as soon as you've got it, and blow their fuckin heads off. It takes a lot of firepower to put these bastards down, so you're probably only gonna have one chance to get the drop on 'em. And if any of 'em get up here on the roof with us, well, that'll be that."

It took thirty minutes.

Mags crouched behind the parapet on her corner of the roof, glassing the darkened streets around her, letting her eyes adjust to pierce the shadows beneath the trees. She'd been in position a while, she didn't know how long, when her eye caught movement and she saw a few deer bounding out of the east. No, not bounding; running. Running from something."

"Any minute now," she whispered to herself, letting her finger dance across the Dragunov's trigger.

From off to her right, she heard a rifle's crack split the night, followed by Connor shouting, "Alright, folks, company's here!"

She scanned the ground in front of her, taking slow, even breaths, and she saw something, a shadowy human-shape flitting from tree to tree. It was too fast to quite make out, but she acted on instinct, leading it by a few inches and taking her shot when it bounded again. The figure staggered, clutching its shoulder, its sprint checked for a split-second, just enough time for her to line up a proper shot. She pulled the trigger twice, and the hunter dropped to the ground, missing most of its head, and did not get back up.

For a moment, the whole roof was a mess of fire and noise as rifle fire lit up the trees and streets below, but it just as quickly died away, and from across the roof TJ announced, "Alright, I don't see shit no more."

"Me neither," Connor called back. "I got one; he's down for good."

"I got one, too," TJ shouted.

"Same here," Mags responded. "But three from five still leaves two."

As if on queue, the ringing in all their ears faded just enough to hear the sound of running boots somewhere underneath them. Jules was the first to react, rushing toward the door leading up to the roof, where Prof stood. The others started to turn around, but not fast enough. The door burst open and a tall, blonde man in a black uniform burst out, almost too quickly to see, and much too quickly for Prof to react; the hunter knocked him aside as it flitted straight for Mags.

Jules, knife in hand, took an almost-blind leap into the hunter's path, startling it just enough to sink the knife into its back. It should've been a superficial wound, but the hunter stopped and let out an ear-splitting howl as the flesh around the blade began to boil and hiss. He collapsed onto the roof, spasming, and didn't get back up.

"Shit," Jules panted, "fuckin . . . thanks, Millie."

Something struck her in the back and she went down to find the fifth hunter kneeling over her, its canines bared, its face twisted into a sneer of hatred. It grabbed her with both hands and slammed her head into the roof, and she heard something pop and saw stars.

As the others rushed forward to help her, a sixth figure stepped through the door, strolling calmly up to the two of them. Coming up alongside them, he drew a revolver from his belt and, seeming unhurried and almost bored, casually shot the hunter in the head, sending it sprawling onto the roof next to the other. He emptied his revolver into the two hunters' heads, dropped it at his feet, and raised his hands up over his head, palms out.

Jules, groaning, blinked until her vision cleared, and she found herself staring up at a short, lithe man wearing a dark green over-coat and a wide, round green hat. He had shoulder-length black hair and a long black mustache, and he was grinning from hear to ear like a boy who'd just been caught misbehaving.

"Oh, no way," she muttered. "Oh, no fucking way."

The stranger looked down at her, winked one of his empty black eyes, and said, "I suppose that means that no introductions will be necessary."

Becky had spent the hour trudging in front of Barns down the high-way, her hand never leaving the radio, and when it crackled three times she snatched it up to her mouth and barked, "What's up? You guys okay?"

"Good evening, dearest," came an old, familiar voice. "I gather that you are one step ahead of me, as always."

Becky stood in stunned silence for a long moment. After a while, her face broke into a smile and, laughing, she replied, "Oh, you are an absolute motherfucker, you know that, right?"

[17]

THE MAN IN THE HIGH CASTLE

JOHN FELT COLD.

The anesthetic wearing off didn't bring lucidity. He became aware—acutely so—of the horrible pain in his leg, and a new pain in his arm, but he continued to drift in and out of consciousness. He felt weak, too weak to move, and dizzy, and so terribly, terribly cold. At times, when the pain in his arm grew worse, it would snap him back to reality, and he was aware of being in the same bed, in the same room, only surrounded by voices. He knew one of them as Todd—*fucking Todd*—but the others were strange, and sometimes the strange voices would ask questions, and, automatically, he would answer their questions in a weak voice that it hurt him to hear coming from his own mouth.

"You do good work," one of the strange voices said, a woman's voice. He was in such terrible shape when Ulfkessel brought him here, I thought that this was all a waste of time."

"All in a day's work, boss," Todd said. "I can't take all the credit, though; the big guy's a real hardass. You could run this guy over with a truck."

"Indeed; he is quite the specimen. But I suppose some

strengths cannot be so easily measured." A sad sigh. "Such a waste."

"Well, not a complete waste."

The woman laughed. "Quite right. By the way, how does he look now, after everything?"

"Oh, we jacked him up pretty good; he's been in shock ever since we stopped, and I wouldn't want to get anything else out today. But the big guy's a tough sumbitch; we get some food in him and let him get some sleep and he'll be good to go."

"Very good. And this report we managed to coax out of him is . . . fascinating. I must go file this, and then, I think, I will make a few calls. Keep up the good work, doctor."

"All in a day's work, boss. You have a good night!"

The sound of boots clapping across concrete as someone walked away, and then, silence.

John took a few slow, deep breaths and felt sense return to his mind, felt his heart stop racing and his limbs relax. He clenched his right hand into a fist, a familiar motion, and it felt good, made him feel more in control. When he clenched his left hand, though, it sent a white-hot lance of pain from his wrist up to his shoulder, and he swore. He opened his eyes to see Todd turning toward him.

"Oh, hey there, big guy," the corpsman said.

Tomassi glared at him and growled, "Aw, fuck you."

"Nice to see you back in the land of the living. Well, figuratively speaking."

"Suck my cock."

"Nah, you'd enjoy it too much. I know way too much about your appetites."

"What the fuck . . . what the fuck did you do to me?"

"Just took a couple donations is all. And you really are a tough son of a bitch; I managed to get four whole pints out of you before you went into shock. Your old man a bear or something?"

At that, Tomassi looked over at his left arm and saw that it had been crudely bandaged and sported a patchwork of sickening black bruises. He tried to make a fist again, failed again, and groaned, "What . . . what the fuck?"

"Hey, man, it's not that big a deal. Everybody does it. That's just the price of admission around here. You pay your dues and take your licks a little while before you can go sit at the big kids' table. All completely routine."

When Tomassi looked up again, Todd's expression had shifted from an easygoing smile back to his soulless, rictus grin, and the corpsman went on: "You though, you're special. Most of the new guys are on lunch detail for a couple weeks, maybe a month at the most before they get to go upstairs, but you? You're a test case. They wanna see how long I can keep you alive before the hypoxemia causes terminal organ failure."

Tomassi stared at him in disbelief. Todd laughed and added, "I know all about you now, big guy. The major was pretty skint on the details when he dropped you off the other day, but you sang like a fucking canary as soon as the delirium kicked in, especially with Frau Mahler asking the questions. Ain't she a piece of work? Anyways, this is what happens when you're a degenerate and a failure."

John's face contorted with rage, and he growled, "I'm gonna fucking erase your ass, you little faggot."

"Oh, are you? That's rich, coming from a guy who can't lift his head up. Double rich, coming from a degenerate who started crying about his pretty little boyfriend first thing when he woke up."

"The fuck did you just say?"

"I already told you, man, you got real talkative when you started to go under. Like, real talkative. He's dead, by the way. Or if he's not yet then he will be soon. Once the major got back, they sent out a team of real soldiers to do what you couldn't. Is that what does it for you, captain? Pretty boys in black dresses?"

"I swear to Jesus fucking Christ and the Virgin fucking Mary that I am gonna rip your head off and fuck your neck."

"Yeah, yeah, keep talking. No, really, this is the most fun I've had all year." And Todd winked at him, and started to roll up his shirtsleeve, revealing a sleeve of stick-and-poke tattoos ending with a grinning death's-head clutching a dagger just below his left elbow, wreathed in their words: "*Non mi interessa davvero.*" *I really don't care.*

"See," Todd said, "I know people like you. My whole life—my whole life—I been taking shit from brainless meatheads exactly like you. You think being big and tall and getting all the pussy means you get to kick ol' Todd around, huh? Well, shit rolls downhill, brother, and guess who's on top of the heap for now? Honestly, man, it's funny as fuck that you think you're gonna threaten me when you can't even take out a squad of reds without getting your entire shit wrecked. But I guess we shoulda expected that from you. Why don't you go cry to your little ladyboy about it? Oh, yeah, that's right; that'd be a bit difficult."

Tomassi was beyond words, his powerlessness making his rage all the more acute, and he snarled like a kicked dog. Todd, leering at him, said, "Let me tell you how this is gonna go, big guy. I give you a month, maybe a month and a half if you're really stubborn; I'm damned good, but ol' Todd's not a miracle worker, he's just a corpsman. And you are going to feel yourself dying, in every breath you take, for every second of every day until you finally do. And, brother, I'm going to enjoy every little bit of this. Y'know what that is, my man? That's the price of failure."

The probates were bringing up all manner of treasures to lay at their leader's feet.

The facility sat on top of a maze of warrens, miles of service tunnels, magazines, and God knew what else; even after being an inmate, staff member, occasional resident of the facility off and on for almost three centuries, Otto still didn't know the half of what was down there. It made good work for the men from Ohio, keeping them busy in between shifts filling his army's field rations. As his army spent its nights on the surface making ready for war, the probates spent theirs beneath the earth, cataloging and drawing forth his army's many armaments.

And what a sight it was. They had found for him all of the typical things one might expect to see in an American magazine, the explosives and Armalite rifles and squad machine guns, but they also brought many more exotic, more interesting things. His army salivated at the vials of polonium, at the sarin gas canisters, at the thorium explosives. At the monstrously heavy, lead-lined crates of artillery shells marked with radiation symbols and words like "Sub-Kiloton Yield."

And they found other weapons as well, these even more grimly beautiful, the sealed cases marked in bright red with the broken triskelion denoting a biological hazard. These treasures, lovely though they were, would stay at their rest beneath the earth . . . for now.

Every night his army and its armament grew. Every night the shining beacon of his Citadel attracted more unaligned hunters out of the wasteland, and every night more of the men from Ohio showed themselves worthy to ascend into its ranks, and Oberst-Gruppenfuhrer Otto von Hochulf watched it all with an eager, hungry grin. Behind his walls, in his very hands, he now had an army worthy of the name, now had a weapon with which to strike out, to avenge the old disgraces, to purge away the filth yet corrupting the world. He had recovered so many of his old *Kameraden-in-Waffen*, all of them eager to taste victory again, and had found so many of the new generation who were more than ready for the task that destiny had laid before them.

It was a matter of days now. Soon, so terribly soon, his gates would open and his terrible, beautiful army would march out to bathe the wasteland in its long-overdue baptism of blood and fire. It would begin in the mountains; he from the east and the Falangists from the north would subdue their foes by their iron and blood and burn away the last remnant of the very same disease that had once trampled and profaned the Volk's last great flowering of hope. And after his revenge, so long overdue, well, the possibilities were endless, for on that night the whole of the world would be helpless at their feet.

And the men in Ohio . . . For the most part, his allies would remember their place, would kneel in proper awe of him and his ascendant army. Some of them, some of the men in Columbus, the Catholic Falange who had the audacity to name themselves *Oberkommando,* some of them were a bit too proud for his liking. But that was nothing. If they made trouble, well, *die Nacht die langen Messer wird bald wiederkommen.*

Otto sat in his personal quarters, high in the tower looming over the walls, with a satisfied smile on his face as he contemplated his imminent campaign and the wonder and horror of it all. He was taking a quick rest from reviewing the readiness reports and had just lit his pipe when a knock at the door interrupted him.

"Ach, who is it now?" he grumbled.

"It's Mahler, Commander," came a woman's voice, a sing-song voice with a thick Austrian accent. "I won't waste your time; I only have a small request."

He rolled his soulless, black eyes. "Come in, then."

A tall, fair hunter in a black uniform bearing a major's insignia stepped into the room and stood ramrod-straight in front of him, clutching a few pages of handwritten notes in her left hand. Upon actually seeing her, Otto smiled, and he puffed his pipe and asked, "What is it you need, Jana?"

"Commander," she said, "I received a report from one of the Blacklanders which piqued my curiosity into one of their camp programs, and I would like to speak to one of the technicians involved. I request your permission to use our direct line to Columbus."

"That does not sound urgent," Otto grumbled. "But . . . ach, no-one is using that channel at the moment. Go ahead, Jana."

"Yes, sir. Thank you, sir."

He waved her away, and when she was out of his presence and with a closed door between them, her eyes narrowed with malicious mirth as she tried to suppress a giggle. She held Otto in great respect and reverence, had for almost three hundred years, and she never liked lying to him, but he might not have granted her request otherwise, and the jape she'd been thinking of since she'd finished talking to Tomassi was just too rich to pass up. A sadistic smile spread itself across her face as she made her way up the stairs to the radio room at the top of the tower.

———

Roland didn't like sleeping in his office, but at times either duty or propriety demanded it of him, as a head of state. Tonight's concern was the latter. He was the Commander and could do as he pleased, and his long-time mistress was a vice that everyone knew better than to gossip about, but still, he thought, the Commander should keep up appearances.

When a loud knock came at the door and the two of them shot awake, he shook off his sleep and growled, "Just a moment! And I certainly hope that this is a matter of life or fucking death!"

"Ignore them, darling," his companion whispered, pouting, her voice slurred with sleep. "You need your rest."

"It's not that easy, Doc," he whispered back, buttoning up his black campaign shirt and straightening his hair. "They all know better than to bother me like this; it probably is a matter of life and death."

Once dressed, he opened the door a crack to see a terrified and trembling signalman standing before it at rapt attention. Roland slipped out of the crack and shut the door discreetly behind him and, towering over the signalman, he sighed and growled, "Please do tell me what could possibly be so important that you've come knocking on my office door at three o'clock in the goddamn morning."

"Sir," the signalman said, "I'm sorry to disturb you, sir, but someone from Baltimore just came on the horn. One of them wants to speak to you, sir."

Roland sighed again. "I might've guessed that that's who would be busy at three o'clock in the goddamn fucking morning. Lead the way, soldier."

And, sighing herself, Natasha fell back asleep to the rhythm of jackboots marching off down the hallway. Only a few minutes passed, though, before the door opened again and her Commander slipped back into his office. He walked up to her, gave her a kick in the shoulder, and barked, "Get up. This one didn't want to talk to me. This one asked me to come get you."

"Me? Oh, goodness! Whyever for?"

"I don't know, I didn't ask. But you'd better hurry up, they tend to get all pissy if you keep them waiting. And don't come back here. When they're done with you, leave through the back exit and go back across the street."

"Yes, sir. Of course, sir."

"Yeah, yeah. I'll send for you when I want you again. Now get out."

She gave him a peck on the cheek before leaving and heading off down the hall.

Mahler sat at the desk in the radio room eagerly counting the seconds, the sadistic smile still plastered across her face. After what felt like ages, an entirely-too-nice sing-song voice came across the wire, saying, "This is Corpsman-Major Natasha Wenden. How may I help you?"

"Good evening, *Frau Kapo*," she replied. "I am *Kriminalrat*

Jana Mahler. I'm terribly sorry to call so late, but you know what sort of hours we keep."

A satisfyingly awkward pause, then, "Oh, it's no trouble at all, dear. How may I be of service?"

"*Frau Kapo*, I've heard of your work in developing medical treatment for antisocial behavior, and just tonight I came across some information that I thought might be of interest to you. I've just finished speaking with a Captain Jonathan Tomassi; I believe you know him."

"Tomassi, Jonathan . . . Well, I wouldn't say I know him, but the captain and I have spoken before, yes."

"Well, I managed to extract a very fascinating story from him. You might know another name: Julia Binachi?"

A long, sad sigh. "Poor Julia. Yes, she was one of my girls. Textbook secondary transsexual, autogynophile, transvestic fetishist. We had intended for her to be a test case in the treatment of antisocial behavior, but she just would not conform to expectations, the poor thing. Such a shame. Why do you ask about her?"

"Because, *Frau Kapo*, the good captain informed of this story's fantastic conclusion. Perhaps you'd like to know that your problem child survived her escape attempt."

Another pause, then: "But . . . but that's impossible."

"I do not know the particulars, but it is very possible. And after that, it would seem she defected to the Bolshevists. She was last seen taking part in the murder of an entire squad of your stormtroopers."

A sharp intake of breath came over the wire, and Mahler savored it before going on: "But she is dead now. Or, if not yet, then she will be momentarily. Nothing for you to worry about; we've taken care of what you couldn't."

After a long beat, Tasha said, "I'm afraid I don't understand. Why are you telling me all this?"

"Oh, very simple," Mahler laughed. "To hurt you."

". . . what?"

"You are a disgusting, hideous abomination, and when I received this information I thought it would be good sport to remind you that you are a failure as well."

There was silence on the other end, and Mahler laughed again and said, "And you can't put on a face and pretend it didn't work; you forget who you're speaking to. I can hear your heart racing, can hear the trembling in your breath. Now, let me guess . . . he's fucking you, *ja?*"

More silence, but to Jana's ears the beat of her heart was answer enough. She went on: "Our records on your adorable little Falange are incomplete, but I know that Rain's old operating group included a medical corpsman, a Nicodemus Wenden. Is that it, then? He protects you because you've been consistently amusing to him? That is all you can ever hope to be, you know."

That elicited an audible gasp. Mahler pounded her fist on the desk in sadistic mirth as she concluded: "Ach, it's worse than I thought! You *love* him! Ach, you damned fool. But that is all I wanted from you, you living abomination, you walking, talking obscenity. Now that I have had my little fun, perhaps you should return to your rest; you have another long, hard day of putting on a costume and pretending to be something you can never be ahead of you."

After another long beat, the too-polite sing-song voice said, "Yes, thank you, *Kriminalrat*. Have a lovely evening." And the radio went silent.

Four hundred miles to the northwest, in front of another communications desk, the Corpsman-Major sat staring into the middle distance. Her face ached as her perpetual smile twitched around its edges, and a barrage of thoughts and emotions threatened to flood into her mind. She, doctor and soldier, ever-loyal, refused to allow any of them, reminding herself as she often did that to serve the state was to serve God. She merely huffed as she stood up, and she muttered into the darkness, "Well, she was certainly *rude.*"

As she left, her sensible heels clicking across the floor, one thought managed to pierce her defenses, and it echoed around in her mind like a warning bell she would never heed: *"Oh, she has no right to speak to me that way!"* it said. *"That is how we speak to the others. I, however, have been good."*

[18]

ON THE RUN

THE OTHERS HAD STOPPED SHORT AT THE APPEARANCE OF THE stranger, but not Mags. Lukash turned to her and started to speak, but she ignored him, dropping to her knees and sliding to a stop next to Jules.

"Oh, fuck," she muttered, her eyes locked on the blood pooling under Jules' head. "Honey, are you okay? How do you feel?"

"Oh, I feel fucking great," Jules groaned. "I feel like I just ate a gallon of Nana's gelatto and then got my dick sucked. How the fuck do you think I feel, you stupid bitch? Jesus fucking Christ. *Ah, cazzo la Vergine Maria! Fanculo ai santi!*"

"What's your name, honey?"

"I'm Julia fucking Binachi, dumbest woman alive."

"Where were you born?"

"Fuckin . . . Somerset, Ohio, the asshole of the universe."

"Do you know where you are?"

"Fuck no! I'm on top of a JC fucking Penny in the middle of bumblefuck nowhere!"

"Okay, okay," Mags panted, "I think you're okay." She turned to the others and shouted, "Hey, does anybody got a flashlight?"

"No lights," Connor barked. "That'll draw God-knows-what else right to us."

Mags fixed him with a withering glare. "Could someone please hand me a flashlight so that I can make sure my girlfriend isn't bleeding inside of her brain, please?"

Prof handed her a flashlight, and she looked back at Jules and said, "Honey, I'm sorry about this."

Jules scrunched up her face in anticipation. "Do what you gotta do, sug."

Mags shined the light into her face and examined both of her eyes, prompted her to follow the light with them, and at last announced, "Alright, I think you're okay. Looks like you're okay."

"Oh, I don't know if I'd go that far," Jules winced, struggling up to her feet. "Bastard split my scalp wide the fuck open and now there's blood all over my favorite fucking shirt."

Mags threw her arms around her and she added, "Aw, great, now I'm getting blood all over my favorite girlfriend, too."

Lukash cleared his throat. When everyone turned to look at him, he announced, "Well, I am glad to see that everyone is alright, and I'm sure that you have lots of questions for me, but I'm afraid that time has gotten away from me. We should get moving, and quickly, if we wish to make the final way station before sunrise."

Prof started to speak, but before he could Connor stormed over and demanded, "Okay, what the fuck?"

The hunter gave him a warm, friendly smile. "Your group has made far better time than I anticipated. My plan, you see, was to come here tonight to meet with my lovely assistant—I assume, based on the fact that I am not dead, that she's told you all about me—and to make plans for our final approach when you lot arrived the following evening, but it seems that everyone is one step ahead of me. Everyone except for dear Otto, of course, but that is to be expected. Now, given the gravity of our situation— time is of the essence, I am afraid—and given mine and Becky's travel restrictions, I suggest that you fine people should break your camp and head east with all speed. We can make our plans in the morning."

Everyone stared at him. Connor growled, "Now listen, buddy, I do not know who the fuck you think you are--"

"Oh, how rude of me! I had thought that my reputation would precede me. I am *Landsritter* Wolfgang Kristops Lichtmann von Lukash, and I believe we share a common enemy. Now, I am aware that this is highly irregular, but you must understand that we are very nearly out of time, and--"

"No. You do not fuckin get to just show up and start tellin us what we ought to do. If you've got some fuckin big ideas, you can slow right the hell down and make a case and maybe we'll like it and maybe we won't, but either fuckin way we do shit by consensus 'round here."

Lukash gave a patient nod. "Of course, of course, of course. I can tell from your rugged look and bearing that you are a man who knows how such work is done. Everyone, please do gather around, for as I've said, time is running short."

The others shared dubious looks back and forth as they walked over to the doorway and stood in a semicircle around Lukash, who cleared his throat again and said, "I will try to keep this brief. I'm sure that you all know your own work perfectly well, and I trust that Becky gave you at least some summary of mine. Is that correct?"

"Yeah," Mags said. "She told us you've got your own beef with the people running the Citadel, or Marion Proving Ground, or whatever, and that you know what's inside it a lot better than we do."

"Ach, excellent. Well, as you know, my associates and I have been keeping an eye on my erstwhile companion as well as we've been able, and to that end I had one or two of my people embedded in his staff. Just a few days ago, I received a report from them which was . . . chilling. Things have gotten well out of hand and are moving much faster than any of us anticipated. Otto is using that place to build an army, a terrible army, and he is more than ready to use it. Thanks to all of the many goodies that our American friends were keeping hidden in their little warren, his army is perhaps better equipped than any now on Earth, and according to our intelligence his plan is to launch a joint strike against your little social experiment in Kentucky, he from the east and your friends in Columbus from the north. As for when this will happen . . . my friends, we have days. Perhaps a week at the most, but probably far less than that, to bring this business to its conclusion."

Mags was the first one to speak. She met Lukash's eyes and snapped, "Are you fucking serious?"

"On my honor, my family, and my name."

She spun on her heels to face Prof. "I need one of your radios."

"Mags, we're too far out," he said, giving her a sad shake of his head. "You'd be damned lucky just to raise Freeside."

"*Give me a fucking radio, old man!*"

With a sigh, he took one of the two-ways off of his pack and handed it to her. She took a few steps away, tuning it with care, and barked, "All call signs, all call signs, this is Crow 12. Commo check. Over."

Silence. With an edge of panic in her voice, she shouted, "All call signs, all call signs, can anybody fucking hear me? Over."

Amidst crackling static, a few garbled words struggled to come through: ". . . 12, this . . . End . . . lot of fuzz, over."

"Bad copy, bad copy, please repeat, over."

". . . Land's End . . . interference . . . can't really . . ."

She repeated herself and received only silence. She dropped the radio at her feet, then sank to her knees, cradling her head in her hands. Jules was the first to reach her, muttering, "Hey, what's going on, sugar?"

"We're fucked is what's going on. It's over. It's all over."

"I'm not following. What's over?"

"Everything! The whole fucking Republic, the entire goddamn

revolution! You . . . you know why we haven't ever taken the war north in all this time?"

"Uh, no, actually. That was always a pretty big mystery."

"Because we fucking can't! We have enough manpower to maintain the stalemate, and that's *it*. We could repel one season of campaigns, maybe even launch reprisals, but two at once? *Two at once?* I was never worried about that because that was never supposed to be a fucking possibility! Hell, this dumbass mission was supposed to be the thing that would finally give us our edge. Well, *fuck me*, I guess!"

No-one spoke. Mags gave Jules a sad smile and said, "I was gonna introduce you to my mama. I was gonna have you live with us. And I . . . I never did get to see your roses before we left, did I?"

Jules laid a hand on her shoulder, but before she could speak Mags felt a hand fall onto her other shoulder, icy cold and deceptively strong, and Lukash asked, "*Yidna*, what is the antidote to despair?"

Mags answered automatically, like completing a catechism: "The antidote to despair is action."

"Good girl. Now, I like to think myself a good judge of people, and I can tell from looking at you that you have iron in your spine, that you are a one-foot-in-front-of-the-other sort of person, and I think that if the worst did come that you would prefer to face it on your feet. Have I read you correctly?"

"I'd say so, yeah."

"Well, then, allow me to temper my bad news with a bit of desperate hope. If we take decisive action, and if we begin at once, then our precious few days should be more than enough time to prevent Otto's plans from coming to fruition."

Mags digested his words for a moment, then looked up into his empty black eyes and asked, "So, *Lichtmann*, huh?"

"*Ja*. My dear mother's family name. May her memory be a blessing."

She extended her hand, and as he grabbed her wrist and pulled her up to her feet, she smirked and said, "Talk about *yiddisher mazel*, eh?"

"Indeed, *yidna*."

"I'm sold. I'm in. Let's do it."

And Jules stood up with her, gripped her shoulder, and said, "And whatever the plan is, I go where she goes."

The hunter nodded his approval. "Excellent. Anyone else?"

TJ was the next to speak: "Well, bud, from all of that, it kinda sounds like we're bent over a barrel and you're the only game in town, but I am gonna need a bit of a harder sell than that. I gather you're in a hurry to get the ball rolling, so maybe we dot all the t's and cross all the i's a little bit down the road, but let's start with what the hell step 2 is. You said something about wanting us to break camp and get moving?"

"That would be my suggestion, yes. This little visit from our friends that I walked into tells me that your location has been compromised, and in any event I think it a good idea to keep our forces consolidated so close to the endgame. If we begin moving right away, I can easily reach our rendezvous with the other two before sunrise, and you lot before mid-morning. From there, we may plan our terminal approach."

TJ rolled their eyes. "Y'know, this sounds like a real fucking bad idea, but I would kinda like to make it through this whole shit alive, and I'd also kinda like to have a home to go back to. I'll do it, I guess, but if we all get killed I am gonna say I told you so."

"Well, I ain't fuckin doin it," Connor growled. "That is goddamn suicide. Hell, it's worse."

"My friend," Lukash said, "I am afraid that there is no choice. As I said, in a few days--"

"Oh, no, I got that part. That ain't the part I got a problem with. The part I don't like is the part where you expect me to go on a fuckin quick-march through the fuckin wasteland in the middle of the fuckin night. You ever heard of roamers? Dogs? Or more creepy fuckers like you?"

Lukash nodded toward the pair of fallen hunters before the door. "I believe that our two friends there should serve as evidence that we make very competent advance scouts. Moreover, though the roamers and the more mundane dangers are still present, I think it's safe to say that the more dangerous sort are firmly under the lash. Those not in Otto's employ will have long since moved off to find less volatile hunting grounds, and these five will not be missed for some hours yet. That you posed any challenge to them at all will be quite the surprise. That you managed to best them completely will be unprecedented."

Connor was silent for a long moment, his face cycling through a series of concerned or unhappy expressions as the logic of Lukash's words struggled against a lifetime of received wisdom and personal experience. After a while, he grumbled, "Y'know what? Fuck it. Reckon I gotta die sometime."

Throughout their exchange, Prof had been giving Mags a stern look, a look that she recognized and knew she was supposed to draw some lesson from but couldn't quite parse. When Connor at last grumbled his agreement, the old man nodded and declared, "Well, I believe we've reached consensus."

"You have no concerns of your own, my friend?" Lukash asked.

"Oh, I had quite the grocery list of them when we began, but they've more or less been addressed. See, this is why I prefer to be last in the queue during these sorts of discussions."

The gunplay had not gone unnoticed.

As soon as the group was assembled on the street in front of the department store, they could hear a chorus of painful keening growing in the southeast, coming closer, and could smell a foul stench on the wind. Connor stepped out to the front of the group, his eyes wide with unease, and said, Alright, if we want this bullshit to work, we are gonna have to move like we got someplace to be.

258 / NATALIE IRONSIDE

It'll be a quick-march through the woods till we hit the 70, and once w'ere on the 70, we're gonna run. Everybody up for that?"

They nodded, and there came another, fresh chorus of moaning, this one from the west, and Connor shuddered and muttered, "We got about four hours till sunrise. Sunrise won't stop 'em, but it'll calm 'em down a bit. Long as we stay ahead of 'em till we reach the highway, we might just be alright. We ready to move out?"

Lukash stepped forward, a perfect image of the past in his green cloak with his Mauser over his shoulder. "If I encounter anything noteworthy," he said, "I will be ahead to warn you of it, but I do not think that I will. Godspeed, my friends, and I look forward to seeing you all again in a few hours."

Connor clapped him on the shoulder and he took off into the northeast at a sprint, disappearing into the darkness between the trees. The others followed, picking their way through the darkness as quickly as they could, Connor taking the lead and Prof the rear as they filled through the trees. They made decent time, moving at a quick march, but as they walked they heard the moaning grow louder, followed by the sound of shuffling feet, and, as they made their way deeper into the forest, the baying of dogs far away.

"Keep the line tight," Connor growled. "Whatever you do, do not fucking fall behind."

The outlines of buildings loomed in the shadows and the oppressive darkness as they picked their way through the forest, the sounds of pursuit always close behind, until a few hours later they broke out onto the greenway of the crumbling Interstate bathed in moonlight and Connor motioned for them to halt and circle up. He looked over the group, panting and drenched in sweat, and whispered, "Alright, let's take 5. Stretch, drink some water, all that shit. Enjoy it, 'cause when we pick it up again, we're running."

They all nodded, grateful. Mags checked to make sure the wind was still coming from the southeast, then hunkered down close to the cracked pavement and lit a cigarette. Connor considered her for a moment, then walked a few feet away and did the same.

While they rested, Prof knelt down beside her and whispered, "Magnolia . . . we should talk."

She gave him a concerned look. "Uh, sure. What's up?"

"May I be completely blunt with you?"

"Yeah, of course. Always."

"The way you handled things with Connor earlier was unacceptable and, quite frankly, disappointing."

Mags stared at him in disbelief, and she started to speak, but checked herself, bit her lower lip, and motioned for him to continue.

"I know that you have a pithy little quote about trains and cliffs on the tip of your tongue, but you're not quite considering the particulars of our situation, or the dynamics of the group. For one . . . . Believe me, I know that the way the Freesiders do things is inefficient and infuriating, but it is the way they do things and good luck talking them out of it. That Lukash fellow picked it up right away; you can't just order them to do things. You have to make a case."

She chewed her lip harder and nodded.

"And for another . . . I told you that one of the people we lost last time was Connor's wife and one of my best friends. Did I tell you how Tanya died?"

"Nah."

"That man Otto—the man we're on our way to see—ripped her head off while we watched. If Connor is a bit overly cautious, he has his reasons, and it's safe to say that I share them, and it has nothing to do with cowardice."

Mags was silent for a long moment. At last, she sighed, and rolled her eyes, and Prof thought that she was about to argue in her defense, but instead she reached out and squeezed his shoulder and said, "Thanks, old man."

Before he could respond, she'd stood up and started walking over towards Connor, where she knelt down next to him, sighed, and whispered, "Uh . . . hey."

"The fuck do you want?"

"I owe you an apology. On the roof earlier . . . well, I fucked up. You're the expert here, not me, and I guess I let that get away from me. I'm sorry."

Connor considered her in silence for a while, then squeezed her shoulder and said, "Yeah, you sure did. But y'know what?"

"What?"

"Well, you turned out to be onto something. Just figure out how to talk to people like they're fuckin people, alright?"

"I will. Are we square?"

"You ever call me a coward again and I'll fuckin kill you."

"I'd expect nothing less."

"Then we're square."

And he stood up, stretched, and hissed, "Alright, break time's over. Let's get ready to roll."

Everyone got their feet, shuddering at how close the sounds of pursuit had grown, and as they grouped together, Mags sidled up next to Jules and took her hand and whispered, "Hey, honey, I, uh . . . When we stop for the day, you think I could talk to you about some stuff?"

"Of course, sug. What's wrong?"

"Nothing, nothing. Well . . . nothing anybody did. I just . . . I've got some stuff on my mind and I'd like to borrow you for a little while. If that's okay."

"Of course. That's what we do around here, right?"

"Yeah."

Connor whistled, and as everyone looked over at him, he barked, "Alright, y'all, time to run!"

And they ran, just as groups of dark human figures began to emerge from the trees, shambling toward them with keening voices and withered, outstretched hands.

The pursuit stumbled blindly after them, the roamers stumbling over every root and crack and hole, their minds consumed with a singular purpose, oblivious to their surroundings, and the runners managed to keep a comfortable difference between them, though one thought burned in the back of everyone's mind: *We'll get tired. They won't.*

The group managed to keep the pace for an hour before TJ and then Prof began to lag behind. Though they could still hear the noise of pursuit, they'd made enough distance that they could no longer see the shambling human figures in the darkness, and Connor waved them onto the span of an overpass for a quick rest. He lit a cigarette as he leaned, panting, against the guardrail, all thoughts of stealth left behind.

"How much . . . fucking . . . farther?" Prof gasped, stopping next to Connor and clutching his knees.

"Ain't got a map in front of me," Connor panted, "but I reckon about seven or eight miles."

"Oh, goddamn shit. Buddy, I don't think I can keep this up for eight miles. I feel like I'm gonna have a fucking heart attack. God, wouldn't that be a stupid way to die?"

"Sun's gonna be up in an hour. Won't stop 'em, but it'll calm 'em down, scatter 'em a bit. You got another hour in you?"

"Do I have a choice?"

"Nope."

Coming up beside them, Mags doffed her rucksack and gasped, "Listen . . . I just got a real bad idea."

Connor smirked. "We love bad ideas around here, red. Hit me with it."

"Well . . . I was thinking about all the stuff I got in my bag of bones here."

"Uh-huh."

"Well, we're on this fuckin . . . bridge . . ."

"Uh-huh."

"Back in Freeside, when we were getting kits together . . . y'all gave me a spool of det cord and four pounds of Semtex."

Connor stared at her, blinking a few times, as the sounds of keening voices and shuffling feet grew closer, and he said, "Alright, girl scout, I'ma need you to take a deep breath and tell me exactly what it is you're tryna say."

"Well, those things are too fuckin stupid to notice a whole in the ground if it's right in front of them, right?"

"Yeah, but--"

"This bridge is so old and shitty, you'd probably only need about half a pound to make one real motherfucker of a hole. Hell, find a big enough crack to stuff it in and I bet it would widen it across the entire span."

Connor blinked a few more times. "Mags, do you fuckin remember how we got into this mess? Remember about bright lights and big loud noises in the exclusion zone?"

"Sweetheart, I'm pretty sure that that ship has fuckin sailed already. And either way, there's no chance we can keep up this pace the whole rest of the night. You know that, right?"

"Yeah. Yeah, I know it. Just . . you sure you know what you're doin with that crap?"

"Hell yeah. I mean, I ain't no engineer, but this ain't exactly my first time."

"Alright. Fuck it. Go for it."

"Yrah. You start herding people onto the embankment across the bridge. I'll be right behind y'all. How much time you think we've got?"

Connor squinted at the far end of the bridge in the direction they'd come from, listened to the growing chorus of moaning and shuffling, and declared, "You got two minutes."

Mags was already on her knees, rooting around her rucksack and coming up with a spool of green wire, a spool of yellow wire, and a brick wrapped in oily brown paper. She unwrapped the brick, drew her combat knife, and started to slice off a chunk of it, declaring, "Oh, hell, that's plenty of time. I'll see y'all in one."

The group had snugly hunkered down on the far side of the embankment when they saw Mags running toward her, unspooling something over her shoulder. When she reached them, she dropped to the ground, cut the wire, and snapped, "Alright, everybody ready?"

A chorus of solemn nods.

"Yrah. I couldn't measure exactly, but when I touch off this fuse we're gonna have about thirty seconds, give or take. Then the fuse hits the det cord, the det cord hits the plastic, and then there's gonna be a great big fuck-off explosion and a little earthquake. So when I say 'now', everybody hit the dirt, facedown, feet toward the bridge, hands over your ears, mouths open. Y'all tracking?"

"Wait, how come our mouths gotta be open?" TJ asked.

"So the air inside your head has someplace to go besides out through your eardrums. Everybody follow? Company is real fuckin close."

They nodded their assent.

"When this pops off, it is gonna sound the dinner bell for every roamer in a big wide radius, so we are gonna have to hop back up and run, but if we're lucky they'll be so worried about this spot that they won't pay us too much mind, and anyways it's gonna go a long way towards wagging the tail we've already got. Okay . . . *NOW!*"

The group threw themselves to the ground as Mags lit the end of her fuse and then followed them. For a very long thirty seconds, they lay on the cool, dark earth, feeling it vibrate under them as more and more roamers—a few hundred, at least, by then—shambled onto the bridge, moving ever closer. Then, in a flash, the earth heaved underneath them, and the sky reared back to sock each one in the head, and for an instant all of existence was replaced with a terrible, ear-splitting roar. It stopped as soon as it began, and they lay covering their heads as pebbles and dust and another, less wholesome substance peppered their backs and the ringing in their ears died away to be replaced by the sickening *creak* and *crack* of the overpass settling around its new, gaping wound.

"Alright," Mags barked, pulling herself to her shaking feet, "sound off. Who's not dead?"

The group rose up to join her, and they looked behind them; they couldn't discern the state of the overpass from over the embankment, but the horde of roamers that had been closing in on them moments before seemed far less intimidating now. A few shadowy humanoid figures were pulling themselves back to their feet, but not many. Not very many at all.

Only a few seconds passed, however, before the still night air was filled again by a doubled, trebled chorus of moaning, coming from all directions at once.

"Alright, alright," Connor growled, "fireworks show's over and we still got 45 minutes till sun-up. Time to run!"

Barns, Becky, and Lukash had sheltered from the sun within the sanctuary of what had once been a church just off of the Interstate, catching up with each other as they awaited their companions. Prof had radioed in at sunrise to let them know they'd survived the night, but it was still a few long hours before the five of them came shambling into the knave, filthy, panting, and exhausted. Luaksh sprung up at once to greet them, but Connor held up a hand in the dark and barked, "After lunch."

"I knew you all would make it," the hunter said with an approving smile. "Now that you are here--"

"Listen, buddy, I been on . . . a quick march . . . and a running fight . . . since after goddamn midnight. We can talk *after lunch.*"

"Ah, yes, of course. I forget how we are different sometimes. Yes, take all the time you need."

The group doffed their rucksacks, and one by one they settled down on the floor, save for the two women. Mags, a pinched and pained expression on her face, squeezed Jules' shoulder and gestured to the door behind the sanctuary, leading to the sacristy.

When they were alone together, they stood staring silently at each other for several minutes as Mags chewed her lower lip, trying to find her words.

Jules lit a cigarette, offered the pack to her, and asked, "So what's this all about, sugar?"

"I . . . I kinda wanted to talk to you about some stuff."

"Uh-huh."

"I . . . do you remember the other day, when we talked about how you don't like to be fussed over?"

"Yeah. Sugar, where are you going with this?"

"Last night I started thinking about some stuff, and I . . . I finally figured out why seeing you and Becky process stuff was making me so jealous."

"Oh, boy. Listen, sug, I'm . . . still not really sure what you're trying to get at, but I promise you can tell me anything. I--"

Mags threw her arms around her and buried her face in Jules' chest. Before Jules could respond, she began to cry, and the crying became sobbing, weeping. Jules held her tight and stroked her hair, not saying anything, until at last Mags sobbed, "I just . . . I just miss her so fucking much . . ."

"Who do you miss, sugar?"

"She was . . . fuck, she was only six years old . . . We were both just little kids . . ."

"Aw, fuck. You're talking about your sister, ain't you?"

Mags sobbed harder, her body shaking with the effort of it. "I . . . I was her big brother! I was supposed to take care of her, and she . . . she . . ."

"Sugar, you were like 11; there was nothing you coulda done different."

"I was her big brother! And I just woke up one morning, and she was gone, and . . . and . . ."

Jules held her tight as they sank to the floor together. Mags shook and sobbed without words for a while, then took a few deep breaths and muttered, "And Dad . . . Dad was such a big guy . . . He was even taller than me, if you can believe that. But by the end of it, he was nothing; just a skeleton lying there in the bed, too sick to move, coughing up blood. And just like with Maggie, I . . . I went to bed one night, and when I woke up in the morning he was just gone."

"I'm so fuckin sorry, babe."

"And the part that . . . the part that I always try real hard not to think about is . . . Fuck, Dad was always so warm and friendly and open, he was the one I was closest to. I love my mama to pieces, but she is a hard woman to get close to. But he . . . he never fucking knew me, did he? He lost his youngest daughter and never got to meet his oldest."

Pulling out of Jules' embrace, Mags sat up, took a few deep, measured breaths, and held her hand out, palm up. Jules surrendered the cigarettes she'd offered earlier. Mags took one, studied the floor, and muttered, "And there's no family plot, no headstones with their names on them. It was . . . it was everywhere. There were so many people dying that we couldn't dig pits for them fast enough. We wound up stacking the dead up like cordwood and burning them."

"Fuck."

"Yeah, that's what I said. Fuck." She wrapped her arms around herself, shivering. "Fuck. Fuck. I . . . I don't know what got into me. I'm sorry."

"Hey, sugar, you ain't got shit to be sorry for. Listen: Thank you. Thank you for telling me all that."

"W . . . what?"

"Hey, I didn't know how to say this without it coming off like I was fussing over you, but honestly? I been really worried about you, sug. I knew that those walls were gonna have to come tumbling down eventually."

A long, sad sigh. "Well . . . there it is. That's what thirteen years of silent grief sounds like all at once, I guess."

"You feel any better?"

"No, Jules, I don't. I feel like shit. I feel . . . naked."

"Ain't we been naked enough times?"

"Oh, you know what I mean."

"Yeah, sugar, I know exactly what you mean. That's how I feel every minute of every day."

"Oh. Yeah. Of course. Fuck, I'm sorry, honey."

"You got nuthin to apologize for, sug."

"It doesn't feel like it. I . . . God, I shouldn't have just unloaded on you like that. I'm sorry."

"No, sugar, listen: I'm glad you did. I'm glad you feel comfortable enough with me to do that."

"I just . . . I'm supposed to be the one who helps people. I ain't supposed to be the one who needs help."

"I know you know that it don't work that way."

"Yeah. Yeah, I know it. But . . . Jules, I feel so shitty. I feel so shitty all the fucking time and I don't know what to do about it."

"I don't have any magic words to say that'll make it all better, much as I wish I did, but I'll tell you this: I know exactly how you feel. We can feel like shit together."

Mags wiped her eyes and smiled. "Yeah. That's . . . that's as close to those magic words as I think we're gonna get. I love you so goddamn much and I'm so glad we're in this together. I just . . . Jules, it hurts so goddamn much. All the time."

"Oh, don't I know it. But, hey, I might just have an idea about that. It ain't gonna be much help right now, but . . . you remember what you said to me after we ran into Frank? About getting out in front of shit?"

"Yeah."

"Well, how about this: We're gonna see this job through—I dunno how, but I know we are—and you're gonna go back home. And this time, when you come back home, you're gonna be bringin along a cute little housewife who can't wait to cook your dinner and shine your boots and all that bullshit. And y'know what that sounds like to me? Sounds to me like the makings of a family."

Mags broke into a smile and leaned against her. "God, I fucking love you. I feel like such a walking, talking lesbian stereotype, because I've known you for like a week but I can't imagine a time without you."

"Is that a lesbian stereotype, sug? Because I feel that, too."

"Oh, yeah. When women fall in love, we do it fast and hard. That's always been a thing. And we sit around comparing trauma before we actually get to know each other." She laughed. "Jules, what's my favorite color?"

"I dunno, sugar, but I'm gonna guess. Is it red?"

Mags socked her in the shoulder. "Okay, that one doesn't count."

"Yeah, yeah. Listen: I fucking love you."

"I fucking love you, too, Jules."

"Now, if you're up for it, I reckon we ought to get up off the floor and go see what we're having for lunch. I bet it's more that soggy mashed potato bullshit you love so much."

Mags laughed as they stood up together, and she kissed Jules and said, "Y'know, honey, I think I know exactly what I'm gonna do when we're done here. I'm gonna do something I haven't done in a long time. Hell, something I've never done, really."

"What's that, sug?"

"I'm taking a fucking vacation."

[19]

THE MASTER'S CALL

As the group dished out bowls of food and Barns got up and went to join them, TJ looked to the two still lurking in the shadows and barked, "Hey."

Lukash perked up in the dark. "Yes, darling?"

"This used to be a church, right? Back in the old days?"

"Yes, it would appear so."

"Well . . . don't that hurt y'all?"

The little man laughed. "Oh, I didn't think that so much lore would survive from the old days. No, my dear, that one is mere superstition. If there's any truth to all the warnings about Christian iconography, well, I haven't seen proof of it in three hundred years."

"But some of the shit is true, then?"

"Dibs and dabs, yes. Sunlight and silver will kill us, and much faster than physical trauma. Salt, some spices, and running water can hurt us, but not badly. That, I think, is all one would need to know about how to deal with our peculiar physiology."

"Well, here's another question: Where did you guys, like, come from?"

Chuckling, Lukash stood up and moved closer to the group, with Becky following him. "Ach, I thought that you all would be full of questions. If you must know, I was born in Blankenhagen, in the Rostocker Wald in Pommerania in 1890. My father was Rudolph von Lukash, a *Ritter* . . . a knight, but I think 'Baron' would be closer in English. My mother, though, her name was Shoshanah Lichtmann, the daughter of one of my grandfather's clerks. Rather the star-crossed romance, you might say."

Becky socked him in the arm. "You know what they mean, dork."

"Of course, of course. As far as I know, we are as old as humanity, just one more aspect of the human condition. But as for how I found myself in this condition, well . . . During the Great War, I was a *Rittmeister*—a captain—leading a company of rangers. I received the Iron Cross for my service at Tannenburg, you know. The Austrians, during their Carpathian campaigns, managed to flush out a coven of such creatures, and the German *Kriegsbureau* found that very, very interesting. That was where Otto got the idea, you see; he is not very creative. And that began Operation Nachtjager."

"Hold up," Becky said, "I thought that Nachtjager started during the Second World War."

"Ach, it may as well have, *Schatzie*. This was not until 1918, with only a few short months left between us and the Hundred Days, and most of those involved would enter the NSDAP after the war. Most, including Otto."

Lukash clenched his long, elegant hands into fists, and he grimaced at the pain of his memories. "You see," he went on, "I . . . I never wished for this. As a captain of rangers, a decorated veteran of Tannenberg, of course they approached me with their offer, and yes yes it sounds nice to be stronger, faster, fiercer than an ordinary man, but this was 1918; those of us with sense knew that there was not much war left, and I would have preferred not to spend the rest of my nights as a monster from a fairytale. But I agreed, because . . . because . . ."

Becky reached out and gave him a pat on the shoulder, and he gave a long, sad sigh and asked, "May I trouble one of you for a cigarette?"

Mags tossed him a pack and her lighter. He struck one, sighed again, and continued: "You must understand that he was not always as he is now. Otto von Hochulf was once a good man, a kind man . . . or at least he appeared so on the surface. But war is a hideous thing. War brings out all that is base in men and destroys all that is virtuous. And Otto, well, he'd already become a beast hungry for blood long before we became monsters. I thought . . . I thought that going through this together would make us close again, as we'd once been close, and would enable me to save him. I was wrong. I was quite wrong."

It was Connor who spoke up next, saying: "Shit. You loved him, didn't you?"

"Did Patroclus love Achilles? But it was . . . terrible to watch him change. When the war began to go poorly, Otto sought meaning with the Romantic nationalists, began to develop notions about race and nation and destiny, and suddenly all of our evening trips to the opera seemed much less innocent. He used to call me *Wolfchen*, his little wolf, but do you know what he called me on the day we parted? He looked at me in my eyes and he called me a rat."

The group gave Lukash a pitying look, and Mags winced, and the hunter shook his head and concluded: "The man I loved died three hundred years ago. All that's left now is a creature, an animal, a mad dog that needs to be put down. And I intend to do just that."

After a beat, Mags spoke up, saying, "So, about that. What exactly is our plan for doing that?"

"Ach, yes, yes, the plan, of course. They headed back north ahead of us at my orders, but until very recently I had two of my people embedded in Otto's staff, and from them I learned many interesting things. His facility is not nearly so difficult to infiltrate, not nearly so secure, as your people presumed, Magnolia. Your man Bartholomew failed because he thought of it in two dimensions, rather than three."

"Yeah, what does that mean?"

"The facility is like an iceberg. Its blast walls and office tower and all of that sit above a warren of utility corridors, underground magazines, that sort of thing. And it has been standing there for two hundred years, crumbling, in spite of Otto's best efforts. There are breaches and boltholes, cracks in the edifice scattered here and there about the area, and not all of them are watched. A small team of professionals, such as we are, could make great use of that."

"Huh. Y'know, that sort of thing is exactly what I came here to look for. And that actually does sound doable, if your intelligence is good. But here's the real question: Once we're inside the place that kills everybody who tries to go inside of it, what the fuck do we do next?"

"Now that, that is deliciously dramatic. I also have some knowledge of the facility's contents, some of the things that were developed and stored there. There are several caches of tactical nuclear weapons."

Amidst gasps and slackening jaws, Lukash went on: "Otto is salivating over some of this, over artillery and rockets and such, but there is a magazine that he is ignoring as unimportant, all flash and no substance as he is. If we can enter the facility, we should be able to make our way to the magazine where the Americans stored their demolition munitions."

Mags blinked a few times. "You . . . you want us to be a green-light team? You wanna crater the place?"

"It would bring all of this unpleasantness to a swift conclusion."

"Yeah, it would, but . . . we kinda need the stuff that's in there. The munitions not so much—and sounds like we wouldn't want a lot of that shit anyways—but there's computer, radio, and power infrastructure inside that place that we can use and that we desperately need. Just blowing it up is, like, a million miles outside the parameters of my mission."

"I understand, Magnolia, but the speed at which things are progressing rather limits our available choices. We have mere days to bring things to their conclusion, and you know as well as I that your people need that place gone far more than they need it looted."

Mags was quiet for a long moment. At last she nodded and said, "Yeah. Yeah, you're right. And that's the goddamn stupidest plan I've ever heard in my life, but like you said, I'm kinda out of choices. I'm in. Probably gonna get my ass crawled when I get back to Central, but fuck it, I didn't want the promotion anyways."

"This is fuckin stupid," Connor barked.

"Lukash gave him a nod. "You have objections, friend?"

"Nah. Well, I got a whole lot of objections, actually, but like the red said, what I ain't got are choices. I just wanted to make sure the record shows that this here is goddamn stupid and we're all gonna die."

"Oh, almost certainly. Now, we are about one day's travel away at this point, yes?"

"Thereabouts. Less, if we really book it."

"Very good. My plan for the next stage is this: Becky and I will go and get a few hours' rest, and at nightfall we will leave together to find a good staging area near to our target. In the morning you will rendezvous with us, as usual, but the following night . . . If all goes, well, we will walk into the lion's den the following night."

A deep, solemn silence fell over the group, the desperation and finality of their plan weighing down on them, until Becky spoke up, saying, "Hey, boss, hold up. What about my nerd?"

"I'm afraid that Steven should stay with his own kind for now, darling. At this stage, stealth and precision are called for, and he cannot keep up with us on foot."

Barns reached out and put a hand on her shoulder. She grimaced, then muttered, "Yeah. Yeah, you're right."

"If our plans are now laid, I suggest that you and I retire for the day. We have a long night ahead of us."

"Uh, you go on ahead, boss. I'm not really that tired right now."

Lukash smiled as he stood up, and he gave her a pat on the shoulder as he turned to walk deeper into the darkness. As the others finished their meal and began to put their dishes away, she got up, slid over beside Jules, and said, simply: "Hey."

"Hey."

"I know you're probably worn the hell out, and things are kinda, well, heavy right now, but if you wanted to keep the game going today, I'd be down."

Jules looked over toward Mags, who gave her a warm smile and said, "Hey, I got what I needed, hon."

And looking back toward Becky, Jules grinned and asked, "So if it's a game, who's winning?"

———

Jules returned to the sacristy with Becky following behind, and the two women sat facing each other without speaking for a long while until Jules sighed and said, "Y'know, this is harder than I thought it would be."

"Hey, you don't have to tell me dick if you don't feel like it. I was just offering."

"No, no, I want to, it's just . . . so much shit has happened *so much* over the past few years that it's kinda funny how short the story actually is to tell. Where'd I stop last time?"

"Something about being 'marked'. Then the other day you mentioned something else about the dress."

"Yeah, yeah. I think . . . I think I'll get us as far as the dress. That's about all I feel like dealing with right now, and anyways, if

I'm being honest, after that it gets pretty repetitive for about eighteen months 'till I made my run."

"Oof. Yikes."

"Yeah, 'yikes' is right. So anyways . . . marked."

And Jules stood up, turned around, and lowered her jeans just enough to show off the small of her back and the top of her buttocks.

"Oof," Becky repeated, "I dunno what that means, but I do not have a good feeling about it."

"Yeah, you'd be right. The word is pretty self-explanatory, but the eyes mean 'This prisoner has no allies and can be abused without consequences'." She sat back down and lit a cigarette. "When they threw me in the stockade, at first I had no idea what the hell I was doing there. The penalty for degenerate sexual deviance while on active duty is death by public hanging without a trial; the law's pretty clear on that. Found out later, what they were doing was trying to make me disappear. Hanging a blackshirt for being a girl would mean admitting it happened, so they threw me in the pit and the marshals told the other prisoners what the score was, hoping they'd kill me and I wouldn't be their problem anymore. It almost worked, but I'm too goddamn mean to die.

"Went all of one day before some people came gunning for me. I think they were just trying to kill me, win favors upstairs, but I tried to kill 'em right back and turned out to be a whole lot better at it. Problem is, though, that they had friends, and a couple days later their friends decided I needed a lesson."

"Oh, shit."

"Uh-huh. They had to bleed for it, but in the end there was four of them and one of me. And . . . afterwards, they decided I needed a souvenir. Hence, the ink." Another sigh. "And that was life, for about a month, I think. Every few days somebody would come at me trying to start shit, and usually I'd win, but . . . sometimes I wouldn't."

"Oh my God. That's . . . I'm so fucking sorry."

276 / NATALIE IRONSIDE

"Yeah. I almost broke, almost, but at the end of that month I got to meet the wildest piece of work on God's green Earth."

"Who's that?"

"Oh boy. So this one day, I was having my morning cry in a corner someplace when one of the marshals came and found me and said to me, 'Hey, faggot, come with me, you got a visitor.' Didn't know what to make of that. Instead of leading me up toward the guard shack he took me into an interrogation booth with two chairs, a desk, and a woman behind it. She was tall, taller than Mags, blonde hair, wearing a black shirt with a corpsman's staff on it—and that's out of the ordinary; women are only allowed in a non-combat auxiliary, and their uniforms are brown. And her face . . . God, that fucking face of hers. Looked like a china doll. There was no life behind her eyes, and she had this forced, empty smile that looked like it had been painted on. She looked over at the marshal and said, 'Thank you, darling, that will be all.' And he kicked me into the booth and shut the door."

"Oof. I have got a real bad feeling about this one."

"Oh yeah. So she looks at me and tells me to have a seat and I sit down, and she says, 'Let's start with names. I am Corpsman-Major Natasha Wenden, women's auxiliary. And you are?'

"'I'm Corporal Jules Binachi,' I says.

"And she fixes me with those empty blue eyes of hers, and she shakes her head and says, 'Tell me, darling: What is "Jules" short for?'

"'It's just fuckin Jules,' I says.

"And she leans across the desk so that her face is right in front of mine, takes a deep breath, and her voice drops a good four octaves and she says 'I suppose you must think that you're the first blackshirt to have ever found herself in this predicament. You're not. You are, in fact, the second. Might I guess that Jules is short for Julia?'"

Becky stared, slack-jawed, for a moment before stammering,

"Wait, but . . . what? How could . . . But don't they, like, kill people like you?"

"Uh-huh. The short answer is that she used to be a medic in Rain's operating group and she's blowing him. Also, her daddy's an Ecclesiarch—an archbishop. Rich girl with friends in high places."

"Jesus."

"Yeah, exactly. She gave me a sales pitch about a program for women like us, where we can get treatment. That was how she talked about it, too; 'treatment', like we're a disease, so we can be made useful to the state again. Now, looking back on it, I shoulda been able to spot the trap a mile away—Uh, that's a poor choice of words. Looking back on it, I shoulda known what it sounds like to be sold a bill of goods, but listen, she . . . she found me in the darkest place I'd ever been in, and she gave me hope, and it made me stupid."

She was quiet as she finished her cigarette, then lit another one and continued: "There's a little compound in the middle of Columbus. Not much, just a parade field, a barracks, a clinic, and an office tucked into a side lot near the Oberkommando building. She gave me hope, and it made me stupid, and I didn't notice the bars over the windows, or the razor wire on top of the fence. They gave me a set of women's auxiliary uniforms, gave me feminizing hormones, didn't give me fuck-all to do except for every couple days Wenden would come talk about how I was getting on and how my 'progress' was. That was life for about a month. Then, during one of those meetings, she told me that I might be ready to move on to the next stage of her little program, enter general population--'meet the other girls', she said—start training for some clerical job. She just needed a little bit more to prove I was meeting expectations. I didn't follow what that meant, on account of that woman is the world's greatest bullshit artist and could write you a novel about soap, but the word 'duty' came up a lot. So did 'heterosexuality'."

"Oh, shit."

"Then, like it was an afterthought, she said that I had a visitor, and that he'd come with a gift. She reached under her desk and pulled out my dress. And that night . . . that night, I got to see John again."

"Oh my God. Jules, I . . . I'm so fucking sorry."

And Becky looked into her eyes, expecting to see Jules on the verge of tears, but instead her face was contorted in a sneer of pure, smoldering hatred, her eyes fixed with a flinty determination that almost hurt to look at. "Mags put words to it for me once," she said. "To be taken seriously as women in a reactionary society—I like that word, 'reactionary'; sounds exactly like what it's describing— we have to overperform everything that's expected of you cis women. And in the Blackland New Republic, what is a woman? A slave. An object. Something that exists for men to use. Hell, John explained it to me, too, with his arm around my throat and his cock up my ass: 'If you wanna be a girl, Binachi, I'll fuckin treat you like one.' And that fucking kapo . . . unlike the rest of us, that fucking kapo never had a problem with that state of affairs."

"Uh . . . not to interrupt, but what the hell is a kapo?"

"Short for *Kameradschaft-Polizei*. A kapo is an inmate in a camp who sides with the camp guards and gets to play boss over the other inmates." A long, sad sigh. "She came and found me in the shower afterwards. When I tried to say something about the whole thing, she threatened to kick me out of the program and send me back where she'd found me, and told me I could just quit and go back to my unit like nothing had happened if I couldn't hack it. And you . . . you . . . no offense, Becky, but I don't think I can even explain what kind of a choice that is in words you'd understand. That bitch was smart, whip-smart, giving me a taste of the good life before springing that on me. They'd kill me deader than Elvis if I ever came back, I knew that for sure, but . . . fuck, even without that, trying to be *him* again would be worse than dying. So I kept my mouth shut. After that, I got to meet 'general population', which was about twelve other women with sad eyes and broken spirits. I never saw anybody besides Wenden who was older than 30. One or two officers from the Oberkommando would come by the camp looking for strange about once a week. We lost a girl to suicide about once every three months. And that . . . that was life, for a solid eighteen months, until I saw a chance and went for it. And here I am."

Jules was on the verge of tears, then, and Becky moved closer and put an arm across her shoulders, and Jules said, "That's . . . that's about all I got in me today, I think."

"Yeah. That's a hell of a thing, telling anybody even a little bit of that story. Thank you."

"Yeah. Thanks for listening. One more thing, though; this just occurred to me the other day."

"What is it?"

"Back in Harper's Ferry, when you asked me who John was and I snapped at you, that was . . . that was the first time I ever actually said the R word out loud. Or, hell, even thought it. I've told Prof everything, and I've really told Mags everything, way more gory details than this, but I . . . I always danced around that word. Felt too concrete. Too real." She sucked in a quick breath through her teeth. "Rape. They were rapists. I was raped."

"That's right, girl. And I know it probably doesn't feel like it right now, but that's . . . that's a really big step. Like, for me, I spent a really long time pretending that everything that happened to me was bad dreams. It's a big deal to call a thing what it is."

"Yeah. Say, Becky . . . you got religion?"

"Nah. Not for me."

"Word. I dunno if I do or not anymore, and if there is a God then I dunno if I would wanna talk to His ass anyways, but these digs y'all picked out have got me thinking about some stuff."

Jules reached into her pocket and took out a small silver medallion on a broken chain. She held it up in front of her face, watching it spin around in the gloom, and said, "When I got conscripted, my mom cried for about two straight days. Then, when I told her I was volunteering for the blackshirts, she didn't speak to me for a year.

Right before she gave me the cold shoulder, the night before I left for selection, she gave me this. Told me, 'I don't know why, but I think you should have this.'"

"What is it?"

"St. Monica of Hippo. Patron saint of abuse survivors and rebellious children."

"Oof. That's a bit, uh, on the nose."

"Yeah. You could always count on Mom's intuition. Damned if I don't wish I'd listened to her."

And Jules stood up and looked to the far side of the room where an imposing crucifix hung on the wall, and she said, "Becky, sweetheart, I want you to do me a favor. It's probably all bullshit, but I think it'll make me feel better."

"Oh, hell, of course. Anything."

"I want you to witness my act of contrition."

"Don't you need, like, a priest for that?"

"No, that's confession. I wanna do contrition. It's like confession, but you don't need a priest."

"Uh . . . alright. What do you need me to do?"

"Same as you been doing. Just listen."

And Jules approached the crucifix and sank slowly to her knees, clutching her medallion in her right hand as she crossed herself and whispered, "Hail Mary, full of grace, the Lord is with thee. Blessed art though among women, and blessed is the fruit of thy womb, Jesus. Holy Mary, mother of God, pray for us sinners, now and at the hour of our death. Amen."

And, staring at the floor, she was silent for a long moment before continuing: "I've . . . I've done some bad shit. I've blasphemed and doubted and apostatized and all that fun stuff, but I've also done, like, real shit. I've hurt people. I've shot and stabbed and otherwise killed people—it was what I did and I was fucking good at it. I guess I'll carry that on my conscience for the rest of my life. And I've . . . suffered. I got sucked in and chewed up and shit out by the very same monster I spent my life working for and I don't think Hell has any more terrors for me. But after that . . . after that, I received so much fucking grace. I found people who took me into their home and helped me, and I found . . . I found *her*. She coulda just left me to rot, and I woulda deserved it, but instead I found love, love that saved and redeemed and defined me. It's a tall order, 'cause the world You made already ain't good enough for her, but as long as I've got the strength to keep going I'm gonna spend every goddamn day trying to be the woman I see reflected in those big green eyes."

After pausing to catch her breath, Jules looked up at the ceiling and concluded: "O my God, I am heartily sorry for having offended Thee, and I detest all my sins, because I dread the loss of Heaven and the pains of Hell, but most of all because they offend Thee, my God who art all-good and deserving of all my love. I firmly resolve, with the help of Thy grace, to confess my sins, to do penance, and to amend my life. Amen."

And, panting, she rose slowly to her feet, locked eyes with the crucifix on the wall, lit a cigarette, and growled, "That good enough for You, You son of a bitch?"

"Well," Becky asked, "you feel any better?"

"Oh, yeah. Hell of a lot better. If there is a God—and I reckon there might be—then now I can go fuck off and die in a state of grace. Either way, though, it would've made my mom happy, and I'm more worried about her than I am about God anyways."

Jules and Becky parted ways in the sanctuary, the hunter going off deeper into the shadows to sleep while Jules went to rejoin the group, who were sitting around stretching the knots out of their muscles and talking. Barns seemed to be the center of attention.

"It doesn't hurt," he was saying, in answer to someone's question as TJ watched him with rapt attention. "I mean, it probably could, but the way she does it just feels like you got stung by a horsefly."

"Huh," TJ said, taking mental notes. "So, like, what made you agree to start doing that?"

"Well, uh, if you really wanna know . . . I kinda get off on it."

They looked at him in confusion for a moment, then said, "Ooooh, so it's like a sex thing."

"A little bit, yeah. Some people are weirded out by it, but . . ."

"Eh, it's not any weirder than anything else you people do. I'll just jot down 'getting fed on by hunters' on my list of shit I don't understand."

"Uh . . . who is 'you people'?"

"You sex-havers and your sexual attraction." They lit a cigarette and sighed. "I'm stuck out in the middle of the wasteland with a bunch of allos and white people. This feels like the setup for a joke."

Prof stifled a laugh. TJ turned to him, grinned, and asked, "Hey, old man, how the hell did we let all these white people drag us into this? Are we stupid?"

"Well," the old man chuckled, "sometimes I do wonder."

"Y'know, I have actually wondered about that, now that I mention it. How exactly did you get dragged into all this? You were like a fancypants college guy; you're like the world's foremost expert on American history and authoritarian red bullshit. Ain't you got better things to do?"

"Allow me to answer that question with another question: Why are *you* out here?"

"'Cause it's the fuckin Citadel. I grew up listening to ghost stories about that hellhole. Too-tall and shortstack over there show up and give me a chance to go look inside of it . . . I'm fuckin taking that chance."

"And there's your answer. I saw it once. It was from far away, but it was with my own eyes, and I . . . I haven't been able to stop thinking about it since."

Connor grunted in agreement, and at once a grim shadow settled over the group, the turn in the conversation bringing home just how close they were. Everyone was silent for several minutes until Connor grumbled, "All goes according to plan, we're gonna see it tomorrow."

"The boss says we might be inside of it tomorrow night," Barns said.

Jules took a seat next to Mags and sank onto the floor, resting her head on her girlfriend's lap. No-one spoke for a long, tense while until Mags began to stroke her hair and muttered, "Tomorrow night. One way or another . . . one way or another, we're gonna be done here soon."

———————————

It looked exactly how the two veterans had described it, with a few dramatic flourishes.

Becky and Lukash saw the lights in the distance from far off as they picked their way through the rotting city, past crumbling skyscrapers that loomed like dead gods in the shadows. As they followed the trail blazed by the doomed expedition years ago, it grew more and more into focus, a relic of a darker and less civilized age.

And, at last, with the moon and stars obscured by gathering clouds, they came to the spot. Amid what had once been a sprawling residential suburb, the trail ended in a football pitch on top of a hill, ringed by the rusting wrecks of trucks, armored personnel carriers, Paladins, and Abrams tanks. It overlooked their ultimate destination, the rings of impregnable blast walls with an office tower peeking over them and an Old American flag fluttering in the night wind. And, in the center of the field, stood a neatly stacked pile of tattered flecktarn uniforms, rusting Kalashnikov rifles, and sun-bleached human skulls.

The two scouts still had many hours of darkness left, and they spent these sneaking carefully around the fallen-in ruins of houses, searching for a secluded place from which to begin the final approach. As they made their way down from the hill and around toward the south of the Citadel, Becky thought that she could almost hear, faintly, from deep under the earth, a sound she couldn't quite identify; a steady tattoo of tapping, like stone against steel.

[20]

A SKY WITHOUT EAGLES

WHEN MORNING CAME, PROF WONDERED IF IT HAD.

He was already awake when TJ came to fetch him for last watch. During the night, a wind had kicked up that shook the crumbling old church and groaned through its many cracks and drafts like a pipe organ. Picking up his battle rifle and heading to the door, he saw that the moon and stars were hidden behind a veil of gathering clouds. Far, far off in the south and east, only just visible, a bolt of lightning split the sky, and even from such a distance Prof could see the inky black thunderhead that birthed it come alive with orange rays of heat lightning and twinkling blue and white spook lights. The tells of ionizing radiation.

Shuddering, he flipped open one of the pouches on the side of his rucksack and pulled out his Geiger counter. After stabilizing, it read out a comfortable 0.01 millisieverts; above normal, but not enough to worry about. He let out a sigh of relief.

The dial jumped again, and again, creeping slowly but inexorably upward.

Rolling his eyes, the old man dug around in his pockets until he

found a cigar—his last cigar. With a salute to the gathering storm, he struck a match and lit it, not caring how far the sight of fire or smell of smoke might carry; they were at the end of it now.

After a beat, Mags shuffled out of the darkness and stood beside him, rubbing the sleep from her eyes. He looked up at her, smiled, and asked, "Trouble sleeping?"

"Eh," she said with a yawn. "I've always been an early riser anyways, but yeah, I don't see how anybody could sleep with all this going on."

"Quite. It's all . . . so horribly familiar, isn't it?"

"How do you mean?"

He gestured to the southeast, and a moment later there was another flicker of lightning and the fireworks show that accompanied it.

"Aw, hell," Mags grumbled.

"I'm keeping an eye on the levels, and presently we're still only in 'dental x-ray room' territory, but . . . I have a feeling they'll go up."

"Eh, it's just as well."

"What makes you say that?"

"Nobody could fly a helicopter out here from Land's End in time, anyways, no matter what the weather is."

Prof gave a humorless laugh. She sat down next to him and lit one of her cigarettes, and he asked, "How many of those do you have left?"

"Four packs. Between me and Jules, just barely enough to keep us from getting grumpy on the journey home."

"Hell. This is my last cigar."

Mags took an unopened pack of cigarettes from her pocket and tossed it into his lap. He shook his head, saying, "No, no, I wasn't going to ask. The way back--"

"Sweetheart, you and I both know that there is no way back."

They sat in silence for a while, until Mags asked: "But, hypothetically, if we were going to live through this . . . what comes next for you?"

"Oh, I'm going back to Freeside. I know that things have improved a lot in the Republic since I took my extended sabbatical —no worries about one of Ken Kilroy's goons putting an ice axe through my skull or anything like that—but I've enjoyed it there. And, of course, they're going to need my help, since you've purloined my gardener."

"Yeah. About that. Y'know, Central offered me a promotion to take this job; it's probably off the table now that we've gone off the shits, but anyways I'll probably get some kinds of atta'girls and accolades and probably some stupid medal for this. But, man . . . I'm not so sure I want it."

"Magnolia, are you asking me for advice?"

"Well, you were the one who told me to apply from the Academy when I finished my associate's, and that was the first good choice I ever made. I value your advice."

"You've spent your entire life in service of others, Magnolia. I think you should take a step back and ask yourself what it is that *you* want."

"Man, please call me Mags; you sound like my mama. But . . . if I could have everything I ever wanted, honestly, I'd keep doing what I been doing the past couple of years: Being a shop steward in my hometown. Only difference is, well, now I don't have to be alone anymore. That's what I want. I wanna take my girl home, settle in with her, and go back to watering the grass and handing out apples."

"I couldn't think of a better life for you, or for anyone. And Mags? I'm proud of you."

"Aw, hell, don't go getting sentimental on me."

"I mean it. You've come very far from a dumb Kentucky girl sitting at a desk agonizing over different kinds of surplus value. If I had any hand at all in you becoming who you are today, then I can go to my grave knowing I did at least one good thing."

"Good Lord, man, that's the nicest thing anybody's ever said to me. And . . . yeah, you taught me everything I know. If it weren't for you, hell, I might still be that dumb Kentucky boy everybody thought I was."

Prof stifled a laugh. She cocked an eyebrow at him, and he said, "Well, about that . . . Let's just say that when you showed up on my front stoop and told me who you are and who you used to be, I was not exactly surprised."

"Oh, God."

"Do you remember the unit on materialist feminism?"

Grinning like a child caught misbehaving, she looked down at her boots and said, "Yes, professor, I remember the unit on materialist feminism."

"We try not to foster cults of personality in the Ashland Confederated Republic, you know. And so most people don't just start sobbing in the middle of reading Lauri Bluecrow's biography. The ones who do, well, they tend to have hideous beards and sad, sad eyes."

She laughed, socked him in the shoulder, and barked, "You're too goddamn smart, you know that?"

"I do. It's what got me into trouble." And, checking his pocket-watch, he added, "Well, it's morning now, for all the good it will do us."

"I can't even see where the sun's coming up. This must be blowing in off the ocean."

"I imagine. We are right in the middle of hurricane season."

"Hell. Well, the sooner we get on with this . . ."

"My thoughts exactly. I'll go wake up the others."

———

The clouds only thickened as the day drew on, and when the darkness gave way to the inky blue gloaming of pre-dawn, it hung there as the curtain of ominous black anvils over their heads grew heavier and darker. The wind from the southeast howled into their faces, peppering them with a light mist of rain, and every few minutes the darkness would be split by a clap of thunder and a bolt of lightning, the storm coming ever closer, the sparks and ghost lights dancing within it growing ever brighter. Everyone kept a close eye on the radiation levels, and though they remained safe, the millisieverts-per-hour reading kept ticking slowly upward.

Around noon—though it still looked like early morning—they stopped to check their Maps, and Connor lit a cigarette without bothering to conceal it and said, "Y'know, there is one good thing about this whole clusterfuck."

"And what's that?" Prof asked.

"Whatever it is we're walking into, at least we're downwind of it. It won't see us coming any more than we'll see it."

"I suppose. I just . . . this rather defeats the purpose of waiting for daylight, doesn't it?"

"Yeah. If there's hunters out there, I sure hope they can't hear us or smell us through all this wind, 'cause this pissant excuse for daylight ain't gonna stop 'em. Speaking of, why don't you try and raise our friends on the radio? We're getting close."

Prof dug out one of his two-ways, held it up to his mouth, and was about to speak when, from off in the darkness, they heard Becky's voice cry out: "Yup, that's a big 10-4, Bandit, I read you loud and clear."

Heads snapped around looking for the source of the voice, and Becky came walking out of the gloom, giving them a friendly wave.

"The hell are you doin out here?" Connor asked, cocking an eyebrow.

"Well, with this nice weather we're having," she said, walking up to Barns and draping an arm across his shoulders, "I kinda felt like taking a stroll. Y'know, for the novelty of it. Nah, the boss is camped out about two hours down the road and since you guys have kinda lost your big advantage, I backtracked to give you some extra eyes. And, like, you're pretty safe what with the wind and all

—I only found you guys because I knew what to look for—but, uh, they are out there."

"Shit."

"Yeah. I clocked three different assault squads on my way back here. They don't know when you're coming or where you're coming from, so that's something, but they sure do know you're coming. So let's get rolling; the sooner we're inside, the sooner this is all over with."

"So y'all found a way in, then?"

"Yup. It was a little tricky, but . . . well, you'll see when we find the boss. Right now, let's get moving." And she perked up like a bird dog, and took a long, deep sniff, and hissed, "Now. We should get moving, like, right now."

And from off to their left, to the northeast, they could just hear the sound of boot-heels clapping across pavement, in slow, methodical steps.

Even in the dark and under the gathering storm, Prof and Connor knew the way. Becky lagged behind the two of them, letting them lead, and their feet carried them at a brisk pace the others struggled to keep up with, so that it was far short of the estimated two hours when they came at last to the hilltop field and its grim monuments, and, before them, their destination, looming like a squatting titan in the darkness, the star-spangled banner yet waving atop its tower.

"Well," Connor pontificated, his eyes locked on the fortress in front of them.

"Yeah," Prof agreed.

The others, one by one, came up to stand beside them, their fear masked by looks of hungry curiosity. Even Barns and Jules, who'd only heard of the place recently and third-hand, felt drawn to it, felt something beckoning them to come see what lay behind its walls.

"Never thought it see the day . . ." TJ muttered.

"Yeah," Mags said. "It's like . . . staring into the face of God."

"Mouth of Hell, more like," Connor grumbled. "Take it from me; seeing it from here is plenty."

Prof, however, was just as transfixed as the others, muttering, "Yes, but . . . but now we're actually going to see the inside. Nobody's done that."

"And nobody else will again, if we got shit to say about it. Snap out of it, old man. Y'know who's in there? That big fucker."

Prof shook himself, his look of awe and hunger melting into one of steely determination. "You're right, of course. He's in there . . . He's in there, and this time we're the ones coming for him."

"Damn right. Shit, man . . . Millie was right. Live or die, this is the next right thing. For our friends. For Tanya."

"Goddamn right. For Tanya."

And they turned away and let Becky lead them down the hill just as the sky broke, just as the rain came down.

Through the overgrown ruins at the bottom of the hill and around to the side of the Citadel, Becky led them to a tumbled-down building of red brick, its barely-legible sign marking it as once having been a police station. At the foot of it was an open storm cellar, and beside it sat Lukash, lying on his back, smoking a pipe in the rain.

"Ach, you've all made excellent time," he said without looking up. "You'll be pleased to know that I have found us a means of ingress."

"I found it," Becky said, walking up to him and giving him a kick in the ribs.

"Of course, of course; it was my lovely protégé and her sharp ears who found our way in." He hopped to his feet, like a cat, and gestured at the cellar doors. "Let's get out of the rain, and then we may talk."

They followed him down a set of stone stairs that led down, down below the ruins, into a wide concrete room cluttered with the flotsam and jetsam of two centuries of floodwater. It was Connor who first noted that, and the lack of standing water; all of the rain that had followed them down the stairs kept flowing across the floor, draining into a crack in the far wall a few feet wide that loomed like an open wound in the darkness.

"Very perceptive, my friend," Lukash said. "That would be the second sign that told us we'd found the correct hole in the ground. The first was this fine mensch."

And he gestured behind one of the piles of debris, where they saw the body of what had once been a human being. Its skin had the sickly grey-green pallor typical of any roamer, but its flesh was shriveled and hardened like cured meat, indicating an uncomfortable ancientness, though the wound in its head that stopped it from getting up appeared to be fresh.

"He heard us stomping around up over his head and wanted so badly to get to us that he made enough racket to alert Becky to his little hideaway. I thought that, yes, he is quite old, but surely he hasn't been trapped down here with no food for two hundred years, and yet those cellar doors plainly had not been opened in all that time. It was then that we noticed the hole in the wall. Now, then!"

He reached into one of his coat pockets and took out a sheet of paper with a crude map sketched onto it. Taking care to keep it dry, he showed it off to the others and said, "That crack leads into a fissure in the limestone which connects—I think—to this corridor right here. The map comes secondhand and incomplete, but if it is still at all close to correct—and I believe it is—then that is very fortunate, because it is not so many twists and turns to get to the magazine we're trying to reach. And if not, well, it is at least a beginning. I poked my head in and took a little look around, and the corridor appears to be unused; I dare to hope we may go in and come back out unseen."

"Alright," Connor said, "now here's the question. Suppose that that there's one of the parts of your map what's incomplete. What's the plan then?"

"Oh, come now; don't you know how to solve a maze? Back-track and take the next turn. Simple."

"Suppose we ain't unseen?" Mags asked. "What's the plan if we run into boneheads?"

"I very much hope that we will not, but if we do, I think that speed will be our ally more than stealth. If we are discovered, we keep moving. If we are waylaid . . . well, we will keep moving."

"Man, you seem pretty calm about this whole thing."

The hunter looked at her with steely determination flashing in his empty black eyes. He reached into his green overcoat and drew a revolver that looked just as old as himself, and he said, "I have been waiting for this day to come for three hundred years, Miss Blackadder. At the end of this night, either this business will be finished, or I will be finished, or my name is not Wolfgang Kristops Lichtmann von Lukash, twelfth and last *Landsritter* of Lukash."

Mags and Connor slung their long rifles and drew their sidearms, nodding. Lukash walked up to the crack and said, "As you fine people struggle in the dark, I will lead the way and Becky will watch our rear. Is everyone ready?"

"Nah," Mags said, "but that ain't gonna stop me."

As the group stacked up, Jules reached out and put a hand on her shoulder and whispered, "Mags? I love you sugar."

"I love you, too, honey."

And Lukash stepped forward into the darkness, and the others followed as he led them slowly downward through the narrow fissure in the earth. the passage, already barely big enough to walk through, grew tighter and steeper the further down they went, and they were just beginning to grow concerned when it opened back up into a wider passage, a manmade concrete corridor. The air was cold, stale, oppressive, and though they couldn't quite see in the darkness, they could almost sense that the tunnel stretched on an uncomfortable distance in either direction. The floodwater trickling in behind them rose only up to their ankles, the rest of it flowing down the gaping black maw of the passage which angled just slightly downward, deeper into the earth.

"It's just as well," Prof whispered, dropping a probe from his Geiger counter into the stream and reading an eyebrow-raising 0.2 mSv. "Between this, the wind, and the lightning, we'd probably be dead on the surface."

"Yeah," TJ said, "instead we get to be nice and safe inside the labyrinth full of Nazis. That's a big improvement."

Lukash motioned for them to be quiet, pointed down the tunnel, and started walking. They trudged through the darkness and the cold, stale air for what felt like hours before they saw any signs of habitation or any break from the sameness of the filthy, crumbling concrete barely visible in the dark, though as they walked they felt a palpable, primal fear building in the backs of their minds, the fear of a prey animal being watched by a predator, and they could sense that this was a place where many hunters had been congregating for a very long time.

From time to time they would reach a dead end, or Lukash would stop at a fork in the path and announce that this was the wrong way, and he would lead them back the way they'd come and down a different side passage, and though they all felt lost and terribly alone, the hunter's seeming certainty about how to navigate the warren was at least enough to keep them going as they wove from tunnel to tunnel, trending ever downwards, deeper into the Earth.

The sameness of the passage made keeping time impossible, but they estimated that it had to be close to midnight when, after yet more twisting, turning, backtracking, and fussing over the map, Lukash stopped in front of another passage, this one sloping upward. He gestured for the others to follow and whispered, "Yes,

yes, this is the way. It's not far, I don't think. A few more twists and turns, and we will be at our destination."

The upward corridor, in contrast with the others, was relatively clean, showing signs of recent use, and as they walked the sense of dread that permeated the warren grew stronger, thick enough to taste. Up ahead, from around a bend, they saw dim, flickering fluorescent light. Near the bend, Lukash stopped, listened, sniffed the air, and whispered, "There are two men up ahead. They're calm, and not expecting us."

He crept forward to peek around the corner, and at once sprinted ahead and out of sight. The others followed, weapons up, and found Lukash standing next to a heavy steel door set into the wall of the corridor. He was holding a blackshirt against the wall by his throat, silently choking the life out of him. The blackshirt was a small, wiry man, his eponymous shirt tied around his waist, and a lit cigarette lay on the ground beside them. The look on his dying face seemed to betray not anger or fear, but rather disbelief.

As the group came up, the dying man locked eyes with Jules, and with his last ragged breath he managed to whisper, "No . . . fuckin . . . way . . ."

Jules ignored him, moving ahead to the door, leading with the barrel of her Armalite as she nudged it open. She started to dart inside and clear the room, but stopped short, causing Mags to bump into her back.

They were staring into a small room, what had probably once been a utility closet, containing a desk, a refrigerator, and a bed. Beside the bed stood an IV pole, and attached to it, handcuffed to the bed, was something that had once been a man.

His skin was sickeningly pale, almost translucent, like a hunter's, where it wasn't covered with ugly black bruises. He was identifiable by his long blonde hair, his wild blonde beard, and the patchwork of tattoos covering his arms, neck, and chest, but he had a withered, sunken, ghoulish look, and they thought that they were staring at a corpse, until his fierce blue eyes turned toward them and his shallow breathing quickened.

After a beat, Jules slung her rifle, took a step forward, and announced, "I'm gonna need a minute."

Mags squeezed her shoulder before taking a step back out of the room and shutting the door behind her.

Unsheathing her knife, examining the blade, Jules walked up to the edge of the bed, looked down at the man lying in it, and asked, "So . . . How does it feel, Johnny?"

Tomassi glowered up at her with a strange look that was somewhere between hatred and relief, and said nothing.

"Looks to me like maybe you got some idea of how it feels to get used up and thrown away. It ain't a lot of fun, is it?"

Tomassi drew in a slow, ragged breath and, weakly, with great effort, muttered, ". . . Jules . . ."

"Uh-huh. Y'know, John, I used to dream about this moment. I found out the names of every man who ever came at me and I used to whisper them to myself every night before I went to bed; a list of people I'm gonna kill, and you were at the top of it. That was the only thing that kept me going when shit got really rough. But now? Brother, you don't look like catharsis. You look like a chore. A mess I have to clean up. Lookin at you like this is like lookin at a sink full of dirty dishes."

"You . . . ungrateful . . . bitch," he wheezed. "I . . . loved you. *I loved you!*"

"Yeah, I know you did. You used to whisper it to me while you choked me out and prison-fucked me."

"Goddamn . . . disgusting, degenerate faggot. . . ought to be grateful . . ."

"Sure, dude. Y'know what? I ain't got time for this. I got work to do."

"Fuck . . . you . . ."

She rolled her eyes. "Yeah, that's exactly what you are. A sink full of dishes."

Jules emerged a moment later, shut the door behind her, wiped her bloody knife on her jeans, and announced, "Well, that's done."

Mags put a hand on her shoulder. "You, uh . . . you alright, honey?"

"Yeah. Yeah, I'm alright. Oh, hey, Becky? Merry Christmas."

She tossed something small and white to Becky, which the hunter caught in the air, examined for a moment, and stuck into her pocket, declaring, "Oh, *nice!*"

"Whatcha got there?" Barns asked.

"A molar!"

The group looked back and forth at the two women for a moment before Lukash gestured for them to keep moving. They hadn't gone far when he stopped, turned to them, and whispered, "There are people up ahead. Quite a few of them. I think one is coming this way."

The group held their weapons ready, stacked up against the wall of the tunnel, and were just about to resume their advance when Lukash perked up like a bird dog and hissed, "Oh, goddamn!"

And the others heard, then, the sound of running feet, coming their way much too quickly.

The hunter came around the corner in front of them moving at inhuman speed, only visible as a dark blur in the flickering light, and Jules—just behind Lukash in the stack—fired on instinct, her round striking the hunter in the chest. *Kriminalrat* Jana Mahler was only saggered for a split second, the sounds already beginning to heal just as they appeared, but it was enough; the rest of the group opened fire on her at once, sending her spinning to the ground where she lay still and did not move.

From where she'd come, further down the passage, they heard shouts, and the sounds of more running footsteps. Many more.

"Well," Lukash declared, "I suppose we are burned. Now,

friends, it is time to run. If anything should happen to me, we are looking for a steel blast door marked 'X-18'. If anything moves, you shoot it, and we do not stop until we reach our destination. *Ja?*"

The group took off at a run, surprising the squad of blackshirts as they came around the corner, gunning them down. They ran, and Lukash led them down this passage and that, and all the while frantic shouting and the sound of boots clapping across concrete seemed to come from everywhere at once. They ran, running into and gunning down the occasional group of blackshirts or pair of hunters, until at last they came to a corridor lined with heavy steel blast doors. Lukash ran down the line of them, laughing like an excited child, until he reached the one marked X-18, along with two other symbols: The yellow and black trefoil denoting a radiation hazard, and the broken scarlet triskelion warning of a biohazard. The others kept watch while he wrestled with the door's mechanism, until, finally, groaning in protest, it swung open.

Lukash, Prof, Mags, and TJ entered while the others kept watch. Pulling out their flashlights and taking a look around in the dark, they saw that they were in a storage room, and it had mostly been ransacked, save for a pile of green canisters about the size of beer kegs. Each canister was marked, "Mk-54 SADM 0.5kt TNT."

"Special atomic demolition munition," Mags muttered. "Half a kiloton yield. Jesus fucking wept. You, uh . . . you sure you know how to work one of those things?"

To her surprise it was Prof, and not Lukash, who stepped forward and hauled one of the canisters into the center of the room. "It's entirely too simple," the old man said, pulling off the canister's cover. "Terrifyingly simple. Here is a timer and a precursor explosive. You merely put the precursor into the 'armed' slot, set the timer, flip the switch, and . . . run. I'm not sure how far underground we are, but with a yield like this it should do more than enough damage to level the facility in any case."

"How . . . how do you know all that?"

"Because it was my job, Mags. I wrote my doctoral dissertation on Old American nuclear proliferation during the Cold War. One small thing, though . . . These devices have been sitting in this room and rotting for two hundred years, and I would like to give them a once-over before we attempt anything overly ambitious. And I may be a fount of fascinating knowledge, but I'm no mechanic."

"I gotcha," TJ said, kneeling down next to the canister. "This looks pretty simple; I should be able to clean it up. You, ah, sure it's safe, though?"

"Absolutely. Triggering a nuclear explosion is no small thing. As long as that precursor is in the 'safe' slot, this is just a hunk of useless metal."

Mags had taken a step back from them and was looking around the rest of the room, where her eyes locked on a storage closet of steel and glass tucked away in the back corner. It was secured with its own blast door, marked with the broken scarlet triskelion and the inscription, "CAUTION: BSL-4." It was hard to see through the cloying darkness and the small double-paned windows, but the closet seemed to contain some simple laboratory equipment as well as stacks upon stacks of storage freezers. Each freezer door was marked with the scarlet triskelion.

"Hell," she observed.

"Chilling, isn't it?" Lukash asked, walking up beside her.

"I take back everything I said before. There's . . . there's nothing in this place that we need. This place is a monument to humanity's sins and it shoulda died along with the barbarians who built it."

"I could not have put it better myself, Miss Blackadder. You have quite the way with words."

"Uh-huh. So, like, what's our plan for getting out of here?"

"You still have your demolition explosives, ja?"

"Yup. Semtex, three and a half pounds."

"Excellent. I think . . . We will need to give ourselves a good stretch of time in which to make our escape, and during that time, this spot should not be accessible to our enemies. When our friends pronounce the mechanism operational, we should seal the door, and use your explosives to seal the passage ahead of us."

"Alright, I like that plan. Y'know, man, call me crazy, but I'm starting to think that this just might work."

From their spot on the floor in front of the canister, TJ announced, "Okey dokey, I think I've got this thing figured out. Gimme about . . . ten minutes."

Outside, the sound of rifle fire echoed through the corridor, and Connor barked, "You've got five!"

The others went to the door and saw men in black shirts and things that were once men in crisp black dress uniforms streaming down the passage toward them, screaming curses, chanting prayers. The group took cover behind the open blast door, trying to pin the attackers down, but more and more came up, their line coming inexorably closer.

Barns stuck a fresh magazine into his battle rifle and leaned over, outside of cover, to fire. In the instant he was exposed, a round struck him in the shoulder, sending him reeling sideways. As he fell, three more bursts punched into his chest.

From the rear of the stack, Becky let loose an ear-splitting scream of grief and rage and ran forward with unnatural speed. She flitted past Barns and into the oncoming attackers, oblivious to the hale of bullets perforating her flesh as she barreled into them, still howling, ripping at them with her bare hands, and with her teeth. The two hunters that had led the assault fell first, and the black-shirts that had followed them turned to flee. Few made it. Bellowing rage, Becky tore into them, not only drawing blood but ripping out chunks of flesh and devouring them until she covered head to toe in gore. At last, when the corridor was empty, she turned and ran back to where Barns lay.

Jules squatted over him, cutting his shirt away, slapping patches over the holes in his chest. Barns spasmed on the ground, foam pooling around the edges of his mouth, trying and failing to breathe.

"His lungs are collapsing," Jules announced. "Pneumothorax. Who's got my fucking trauma bag?"

She drew in a deep breath, pinched his nose shut, and put her lips to his, breathing for him. When she broke away, her mouth was covered in frothing pink blood.

"There's a pack of aspirators in the trauma bag. Hurry the fuck up! I need to tap this guy before he suffocates!"

Becky pushed her aside. Kneeling over Barns, she raked her fingernails across her wrist until blood flowed, viscous and black, and she held the wound to his mouth and muttered, "Come on, come on, come on . . ."

Barns managed to take in some of the ichor, but nothing changed. He drew a weak breath and wheezed, "I think . . . we waited too long . . ."

"No, no, no! No, no, we have time; it only takes a second. Come on."

As Barns' spasms and then his ragged breathing stopped, Becky grabbed his shoulders and shook him, howling, "No, no, *no!* We have time, we have time . . . it only takes a second . . . *Goddammit, Steve, look at me!*"

Lukash walked up behind her and laid his hands on her shoulders, telling her, "Becky, my sweet . . . It takes longer than a second to turn someone. You know that."

"No. No, he's gonna be fine . . . In a minute he's gonna wake up and ask what's for dinner . . . just like I did . . ."

"There's . . . not really anything I coulda done, either," Jules added, wiping her mouth. "Those are some pretty gnarly holes. Without a blood transfusion, aspirating the pneumothorax woulda bought him maybe five minutes. Hell, even with a blood transfusion, he'd still be a dead man walking without major surgery."

"And you know that that's still not long enough," Lukash said. "I'm . . . I am so, so sorry, Becky. He's gone."

Becky fell backwards onto the floor, and as she fell they heard more footsteps coming down the passage toward them, and they just managed to duck back behind the door and pull Becky along with them before the bullets began to fly again.

"This is fucked," Mags declared. "There's too many of these jokers; I dunno if we can keep them off of TJ for long enough. And before we even start the countdown, I need that tunnel clear so I can set my demo charges. Otherwise they're just gonna come in behind us and fuckin turn it off."

"We need something to keep them busy," Lukash said, sounding far away.

Mags nodded. "Five minutes of peace and quiet. That's all I need."

"A distraction. A way to buy some time."

"Yeah. Say, man, are you . . . are you okay?"

Lukash stood up between the door and the wall, holstered his revolver, and out of his green ranger's overcoat he drew a gilded, basket-hilt officer's saber. "You will need longer than five minutes," he mumbled. "It might take all of you to hold her back."

He locked eyes with Mags, and the two of them shared a silent conversation in that split second. She nodded, put her hands on his shoulders, kissed his cheeks, and said, "Your . . . your memory will be a blessing, Lichtmann."

He turned away from her and walked over to Becky, where he helped her to her feet and said, with a fatherly smile, "Becky, my sweet . . . I am so, so proud of you."

"Huh?" she sniffed.

"I love you, Becky. I love you like my very own daughter, and I'm so proud of you. And, Becky . . . I am so very sorry."

Without waiting for a response, he reared back and drove the hilt of the saber into her face, sending her flying into the doorframe and collapsing to the ground with her head twisted at a sickening angle. At once they could hear the awful crunch of bones knitting back together as she shakily came to, but before they could even register their shock, Lukash was gone, running off down the passage, into their attackers. There were gunshots, and screams, and then only screams, and as the echo of his footsteps faded into the distance, it was replaced by the sound of a saber hilt banging against concrete, keeping time, and a hearty, determined voice singing:

"Auf, auf, zum Kampf, zum Kampf!
Zum Kampf sind wir geboren!
Auf, auf, zum Kampf, zum Kampf!
Zum Kampf sind wir bereit!
Dem Karl Liebknecht, dem haben wir's geschworen,
Der Rosa Luxemburg reichen wir die Hand! . . ."

The *Oberst-Gruppenfuhrer* paced around the parade field in the rain and darkness as lightning danced overhead, lightning and spook lights, and he demanded answers that no-one had. His facility was under attack, that much was apparent; but the attack had come from inside, and none of the teams sent into the warrens had yet returned.

As Otto demanded more answers that his staff could not give, an officer came running toward him out of one of the magazines, shouting, "Commander, someone is . . . someone is coming!"

"And who is coming?" Otto growled.

"We . . . we don't know. It is just one man—a hunter. He's run right through everyone we've sent to stop him."

"One hunter? How on Earth?"

"I don't know, Commander. He--"

And from the direction the officer come, Otto heard, just over the howling wind, the sound of steel banging rhythmically against stone, and a voice he almost recognized singing:

"Es steht ein Mann, ein Mann
So fest wie eine Eiche!
Er hat gewiss, gewiss,
Schon manchen Sturm erlebt!

Vielliecht ist er schon morgen eine Leiche
Wie es so vielen Freiheitskampfern geht . . ."

The singing stopped, and Otto stared at the blast door in shocked disbelief as a short, lithe man with long black hair and a perfectly manicured black mustache, wearing a wide green *Heckerhut* and a long green *Forstermantel* and swinging around a baskethilt *Offiziersschwert* pranced out onto the parade field, locked eyes with him, and shouted, "Otto, my darling! It has been far too long!"

Otto took a step forward and growled, his voice thick with hatred: "You. Why—*how*—are you here? You should be dead!"

"Only to see how you're getting along, my darling, my dearest, my bear! We have not spoken in many nights. You are doing very well for yourself, it seems; your own base, your own army . . . and to think, it only took you three hundred years."

And Lukash looked around at the gawking crowd of blackshirts and newly-inducted hunters and old-guard *Schutzstaffel Nachtjager* that were gathered around and staring at him in bemused disbelief, and he twirled his saber and shouted, "Ach, you all seem so surprised to see me! Has he not told you about me? I am hurt, Otto! How could you not tell all your friends about your little wolf? Or are you still embarrassed? Ach, you are, aren't you? That is adorable, darling!" He blew a kiss.

Otto, bellowing rage, began to walk toward him, and Lukash laughed, and brandished his saber, and cried out, "Yes, yes, that is what I wanted to see! The fire! The passion! Ach, the passion! Yes, darling! Come here, and let us put to rest the business we should've finished on that rainy night in Russia three hundred years ago."

At those words, Otto's look of rage twisted into an eager, hungry grin, and he called back, "Very well! I don't know how you survived so long, nor how you found your way here—though I suppose it is the wont of a rat to sneak and scuttle around. But if you want to die so badly, little rat, I will be happy to oblige you."

And he drew his own blade, a long, broad steel dagger inscribed with the motto of his former order: *Meine Ehre heisst Treue.* My honor Is Called Loyalty.

Lukash laughed again and shouted, "Yes, yes! Two estranged lovers crossing swords under a raging sky—Euripides might have written it! And this setting? Even more romantic a stage than the opera house."

Otto lunged forward, bellowing like a beast. Lukash danced out of the way and struck out with his saber. Otto parried the blow and lashed out, and Lukash, leaping back, laughed louder and cried out, "You know, Otto, there is something about a swordfight that's just inherently homoerotic, don't you think?"

The big man howled with rage and drove his dagger toward Lukash's heart. Lukash danced out of the way, sending Otto off balance, and he thrust his saber forward, burying it in Otto's stomach. Before he could retrieve the blade to strike again, Otto, with a grim laugh, took a long step forward, walking up the length of the blade, and slashed his dagger across Lukash's stomach, splitting him open. Lukash howled with agony as ichor stained his green overcoat, and he sank to his knees.

"Otto," he wheezed, looking up into the other man's eyes, "Otto, it is ... it is annoying to have to touch a sick man."

That gave Otto pause. He held Lukash's gaze, and his sneer of hatred twitched around its edges, and he muttered, "Not to me. Not if it's you."

And before Lukash could speak again, he thrust his hand forward, into the wound, and hoisted him into the air. Otto meant to kill him, but was stayed as the little man's howls of agony turned into weak, painful laughter and he wheezed, "Ach, I win again!"

"Win? I'm killing you, you damned fool!"

"Otto ... Otto, I ... I have to tell you a joke ..."

Lukash felt Otto's fingers wrap around his cold, still heart, and he groaned, "In the Second World War ... the Soviet Union made a non-aggression pact with the Nazi Germans ... but they knew that the Nazi Germans were their bitterest enemies, and would surely betray them. . . . Otto, why did they do such a thing?"

Otto growled in rage and confusion, and as his vision dimmed, Lukash groaned, "Because, they were . . . Stalin . . . for time! Isn't that . . . a good joke?"

And Otto squeezed, and as Wolfgang Kristops Lichtmann von Lukash, twelfth and last *Landsritter* of Lukash, died his second death, they all felt the ground tremble under their feet, and just faintly heard the roar of three pounds of Semtex detonating.

It took time—far too much time—for the group to find their way out of the warrens, stumbling half-blind through the darkness with Becky trudging along in silence behind them, but eventually they found the fissure in the tunnel that led them up to the storm cellar below the street. They met no resistance and heard no pursuit, their enemies still scrambling to make sense of the mess they'd left and whatever Lukash had done to buy them time.

Prof stood looking up at the stairs with his Geiger counter in one hand and pocketwatch in the other, and he announced. "It looks like it's safe to go topside. Well, not 'safe', but we'll be okay so long as we keep moving. Getting back here took a bit longer than I would've liked, but . . . Oh, Hell. Oh, fuck. Um, TJ, remind me again, how long did you put on the timer?"

"Two hours," they said.

"Ah. How far do you think we can run in 45 minutes?"

The group stood staring back and forth at each other, their eyes wide and mouths agape, for a beat, but only for a beat before all of them—even Becky—dashed up the stairs.

They hit the street at a dead run, moving northwest, back the way they'd come as best they were able, ignoring the rain and wind. They passed the hilltop field with its gruesome monuments, hit the trail blazed by the doomed expedition years ago, managed to put a good few miles behind them before Prof glanced at his pocket-watch, sprinted to the head of the group, and shouted, "One minute! We have one minute!"

They dove behind the lee of a road embankment and hunkered close to the ground, eyes closed, heads covered, waiting. After several eternities, the ground shook like an earthquake beneath them, and a deafening roar that drowned out the howling wind split the night. When the Earth stopped quaking, Mags looked up, looked around, and announced, "Well . . . I guess we did it."

"Yeah, girl scout," Connor said, clapping her on the shoulder. "I guess we did."

Pulling herself to her feet, Mags said, "Y'know, if we are alive and this ain't just a dream, then we just blew open a corridor straight through the Zone north of Old DC. I might just be the last girl scout."

"Heh, I reckon we did. Well, last girl scout, thanks for making us rich."

"Red or black, Connor, we're all communists. The money is pretend."

"Yeah, but it makes a nice jingle-jangle in my pocket that makes me feel like I did something."

"Word. Y'know, all things considered, it feels pretty good to save the world."

Becky, who hadn't spoken since waking up to find Lukash gone, locked eyes with her and said, flatly: "Not worth it. Fuck the world."

The group stood in the rain studying their shoes for a beat, and she added, "Everyone I ever loved is dead. Fuck the world."

Amidst the awkward silence, Jules walked up to her, and took her hand, and said, "Hey. I'm . . . I'm so fucking sorry, about all of that, but y'know, you've still got something."

"Oh? And what's that?"

"You got friends."

Becky looked into her eyes, and her face broke into the barest hint of a smile—a sad, tired smile, but genuine—and she said, "Yeah. I guess I do."

The group decided not to stop in Winchester.

Though no-one had quite guessed what had happened, they knew from radio chatter as soon as they reached Harper's Ferry that people knew, that scavengers were already talking about the group that went to the Citadel and was on its way back, that they were already legends. And they decided almost without talking about it to avoid the B&B, avoid human contact, avoid questions. So, several days after the battle under the Citadel, five tired and filthy scavvers and one strange young woman veiled head to foot arrived back at the clinic in Parson's Hollow without fanfare just as the sun began to set.

Kat and Keith were there, and greeted them warmly and without too many questions. As they filed inside and took off their boots and doffed their rucksacks, Jules took Becky by the hand and led her up to the two nurses, saying, "Kat, Keith, I, uh . . . I want y'all to meet somebody."

"Hell yeah," Kat said. "Any friend of yours is a friend of ours, sis."

"Yeah, I hope so. Listen, this is Becky, and she's my best friend in the whole world, and she's kinda, uh . . . different. She's had a bit of a rough go of it and she needs someplace safe to rest up. I'm gonna be taking off with my girl tomorrow, so I was hoping I could put her up in my old room, if that's okay with y'all."

"Of course. But what do you mean, 'different'?"

And Becky took off the hat and veil she'd worn to hide herself from the sun, and she looked at them with her empty black eyes, and as they recoiled in fear she danced her tongue across her canines and said, "Aw, come on. You act like you've never seen a dracula before."

They were silent for a long moment, as the scavvers tried to suppress laughter, and at last Keith stammered, "Jules, that's . . . you know that's a hunter, right?"

"Uh-huh, and her name's Becky and she's my best friend. When I got dropped off here, y'all told me that this is the right place for misfits and outcasts; and if traumatized ex-Nazi ladyboys can fit in here then I figure draculas probably could too."

Keith stepped forward and clapped Becky on the shoulder. After flinching from the unexpected cold, he said, "Y'know what? I think you're right. Welcome home, Becky."

Becky examined the floor and smiled as they shuffled toward the dining room. As they walked, Keith turned back toward Jules and said, "Y'know, we figured that you and the red were gonna end up shacking up, so while you were gone we asked around and called in some favors and got you a little going-away present."

"Aw, hell, really? What is it?"

"You'll see tomorrow."

"Ah, fuck you."

After dinner, Jules and Mags lay snuggling in her bed while Becky reclined on the floor like a cat. Jules looked around at the space she'd come to think of as hers and said, "Y'know, I'm really gonna miss this place."

"It is nice," Becky muttered. "It . . . it feels like home a little bit."

"When the old man brought me up here and told me 'This is your room now', I cried like a little baby. And y'know what the first thing I did was? I locked the door. And I cried again."

"So is this clinic just like a halfway house for sad bitches?"

"Honestly? Yeah, kinda."

Becky stretched and said, "Well . . . my dad's dead. My boyfriend's dead. And I'm . . . I'm definitely not okay right now, and right now it kinda feels like I might never be okay again. But you were right about one thing."

"Yeah?"

"I guess I do have friends."

"You sure do, sweetheart. Hey, I just thought of something; I've got something I wanna give you."

"Huh?"

"Open up my bag; she should be packed near the top."

Becky opened Jules' rucksack and found, right at the top, a sock doll in the shape of a black cat. She held it up, smiled, and said, "Oh my God, Jules, I love her."

"Mmhmm. She's soaked up a hell of a lot of tears over the past year."

"I love her. Does she have a name?"

"You're not allowed to laugh."

"I won't laugh, I promise."

"Her name's Carmilla."

Becky laughed, laughed long and hard, but as she did she clutched the sock cat tight to her chest and smiled.

———

Behind the clinic, tucked between the back wall and a raised bed of pole beans, grew a row of briar roses. Four of the bushes bore bright red flowers, but near the end, stunted and ragged compared to the others, grew a tangle of vines sporting rich, black blossoms. Jules beamed with pride as she plucked one of the black roses and presented it to Mags, saying, "Pretty nice, ain't it?"

"It's beautiful, honey. Almost as beautiful as you."

"Mags, that's gay."

"This kinda reminds me of you, actually. A snarl of thorns growing out of toxic dirt blossomed into something this beautiful."

Jules threw her arms around her and kissed her. "Mags, *that's* really gay."

"And it's true. But hurry up; we ought to get going soon. We might have to walk all the way to Land's End."

And Jules broke out of their embrace and went back to the rose-bush. She dipped a shovel into the soil and carefully, expertly, cut a circle around the tangle of brambles, lifted it up, and set it into the bucket at her feet. Smiling at a job well done, she said, "Y'know, I really fuckin hope we don't have to walk all that way. I'm gonna have to carry this thing."

And, walking around to the front of the clinic where the others waited to say goodbye, she saw her going-away present waiting for her. The others stood grouped around a sleek, black motorcycle.

"Oh, no goddamn fucking way," she shouted, shoving the rose-bush into Mags' hands and running forward. "Is that a fucking Triumph?"

"Sure is," Kat said, beaming with pride.

"W--where? How?" .

"The engineers down the road were restoring it. We managed to talk them into handing it over."

"Fuck. I . . . God, I used to have one exactly like this."

"We know."

"Yeah. Jesus, I . . . I don't even know what to say."

"You ain't gotta say nothing, sister. Just remember that now you don't have any excuse not to come back and visit us."

"Oh yeah, for sure. I . . . Hell, this is the nicest thing anybody's ever done for me."

Mags put her arms around her nuzzled the top of her head. "I don't know dick about motorcycles, honey, but it does look real nice."

"It is! Now hop on behind me and we'll be at your mom's place in no time."

Jules grinned like a kid at Christmas as she felt Mags' hands lock around her. She laughed as the bike turned over and she felt it roar to life between her legs, and as she puttered out onto the road and started to open up the throttle, she turned her head toward Mags and barked, "Hey, sugar, guess what?"

"What?"

"I'm finally going home!"

Interlude: On Top of the World at the End of the World With You

[21]
THE CORPSMAN

[2255 AD; Cincinnati, Ohio]

BRADDOCK WAS BALLS-DEEP IN THE DOC'S ASSHOLE WHEN THE
MPs came for them.

As she unbuttoned the blouse of her purloined women's auxiliary uniform—which didn't quite fit her; she was almost seven feet
tall—Braddock looked her up and down and thought about how
he (and so many other men) found her at once alluring and terrifying. The subway map of tattoos she sported, ubiquitous to their
order, was unique; rather than fasces and eagles, numbers and
occult symbols, the doc's skin was decorated neck to crotch with
religious iconography. There were the crosses on her hands, an
Orthodox cross on the back of one and a crucifix and rosary on the
back of the other. Or the detail of a martyred St. Vitus on her left
bicep, or the sword and fiery cross on her right. Most of all, the
massive crucifix spread across her chest and abdomen could make
sex a bit awkward, especially since it had been inscribed before
her breasts had begun to bud, giving the arms of the cross a
warped and otherworldly look. Not that things were any better

from the other direction; the doc's back was a ruin of vertical scars harrowed into her skin by a lifetime of countless scourges, most of them self-inflicted. But, of course, that was to be expected of a preacher's daughter.

She kept her skirt on—she always insisted on keeping the skirt on—and Braddock liked that, though as she threw her legs over him he couldn't help but notice it bulging and tenting where those legs met.

And that was where they were when the door to Braddock's room flew open and six armed men stormed in. The doc reacted quickly, as a seasoned expert, springing up from the bed like a cat, and the MPs hadn't come expecting a fight at all, let alone expecting to throw down with a silent, grinning giant wearing nothing but the bottom half of a women's auxiliary uniform, a combat knife, and a smile. She'd already gutted Waskonski before Braddock had even pulled his pants back up, and of the six men who'd come to arrest them, only three were left to beat them half to death and drag them back to the station house.

And there they sat, shackled to chairs in the late Inspector Waskonski's office, and the doc's perpetual smile never left her bruised and bloodied face. She'd managed, like a contortionist, to free one of her long, spidery arms, and she jigged open one of Waskonski's desk drawers and helped herself to the late inspector's cigarettes, and she sat reclining back with ease, her legs crossed, a smoke dangling from her swollen lips, looking as if this was all a perfectly normal Saturday night and not at all a nightmare.

She looked over at Braddock, who was hyperventilating, muttering curses under his breath, and said, "Do try to calm down, darling. All of this fuss is unbecoming."

"How the fuck can you be calm at a time like this?" he sputtered. "We're fucked, man. You know what's about to happen, right? We're fucked. We're dead."

"Oh, they're not going to hang me."

"The hell they're not! We're made, man. We're burned. Right

in the fucking act. Right in the fucking act! Your old man's not gonna be able to get you out of this one, Nick."

She winced at hearing that name, but her smile didn't waver. "They're not going to hang me, dear. I've been planning for this."

"Planning? What the fuck kind of plan could you possibly have, weirdo?"

"Oh, relax, darling. You worry too much. Trust me, and trust in the Lord."

Braddock looked dubious, but he shrank into his chair and tried —and failed—to relax. Several eternities later, the door swung open and a tall, scarred man entered the room; he wore a black shirt with a major's palms, a stetson hat, and a hungry, sadistic grin. Braddock hung his head and said nothing, but the corpsman made a dumb-show of trying to stand up and barked, "Good evening, sir!"

The major smirked. Approaching the desk, he looked them over and said, "So we've got us a couple of lovebirds, I take it."

Neither prisoner reacted. He locked eyes with the corpsman, clucked his tongue, and said, "Corpsman-Lieutenant Wenden. Y'know, when Waskonski told me there was faggotry afoot, I guessed you were involved, you goddamn weirdo. Least now I know why I haven't seen you without a shirt on in the past few whiles."

Her smile didn't waver. "I have a medical condition, sir."

"I'll fucking bet. What about you, Staff Sergeant? Traps what do it for you?"

Braddock looked down and said nothing.

"You know what the first thing I did was when they brought you in, Lieutenant? I called up Father Wenden to have a little chat. He is not very happy with you, Lieutenant. Not very happy at all. Hasn't been for a while, in fact."

"Well, I'm terribly sorry to hear that, sir."

"Don't give me that crap, you goddamn degenerate. This is it, Wenden. You've fucked around for the last time, and goddamn but I can't wait to watch you swing. Tonight's my lucky night if I get to string up Elias's oldest boy—and I will. Daddy ain't coming to save you this time."

"That's quite alright, sir. I don't need him to. You're not going to hang me."

"And what the fuck is that supposed to mean, you goddamn mutant?"

"I would like to speak to the colonel, sir."

"Oh, you want a fucking lawyer, too, while you're at it? You don't get any requests, faggot."

"So you are planning on publicly disposing of a decorated stormtrooper, and Father Wenden's oldest, without consulting your superior officer? That's very interesting, sir."

The major's eye twitched, and his sadistic grin twisted into a sneer of rage, but he didn't respond. As the corpsman's words sank in, he turned and stormed out of the office.

"How the hell did you do that?" Braddock hissed.

"Sometimes it's helpful to be a disappointment, darling. Didn't I tell you to trust me? Soon the colonel will be here and everything will fall into place."

"Rain? Wait . . . Oh, Lord. Him, too?"

"Him primarily, dear. You might be generously called a diversion."

"Yeah. Alright. But what the fuck is Rain gonna do?"

"You ask too many questions, darling. Just relax. And do try to stop all of that whimpering; we are Arditi and it is unbecoming."

"Aw, fuck you, Doc. I wouldn't be in this mess if it wasn't for you, you goddamn freak. This is all your fault."

That made the corpsman's smile twitch, but only just. She fixed him with a withering look and said, "Oh, darling, it's been quite the team effort, I assure you; as they say, it takes two. Or was it all my fault that you were gargling my cock last night?"

They were quiet until, several more eternities later, the door swung open again and the major returned accompanied by a grim, fair-haired man sporting a colonel's bird on his black shirt. He and the corpsman locked eyes for a moment, and she watched with delight as fear flashed across his eyes. When the two men shut the door behind them, Colonel Rain nodded at Braddock and asked, "Is this our guy, Roy?"

The major nodded. "Sure is, sir. Staff Sergeant Frank Braddock. Caught him right in the act."

"Do your thing, Roy. He's all yours."

The major laughed as he moved over to Braddock's chair and started to subdue him. The staff sergeant, weeping now, turned to the corpsman and barked, "You rotten bitch! You said we'd be okay!"

"I most certainly did not," she said, her smile unwavering. "I said that *I* would be okay."

"You goddamn backstabbing faggot whore!"

"Words, words, Frankie."

When Braddock and the major were gone, Rain pinched the bridge of his nose and grumbled, "Him? Really?"

"I make no excuses, darling. I was bored and he was available."

"Tasha, do you want to tell me what the fuck you're trying to accomplish here?"

"You're not going to hang me."

"See if I fucking don't."

"Oh, come now, dear. Charging an Arditi officer with degenerate sexual deviance is already a national embarrassment on its own, and in this case said officer is both a decorated life-saver and the prodigal son—for lack of a better turn of phrase—of an Ecclesiarch. I would say the prodigal son of the presumptive future Patriarch, but, well, tonight may prove inconvenient for Father's career. In any case, darling, you and I both know that there will be no public hanging. There's only one thing for you to do with me: Quietly make me disappear."

"Oh, we're fucking going to."

"I know you are, my dear. In fact, I've planned on it. The question, however, is how."

"Tasha, unless your bigshot daddy tries to stop us—and he won't, not this time—Roy Farley is gonna take you out back and put a bullet in your head. You know that. I know you know that. Get to the goddamn point."

"Of course, darling. What I want to do is offer you . . . a sustainable option. I want to help you avoid any future embarrassments. You see, Roland, I know I may not look the part at the moment, but you know I'm a medical professional; and yes, I made my bones digging bullets out of people, but my preference is psychology. And I've learned some truly fascinating things over these past few years. Did you know that women who share my illness are not so uncommon? There is a group of us in every major settlement."

The colonel blinked in surprise, and the corpsman went on: "You were the first one to notice the changes my body has gone through; did you think I found a pair of tits lying on the ground somewhere? Every major settlement, Roland. I could give you names and addresses, of course. I write everything down. But I have far, far grander ideas than merely saving myself. So, I would have you consider this: You're going to be the Commander someday, Roland, everyone knows that. There's no other man in the entire Falange who's half as worthy. Imagine being the Commander who put an end to all of these embarrassments once and for all."

"This sounds like bullshit, but you have my attention."

"Oh, good. Now, Roland, you must understand: I have a disease. But, as a medical professional, I understand this disease and I understand how to treat it. It will be better for everyone if this little incident were forgotten, so you should free me, keep me on as a corpsman . . . but transfer me from active service to your administration staff. I will give you names, addresses, and affiliations for all the networks I've sussed out, and you can send your little marshals out to round them up, but instead of throwing them away you can give them to me. I can treat antisocial behavior, have them be inoffensive and useful while at the same time rendering them invisible. Of what use is a corpse, darling?"

Roland was quiet for a long moment. At last, he shook his head and said, "God, but you've got some balls."

"That is, unfortunately, correct."

"For a beat there, I thought you were gonna try and blackmail me."

"Oh, heavens no, dear! That would be gauche. A lady *does not* kiss and tell. Why, I believe you once asked me if I knew how to keep my mouth shut."

Shaking his head, the colonel walked behind her chair and began to loose her bonds. Smiling, always smiling, she added, "Oh, and I have one more condition."

"'Condition,' my entire ass. What now?"

"I'm going to wear a skirt."

[22]

THE COURIER

[AD 2260; Columbus, Ohio]

THE COURIER ROLLED OUT OF BED AT 0600 AND STRUGGLED TO her feet, her entire body aching from head to toe and her mind still swimming with nightmares. As she stretched the knots out of her muscles and prodded the fresh bruises blossoming on her arms and around her neck, she idly thought: The sheets are gonna need to be washed.

She shook the ghosts out of her head and pulled a clean women's auxiliary uniform out of her wardrobe, a khaki skirt and a drab brown button-up blouse, along with her boots. The women's auxiliary uniform included sensible flats, but her boots—high-topped, steel-toed black combat boots—were something she'd never been willing to part with. Their size, weight, and associations were comforting, and she reveled in the small act of rebellion. None of the trustees, and not even Tasha, had ever given her any grief for being out of uniform; some of them, she thought, were afraid of her, and rightly so; others were probably content to allow her a small act of rebellion if it meant avoiding something more dramatic; and Tasha, well, Tasha was probably happy that she'd so willingly marked herself as someone to be watched.

After getting dressed, the courier opened the drawer of her nightstand and took out the only thing she owned besides the boots: A little silver medallion bearing the image of St. Monica. She pulled her long black hair back into a ponytail, slipped the chain over her head, and muttered, *"Hail Mary, full of grace, the Lord is with thee. Blessed art thou among women, and blessed is the fruit of thy womb, Jesus. Holy Mary, Mother of God, pray for us sinners, now and at the hour of our death. Amen."*

And she left her little dormitory room and walked out into the hallway, examining the floor as she went. They'd be serving breakfast downstairs, but she had no appetite and didn't feel up to speaking with anyone, and she certainly didn't want to be alone with her thoughts. Better to head out and see what work was available for the day. Better to stay busy.

As she walked, the courier heard the sharp metronome of sensible heels clicking against the tile floor, and she felt an icy knot of fear clench in her guts as she lifted her head and rolled her shoulders back to stand up ramrod-straight. That would be Natasha.

Coming toward her in the hallway was another woman, towering well over a foot above her, wearing a black button-up shirt and a long black skirt, her blonde hair styled into a perfect pageboy, her cold blue eyes boring into and through everything, a sickening empty smile plastered across her face. She carried a clipboard under her left arm, and her lapels sported a major's palms and a corpsman's staff. The courier had no rank now, but she'd been a corporal once.

"Good morning, Julia!" the director called out in a too-happy, sing-song voice, stretching "good morning" out into too many syllables. "You're up bright and early as always, I see."

The courier only gave her a polite nod and an obligatory "Good morning, major." Tasha patted her shoulder as they passed each other.

Over the past eighteen months, the courier had become an expert at playing the part assigned to her, meeting expectations, hiding in plain sight, but no matter how much time passed she could never bring herself to be pleasant to Tasha. She hated her for the things she'd done as much as she feared her for the power she wielded, and as she walked she reveled in a fantasy, imagining how good it would feel to wrap her hands around the flesh-merchant's throat and *squeeze . . .*

She made her way outside and onto the facility's grounds, which weren't much—a two-story dormitory, a clinic, and an office —but it was ringed with a high fence topped by double spirals of razor wire, and there were bars across all of the windows. She walked around to the usual pickup point, a kiosk off of the side of the office, and saw that Tabby was working pickup today. That made her smile; Tabby, at least, was someone she could talk to. Coming closer, she saw that Tabby was also sporting a constellation of fresh bruises, and that her eyes were red and swollen from crying, but even so, as the courier approached, Tabby gave her a warm smile, waved, and called out, "G'morning, hon!"

"Mornin, Tabby. What do they got for me today?"

Tabby rummaged around in the kiosk and brought up a canvas messenger bag, a motorcycle key, and three brown envelopes. "Good day for you," she said. "Only three stops, but they're all over the place. You'll probably be out until after lunch."

And as the courier took the items, Tabby gave a conspiratorial look around and added, "And, listen, today—and tonight—would be a really good time to stay busy. They posted six new staff officers across the street yesterday."

The two women made eye contact and shared a solemn nod, nothing more needing to be said. The courier was about to walk off, but as she read over her itinerary for the day, she couldn't stop the look of surprise from spreading across her face, surprise mingled with the first stirrings of another emotion she hadn't felt in a long time: Hope.

"Hey, Tabby?" she asked, looking up, taking another look around to make sure they were alone.

"Yeah, hon. What's up?"

"Listen, I just wanted to say, you . . . you've been a really good friend all this time."

Tabby looked confused. "Uh . . . you, too, Jules. Say, I've got my day off tomorrow, do you wanna hang out or somethin?"

"No, Tabby, listen, I . . . I really don't think I coulda lasted in this hellhole if you weren't here with me. You're my best friend. And I . . . Tabby, I'm so fucking sorry."

"Sorry? For what?"

"Ah, nuthin. Forget about it. I'll, uh . . . I'll see you around, hon."

And the courier shouldered her messenger bag, turned, and headed around to the back of the office, trying her best to keep her composure as too many emotions roiled up inside of her. That proved easy enough as the rudiments of a plan began to come together in her mind, and the plan became a job, a mission; it was the easiest thing in the world for her to be a soldier with a mission.

There were a few bikes parked in the back of the office, and she noticed that Tabby had handed her the key for the one she preferred to take for courier work, a Honda which she hated on principle but which ran okay, at least for going around town. It felt good, in any case, to feel the engine rumbling between her legs, though it always brought back an uncomfortable pang of memory, recalling the Triumph she'd once owned, back in another life.

She puttered up to the gate and handed the guard her itinerary. He looked it over, made a few notes, handed it back, and asked, "When do you plan on being back?"

"A little after lunch, sir. Not that many drops, but the route's all over the place."

"Uh-huh. See that you're checked back in before 1400, or you know what'll happen."

"Yes, sir. Understood, sir."

Once clear of the fence, she let her stony expression fade away into one of desperate hope as she turned onto State Street and headed toward the first drop. One of the addresses on her list was a fair piece away, well outside of the downtown cordon, almost on the old highway, and she had a reason to be there, and had a reason to be away from the facility for a solid few hours, and maybe the Honda wasn't the best bike but it was small and quiet and smooth and had a full tank of gas and it would go fast enough if she told it to.

As she puttered off down the street, past the throngs of men under arms in their brown and black uniforms, past the groups of women walking quickly with their heads down, past the martial statues and tanks up on blocks and the murals sporting slogans like "Stand Up, White Man!" and "One God, One State, One Chosen Race," and past the street corners where murders of crows and swarms of flies lingered over lampposts and scaffolds where condemned men were left hanging, the courier tried her best not to laugh, and in time with the cycling of the engine between her legs, she muttered, *"Never going back . . . never going back . . . never going back . . ."*

The second drop lay on the far east side of town, past the military cordon, at the permanent city guard camp between Deshler and the old 70. Eastward still, across eight lanes of crumbling highway, lay the decaying ruins of what had once been miles upon miles of sprawling suburb, now abandoned save for a few small settlements at important highway intersections. East of that lay God-knows-what, and a lot of nothing, but southeast . . . south or southeast, barely a day's run by motorcycle, lay the Ohio Valley, and on the south bank of the Ohio, well, they all knew the stories. Across the Ohio lay the Ashland Confederate Republic, a society of degenerate Bolshevist atheists where Jews and muds and queers ran things in defiance of God and all natural laws. The courier knew enough about the Ashlanders and their society, having once made her living shooting and stabbing and blowing up Ashlanders, and she'd been quite good at it, back in another life. She knew enough to know that they would probably shoot her on sight as soon as she crossed the river, but getting shot still sounded like a better afternoon than going back to the Institute. Her bruises reminded her of that as she hit a bump in the road and bounced up and down on her seat, and Tabby's words rattled around in her mind: Six new staff officers posted across the street yesterday.

She stopped in front of the guard shack outside of the camp, took one of the big brown envelopes out of her messenger bag, and approached the door. The guard shack was only staffed by one soldier, but he was enough: He didn't wear the ugly brown uniform of most soldiers, but rather a black button-up shirt with silver eagles embroidered on the collar. His sleeves were rolled up to the elbows, showing off forearms covered in stick-and-poke tattoos. The courier was intimately familiar with that uniform and with those markings.

As she walked up, the guard gave her a polite nod, lit a cigarette, and said, simply, "Yo."

"Got a parcel for Father Donovan," she said.

"Cool. He's out right now, but I can sign for it."

"Works for me. Say, uh . . . can a girl borrow a smoke? Sir?"

The stormtrooper cocked his head and gave her a quizzical look, and she felt an icy knot of terror clench in her belly, and she watched his eyes to try and determine if they were lingering on her trachea, hands, shoulders, the shadow under her chin. The moment passed, though, and he shrugged and tossed her a pack of cigarettes and a book of matches. She lit one, took a long drag, moaned with contented relief, and said, "Oh, *Mama Maria, Madre di Dio*. Thank you, sir."

"Sure thing, lady. Been a minute, huh?"

"You have no idea, sir." And she glanced behind him and noticed a tin pot simmering on a hot plate inside of the shack. "Say is that coffee?"

"What about it?"

"Well, uh . . . do you mind?"

He gave her a funny look again, plainly registering that her behavior was far out of the ordinary, but he shrugged again and said, "Help yourself."

"You are a real pal, sir."

The courier walked into the guard shack, and the blackshirt followed her. All according to plan. As she stood in front of the desk, pouring herself a cup of coffee with her back to him, he cleared his throat and said, "Hey, lady, let me ask you a question."

She tightened her grip on the tin pot; this would be it.

"Yeah, shoot."

"How the hell come a women's aux courier is wearing stormtrooper boots?"

The courier spun around quicker than thinking and slammed the coffee pot into the side of his head, stunning him, spraying boiling liquid across his face and chest. Before he could recover or even shout, she was already moving, slipping behind him and throwing an arm across his throat, pressing his head forward into the choke, hooking her feet behind his knees as they sank to the floor together. She held him tight until he stopped struggling, kept hold a minute longer for good measure, then sprung up, opened her messenger bag, and started filling it. There were a few tins of food in the shack, as well as the guard's combat knife, and his ammo bag, and his Armalite rifle, which fit in the bag once it was broken down.

For a beat, she thought about stealing his clothes. Her women's aux uniform stuck out like a sore thumb, whereas an Arditi stormtrooper could go anywhere in the BNR without too many questions, and he wasn't that much taller than her, and maybe her breasts weren't too big, and maybe her face wasn't too soft, and she already had the boots . . . but no. No, never again.

She looked down at her khaki skirt, drawing comfort from it, and she kicked the dead man, laughed aloud, and declared, "Never again. Never again!"

Hopping back on the Honda, the courier puttered out onto the road at a lazy pace until she was out of sight of the camp, then turned onto the highway and let the throttle out, building speed. Too much speed, she knew, but she found it difficult to care. As she sped away, she broke out into laughter, howling laughter, mixed with tears of joy and relief.

She saw few people, and none of those she did see made any attempt to stop or to follow her. Perhaps nobody had made the connection between the motorcycle courier and the dead guard, or perhaps they were slow in getting the word out. Perhaps they were just that happy to finally see the back of her, to not have to deal with her anymore, just like when they'd tried so hard to make her disappear eighteen months ago. Very unlikely, but, she thought, sometimes it might be useful to be a national embarrassment.

It was mid-afternoon when the courier decided it might be time to turn south, to get off of the exposed highway and into the hills, to head for the river. When she was sure there were no people around, she made to turn onto a side road heading that way.

The crumbling pavement, first laid over two hundred years before and barely maintained even when it was new, heaved under the Honda's weight, and in a moment the front wheel caught nothing but gravel, and before she even had time to curse the courier found herself tumbling through the air before landing hard in the dirt with a sickening thud. She lay there groaning for what felt like hours before at last deciding that she wasn't dead, and she pulled herself to her shaking feet and found that though she now sported all new constellations of bruises, nothing seemed to be broken. A miracle; the Honda had spun into a tree a few yards away and would never run again.

328 / NATALIE IRONSIDE

"Hail Mary," she muttered, fishing the St. Monica medallion out of her blouse, "full of grace, the Lord is with thee, blessed art thou among women and blessed is the fruit of thy womb, Jesus . . ."

Stretching, and picking up the messenger bag which had fallen next to her, the courier turned south and looked into the forest and, beyond it, the hills. With a heavy sigh, she tightened her boots and started walking.

[23]
ON TOP OF THE WORLD AT THE END OF THE WORLD WITH YOU

Emma Blackadder finished her day's work in the early afternoon. She went home, took off her shoes, and decided to spend an hour or two catching up on her reading before she thought about what to do for dinner. Every day someone invited her to one of the communal meals that were always on offer at the union hall or the schoolhouse or someone's home, and she knew that they fretted over the aging woman eating alone in an empty house, but she preferred her solitude. Not that she didn't love her comrades, her neighbors, the children, but moving through social situations could be exhausting and she cherished her moments of peace and quiet. Even her daughter, who had inherited her mother's temperament and always kept to herself, was enough of a presence that Magnolia Jane's absence made the house feel bigger, more serene.

Emma worried about her, from time to time, but not often. Magnolia Jane could take care of herself.

The hardest part of the day was agonizing over which book to pick up. Surveying her bookshelf, she shillied over whether to start a new volume of Lenin or to re-read one of her old fantasy novels. After several minutes of careful deliberation, she settled on the novel—no sense in working all the time—and she walked out to her porch and her rocking chair with a cup of coffee and an ancient copy of *A Wizard of Earthsea* and sat down to the sublime music of birds chirping in the trees and bees buzzing through the fields.

She'd only just opened her Le Guin when the picturesque scene was shattered by the roar of a motorcycle engine coming down the lane. Rolling her eyes, she looked around and spotted a sleek black Triumph T120 which was, comically, being driven by a very small woman with a very tall woman seated precariously behind her. She was about to return to her book when she noticed the tall woman's distinctive mane of wild red hair.

The bike puttered to a stop in front of Emma's porch, and Mags hopped off, leading her companion by the hand. The stranger wore her long, black hair pulled back into a ponytail and glowered forward with a pair of fierce brown eyes set into a scowling face; she would've looked intimidating, if her face wasn't contorted into a look of abject terror.

"Hey, Mama," Mags said with a wave as she approached the porch.

"Hey there, Magnolia Jane. Job go okay?"

"I dunno about 'okay', but it went."

"Sounds about right. So who's the foreigner?"

Mags pulled Jules forward. "Somebody I'd really like you to meet. Mama, this is Julia."

"A pleasure."

"Mama, I'd, ah . . . I'd really like it if Julia could stay here with us for a while."

Emma gave them the vaguest hint of a smile. "Is that right? Well, what are y'all waitin for? Come on up here."

They ascended the steps onto the porch, with Mags pushing Jules in front of her, and Emma turned toward Jules and asked, "So where'd you come from?"

"Uh . . . From Freeside, Mrs. Blackadder."

"Anarchist?"

"Uh . . . I don't know, Mrs. Blackadder."

Her smile broadened, and she nodded toward Mags and said, "Magnolia Jane, go inside and put on some more coffee."

Breaking away to head for the door, Mags planted a quick kiss on Jules' lips and said, "Relax, honey. There's nothing to be worried about."

And when they were alone, Emma took a sip of her coffee and said, "Child, you ain't got nuthin to worry about. I'm glad you're here."

"R-really?"

"If you've known my daughter for longer than a minute, you know how she is. And I ain't seen her smile like that in a whole lot of years."

Jules relaxed a bit, and Emma went on: "Let's try it like this. Tell me about my daughter."

At that, Jules' eyes sparkled, and her grim expression curled up into a smile. "She's . . . she's amazing. She's so smart; she's the smartest person I've ever met. And she's so sweet and so strong . . . God, since the moment we met, she's all I've been able to think about."

"Yeah, you ain't got nuthin to worry about. Listen: I trust my daughter, and if she wants you here then that's good enough for me on its own. And if you look at her and see the same woman I do, well, that's a whole hell of a lot."

"Oh, jeez. Thanks, Mrs. Blackadder."

"Now what the hell is you so nervous about?"

Jules looked into her eyes and saw that the question was genuine, that Emma did not understand why the interaction should be difficult, and she chuckled and said, "Well, Mrs. Blackadder, I guess I still got a lot to learn about the way things work around here."

"Reckon so. By the way, please quit callin me that. My name is Emma."

Jules stammered, gave a nervous laugh, said, "I, uh . . . I don't think I can do that, Mrs. Blackadder."

"Well, then, you can call me 'Mama,' like my other daughter does."

And when Mags stepped back out onto the porch a moment later, she found a somewhat bewildered Emma standing up and holding Jules, who was weeping happy tears.

The afternoon passed slow and easy. Jules pulled her bike around to the back of the cabin, dumped her few meager possessions in Mags' room, and as she took the Armalite rifle off of the top of her rucksack and leaned it against the wall in the corner, she stood there in silence and considered it for a long moment.

"Gonna need another gun rack as well as a bigger bed," Mags said. "What a pair we make, huh?"

"Yeah."

"Something on your mind, hon?"

"Yeah."

"You wanna talk about it?"

"I don't know. I . . . It's complicated, I guess. I just know that every time I put that thing down, I'm gonna have to pick it up again. War is the only thing I've ever done, the only thing I've ever been any good at, for years, but now? It hurts me to look at that thing, sugar. I wish it could just sit in that corner and collect dust forever."

Mags put an arm across her shoulders, and she leaned into the embrace and recited:

"Let the boy try along this bayonet-blade
How cold steel is, and keen with hunger of blood;
Blue with malice, like a madman's flash;
And thinly drawn with famishing for flesh."

"I love it when you do that," Mags said.

"Aw, hell, really?"

"Yeah. I'm the luckiest woman in the world; I got a girlfriend who recites war poetry by heart and talks yearningly about beating her sword into a plowshare."

Jules blushed. Mags held her tight and asked, "You ever write any original verse?"

"Nah, nah, that ain't me. I'm not smart like you are."

"Yes the hell you are."

"Ah, c'mon. I never went to school."

"Yeah, but you're bilingual."

"Ah, *non e niente*. So are you."

"Exactly. And a year ago you were functionally illiterate, until you memorized two books of Yeats and Owen. You should cut yourself some slack."

"Huh, maybe you're right."

"Yeah. You've spent your whole life being told who and what you are and what you have to be, but that's over with; you can be whoever you want to be."

"Aw, jeez, that's a tall order. Honestly, I . . . I don't know what that would look like."

"We've got all the time in the world to figure it out, hon. Right now, let's go eat; it's almost dinnertime."

"I like the sound of that. What are we having?"

"Dunno. Depends on whose turn to cook it is."

Jules' eyes lit up at that, and she pranced back into the kitchen and asked, "Hey, uh . . . would it be cool if I took care of dinner? I promised Mags I'd cook for her."

"I reckon so," Emma said. "What were you figurin on making?"

"I was gonna make a minestra."

"Alright. Whatcha need for that?"

"Gonna need garlic, onions, beans, sausage, broth, and chicory. We got all that?"

"'Do we got all that?', she asks. Of course I got all that. What kinda barbarian you think I am?"

Jules grinned as she began rooting around through the cabinets and the ancient, rumbling refrigerator and Mags lit the old cast-iron stove, and as they worked she drew in a deep breath and in a high, exuberant voice, began to sing:

"E le genti che passeranno,
O bella ciao, bella ciao, bella ciao, ciao, ciao
E le genti che passeranno
Mi diranno, 'Che bel fior!'
"Questo e il fiore del partigiana
O bella ciao, bella ciao, bella ciao, ciao, ciao
Questo e il fiore del partigiana
Morto per la liberta . . ."

———

After midnight, the portraits on Mags' bedroom wall rattled in their frames as she slammed Jules against the door again, holding her tighter, kissing the back of her neck and panting, "That feel good, honey?"

"So fuckin good," Jules moaned as she thrust into the hand between her legs. "So fuckin good . . . God, Mags, your clit's so fucking huge . . ."

"Good . . . I gotta make my girl feel good . . ."

"So fucking good . . . Aw, fuck, sugar, I'm getting close . . ."

"Oh, yeah. Come for me, honey."

Jules shook and screamed as she released into Mags' hand, and Mags whispered, "Yeah, that's my good girl . . . that's my fucking good girl . . . God, you're so pretty when you come . . ."

And, a moment later, she finished herself, pressing herself tight against Jules' back and gasping, "I love you . . . I love you . . . I love you . . ."

And the two women tumbled backwards onto the pile of blankets that would serve as their bed until Mags could find something bigger than her cot in the corner, gasping for breath, giggling, and as they held each other, Jules buried her face in Mags' chest and panted, "I fucking love you."

"I fucking love you, too, honey. You're so goddamn beautiful and I love you so fucking much."

"Fuck, that was incredible. Mags . . . Mags, is this real? Did today really happen?"

"It sure did, honey. Every little bit of it."

"Holy shit. Mags, I . . . I'm home now, aren't I?"

"You sure are. This is your home—our home. This is our room, where we live together. As soon as I get a bed in here, that'll be our bed."

Jules laughed and wept into Mags' chest, and Mags held her tight, and after a moment she caught her breath and laughed, "Crying after sex, but in like a good way. Call that growth."

Mags lay there in silence for a beat, unsure how to respond, and Jules kissed her and added, "Today doesn't feel real because every day since I met you has been the best day of my life."

"Aw, hell," Mags yawned, "now you're trying to make *me* cry."

It wasn't long before Mags' yawns turned into snores, and Jules luxuriated in the warmth and smell and closeness of her for a few minutes, but she felt restless. Disentangling herself from Mags' arms, she got up and started to pull her jeans back on but stopped when something occurred to her. The whim felt ridiculous, but she ran with it, tiptoeing over to the chest of drawers against the far wall and looking through Mags' clothes. At first Mags seemed to own nothing but uniforms, but hidden amongst the flecktarn pants and blouses and sleeveless blue-and-white undershirts, she managed to find a t-shirt. It would've been a little too long for Mags, and on her it hung almost down to her knees, which made the exercise feel all the more adorable.

The front of the t-shirt was emblazoned with the crude abstract of a map and the words "Gettin Lucky In Kentucky."

She grabbed a pack of cigarettes and Mags' zippo and tiptoed out of the bedroom, through the darkened kitchen, and out onto the porch, where she stopped dead in her tracks as she saw Emma sitting in her rocking chair, reading by a miner's lamp.

"Evenin," the older woman said, without looking up. "Or, mornin, I suppose."

Jules kept silent, stood frozen in place, and Emma did look up and saw that she was trembling, a pained look frozen on her face, and she closed her book and asked, "Somethin the matter, child?"

"We were . . ." Jules stammered, "and you . . . Aw, fuck. I . . . I'm sorry."

"Nah, it ain't nuthin. I was already up."

Jules stayed frozen in place, and Emma recognized the same anxiety she'd seen earlier in the day, and she sighed and said, "When folks live in the same house, they do human activities and sometimes they make noise. That's just life. I dunno how they do things wherever you come from, but I promise I don't give a half a damn what you and my daughter get up to. I just wanna read my goddamn book."

Jules relaxed a bit, but only a bit, and Emma furrowed her brows and said, "You don't act like no Freesider I ever met."

With a sigh, Jules took a few awkward steps forward, into the light, and Emma raised her eyebrows as she looked over the tattoos covering her forearms, and, steeling herself, she said, "Well, Mags did find me in Freeside, but yeah. I'm from Ohio."

"What in the goddamn . . ."

"Yeah. I, uh . . . I got some history."

"Oh, I'll bet. And I know women ain't got tattoos like that. You and my daughter have got a lot in common, huh?"

"Yeah. I, uh . . . I was a part of somethin I shouldn't have been, until I wound up on the wrong end of it. And now I'm here."

"Well . . . I'ma stand by what I said earlier. I trust my Magnolia Jane. If she says you're alright, you're alright."

Smiling sadly, Jules sat down on the porch next to the rocking chair, lit a cigarette, and said, "I sure hope so, 'cause that's what I been tellin myself, too."

"You, ah . . . You been hurt, ain'tcha, child?"

"Yeah. Yeah, Mama, I been hurt pretty bad. By a lot of people."

"I can tell. I can see it in your eyes, the way you carry yourself. Did Magnolia Jane tell you what happened to her sister?"

"Yes, ma'am."

"Please cut it out with that 'ma'am' shit already. I work for a living." And Emma shut her book and said, "I'll never forget Abe or our baby girl. I loved that man, loved him with my whole heart. Never been able to get close to anybody again the way I was close to Abe. Raised two babies together, two beautiful daughters—Magnolia Jane says she didn't know for a long while, but I always sorta guessed—and then . . . well, you know the rest. We all grieved together, but Magnolia Jane took it especially hard. She blames herself, y'know. Survivor's guilt."

Jules looked up at Emma in wonder. In all ways, Emma Blackadder had seemed cold, distant, almost austere, even more so than Mags, but this raw weeping wound in her heart had opened up as readily as if they were discussing the weather. Emma read the surprise on her face and said, "Let me guess: Magnolia Jane is the first Ashlander you've actually met."

"Yes, m—uh, yeah."

"I'm glad to see you here, child, because my daughter's kept herself cut off from the world for way too long. It ain't healthy. You've heard what we say around here, right? 'All is for all.'"

"Yeah. All is for all."

"We share everything in common around here, the bad along with the good. When there's work to be done, we work together; when there's plenty, we eat together; when there ain't, we suffer together; and when we pass away, we bury our dead together, we mourn them together, and we weep together, and we heal together." She held out her hand, as though going for a shake, and asked, "You see what that is, child?"

"I don't follow."

"An empty hand, same as yours. You came to my door with an

empty hand, and I'm glad to offer you the same right back; two empty hands can clasp in solidarity. I own nothing, I command no-one, and no-one can command me, and because I own nothing, I'm richer than God. All is for all."

Jules sat digesting her words in silence for a while, watching the fireflies dance in the fields out beyond the yard. At last, she took a long drag on her cigarette, sighed, and said, "I was . . . I was fifteen years old the first time I killed a man."

"Tell me about it, Blacklander."

"Firefight along the Ohio Valley. I caught a red in my sights and I put a hammered pair right through the center of his face, watched him spin around as he pitched backwards. I pissed and shit all over myself, and then when it was over I threw up and I cried. The old guys just clapped me on the back and told me I'd get used to it. They were right."

"You never shoulda been there."

"Thank you. Thank you for that. I . . . I was a kid. I didn't know shit about shit. All I wanted to do was play stickball and make out with Jane Braddock and skip church. But apparently when you're 15 you're a whole adult and you've gotta go fulfill your civic duty."

"Fuckin monstrous, that is."

"Yes. Thank you. And I . . . I know a thing or two about survivor's guilt. Getting from there to here was a hell of a long, hard road with a lot of twists and turns, and I . . . I can't tell you where I ended up. Maybe someday I will, but not now. Enough to say it was Hell; like somebody had custom-built a special Hell just for me. And I . . . I . . . I had to leave my best friend behind to make it out. I just . . . I just fucking left her there."

"Say her name, child."

"Tabby. Tabitha Lynn Markhov. She . . . she was like me, and like Mags, and that was how we ended up there, except for she was innocent—she was like a filing clerk or something before she broke bad. And I . . . I just left her behind. There was nothing I coulda done different, I *know* that, but . . . fuck . . . Tabby was the one who should've gotten out. It should be Tabby sitting here with a new home and a safe place to heal and a girlfriend, not me. I don't deserve this." And she drew in a long, rattling breath and said, "If I could, I would go back. I would go right back there and switch places with her. She's . . . she's probably dead by now, and if she ain't dead then she's got more salt in her than I ever will, but if I ever saw her again I could fall on my knees and beg forgiveness a thousand times but I'd never be able to look her in the eyes again."

Jules was surprised, almost unnerved by how easily the story came spilling out of her, but Emma seemed to expect it. She reached out and laid a hand on Jules' shoulder, and Jules, tears streaming down her face, continued:

"F-five times. I've tried to kill myself five times. And every time, I got closer to making it stick. That place is locked down tight, but I'm a fucking operator, I can turn anything into a weapon. Every time . . . every time, it was Tabby who found me, patched me up, got me back on my feet—she had a sense for when I was about to break. The fifth time, when I came back around, I . . . I begged her to stop. Begged her to just let me die, let it be over, let me finally have some peace. She held me tight and she said, 'Jules, I need you. Please don't go, not where I can't follow. Please don't leave me here alone. I need you.' And that . . . that was the day I decided I wanted to live. And y'know what I did, in the end? Y'know what I fucking did? I went where she couldn't follow. I left her there alone. Some fucking friend I am."

Emma was quiet for a long while. At last, she said, "I can see why you and my little girl get along so well. You sound exactly like her."

Through her tears, Jules smiled, and she muttered, "Aw, hell, I sure do, don't I?"

"Mmhmm. Magnolia Jane still blames herself for what happened to Margaret, and I bet you know all about that. But she was just a baby herself when it happened; she was as much a victim as my Margaret, and nobody coulda helped it. That sounds about like you and your friend. Sounds like you were in an impossible situation and did the only thing you coulda done. Whatever happened to your friend, you're blameless; fault lies with the people who hurt y'all."

"Fuck. Thank you, Mama. Thank you so goddamn much. Nobody's . . . nobody's ever told me that before. I've . . . I've done some bad shit and I've got a lot of atonement to catch up on, but . . . but at least I never did *that*."

"Mmhmm. I do know exactly how you feel, though. Not a day goes by that I don't grieve for my husband, or my baby girl, or Magnolia Jane's childhood, and a part of me is always gonna blame myself for it. But the rest of us, we turned our pain outward, and we carry the weight of it together, as a community, same as anything else—all is for all. A lot of backs make for a light load. My oldest, though, she . . . she turned inward, internalized all that blame, tried to bear the burden all by herself. Now she smokes too much, drinks too much coffee, never sleeps, works all the goddamn time. Trying so hard to save everybody else that she's killing herself, and I worry about her."

"Yeah. Yeah, that sounds like Mags."

"I'm glad you're here, child. I don't think she has one single friend. The last time she mentioned a relationship was about four years ago. She's been needing somebody to share all that hurt with who ain't a bitter old widow sharing a house of death."

Jules blinked as she digested those words, and she muttered, "I never even thought of that. Mags and I made love in the room her sister died in."

"Mmhmm."

"Jesus Christ. Why . . . why wouldn't y'all move to a different place?"

"Because this is our home. There's a lot of grief in these walls, but there's so much love and life, too, and anywhere else would feel . . . sterile. Empty. Listen: Did Magnolia Jane tell you about the mass graves?"

"Yeah. She said it's tough to mourn when there's no headstones."

"She would say that. I bet she didn't tell you the end of that story. Y'know what those plots of ground are today?"

"Nah."

"They're orchards, Julia. All our pain and suffering and bitterness went into that ground, and when things got better, it came right back up as strong, green trees and beautiful flowers. That's a better monument to my Abe or my baby girl than any cold piece of stone could ever be. And that's about how I feel, thinkin of you two in that room together; we'll always remember the pain, we'll always carry our scars, but scars are what forms when you grow and heal."

"That's . . . aw, hell, that's beautiful."

"Glad you agree, Ashlander."

Jules gave a contented sigh, and she said, "So, in light of that, I gotta ask . . . A minute ago, before I came out here, that . . . that wasn't weird?"

Emma opened her book and replied, in her frank and direct way, "Well, no, it was pretty fucking weird to have to listen to my daughter destroy somebody's asshole while I'm trying to finish my goddamn novel two rooms over, but I wasn't gonna say anything about it. We're all adults here."

Jules grimaced and blushed bright red. Emma patted her shoulder and concluded: "Listen, kid. The secret to harmonious communal living is all about what we choose not to hear. You go get some sleep, and we'll go on with our lives pretending that this didn't happen."

The next morning, Mags woke up just before dawn and woke Jules up as she stirred. They held each other close under their blankets and shared soft, sleepy kisses until Mags started to nod off again and broke off the embrace to sit up and rub the sleep from her eyes.

"Sugar," Jules yawned, "we should do something today."

"Like what?" Mags asked, pulling herself to her feet.

"I don't fuckin know, I ain't never been here before. But, like . . . If this is where I live now, I'd like to go check it out."

"I like the sound of that. I dunno what's going on at the moment, but after we've had some coffee we can go next door and see what's posted on the notice board." She yawned and stretched. "I've been on vacation for eighteen whole hours and I already don't know what to do with myself."

"How long you think we've got before shit picks back up, anyways?"

"Not as long as I'd like. I give it a week, two at the most, before Central finishes processing that report I dropped off in Land's End, then a couple days before they send somebody here to collect us. They'll want to debrief both of us, go over the report with me, do your official onboarding interview . . . Gonna be a lot of repetitive questions in both of our futures."

"Back when we first met, you mentioned that that interview might not be a whole lot of fun. There anything I need to be worried about?"

"Well, that was before you became a war hero. I really don't think your loyalties are gonna be in any doubt."

As Mags went to her dresser and took out another pair of flecktarn pants and another tank top, Jules laughed and asked, "Sugar, is that really what you're gonna wear?"

"Yeah. Why wouldn't I?"

"You're on vacation, sug."

"Well, uh . . . These are pretty much the only clothes I own."

They dressed and walked into the kitchen, where Emma was already awake with a pot of coffee going. She gave them a curt nod and said, "Mornin, girls."

"Mornin, Mama," Mags yawned. "Early day today?"

"Mmhmm. We're doing library inventory today. Probably be busy till dinnertime."

"Oof. Y'all need any help with that?"

"No. No, we don't."

"I could--"

"No. You're too busy."

And Mags glanced over at Jules and said, "Yeah. Yeah, my time's spoken for. Speaking of: You know if there's anything going on in town today?"

"I hear they're putting on a show at the union hall."

Mags rolled her eyes as she and Jules poured cups of coffee and sat down. "Let me guess: They're fucking doing *Fiddler On The Roof* again?"

"Nah, not this time."

"Well then it must be *Les Mis*."

"Mmhmm."

As Emma headed out the door, Jules threw back another cup of coffee and said, "Y'know, sugar, I must be pretty bad at being on vacation, too, 'cause I keep thinking . . . What am I gonna, like, do?"

"Eh, we'll figure it out. We've got all day."

"No, I mean, like . . . with the rest of my life. I don't wanna spend another minute doing the only thing I was ever any good at."

"Oh, honey, you're good at lots of stuff. You love your roses, right?"

"Yeah. I do love my roses."

"Well, you're in the heart of our agricultural base. You can be a gardener. We always need more of those."

And Jules stared off into the middle distance, a hopeful smile on her face, and muttered, "God, that . . . that sounds nice as hell. I . . . Fuck, that's it. That's what I want. I wanna throw my Armalite away and grow plants till I'm an old lady."

And Mags laughed, and declared, "Julia, honey, I know what we're doing today."

"Oh, really? What are we doing today, Magnolia?"

"I'm taking you to the model forest."

"What the fuck is a model forest?"

"You'll see."

A few minutes by motorcycle to the south, between Boone Creek and the Kentucky River, stood a few acres of woodland. Orchards of fruit and nut trees were blended seamlessly in with the native hardwoods, and each tree sported a bird feeder, or bat box, or beehive—the whole area was the thick with the droning of a hundred different species of bees—or a trellis thick with hanging beans, melons, or cucumbers. With ample space between each tree, the forest floor was an unbroken carpet of herbs and wildflowers and prairie grass. Mags and Jules stood at its verge, next to a group of rammed-earth buildings and a sign proclaiming, "Ashland Agriculturalist Syndicate—Bureau of State Ecology—Weyepiersenicah Agriforestry Laboratory."

Jules gawked at the trees like a kid at Christmas, her sad eyes sparkling, her mouth agape, and declared, "This is fucking great."

Mags nodded. "Ain't it, though?"

"I love it! What the fuck is it?"

"This is how we make sure nothing like the Hunger ever happens again. This whole area is a laboratory where we're coming up with new ways to integrate agriculture into the native forest ecology."

"I fucking love it. I love everything about it. I've never seen anything better than this. I . . . Mags, I never wanna leave."

From off to their left, a tall Black woman in a blue gingham dress and heavy work boots who'd been leaning against one of the buildings having a smoke noticed them and came walking over. She waved as she came up and said, "Oh, hey there, Mags. You here to see the kids?"

"Nope," Mags said, beaming with pride. "I'm on vacation."

The woman laughed. "Really? Comrade Political Commissar is on vacation? Is the revolution over?"

And Mags grabbed Jules' hand and smiled sheepishly. "Well, I'm, uh . . . I'm here with my girlfriend."

"For real? You? Well, I am agog, I am aghast; has the commissar found love at last?"

"Lilly, this is, uh, this is my girlfriend, Julia."

"Oh, congratulations! I don't think I've seen you around here before. Where you from?"

"Nowhere," Jules said.

"Well then it sounds like you're in the right place. Welcome to New Lawrence."

"Jules, this is Lilly," Mags said. "She's one of our state ecologists. This whole thing is her baby."

And Jules' eyes lit up again, and she stammered, "This . . . this place is incredible. I've never seen anything like it. It's . . . it's so beautiful. I feel like I just walked into a fairytale."

Lilly nodded her approval. "You like plants, Julia?"

"Call me Jules. And yeah, I love 'em. They're kinda my thing."

"What's your favorite?"

"Roses! I've got a sweetbriar rose back at Mags' mom's place that's sorta my baby. It's black, if you can believe that."

"Wait, you've got a black *rosa rubiginosa*? I didn't know that was possible."

"Neither did I. I found it growing wild in an old homestead in Freeside, and it is *definitely* an eglantine, but when it bloomed for me they were the most gorgeous black you ever saw."

Lilly smiled at Mags and said, "Sweetheart, I think this one might be a keeper."

Mags blushed. "Yeah, I sure think so."

"Jules, I think you and me are probably gonna see a lot of each other."

"I sure fuckin hope so," Jules said, beaming. "I can't believe all this is real; I feel like I'm trapped in one of Nana's fairytales. It's so beautiful, I . . . I just wanna stay right here and learn every goddamn thing about it."

Mags put her arms around Jules' waste and said, "Hey, I just thought of something. Lilly, I think I would like to see the kids, actually. There's somebody here I think that Jules should meet."

Just within the shade of the forest, a group of children of various ages were playing, some of them rolling around in the grass, others running from tree to tree, and a few had taken up sticks and were engaged in mock swordfights. Mags led Jules by the hand up to one of the pairs of children stick-fighting and called out, "Hey! Hey, Iris!"

A gangly, awkward girl of about 12 threw down her stick, put her hands on her hips, and barked, *"What?"*

"Hey, come here for a second."

Rolling her eyes, the girl ran over and said, "Mags, I'm glad you're back, but I don't wanna talk about Lenin or whatever. I'm *playing.*"

"I just want a second; I want you to meet somebody. Iris, this is my girlfriend, Julia."

Iris gave Jules a bored wave and started to roll her eyes again, then stopped, looked up her and down, and said, simply, "Oh."

"Kiddo, do you remember when we were talking about girls like us, and I told you about how the Republic is special? How girls like us have a real hard time in lots of other places?"

The girl nodded.

"Well, Julia grew up in one of those places. Julia had to pretend to be a boy for a really long time."

With another, very serious nod, Iris walked over to Jules and threw her arms around her. And, as Jules began to cry, she looked up into her sad, brown eyes and said, simply: "Welcome home."

"Thanks, kiddo. You can get back to playing now."

Iris lingered long enough to squeeze Jules' hand before running back to rejoin the other children.

And Jules gawked at her with a wide, ecstatic grin splitting her face and rivers of tears streaming down her cheeks, and she stammered, "No way. No fucking way."

"Way," Mags said, putting an arm around her.

"No fucking way. That . . . Mags, that was a little girl. That was a little fucking girl just playing with the other kids, just . . . being a little girl."

"Mmhmm."

"Mags . . . Mags . . . Oh, fucking Hell . . . *Little girls get to be girls here!*"

"They sure do, hon. And little boys get to be boys, and outside and in-between and whatever else they happen to be. One thing I've thought about a lot ever since we met, I can't really understand the stuff you've been through, not because I don't sympathize, but because I literally can't understand it; I have no frame of reference for it. It really shook me to think about just how good I have it; meeting you was like seeing an Old American transsexual come walking out of one of my schoolbooks. But even with how fortunate I am and how easy I've had it compared to other people . . . Jules, that little girl is growing up without anyone telling her who or what she has to be. She can choose her own destiny without having to fight anybody for it. And as she gets older, she'll only have to go through one puberty."

Jules couldn't find her words, but laughed through her tears. Mags lit a cigarette, handed one to her, and said, "And, y'know, little miss Iris Shanks loves the trees. She says she wants to be a state ecologist when she grows up, like Lilly. You'll probably be seeing a lot of each other."

"I can't . . . Mags, I can hardly process what you're saying to me. It's . . . it's like this forest we're standing in; even though I'm looking right at it, it's just too beautiful to be real."

"It's really real, honey. Welcome to the Ashland Confederated Republic."

"Hell. I'm . . . I'm really home, aren't I? I'm home."

"You are. You belong here, and you're welcome here. This can be your town as much as it is mine, and these your people, just like how tonight we're gonna go to bed in *our* room." And Mags choked up herself, muttering, "Oh, it's . . . it's not just *my* room anymore."

Jules digested those words for a long, quiet moment, before she at last wiped her eyes and said, "I hate fighting, sugar. I hate violence. I'd love to never do any more of that for the rest of my life. But, I swear to God, I will *destroy* any motherfucker who so much as thinks about trying to put a stop to all this."

———

It took two weeks.

After two weeks of sex, late mornings, days out, long motorcycle rides, and walks in the woods, Mags and Jules came back to the cabin one afternoon to find a flatbed truck parked out front and a woman Jules hadn't seen before standing on the porch having a spirited conversation with Emma. As they approached, the conversation halted at once as the woman saw Mags and broke into a wide, warm smile. Mags, rather than smiling, honked with excitement and ran up unto the porch to embrace her.

The stranger looked to be about sixty years old, with long, grey hair and a grim, scarred face, wearing the same uniform as Mags as well as a wide black hat and a necklace of turquoise and bone. And as Jules caught up to them, she noticed that she had a patch over her left eye, and that she was leaning against the wall of the cabin with her mostly-empty left pant leg billowing in the wind.

"Oh my God, Miri!" Mags cried out, throwing her arms around the old woman and kissing her cheeks. "It's so nice to see you again! God, it's been years."

"You too, kid," the old woman said. "You look like you've done pretty good."

"Jules," Mags said, spinning around to face her, "this is . . . this is the person I told you about. This is the TI who cracked me."

"Political commissar Miriam Methotaske. Chief warrant officer 5, brevet major general. You must be Julia."

"Yes, ma'am."

Miri's smile widened. "Don't call me 'ma'am'; I work for a living."

"Well, then, you can call me Jules."

"Cool. Well, ladies, much as I'd like for this to just be a friendly visit, I think y'all know why I'm here. Honeymoon's over. We've got business at Central Soviet."

She lit a cigarette and offered one to Mags, who took it and said, "Yeah. Back to work."

"Yeah. But the reason I came here myself—other than 'cause I wanted to see you—is that this is bigger than dotting the T's and crossing the I's, and it's bigger than finishing your girlfriend's onboarding. That report you filed in Land's End when you got back is starting to light a lot of fires under a lot of asses, and some wheels have started to turn. They're calling an All Soviets Congress in a few days. And you remember the Women's Caucus?"

"Well yeah, I'm a member of it. Wait . . . what do you mean, 'Remember'?"

"It's gone. Last week, we voted to dissolve and reform. Welcome to the Militant Feminist Faction."

"Oh, shit."

"Yup. And I wanna make double sure that the people who saw all that shit firsthand are there to be heard when the arguing starts. One way or another, kid, and I think sooner rather than later, this cold war we're in is about to get real, real hot."

[PART 2]
NOT ONE STEP BACK!

[24]

PREACHER

JULES STAYED QUIET AND WORE A SOUR EXPRESSION THROUGH the rest of the afternoon. Around evening, when they began to talk about leaving for Ashland the next morning, she spoke up and insisted on driving herself.

Looking at a map, the road from New Lawrence to Ashland was a straight jaunt down the old 75, which as the region's main artery would be well-maintained and easy to travel, even for someone who'd never been there before. Miri and Mags both gave her funny looks, given that Miri had made sure to come in a vehicle with plenty of room for the three of them, but Jules laid a hand on Mags' shoulder and said, "Sugar, I got a feeling that pretty soon we might not have a whole lot of time for just us."

Over a dinner of cornbread and beans, the four women sat around Emma's kitchen table, keeping a solemn silence until Mags, staring off into the middle distance, whistled and said, "An All Soviets Congress, huh?"

"Sure is," Miri replied. "Like I said, some big wheels are turning. When I left, everybody was trapped in 'We know we have to do something but we don't know what' mode."

Jules made a throat-clearing noise and asked, "So do y'all mind telling me what the hell an All Soviets Congress is?"

Mags laughed. "Oh yeah, I'm sorry, hon. This must all sound like a word salad to you."

"Yeah, it does. I don't know what any of this crap means—y'all haven't explained dick. Hell, I don't even know what you do; what the hell does a commissar do, anyways?"

Emma suppressed a chuckle. Miri gave Jules a quizzical look and said, "What, you mean you've been dating *her* of all people and she hasn't been talking your ear off about all this stuff? I'm surprised you'd find the time for anything else."

Jules' grumpy expression softened a bit at that. "Well, I guess I can forgive her for being polite by not talking with her mouth full."

Emma's chuckle escaped. Miri roared with laughter. Mags grew red in the face and said, "So, uh . . . a *soviet* is a council of deputies. the Republic is organized industrially by syndicates and regionally by soviets. Every town has one, which sends delegates to the canton soviet, which sends delegates to the Central Soviet General Assembly down in Ashland. The General Assembly is the decision-making body for the Republic, but for really big stuff—like, for instance, a war council—we'll call an All Soviets Congress that includes the whole commonwealth."

"Commonwealth?"

"Such as it is; we're kinda, uh, isolated. So it'll be us, and Musko will send some people from down south, and the Oceti Sakawin and Miami and Potawatomi nations will send some people from out west if they can. Which, like, I hope they can, 'cause when the war heats up we're gonna be playing in their backyard. Ooh, I wonder if Kim will be there."

"I'll be shocked if they're not," Miri chuckled. "Kim Strongbow would fight their way through the entire Blackland New Republic for a chance to yell at us."

"Hold up," Jules said. "The Sioux and Miama are . . . your people? Well, ours now, I guess."

"Mmhmm," Mags replied. "We're in solidarity with all oppressed peoples. We can't do a whole lot where we're at, with the Blacklanders and the Indianapolis Exclusion Zone between us, but we help each other out where and how we can. Ashland mostly runs guns."

Jules smiled with admiration. "Hell yeah. I never got sent to the western theater, myself, but we all heard the stories, and I thought that those guns looked familiar."

"Nice. Glad to know we're doing some good in the world."

Miri's face broke into a sly smile, and her one good eye twinkled, and she said, "Say, Magnolia, speaking of syndicates and deputies and delegates, before I came here I stopped by the New Lawrence soldiers' syndic and they had a little welcome-home present for you. They were keeping it quiet on account of they didn't want to interrupt your little honeymoon, but if we're heading south tomorrow then I figure now's a good time."

Mags furrowed her brows. Miri reached into her pocket and took out a rectangle of red construction paper with a black start stamped on it, along with some words that were too small for Jules or Emma to read. Mags took the card, sat staring at it for a long moment, and said, simply, "No."

Miri clapped her on the shoulder. "Congratulations, comrade commissar."

"No."

"You don't have a choice, kid. Your syndicate said 'jump'."

Jules leaned closer, trying to read the message on the card, and asked, "Well, sugar, what is it?"

A long, defeated sigh. "I . . . I have been elected by a majority vote of the enlisted soldiers of the New Lawrence Militia to represent our syndicate as a voting delegate to the All Soviets Congress."

"Is that . . . bad?"

"It's not bad, it's just . . . It's a lot of responsibility, and it's awkward and weird and it's not my job, and worst of all—worst of all—it's *prestigious*." She spat the last word, like a curse.

356 / NATALIE IRONSIDE

"This is what happens when you're a war hero," Miri said with a shrug.

"But that's my whole point! I *hate* heroes. *We* hate heroes. They should've given this to some corporal."

"Oh, I agree. But they gave it to you."

"This ain't my job."

"Yeah, it ain't your job; it ain't anybody's job. That's the principle our democracy is built on. And the more you whine about not wanting to do it, the more convinced I'll be that you're gonna be good at it."

Emma spoke up, then: "It's your civic duty as a member of this commonwealth, Magnolia Jane. Workers' democracy only functions when we participate in it. 'All shall govern in their turn--'"

Mags hung her head. "'--and soon become accustomed to having no-one govern.' Yeah, Mama, you're right."

"I know I'm right. What you want we should do instead? Have a professional bureaucracy? When a party has a professional bureaucracy--"

"I know, Mama, I know. Hell. Alright. Anyways, the congress can't last longer than, what, a few days?"

"If that," Miri said. "And it'll be good to have at least one delegate already on our side when we get there. You know there are a lot of people who still think that winning the war is impossible."

"Well, Miri, about that . . . It is kinda impossible."

"Pfft. You're thinking like a profiteer. Thinking like a settler. Think like a revolutionary."

"What the hell does that mean?"

"What makes you say it's impossible, Magnolia?"

"Well, in a force-on-force conflict, the Blacklanders could walk right over us. The projections show that, between professionals, marshals and conscripts, the Oberkommando could field up to a million men in a total-war situation; we have more citizens under arms than they do, but they have something like twice as many regular troops. Seizing and holding territory north of the Ohio Valley would require troop numbers that we just don't have."

Miri scoffed louder. "Alright, Karl von Klausewitz. You're not wrong, but if you'd stop for a minute and remember any of the lessons I tried to teach you, maybe you'd remember that winning a war isn't about meeting force with force. Winning is about exploiting vulnerabilities. Hell, if we were talking about just invading Ohio and annexing land into the Republic, then I'd be the biggest dove here, because that's both impossible and unconscionable. Good thing we're not talking about that."

Mags chewed on her words for a minute. Thinking it over, she muttered, like a catechism: "The fascist social order is inherently unstable because it's built on the same contradictions that are tearing it apart."

"You're getting there. Jules, sweetheart, would you say that where you grew up, people were satisfied with the state of things? Would you describe it as a peaceful existence?"

"Well, no," Jules said. "It's painful, violent, shitty, and weird. Honestly, the only thing holding it together—other than fear—is that so many people have all bought into the same lie."

"Uh-huh. Our belligerent northern neighbors are sitting on a pile of dry kindling, kid. We solve the problem with a few well-placed matches."

"Aw, fuck," Mags muttered, "you're right. We don't conquer the BNR, we break it. We make it consume itself. Just like Kitty is always saying."

"Precisely. Between its own instability, our external allies, and all the intelligence that your asset has got in her head, we'll figure something out. But that's for later. The struggle in front of us will be convincing the other delegates."

"'Asset'," Mags repeated, chewing on the word. "She has a name, y'know."

"No, no, I kinda like that," Jules broke in. And she looked off in the middle distance with a self-satisfied smile and muttered, "I'm an *asset*."

"You sure are," Miri said. "Your service to the Republic is invaluable and appreciated. And Mags? You really are something else, kid. I don't think we've ever seen a blackshirt catch religion before, and then you went out on a job and found me two."

Jules perked up. "So Peterson made it in okay? I need to tell that ugly piece of shit thank you again; I only thanked him about a hundred times the first time."

"I haven't had a chance to see him myself, but yeah, we got him down there. From what I hear, the DIS spooks went from wanting to make him talk to not being able to get him to shut up. Both of you ladies are something else." She yawned. "Hell of a big day for everybody tomorrow. Let's not stay up too late; if we get an early start, we'll be in Ashland before lunch."

"Oh, that won't be a problem," Mags said. "I still wake up at 5 AM every day."

They laughed, and as they laughed Emma gave her daughter a serious look and said, "You mind yourself down there, child. Don't let none of them big-city bureaucrats give you the run-around."

"I ain't worried about no bureaucrats, Mama. It's them ought to be worried about me."

"That's my girl."

[*That same evening, on the outskirts of Somerset, Ohio*]

Jack Binachi was dead, and that much, at least, was good news.

Jack Binachi was a veteran, and so Chaplain Pete and the other presbyters had spared no trouble rolling out the pageantry for a hero's funeral, even though Jack had never done anything more heroic than put in two turns with the brownshirts along the border before coming home to pursue a career in drinking; all the men had to serve one turn, and anyone who voluntarily re-upped his enlistment was entitled to the hero treatment whether he'd done anything noteworthy or not. Maria didn't really mind so much; an official state funeral for a war hero involved cremating the corpse so that an urn could be displayed on the hero wall in the local church. And there was small chance of anyone digging around in Jack's ashes to find the rat poison that had been in his stomach.

What Maria minded was that Jack was a cruel, worthless man and a mean drunk who'd never done anyone a lick of good, and she could think of a few people who were far more deserving than him, but those people had never gotten funerals.

She managed to keep it together through the service. Managed to keep it together as Chaplain Wenden stood in front of the church and gave a stirring speech all about how beloved husband and father Jack Binachi so greatly embodied the spirit of the Blackland New Republic, the Falange, and the High Church in his character of service and self-sacrifice, a character that had earned him a hero's grave and should stand as an example for all to emulate. Maria thought bitterly that a hero's widow ought to at least get a hero's pension.

And she'd kept it together as the chaplain folded up the flag—the flag of the New Republic with its horizontal black and blue stripes and the big Orthodox cross in the top left corner—and kissed Jack's urn and kissed the flag and handed it to her, thanking her for her husband's sacrifice. She promised herself that she would burn that flag just as soon as it was safe to do so.

And she went back home to her mother's old house that had once been so full of life but now stood empty save for one bitter old widow, and she found a tall, black candle and a bottle of red wine.

It had been a hard thing to finally come to, deciding to kill Jack, and though she didn't regret it in the least, though she was ecstatic at the thought of never sharing a bed with that man again, still, it was a hell of a thing, and it weighed on her as the sun set and the empty house grew dark. She'd need to clear her head before getting drunk and going to bed.

The family altar stood against the far wall of the kitchen, across from the dining table and next to the stove, and bit-by-bit it had grown less ornamented, less tended in the decade since Carlotta went away. By the time of Jack's funeral, it was bare save for the incense burner, the crucifix, the silver Madonna, the taper candlestick, and, tucked away in the back, a little reliquary. The reliquary had once contained what she'd been told was a lock of Murphy Covington's hair, but a few years ago she'd cleaned it out and thrown that away. It now held a handful of baby teeth, a hair clip, and a pair of brass corporal's chevrons; far more sacred relics, of a far more deserving saint.

Maria wasn't sure if she had any faith left, but Carlotta had had enough faith to sustain a family, and, thinking on her mother, she crossed herself and whispered, "Mom, I wish you were here. Goddammit, Mom, but I wish I'd listened to you."

Thinking on her mother, and on what her mother would've wanted, Maria lit a cone of incense, lit her candle, kissed the Virgin's forehead, and knelt down onto the floor, her knees slotting into the worn spots where so many knees had rested before. And after chanting her ave and her paternoster, she repeated the prayer she'd said every night for twenty-five years, along with all the additions and alterations that the events of a lifetime warranted, and she said it loudly now, no longer afraid that Jack might overhear.

"Do one thing for me," she said, her words echoing through the dark and empty house. "Watch over him. Keep him safe. Show him the right path; save him from temptation, and save him from myself. And . . . and bring him back to me. Bring my little boy home."

And, with tears in her eyes, she looked up, and she locked eyes with the brass image of the crucified Christ, and she growled, "And if You can't do that much, then what the fuck are You good for?"

And, taking up her bottle of wine, she got up and sat down at the kitchen table, to drink and to cry.

Jack got a funeral, and pieces of shit like him got funerals, but some people didn't. Sometimes old grandmothers got taken away in the middle of the night. And sometimes . . .

Maria kept going back to the last conversation she'd had with him, during one of his visits home. He always made time for his mother, and as much as it hurt her to see him wearing that uniform —and she never missed an opportunity to remind him—she still loved to see him. But, toward the end, she could tell that something was eating him up inside, could see conflict raging behind those big brown eyes. Her mother's eyes.

The last time they'd spoken, she'd gotten up early and gone to the kitchen to start an early breakfast and had found him there, kneeling in front of the family altar, whispering the ave over and over again as tears ran down his face. And she'd knelt down next to him and put an arm across his shoulders and asked, "Baby, what's wrong? What's got you like this?"

And he'd turned to look at her, and looked at her just the way a drowning man would look at a life preserver, and he'd stammered, "I . . . I'm not doin so good, Mom. I'm all twisted and torn up inside and I don't know what to do. I don't know what to do."

And she'd kissed his forehead and whispered, "Tell me what's got you like this, baby."

He stared at her in silence for a long moment, and for a little while she'd seen hope flashing in those sad brown eyes, and several times he started to speak and she watched the words catch in his throat. At last he sighed, and dropped his gaze, and whispered, "I can't tell you. I'm sorry, Mom, I . . . I just can't."

And, later that morning, as he was getting ready to hop on his bike and head back to Cincinnati, they'd shared a long, warm, solemn hug, and he'd looked at her with tears in his eyes and said, "I love you, Mom, and I'm sorry. I'm sorry I can never be the son you deserve."

She'd puzzled over those words ever since, replaying the inter-action in her mind every day, trying to suss out the hidden meaning behind them, but always felt like she was missing a piece of the puzzle. Like what he'd tried and failed to confess in front of the altar was the piece she needed, but would never find, to unlock the puzzle that was the troubled, inscrutable mind of Jules Binachi. And, a few weeks later, an officer and a war cleric from the Cincinnati garrison had shown up and handed her a flag and told her that Corporal Julian Binachi had died a hero's death defending the New Republic from an invasion of godless Bolshevists. But there was never any funeral, never any memorial put up on the wall in the church, never any other word about it, and though Maria never knew what really happened to her son, she at least knew bullshit when she smelled it. Partly from experience and partly from intuition, Maria Binachi could guess at the truth: Her little boy had not been lost, but rather stolen.

"They take," she grumbled as she threw back another long drink of wine. "They take and they take and they take, and now there's nothing left."

There was a knock at the door.

Grumbling curses, she got up and staggered to the front door and found herself staring at a man in his mid 20s—*My Jules is about that age*, she thought—wearing a black robe and a pistol belt. He had close-cropped blonde hair, fierce blue eyes, and a painfully artificial smile.

"Good evening, chaplain," she slurred, not bothering to hide the edge of displeasure in her voice.

"Please, Maria," the priest said, "call me Peter."

"What do you want, chaplain?"

He took a step into the house. "I wanted to check in on you. These past few days must have been very difficult."

And, walking back to the kitchen table, she sighed and asked, "Would you like a drink? Cigarette? I haven't started dinner yet."

"No, thank you," he said, pulling out a chair and sitting down. "I don't indulge. A glass of water would be wonderful, though."

Maria poured him a glass, found herself another bottle of wine, and sat down across from him, saying nothing.

"I see you've been praying," Peter said, glancing at the altar. "That's very good. We should lean upon the Lord and His Church during such times. A candle for your late husband, I presume?"

"No. It's for my son. I light a candle for my little boy every day."

"Of course. You, too, are a hero, Maria; you've given as much as can be expected of any woman, and the New Republic appreciates your service."

"Do they?"

"Of course. What kind of question is that?"

"Why are you here, Peter?"

The smile didn't waver. "I wanted to be sure I make my rounds and check in on the flock. Word has not yet gotten around, but I'm going to be leaving soon; the Ecclesiarchs are sending me to the western districts. Lots of souls in need of saving out there."

"Well, I'm happy for you."

"And I wanted to see you especially, Maria. To see how you're faring after your husband's . . . untimely . . . passing."

The word "untimely" hung in the air like cigar smoke, and Peter's eyes bored into her as though he were staring into her soul, and in his face she saw the authority of a hundred priests and marshals and soldiers who'd made cowing her their life's work, and for a moment she was cowed and wanted to shrink back into her chair and lower her gaze, but she resisted the instinct. She met his eyes, and in a cool, flat voice she said, "You know, Chaplain Wenden--"

"Father, if you please. My reassignment came with a promotion; the Ecclesiarchs, in their grace, have made me a war cleric."

"You know, Father Wenden, it's too bad that you're going away, since you and I haven't spoken much. Tell me . . . how's your brother?"

The priest's smile wavered around its edges, and his eye

twitched, and he said, "We don't, ah . . . we don't see each other much these days—his work keeps him very busy—but Nicodemus is doing quite well for himself. He's on the Commander's administration staff, you know."

"So I've heard. Your father must be very proud."

"Maria, is there something you're trying to tell me?"

"Just that I'm a poor old widow and I'd like to be left alone to grieve. You can see yourself out, Wenden."

Peter felt a terrible, ice-cold rage building inside of him, an impotent rage because he knew that she had won. Though he ached to spring up from his chair and punish her for her insolence, he only nodded, and bade her good night and God bless, and left.

He thought the interaction over as he made his way back to the church. The widow Binachi had murdered her husband, he was sure of that much; he'd all but accused her, and she hadn't voiced any denial, nor made any show of grief. Indeed, she looked as though a great weight had been lifted off of her shoulders. And, doubtless, she was as full of sin and sedition as her troublemaking bitch of a mother had once been; the elder presbyters had warned him about that. But, what to do with this information?

After some thought, he decided that, really, the ramblings and sins of a bitter old widow were not worth his time, not in days like these. Maria, and all the weak and wayward folk like her, they would receive their comeuppance soon enough. He didn't know precisely when, but soon, terribly soon, war would come. War would come like a hurricane, a holy war, the great purgative that would burn away all that was impure and base, and he relished the thought of it.

It bothered him that he had no inkling of the when or where of the coming war, other than that it would be soon, but there was little he could do about that. He was a man of God, only newly minted as a soldier, and declaring and prosecuting a war was Falange business, not High Church business, and he had precious few contacts within the Falange, especially at the upper echelon. Within the Oberkommando.

And, with a long, loud sigh and a roll of his eyes, he thought, *Well, that's not entirely true. I suppose I do know* one *person who's close to the Commander.*

[25]

FREE AND GREEN

THE 75 WAS MAINTAINED IN MORE OR LESS ITS PRE-WAR state, a sprawling eight-lane monstrosity of ancient asphalt patched all over with hempcrete and reclaimed plastic and whatever other materials had been to hand, winding a lazy path through the hills and south into the mountains. Maintaining the existing roadbed created far more highway than the Republic's transportation needs actually called for, which made for fast and easy traveling, with Miri and Jules negotiating a light load of buses, trucks, and the occasional bike. The two lanes on the far left of the southbound side had been converted into light rail tracks, and the trains were always running, hauling produce in one direction and finished goods in the other.

At first, Jules had been nervous about following in the exhaust of Miri's rock-crawler, but she found that the big diesel's fuel gave off a light discharge that reminded her of the smell of frying chicken.

The road wound lazily through rolling green hills, a patchwork quilt of forest and farmland, and regular clusters of buildings. At intervals, the buildings clustered closer together around a machine shop or factory or distribution center, but even the towns seemed to built around the landscape rather than on it, the whole affair blending together as seamlessly as the fields blended into the forests.

A couple of hours into the trip, the hills began to rise up into sharp, fierce mountains, with the farmland hugging the coves and valleys and the forests dominating the slopes. And, passing around a hair-raising bend in the road overlooking a wide, flat cove, Jules saw her first real Ashlander city. She almost crashed.

The floor of the cove was a grid of sturdy, brutalist tower blocks, broken up by the occasional warehouse or factory. The roof of every building sported a bank of solar panels, or a cluster of eggbeater windmills, or a vibrant garden, and crawling or hanging plants grew over many of the walls. As the road wound down into the cove, Jules saw trees lining the roads and sidewalks, and hints of wide, green spaces tucked between many of the buildings. A billboard in front of the canton checkpoint informed her that the city was called Refuge, and that they were entering Ashland Canton.

The controller at the southbound checkpoint was a young Shawnee woman who seemed supremely bored with her job, sighing as she glanced over passes and manifests and passengers and waved people through with a cigarette dangling form her lips. As Mags and Jules came through, though, her eyes lit up, and, grinning, she said, "Holy shit, that is a sick bike."

"Thanks," Jules said, returning the grin as she fumbled around in her pockets. "It's a Bonneville."

"I don't know what that means, but it sure does fuck."

"It does what, now?"

The controller noted Jules' confusion at a common Ashlander figure of speech as well as the way her eyes sparkled as they lingered on the city in front of her, and she remarked, "You new here, ain'tcha?"

368 / NATALIE IRONSIDE

"Oh, yeah. I . . . I've never fuckin seen anything like this. This place is amazing."

After a beat, she found the pass she'd been issued in Land's End and handed it over along with Mags'. The controller looked them over, handed them back, and said, "You come a long way from Freeside, huh?"

"I come a long way just in general."

"So where y'all headed?"

"We, uh . . . Sugar, where *are* we headed?"

"Ashland," Mags said. "Business in Central."

"Oh, I'll bet. Y'all have a nice day!"

They fall back in behind Miri, but hadn't made it far when she stuck her hand out of the window and motioned for them to pull over. The highway butted up against a parking lot next to a wide, sprawling park dominated by shady groves of hemlock trees. The truck rumbled to a stop underneath one of the hemlocks, and Jules pulled up beside it as Miri threw open the door and started to pull herself out.

"I need a fuckin break," she said, rubbing her knee. "The good leg's starting to lock up. Plus, I could go for some chow, and I spotted those saints."

She gestured over her shoulder to the edge of the park, where a small group of people stood around a bicycle trailer, dishing out food to passers by, filling the air with a toothsome smell. They walked over to the cart, and Miri gave the vendors a jaunty wave and asked, "So what do we got?"

"Catfish," one of them offered, "and fry bread, and elotes, and pickles. Everything's brass except the pickles. Pickles are free."

"As it should be."

And Miri dug around in her pockets and took out a few loose rounds of 5.45 ammunition, handed them over, and said, "That's for me and the girls. I'll take the fry bread and a pickle."

As Mags and Jules queued up, Jules took a long sniff and said,

"This all looks amazing, but . . . I ain't from around here and I don't know what any of this is."

"Try an elote," the vendor offered. "You look like an elote kinda gal."

"The hell is an elote?"

"Good Lord, you're white. Eat this."

And they handed Mags and Jules each a roasted corn cob on a stick, slathered in mayonnaise and cheese, and a pickle. Mags tore into her pickle first, devouring it in three massive bites with a long, satisfied moan. Jules laughed and said, "Damn, sugar, I didn't know you liked those so much."

"Do you not? Or are you an olive girl?"

"Am I a what?"

Mags smirked. "Honey, what kind of blockers are you on?"

"Uh . . . the orange ones?"

"You need to eat that pickle."

Jules shrugged and took a bite. She stopped mid-chew and stared at the pickle for a moment, her eyes widening in amazement, and she destroyed it in one more massive bite, moaning in sublime satisfaction. Miri, Mags, and the vendors were trying not to laugh, but Jules rushed back over to the cart and stammered, "How many more of those can you give me?"

The vendor, who had by then failed at trying not to laugh, ducked behind the cart and came up with an earthenware pot full of pickles. They handed it over, saying, "Enjoy, sister. And congratulations."

Jules held the pot up to her lips and took several long drafts of brine. Still grinning in amazement, she declared, "That is the best fucking thing I have ever tasted in my life. Jesus fucking Christ, it's like I just found water in the desert."

"Honey," Mags asked, "how long have you been on E?"

"Uh . . . About two and a half years now."

"Well, then, you've had a debilitating sodium deficiency for about two and a half years. And, like, I'm not surprised that the first go-'round left a lot to be desired, but I'm kinda surprised that Prof at least didn't tell you that."

"He probably just assumed she already knew," Miri offered.

By then, Jules, had started on her third pickle, and Mags said, "Well, I guess we might as well make this our stop for lunch, then. Probably won't make it to Ashland till this afternoon."

And Jules finished the pickle, fished out a fourth, and asked, "Why's that?"

"Because you are about to take just the worst shit."

[*The previous evening; Columbus, Ohio*]

It was time to take minutes again.

She knew, and accepted, that a condition of her existence was her continued near-invisibility, that she be kept in her dollhouse with her typewriter and her sexology textbooks, appearing to most people as little more than a name at the top of the occasional research paper. It didn't matter now nearly as much as it used to—nearly everyone from the old days had either been promoted into other districts or placed firmly under the Commander's thumb; to most of the Oberkommando, she was only Rain's anonymous secretary and their occasional fixer—but still, her un-existence gave her occasional dalliances with the Commander a delightful flair of drama, and in any case, a lady should be discreet.

From time to time, he would send for her and insist she needed to be present at this or that meeting in order to do some secretarial job or other. She gathered right away what these summons were really about: The Falange would trot out the Wenden family's dirty secret in order to bully and cow the Ecclesiarchy. She took satisfaction in that, and noted with great satisfaction that Father Elias Wenden, who'd once upon a time been the presumptive heir to the Patriarchy, had long ago stopped attending to the Patriarch at Oberkommando meetings entirely.

And, as she set up her typewriter at the little note-taker's table in the far corner of the war room, most of the men in attendance took no notice of her, and a few gave her quizzical looks and glanced back and forth between her and the Commander before merely ignoring her, but Father Donovan, Patriarch of the High Church and head of the Ecclesiarchy, glared at her with smoldering, undisguised hatred and revulsion. She met his eyes and gave him her biggest, coldest smile.

Roland was in rare spirits that night. He'd gotten up out of his big chair at the head of the table and stormed over to stare down the attending officer who'd been speaking, one of those creatures with sallow skin and dead, black eyes, wearing a crisp *Waffen*-SS uniform.

"Excuse me," the Commander bellowed, his hair out of place and his face contorted in a sneer of terrible rage, "it is fucking *what?*"

"Gone," Ulfkessel said, seeming bored. "I was out on a mission when I received a call that we were under attack. While I was on my way back, there was a terrible explosion, and when I returned I found a crater where our home had been. *So-wie-so.*"

"How the fuck did that happen?"

"I do not know. I did not see. I've no doubt that others will be trickling in soon; perhaps one of them saw something. But, if you want my guess, I would point to the Bolshevists. A few nights previously, I had redirected a squad of your men to deal with a group of Bolshevist agents. They failed spectacularly. We sent some of our own people to finish the job, and I am ashamed to say that they failed as well. *So-wie-so.*"

Natasha stopped typing and sucked in a quick breath through her teeth. Ulfkessel's words recalled for her a conversation she'd had a few nights previously, and brought up implications she didn't want to contemplate. And, not wanting to, she didn't, and resumed her typing.

"What the fuck does that mean?" Rail growled.

The hunter shrugged. "*So-wie-so*. So it goes. Things are as they are."

"You mean this is fucking why there's been radio silence for almost a goddamn month? I had a thousand goddamn men in that place! A thousand goddamn stormtroopers, a thousand goddamn Arditi! Your man was the keystone of the entire fucking plan! I want you to tell me how the fuck in the whole goddamn hell you allowed this to happen."

Ulfkessel cocked his head to the side. "Such insolence. What makes you think you can speak to me like this?"

"Because I'm the fucking Commander, *major*."

"Pfft. 'Commander', you call yourself. I am *not* a major, your stupid, superstitious reactionary, I am a *Sturmbannfuhrer*. You call yourself a Commander, but I walked with the Fuhrer. I spoke with him. I was there for the crusades against Bolshevism and Jewry. I--"

Rain had drawn his Colt while Ulfkessel was distracted, and the rant was cut short as he emptied all six of its chambers into the hunter's head. When the hunter fell to the floor and at last stopped twitching, he turned to face the Ecclesiarchs and general officers seated around the table, and he declared, "Here's an order, an order I want sent out fucking yesterday. If we encounter any more of these . . . things, I want them to submit to our authority unconditionally, and if they can't do that then I want them exterminated. Farley, I'm putting them all under your command; you can use them or throw them away, whichever you'd like. They already failed the race once; and God gave them a second chance, and they failed that, too, and it may have cost us everything; and I don't have any use for failures."

A man in a stetson hat and a black shirt with a brigadier general's star who'd been sitting with his feet propped up on the table and who seemed to be unimpressed with the spectacle, alternating between cleaning his fingernails and occasionally glaring at Natasha, spoke up at last. Clearing his throat, he asked, "Say, boss, about that . . . What is the plan, now that we've lost our assist?"

The Commander was silent for a long moment, and in his silence his face changed from a look of rage to a sadistic, toothy grin, the grin of a shark smelling blood in the water, and he said, "Oh, we're going ahead, Farley. The preparations are already made and the troops are already mustering. The plan is still the same. With or without these freaks, we're about to win this war."

[26]

MANY MEETINGS

The road south led deeper into the mountains, through rolling hills and high ridges covered in a carpet of verdant late-summer green and past more of the blocky, intentional factory towns nestled into the coves and valleys. Though the region was plainly—and evenly—populated, even the bigger towns seemed to blend into the landscape in a smooth, organic sort of way, and as the mountains grew more rugged and forests more dense, they passed signs warning drivers to be careful of migrating elk.

By early afternoon, the landscape in front of them flattened out into a broad, gentle valley, and the buildings covering the valley floor spread out in a tapestry of mossy tower blocks, green rooftops, and glistening banks of solar panels stretching all the way to the next ridgeline shimmering blue in the distance. As they descended into the valley and into the maze of buildings, the highway began to melt away, narrowing as lanes branched off into side streets, and the traffic rolling across the ever-narrowing path seemed to consist only of buses. To either side, Jules saw a city full of vibrant life, with people of all sorts filling the sidewalks, darting in and out of shops, standing on street corners and talking, lounging on benches.

The carts and bicycle trailers handing out food were ubiquitous, with one on almost every block, and the smells of food and of life filled the crisp, clean air.

After a while of inching their way through the city—requiring Mags to hop off and walk the bike along in a few spots—the buildings broke away at once into a broad, open belt of prairie grass stretching all the way to the banks of a slow, blue river. At the river's bank sat a tight cluster of tower blocks and concrete pillboxes, surrounded by heavy diesel trucks similar to Miri's. A red flag embroidered with the hammer and plough flew over the whole affair, and a sign by the road leading up the buildings proclaimed, "Ashland Central Soviet General Headquarters."

Miri pulled off of the road and stopped near the compound's main entrance, and Jules rolled to a stop beside her. In front of them, standing before the entrance, was a statue of a tall, wiry old man with fierce eyes and a great bushy beard, holding a sword high over his head. The statue had a rough, oddly textured look, and its color was the dull yellow of old brass, green in a few places. On a second look, Jules realized it was made out of spent rifle cartridges.

"So who's that?" she asked.

Mags beamed with pride, smiled up at the statue, and said, "That there's John Brown."

The three of them stood taking in the scene in silence for a moment until Jules asked, "So, uh . . . what's the plan?"

"There's some people at or near Liberty Hall we ought to meet up with," Miri said, "and before we do that, some other people are gonna want to talk to you two, and then Mags is gonna need to head to Liberty Hall and check in with Jimmy anyways. Just go ahead in; there'll be somebody just inside checking people in, and they'll tell you where you need to go. And let's see . . . just inside and to the left, there's a bar. You can't miss it, and anybody here will know where it is. That'll be our rally point; we'll meet back up there and go over what's next once all the howdy-do's are over with."

Mags smirked. "Ah, the good ol' Hundred Rads. I wonder if Kelly still works there."

"She does."

The three of them walked into the gap between two of the brutalist hempcrete tower blocks and came upon a guard shack staffed by two soldiers. When they noticed new people, one of them rolled his eyes, but the other—a small, lithe woman with brown skin, long black hair pulled back into a bun, and giant coke-bottle glasses—looked downright excited. She hopped up from her chair, stepped out onto the sidewalk, and hollered, "Oh, hey there! How can we help y'all?"

"I'm here to check in with Jimmy and drop off a couple of VIPs," Miri replied. "Somebody should be expecting them; I got Magnolia Blackadder and Julia Binachi."

The soldier nodded without a moment's pause, her gaze lingering on Jules. "Would you be Miriam Methotaske, then?"

"The one and only."

"Okey dokey. Yeah, you're all expected. Blackadder, they want to review a report with you; you know where the Commissariat headquarters is, right?"

"Sure do," Mags said.

"Awesome. And, Julia, you come with me."

Mags and Jules shared a serious look and squeezed each other's hands before parting ways. The soldier led Jules back behind the guard shack and into the adjacent building. It seemed to be part barracks or dormitory and part office tower, the air thick with smells of coffee, cigarettes, and ink, with most of the available space devoted to filing cabinets and messy desks. Entering the building, she took note of the symbol carved into the big oak door: A clenched fist clutching a lightning bolt, and below that, an open book and two quill pens crossed like swords. She'd never actually seen DIS's unit insignia before, but she did know a spook shack when she saw one. She sucked in a quick breath through her teeth.

The soldier led her down the hall to a room containing a desk, two chairs, and a bank of filing cabinets. Jules took a deep breath and crossed herself as she stepped inside.

"Feel free to have a seat, sweetheart," the soldier said, heading to the filing cabinets. "This shouldn't take very long; Blackadder's report was real thorough. I just need to cross some I's and dot some T's. You want some coffee or water or something?"

"Nah," Jules said, pulling out one of the chairs and sitting down. "Do, ah . . . do you mind if I smoke, though? Nerves, y'know."

"Oh, yeah, for sure. I think there's an ashtray in one of those drawers."

She lit a cigarette and relaxed just a bit. After another moment, the soldier came prancing over juggling an accordion folder, a box of pens, and a tape recorder. Taking a seat in front of Jules and spreading the items out between them, she said, "Mmkay, let's get this started. My name's Lynn, by the way."

Jules nodded. Lynn took out a pen and a blank sheet of paper, started the tape recorder, and said, "Okay, okay, uh . . . shit . . . Uh, this is Commissar Lynn Ramirez, warrant officer 2, brevet captain, conducting the onboarding interview for a Julia Carlotta Binachi. Now, Jules—can I call you Jules?"

"Yeah."

"Awesome. Like I said, this shouldn't take very long. Commissar Blackadder's report was very thorough, and I'm given to understand that you've endured some prolonged and, uh . . . let's call it *specific* violence at the hands of your former affiliation."

Jules sucked air through her teeth. "Yeah, that's, uh . . . that's one way to put it."

"We won't be talking about any of that today, don't worry. I'd like to—I'd like to find out everything I possibly can about this Natasha Wenden character—but we'll save that line of inquiry for a more, ah, comfortable environment. Now, the information we have paints a very hopeful picture of your present character and state of recovery, and we trust Blackadder's judgment, so really I just want to clarify a couple of things about your life and actions prior to your defection."

"Sure. What did you want to know?"

"What unit were you with, and where were they stationed?"

"Third Special Operations Group, Echo Company, First Assault Battalion, First Infantry."

"Roy Farley's brigade?"

"Yeah, that weird motherfucker. And we operated out of Cincinnati."

"Mmkay. What was your rank and your military occupational designation?"

"Corporal, Bravo fire team leader, heavy assault specialist."

"Okey doke. Tell me what a heavy assault specialist does, and tell me about Third SOG's mission more generally."

"A heavy assault specialist takes the forward position during offensive operations; so I was the head idiot in charge of climbing over walls and kicking down doors. And our job was knocking out Ashlander defensive positions along the Ohio Valley."

"No deeper incursions, or so-called peacekeeping operations?"

"Nah, nah, none of that mess."

"Mmkay. Tell me how you wound up in that line of work."

"Well, all men in the Blackland New Republic are required to do at least one enlistment in the regular Army—I'm not a man, obvs, but they didn't know that at the time. During my time, I sorta . . . lost myself in it. Used the Army as a way to run away from myself, to try and fix what I thought were flaws. I thought that if I could just . . . be a man, conform to what everybody expected from me, that I could, well, be a man, and quit hating myself. So when my mandatory enlistment ran out, I said 'bet' and volunteered for the Arditi." A long, sardonic sigh. "And you can see how well my brilliant plan worked out. And I ain't proud to admit it, but yeah, if we're being honest, I didn't really start questioning the things I was raised with until I wound up on the wrong end of 'em."

"Hmm. Why do you say you aren't proud to admit it, Jules?"

She squeezed the arms of her chair and examined her lap. "Because I shoulda fuckin known. They made my life a living Hell from the day I was born, and I . . . I just threw in with the same people who were killing me, the same people who were killing my mom and my best friend and who'd already killed my nana, just 'cause I thought maybe life could be a little bit bearable if I was the biggest piece of shit in the turd pile. I'm ashamed of who I used to be, and I'm ashamed of what I was part of, but most of all . . . most of all, I'm ashamed that I didn't ever decide to stop being a piece of shit until it became my problem."

And, looking up into Lynn's eyes, she went on: "You know something? That's why I latched onto Mags the way I did. When I showed up in Freeside, most everybody felt bad for me and wanted to fawn over me and make sure I was okay and whatnot, but . . . nobody wanted to acknowledge where I'd come from. And it didn't help. Then she showed up, and she told me about myself and what I ought to do about it, and y'know what? I used to have nightmares, horrible nightmares, PTSD flashbacks, pretty much every night; but a few days into our trip, they just stopped. I've had maybe one or two since then."

The room was quiet for a moment, and Lynn nodded and said, "Jules, I'm very happy to hear you say that."

"Why's that?"

"Because that's exactly what I wanted to hear. With this, I agree with Blackadder's assessment that your recovery is coming along in leaps and bounds and that your loyalty is above suspicion. I think we're almost done here. You don't have any reservations about being our intelligence asset for however long?"

"Not at all. I'm happy to help; y'all just say the word."

"Awesome. There is one more thing I want to ask you. And not just as part of the report, but as me asking you, one soldier to another. Jules . . . how many?"

"You really wanna know?"

"Yeah."

"Twelve. There are more, a lot more, that I ain't sorry for—self-defense, the guard I merc'd on my way out, all those blackshirts me and Mags got on her mission—but I know that I'm gonna owe God twelve souls when I die."

"Good Lord."

"Uh-huh."

"Well . . . one more question. If I put on this form that I as your interviewer recommend clemency, and you officially become a citizen of the Ashland Confederated Republic, what are you planning on doing with the rest of your life?"

She answered without hesitation, without pausing to think: "I wanna be a state ecologist. A forester."

"Really?"

"Oh, yeah. I . . . I love plants, I always have. And seeing what you people's cities actually look like, shit, I still feel like I'm in the middle of a fuckin fairytale. And when we came to New Lawrence, Mags took me to see one of you guys's forestry projects, and I haven't been able to stop thinking about it since; God, it was the second most beautiful thing I've ever seen. And there was this lady working there, Lilly, she and I talked a whole lot, and she told me all about what she does as a state ecologist, and I . . . I can't fuckin think of anything I'd rather be doing. I'm tired of taking life; I wanna make some."

Lynn nodded again. "That's good. Well, I think I've got everything I need right now. We'll be in touch with further questions regarding intelligence you might have, but for now I think we're done here."

"Really? That it?"

"Between what we know about your recent past, the assistance you gave to Blackadder, and all your enthusiastic cooperation, I'm satisfied that you're okay. And you want to be a part of all this, right? Part of the Republic?"

"Y--yeah. Hell yeah I do."

"Well then, welcome home, comrade."

Jules broke into a wide, delirious grin and examined her lap again, unsure of what to say. Lynn shut off the tape recorder and asked, "So what are you gonna do now, sweetheart?"

She laughed. "I . . . Well, I wanna go hug my girlfriend, but I dunno when I'll catch her. I thought that this would take longer."

"It's Blackadder, right?"

"Yeah. Yeah, it sure is."

"Yeah, she's probably gonna be a minute; they do like to chew on the details finalizing reports. Y'all gonna meet up at the bar down the way?"

"Uh-huh."

"Go there. There'll be food and music and real nice people. And here."

Lynn fished around in her pocket and brought up three loose rounds of the funny-looking 7.62 revolver ammo and handed them to Jules.

"Have a few drinks on me."

Jules walked back out into the sun and wandered down the sidewalk with her hands in her pockets. Sure enough, Miri and Mags were nowhere to be found, and the people milling about seemed to take no notice of her, so she walked straight ahead, towards where Miri had said the bar was.

Most of the buildings were the same as all the others she'd seen —painfully intentional brutalist crackerboxes made from greyish-brown blocks of cementatious cellulose, saved from looking like a prefabricated nightmare only by the verdant plants growing up and down their walls and the trees lining the streets—but as she walked, one of them caught her eye, far off to her right. Standing apart from the others in the middle of an open green park was a big, archaic, pre-War building of marble and granite with an imposing domed and gabled roof. She recognized it on sight—this was, or had once been, a cathedral—but it bore no religious iconography. Instead, a collection of red and black flags sporting various insignia flew from its eaves, and a big signboard like a movie marquee hung over the door, declaring, "ASHLAND CENTRAL SOVIET GENERAL ASSEMBLY – LIBERTY HALL."

"Yeah," she said out loud as she passed by, "I could get used to this place."

Up ahead, tucked between two buildings, she saw a low, broad structure of plywood and tin that looked delightfully out of place amongst the compound's ordered chaos, with a sign over the door bearing the yellow and black radiation trefoil and the words "HUNDRED RADS TAVERN." It looked as homey and inviting as Lynn had suggested, but as she approached, her mood began to change. As she heard the sounds of music and laughter coming from inside, she found herself growing acutely aware that the people making those sounds were strangers, that the friend and the companion she'd come here with were nowhere around and that she did not know for how long they'd be gone. The groups of Ashlanders moving around the compound, normal people minding their business, took on a malevolent aura in her sight, and she felt the edge of panic creeping into the back of her mind.

Taking slow, deep breaths, she ducked into the gap between the bar and an adjacent building, leaned against the wall, and lit a cigarette, trying to rationalize. As her muscles tensed and her eyes darted around, scanning for threats, she reminded herself that this was a safe place, that there were no threats here, that Mags would come along sooner or later, and that, until then, she belonged here, and these weren't strangers, but *her* people, her friends.

It did not help.

"Dammit," she muttered aloud, "God fucking dammit, I thought I was done with this shit. Thought I was *better*." And she crouched down in the shadows, and thought about how ridiculous she must look, and the rising panic mingled with a sense of shame.

To her surprise, the voice that answered her in her mind wasn't her own, but Emma's, saying, in that blunt and factual way: *"You know that ain't how it works. A person don't just 'get better' like it's the flu. Don't put that on yourself."*

"Yeah," she muttered into the empty alley, "yeah. This is fine. I mean, it's not *fine*, but it's fine."

She considered gathering up her resolve and forcing herself to go inside, but she was sure that she'd strangle the first person who touched her, so she resolved to stay put and wait for Mags to get there, though it made her feel pitiful and ridiculous.

She'd only been there a moment, though, when a short, heavyset woman wearing blue jeans and a black tank top walked past on the sidewalk, noticed her, and asked, "You, uh . . . you okay down there, sweetheart?"

"Yeah, I'm good," Jules snapped, then sighed and added, "I'm just having a little panic attack."

And the stranger looked at the small, scared woman shivering in the bushes and said, "God, you're valid. You, like, need some help or anything?"

Jules started to wave her off, but something about the woman's demeanor was homey and disarming; in a way that Jules couldn't quite describe, and in the same way that Mags had, this person looked like a friend. She drew in a deep breath and stammered, "I . . . I'm new here, and I don't know anybody, and I came here with my girlfriend, but she's busy right now, and we were supposed to meet up back here, but I don't know when she'll be done, and I don't like crowds and I don't like strangers and I don't like being alone and I . . . I . . ." She took a long drag from her cigarette and examined the ground. "So I'm having a teeny little PTSD flashback. And this hasn't happened in a long time, so my girl probably didn't even think about it 'cause, shit, I sure didn't. Fuck, I'm sorry, I'm sorry, I . . . you don't even know me."

"Hey, don't even worry about it. I asked, didn't I? My name's Kelly; I tend bar inside."

"Thanks. My name's Julia. You can call me Jules."

"Fine to meet you. So what brings you to Central, Jules?"

Talking to Kelly, the panic began to die down. "I'm here with my girlfriend. She's one of those political officers, and we did a job together not that long ago, and they wanted to like go over it with us. Mine didn't take that long, but hers is probably gonna be a minute. I was gonna just head down here and have a drink or whatever and wait for her, but . . . strange places full of strange people aren't so good for me, turns out."

"Oh, I feel you on that. Say, if you're feeling any better, you can come inside with me. It's dark in there."

"Yeah?"

"Dark, not too loud, lots of corners to disappear into. I'll walk you in."

Jules looked up at her and grinned. "Y'know what? That sounds nice as hell."

Kelly stepped forward and offered her a hand up. Jules hissed, shuffled backwards, and muttered, "No, I, uh . . . you, uh . . . Don't touch me. Please don't touch me."

"Aw, hell, I'm sorry."

"No, no, it's fine, I just . . . There's one person on Earth who's allowed to touch me, and she ain't here yet."

The interior of the bar was, as Kelly had promised, nice and dim, with a wide open floor plan, a few tables scattered here and there, and a long bar across the far wall. The noise of music and conversation from the patrons—not too many—lingered in the smoky air, and decorations hung along the walls; there were portraits, and flags in shades of red and black bearing various insignia, but what caught Jules' eye right off were the decorations hanging behind the bar. Just over the shelf of bottles and jugs hung three dusty and beat-up Armalite AR-10 battle rifles, and another flag, badly torn and slightly burned, bearing thirteen blue and black stripes with a big Orthodox cross in the top left corner. The words "BOUND TO LOSE" were scrawled across the flag's white fringe in a dull rusty brown. Old blood.

Somewhere off in the shadows, a patron was strumming an acoustic guitar and drawling, "*. . . but people in this world are gettin' organized . . . You're bound to lose, yeah, all you fascists bound to lose . . .*"

Jules took a seat on the far end of the bar, away from any other patrons, with her back to a wall and her eyes on the door. Kelly slipped past her behind the bar and asked, "So what'll you have?"

"You got any food?"

"Nothing to write home about, but we got a couple plates left over from lunch. Just a sec."

And Kelly ducked under the bar to the sound of crockery being moved around. Jules fished around in her pocket and brought out a loose round of ammunition and set it upright in front of her. Kelly came up a second later with a plate of crisp, flaky flatbread sprinkled with powdered sugar. She snatched up the brass and examined it for a moment before stuffing it into her pocket, giving it a funny, suspicious look, and in that moment Jules realized that she'd handed over one of her own .303 Winchester rounds. Wanting to move things along, she gestured at the plate and said, "This smells amazing. What is it?"

"Fry bread. It's a bit cold, but it'll fill a hole. You want anything to drink, sweetie?"

"Y'all got wine?"

"'Y'all got wine?' she asks. What kind?"

"Uh . . red?"

"Yeah, sweetie. Coming right up."

Jules dug into the food, which tasted as good as it smelled, greasy and hearty and sweet, and a moment later Kelly returned with a jug of wine, poured her a glass, and asked, "So where you from, Jules?"

"Nowhere."

"Alright. So who's this girlfriend you were talking about? I probably know her."

"Her name's Magnolia, Magnolia Blackadder. About six and a half feet tall, skinny, giant red hair. Goes by Mags."

Kelly's face contorted in amusement, and she tried not to laugh, failed, and gasped, "No shit? You're dating Mags fuckin Blackadder?"

"Uh ... yes?"

"Wow, what a small world. Yeah, I sure do know her. That's my ex."

Jules chewed her lower lip, unsure of what to say. Kelly laughed again and asked, "So is she still, y'know, wound up tighter than a rattlesnake?"

"Yeah, that's, uh ... that's a way to put it, alright."

"You're a bigger saint than me if you can handle that woman. Does she still wake up at five o'clock in the goddamn morning every day?"

And Jules laughed, and said, "Oh yeah, she sure does."

She reached for another hunk of bread, and as she did she noticed Kelly's eyebrows raise and her eyes lock onto her wrist. For a beat she thought that the barkeep was examining her scars, until Kelly, in a soft and sweet voice, asked, "Hon, can I see your hand?"

Disarmed by Kelly's presence, Jules presented her hand, which Kelly took gently in her own. The barkeep hiked up the sleeve of Jules' lavender plaid shirt a couple of inches, revealing just enough of a stick-and-poke tattoo that seemed to radiate malevolence.

"So you are from that part of nowhere where they shoot AR-10s."

Jules started to panic again, but Kelly released her hand and continued: "Hey, I know who you are. You were part of that team that cracked open the Citadel."

"Wait, y'all ... y'all know about that already?"

"Well yeah. A story that big ain't gonna stay quiet for long."

At that, Jules did panic, though it was panic of a different sort, and she snapped, "How much do you know? How much do people know about me?"

"Not hardly. I know you're from the wrong side of the river and I know you came over to ours and gave us some pretty big help; that's about it."

"Okay. Okay. I'm sorry. I just . . ." And she turned her palms up, showing off the mats of layered scars on her wrists. "There's some shit I'd really rather stayed in the past, y'know?"

"Oh, I'll bet. I'll bet you've been through some real shit. But don't worry about that, sweetie; we mind our business 'round here."

"Thanks."

"So, on a lighter note . . . How'd you and ol' Comrade Commissar meet each other?"

Jules smiled at being reminded of Mags. "I was staying in Freeside when she came through, and she wanted to know all about me and where I came from and the horror of it all, so I told her, and she . . ." A long, wistful sigh. "God, she was sweet. Like, sweet but also mean, and in just the right proportions. And that was all it took."

"Yeah, sounds about right. When we met, that was about, oh, about five years ago now, and it was right here, actually. She was fresh out of the Academy, I think about a year into the big change, still figuring herself out, and goddamn if she wasn't the cutest girl I'd ever seen."

"What happened? If you don't mind me asking."

"Eh, you know her, you know how she is. I never liked being a third wheel, and that woman is married to her work; it's always revolution first and being a human being second. I just couldn't put up with all that. Say, what is it you do around here, anyways?"

"Well, nothing at the moment—I kinda just got here—but I wanna be a state ecologist when I grow up."

"No shit? Well then you two are probably made for each other. Me, my political shit begins and ends with the service workers' syndicate. The ol' Hundred Rads is as high as my ambitions go."

"Y'know, I heard that someplace before. Do you know a guy named Knives?"

"Runs a safehouse east of Freeside? Short, twitchy guy, wears slutty dresses?"

"Yeah, that's the one."

"That's my big brother."

Jules laughed. "*Mama Maria*, everybody around here just knows each other, huh?"

"Well, I mean, red or black, we're all communists."

As they were talking, the front door opened just a crack and a small, nervous young Black man wearing tortoiseshell glasses and holding a clipboard under his arm came shuffling into the bar, examining the floor. Jules recognized his behavior and manner as that of a man who preferred not to be noticed, but he was only a few steps inside before someone took notice and called out, "Aw, shit, y'all! Jimmy's here!"

All of the patrons turned to look and called out greetings to Jimmy, how gave a half-hearted wave, rolled his eyes, and shuffled over to the bar. He sat down next to Jules and, without looking up, asked, "Kelly, could I please get something stiff?"

"Sure thing, hon," the barkeep said. "Anything in particular?"

"Gimme . . . gimme a jar of shine, please."

"Coming right up, hon. Rough day?"

"Oh my God, you have no idea. Kelly, the delegates have started checking in."

Kelly slid him a canning jar full of crystal-clear liquid. He held his nose, threw back a mouthful, coughed, and muttered, "Two of the Freesiders were already here when I woke up this morning, and you know they had a lot to say. And then Tara and a few other people from Musko showed up, and I mean, they're nice enough, but . . . Kelly, they brought Kilroy with them."

"What? That motherfucker? Hell. I thought he was gone for good."

"They don't want him any more than we do. And we still have to check in the regional delegates, and the syndics, and the rest of the international and their proxies, and . . . Kelly, this *sucks*."

"I know it, hon. I sure don't envy you."

Jules lit a cigarette, and Jimmy at last took notice of her, muttering, "Oh, hey, you're, uh . . . it's Binachi, right?"

"Uh-huh," she said. "You can call me Jules."

"Jules. Yeah. Well, uh . . . You did the Republic a hell of a great service. Thanks for that."

"Uh . . . you're welcome, I guess. Who are you?"

"Oh, that's right, you only just got here." He rubbed his hands together and stammered, "I'm, uh, I'm Jimmy, Jimmy Mahon. I'm the, uh, general secretary-treasurer."

Jules stared at him in disbelief. "You're the what?"

"General secretary-treasurer of the Ashland Farmer-Worker Union. Well, only for a few more months, thank God. And I guess it's a little bit your fault that I got stuck with chairing an All Soviets Congress. Oh, shit, I didn't mean that in a bad way, that was supposed to be a joke."

"I guess I'm a little, uh . . . Well, it's something else to be just sitting here talking to a head of state like it's nothing."

Jimmy and Kelly both laughed. Jimmy took another drink and said, "Well, see, we don't really, like, have a head of state. The General Assembly makes all the decisions; I just chair meetings, keep the books, and cast tiebreaker votes. I don't . . . I don't even know why I'm here, honestly. A year ago I was a journeyman machinist at a biomass plant in Land's End, and then my turn to be shop steward came up, and I guess I did a good job because my syndicate put my name forward for . . . this. This sucks and I can't wait to just go back to my mom's place."

"Does . . . does *everybody* in this country live with their mom?"

Jimmy gave her a funny look, but Kelly burst into a long, deep peal of laughter.

A moment later, the door swung open again and Mags came walking in. At once, Jules sprung up from her seat, rushed across the room, and threw her arms around her. Mags planted a kiss on

her lips—prompting a chorus of cheers from the rest of the patrons
—and asked, "You miss me, honey?"

"Oh, you have no idea. Can we . . . can we talk outside?"

"Of course. Did something happen?"

"Eh, not recently."

They slipped out of the door and into the alley where Jules had
been cowering earlier, and before Mags had a chance to ask, Jules
said, "So today sucked ass."

"Oh, shit."

"The interview went well, went really well; they said I'm rehabilitated or whatever. But after that, after I left . . . Sugar, you
remember back in Harper's Ferry, when I made that crack about
how it's too bad there's no instruction manual for taking care of
your pet ladyboy?"

Mags cocked an eyebrow, but before she could speak, Jules took
one of her hands and said, "I think maybe we ought to sit down and
write that instruction manual. Today . . . Well, when I left the interview and headed here, I had a panic attack. Nobody, like, did
anything, but it turns out I don't do new places and I don't do
crowds and I don't do strangers, and if that lady who runs the bar
hadn't been so sweet then I'd probably still be right here, hiding in
the azaleas and waiting for you."

"What is it you need, hon?"

"Don't ever—don't ever fucking leave me alone again."

"I won't, hon. I promise. Fuck, I am so sorry."

"Eh, don't be. It's no big surprise you didn't think about it,
'cause I sure didn't either. But one more thing: It was your idea to
send me here; why didn't you tell me I'd run into your ex?"

Mags looked confused for a moment, baffled as to what Jules
was getting at, then asked, "Oh, is this like when my mama heard us
fuck?"

"Yes, Mags, it's exactly like that."

"Shit. I'm sorry, I . . . I never thought that that would be
awkward."

"Well, I did. Listen, I . . . I feel like a fuckin space alien in this place. I don't know what any of the rules are. Where I come from, you're supposed to hide shit from your girlfriend's mom because sex is dirty and parents are possessive about their daughters, and meeting somebody's ex is supposed to be awful because we carry around our hard feelings. And you're about to tell me how dumb that is, and it is dumb, I know that, but . . . my whole life I lived like that, Mags. That's what 'normal' is to me. I love this place, I want to fit in here, I want this to be the new normal, but . . . I don't know what the rules are, what the script is. I've been on edge ever since we got to your mom's place because I got no idea what to expect."

"Fuck. I did not even think about that. You're right, and I can't even imagine how super weird this must be for you. Tell you what: From here on out, we stick together, and I'm not leaving you alone again, and if anything is new or weird then I'll be there to explain it."

"Ah, you're too good to me, sugar. But, there is . . . there is one more thing."

"Yeah?"

"They know about me in there, Mags. They didn't, like, recognize me, but they know my name because they know what we did together. That means they know where I came from."

"Is it a secret?"

Anger flashed in Jules' eyes, and she snarled, "Oh, parts of it sure the fuck are. Ask me which parts."

"Oh. Hell."

"Is that a thing I'm gonna have to deal with, Mags? Am I gonna run into strangers who know about . . . about *that?* I get the feeling that that's another one of those things that Ashlanders don't attach any stigma to, but I *need* you to understand, Mags, I can't . . . I can't talk about that with anyone but you. I just can't."

"Of course, hon. And no, we don't attach any stigma to being a victim, and anybody who did know wouldn't think any less of you, but we *also* mind our goddamn business. I put it in my report, but the only people who've seen that are the people who need to know —DIS and whatnot--and they know better than to talk. Nobody else knows anything, and they're gonna redact all the personal shit before it goes public."

"Okay. Okay. Thank fucking God."

"Speaking of, though."

"Aw, Hell."

"Miri is on her way back here, and she's bringing some company. It's our official faction meeting, to hash out what our position is and what our arguments are. They're all . . ." She pondered over the right word for a moment. "They're all people who aren't men. Nobody knows shit, and we made it absolutely clear that you're not to be asked any questions, but they sort of guessed that whatever happened to you before you came over the river might be, well, relevant. They want to meet you, like an official welcome type deal, and they're extending an offer for you to join us, if you'd like."

"Huh. What exactly is this all about, again?"

"We're the Militant Feminist Faction."

"Yeah, I don't know what that means."

"Shit. Of course. We're a bunch of fed-up people who are forming an organization within the Union to argue and vote as a bloc."

"Alright. And what are we arguing for?"

Mags smirked. "What else? War."

[*Later that evening; Columbus, Ohio*]

Her room, like everything else in her life, was kept in perfect order. The big four-poster bed with its silk sheets—difficult to acquire, their value in brass immeasurable—was made inspection-ready every morning, like a barracks bed. Likewise were the special uniforms hung up in her wardrobe, the writing desk in the corner by the window, and the footlocker under that desk all kept neat and tidy beyond reproach. She hadn't used any of the footlocker's contents in years and years, but she still kept them all parade-ready, just in case, just in case: The green canvas trauma bag with the red cross on its flap, the Browning automatic, the combat knife, and those hideous boots, steel-toed, high-topped black leather combat boots.

The bookshelf just by the desk took pride of place, and its contents were some of her most precious possessions, all of them hasty reprints of tomes some two hundred or more years old, acquired at great pains and often by dubious means; nobody was printing sexology textbooks in the Blackland New Republic.

The most precious item of all, however, was the icon. A gilded portrait of Christ in His passion hung on the far wall, watching over everything. And she, topless, knelt in front of the icon and met the crucified Savior's eyes as she prayed.

She flung the scourge over her shoulder, and no sound escaped her lips as the leather struck her flesh and the tack nails braided into it dug furrows that would form new scars. And as the wave of righteous, purifying pain swept over her being, a word echoed through her mind, and it changed with each stroke, with each fresh wave of pain.

Filthy...
Disgusting...
Degenerate...
Impure....
Deviant....
Unworthy...
Unworthy...
Unworthy...

The act put her into a sublime place, beyond the loathsome flesh, beyond the care of the material world, so that there was only passion, the passion of pain, righteous and good, and, with it, peace; the only peace she had ever known. At the end, her resolve wavered and she let out a small, pitiful gasp, and at that moment a knock came at the door.

"*I am indisposed!*" she snapped.

"Ma'am, it's 8 o'clock," came a woman's voice from without. "You asked me to bring a report."

"Ah, yes, yes, of course. Just a moment, darling!"

And, springing up from the floor, she pulled her bra and shirt back on, wincing at their touch, internally berating herself for losing track of time and wondering if she would ever get the blood out, and she straightened her hair and went to the door to find a young woman in a crisp brown uniform sporting a second lieutenant's bars. Though they were all technically members of the Women's Auxiliary, Claire was the only one besides the major who officially held rank.

"Come in, come in, darling," she cooed, stepping back from the door. "And what does my best girl have for me?"

"Things are mostly routine," Claire said, following the director as she went to take a seat at her desk and winced as her back met the chair. "There's just a couple of points of concern."

"Oh?"

"We lost Margaret Weiss today, the girl in 2B. Suicide."

"A pity. But not unexpected. We must, as they say, separate those who can from those who cannot."

"And one more thing. Tabitha has been talking again. Stirring up rumors about you-know-who."

"Oh, goodness. Will that girl never learn?"

"I'm concerned about that one, ma'am. When Tabitha talks, the others listen to her; this sort of sedition could threaten the program."

"Quite right. Tell me, lieutenant: What do you think we should do about Tabitha?"

"She should be gotten rid of. Restore her previous status and send her back to Indiana; whether she makes it that far or not, and she probably won't, she won't be our problem anymore."

"Hmm. Your willingness to take decisive action is laudable, but this calls for a bit more subtlety. People who disappear can become martyrs; I believe we've learned that lesson in spades."

"Oof. You're right as usual, ma'am."

"Take mundane action against a mundane problem. Move Tabitha's work assignment to sorting or something equally strenuous, and add her room to the short list for visitors."

Claire stood digesting her words for a moment, then asked, "Miss Tasha, can I make a suggestion?"

"Of course, darling."

"Tabitha is only a part of the problem, and singling her out would reinforce her status as someone special. I'd suggest that we keep her at distribution, and strike her room from the lists entirely. Then we move her friends to sorting, and put their rooms at the top of the short list."

Tasha's perpetual smile widened, curling around its edges. "Oh, that is brilliant, darling. Delightfully devious! Yes, do that at once."

"I will, ma'am. And thank you."

"Of course, my dear. Not to be too terribly sentimental, but it is earned praise. I'm proud of you."

Claire gave a bashful smile and looked down. Tasha went on:

"You've adapted well and you've learned well, darling; I could not have asked for a better protégé. Indeed, none of the other hopefuls ever made it nearly so far."

Claire looked on her with awe and reverence. Her smile twitched as she winced in pain again, and she asked, "Claire, darling, we're, ah . . . we're both adults here. Do you mind if I stepped down from my dignity for a moment?"

"Uh . . . whatever you say, ma'am."

"Shut the goddamn door."

She did, and Tasha began unbuttoning her shirt. At first, Claire stared with renewed reverence at getting to see the director's legendary tattoos, then winced herself as the shirt came away from the director's back with a wet, peeling sound. Tasha sighed with relief and said, "I'm terribly, terribly sorry, dear, but I lost track of the time this evening; I'd only just concluded my prayers when you stopped by."

Claire's gaze wandered back and forth between the discarded bloody shirt and the leather scourge lying in front of the icon, but at last locked on the director's left bicep, which bore a tattoo of a young boy standing upright in a cauldron over a roaring fire. Not recognizing the symbol, she asked, "Ma'am, what does that one mean?"

"The martyrdom of Saint Vitus, darling. I was born on his feast day, and he is the patron of actors, comedians, and dancers."

Claire nodded—the symbolism, though esoteric, was perfectly clear to the two of them—and Tasha added, "Claire, dear, have you ever heard the legend of St. Vitus' Dance?"

"No, ma'am, I haven't."

"This was many, many centuries ago, in Aachen, in the *Erstes Reich*. During a time of great hardship, many of the faithful were overcome with madness and began cavorting about in the streets uncontrollably. Crowds would revel and fornicate in the streets, and they would wander from town to town dancing until their feet bled and their ribs cracked and people fell down from exhaustion. The plague was called St. Vitus' Dance because it began close to his feast day, and that was how it was put a stop to: In Vitus' name, the church fathers prayed, imposed discipline, and reinforced order. The sheep had merely forgotten their shepherd. I've always liked that story, ever since I was a little girl. I find it to be a broadly applicable metaphor."

"Oh, that's clever, ma'am. That's a lot like what you do: The shepherdess imposing order on the chaos."

"I do like to think so, darling."

"You should feel proud of yourself, ma'am; everything you've accomplished, everything you've built. I really don't know where I would be if it weren't for you. I suppose I'd be dead."

Tasha's smile widened. "Thank you, my dear. It's nice that *someone* has some appropriate gratitude."

"Of course, ma'am. You're a lifesaver; you've drawn us up from perdition."

"Thank you, dear." She rested her hand on the inside of her left elbow and muttered, "*Non mi interessa davvero*; do you know what that means, darling?"

"Ah, no, I'm afraid not."

"*I really don't care.* A maxim of enduring great suffering, to triumph over great odds. A slogan for those of whom much is asked and to whom little is given. That is us, darling. We are the women of whom much is asked. You're dismissed, Claire; go on and harden your heart and do the Lord's work."

"Yes, ma'am. Good night, ma'am."

And Claire snapped a crisp salute, turned on her heels, and left, leaving Tasha alone with her thoughts. She knew she should get up and tend to her cuts, but she couldn't bring herself to move. Her attention was fixed on the sign and seal carved into the flesh of her forearm, and she brooded. Her skill at choosing not to think about things best not thought about, a skill she'd honed to a razor's edge over a lifetime, was eluding her, had been eluding her more and more over the recent days, and, against her will, she brooded.

Easily a hundred women had disappeared into her little program over these few years, and only one of them had ever been particularly memorable or particularly special, and in truth she was overall disappointed with the clay she'd been given to sculpt. But there had been one that stuck out, one that she'd been hopeful about. And her hope had proven to be rebellious, recalcitrant, a disappointment, and, at the end, a traitor.

"Sister," she whispered into the empty room as she traced the outline of the skull with her forefinger. "We were of one order, and I drew you up from perdition. Why couldn't it have been you?"

She lost track of time as she sat brooding in her chambers, and it might have been minutes or hours before another knock came at the door. She called out "Who is it?" in her sing-song voice and received no answer. She rolled her eyes as she got up and threw on a clean shirt. The knock repeated a moment later.

"Who is it?"

A man's voice, meek and quiet: "It's . . . ah, it's me."

And she knew that voice. Though her smile didn't waver, her cold blue eyes went wide with shock as she ran to the door and threw it open to find a young man with buzzed blonde hair wearing a priest's black robes and a pistol belt. "Oh, darling," she cooed, "come in, come in! It's so lovely to see you again!"

"Hello . . ." Peter said, awkwardly, her name sticking in his throat. "I'm, ah, in town on business, and I thought I'd drop by. It's protocol, of course, for servants of the High Church to avoid this . . . place, but I think that that will be overlooked, given that you're my . . . sibling."

Her smile widened. "Oh, how nice of you to think of me. Come in, come in, Peter, and have a seat. It's been far too long, so much catching up to do; tell me, darling, what sort of business brings you out of your little parish?"

"Well, Ni . . . Na . . . I've received a promotion. I'm a war cleric now."

"Oh, congratulations, darling! Look at you, *Father* Peter Wenden, war cleric of the Falange. Our father must be very proud."

Peter winced. "Quite. And they're sending me west, to the frontier in Indiana."

"Not the most prestigious of assignments, but very important. That will suit your substantial abilities."

They stood in awkward silence for a moment until Tasha smirked and said, "My dear little brother, let's dispense with all these pleasantries. Tell me what it is you want from me."

"Can I not just pay a cordial visit to my . . . my . . ."

"And there it is, darling: You don't dare to call me your brother, at least not to my face, but you can't bring yourself to call me your sister. Even disregarding the obvious, Father and I have been on the outs ever since I first joined the Falange. And how long has it been since I last saw you? How many years?"

"Fine. I don't have any contacts within the Falange yet, but you've always been a person who knows things, and I know that you and the Commander are . . . close. I know that war is coming, and soon. I know it will be in the south, and that I'm being transferred to help shore up our western flank while so many troops are occupied. But that's all I know. None of the officers and no-one at the Ecclesiarchy will tell me a damned thing. I don't know the when or where of it, and I . . . I need to know."

"Perhaps you should learn to trust in your superiors and to trust in the Lord."

"I know you know. You make it your business to know things. Tell me."

"Yes, darling, I know, and I'll tell you. But you have to do something for me first."

"And what?"

"Peter, dear, what is my name? What's my name, and what am I to you?

Peter rolled his eyes and sighed. "Your name is Natasha. You're my big sister."

"Thank you, dear. The plan is to have a repeat of the old Sunrise operation, but faster, and on a much grander scale. All the troops we can spare—I believe Roland said a quarter million, or close to it—are presently massing north of the Huntington salient, where they will assault through the defenses there and spread into the Bolshevists' industrial base, leveling their settlements and breaking their ability to produce or ship arms. If all goes well, we will have bisected the ACR and begun laying siege to Ashland itself in no time at all. The assault is scheduled to begin in two weeks."

Peter absorbed her words with an eager, hungry, malevolent

grin spreading across his face. "Glorious . . ." he muttered. "And in only two weeks. Such a damned shame I'll be missing it."

"Oh, I don't think you need to worry about that, darling. The west is not the most famous of places, but they have no shortage of bandits and savages out there, and most likely they'll be eager for a little war of their own. I spent some time in Indiana, myself, early in my career; I was quite the snake-eater once upon a time, you'll remember. The west is a lawless and heretical place."

"Yes, I suppose you're right."

"I'm always right, dear. I'll tell the Commander you stopped by; he's rather fond of me, you know."

Peter sighed. "Yes, Tasha, I am acutely aware of that fact."

"Rather enamored with our little family, too. Roland's always playing his little games with the Ecclesiarchy."

"Believe me, I am acutely aware of that as well."

[27]

HOMESICK

As Jules turned to head back into the bar with Mags, she spotted a group of people further down the block, headed toward them, and recognized one of them as Miri. She gave her a slight wave as she turned away, but stopped when someone in the group cried out, "Holy shit! Binachi! Hey, Binachi!"

And she looked and saw that a person had broken away from the group and was sprinting towards her. The stranger was barefoot, wearing a long yellow dress and a wide straw hat and obnoxious sunglasses, and as they drew near she noticed that they were exceedingly thin, almost emaciated, and sported track marks on their joyous, flailing arms. As the stranger drew close without slowing down, Jules prickled and started to back away, but they slid to a stop a few feet in front of her and declared, "Holy shit, it really is you! I heard they'd found a *Julia* Binachi, but I thought, nah, couldn't be."

Jules cocked an eyebrow. "Do I . . . know you?"

"You don't recognize me. I didn't figure you would; I barely recognized you. You look amazing, by the way. But take a look and think real hard; Father O'Brien's Sunday school class . . . you used to whup my ass at stickball . . . you went out with my sister . . ."

And recognition flashed in Jules' eyes, and she laughed and said, "Holy shit! You're . . . well, I guess I should probably know you by a different name now."

"Yeah! It's Kitty; Kitty Braddock. Holy shit, what a small world."

"How the hell did you get here?"

"Ran for it. I was living in Cincinnati a few years ago when shit started getting really bad, and I was like, y'know, the river is right there. And here I am! There's a few of us, actually."

"No shit? God, I've got so many questions, I--" And she turned toward Mags, who was watching the two of them with a warm smile splitting her face, and said, "Sugar, this . . . this was one of my friends growing up. We were kids together."

"Well it sure is a small world, I guess," Mags said. "I've known Kitty off and on, but like they said, there's other defectors around. I had no idea."

"Kitty," Jules said, "this is . . . this is my girlfriend."

"Oh, cute!" Kitty cooed. "That's awesome."

"God, I . . . I've got so many things I could ask you."

"Oh, right back at you. I would love to grab a drink and swap war stories; I'm sure there's some shit you don't know about, and I bet you could answer a lot of my questions. But for now, nah, we're here and we're alive and we're who we are and this is a happy moment."

"Hell yeah it is. Man, what a small world; I never thought I'd see anybody from the old days again, let alone, y'know, another girl."

"Sweetheart, I'm not a girl."

"Aw, Hell. Sorry."

"We've got a whole lot in common, but I could never be just one thing or the other. I contain multitudes!"

"Nice. Y'know, that suits you."

"And what you are suits you, and you're rocking it. Say, you're sticking around for the meeting, right?"

"Yeah, I guess so."

"Good. I'm sure you've got things to say that they need to hear. Speaking of . . . Not to dwell on darkness, but, like, good job being alive."

"Hey, you too. I dunno what all you've been through, but I know it couldn't have been easy."

"Yeah, that's an understatement. But I'm here now, and so are you, and oh, hey, look at that."

Kitty pointed down to Jules' right hand, where her sleeve was still hiked up enough to expose her scars. She started to step back, hurt and confused, but Kitty gave a wide, warm smile and presented their arm, showing off their tracks, and declared, "I guess we're twins, huh?"

"Yeah, I guess we are. And hey, y'know what that is? That's battle scars. It's survivors who get to show off their battle scars."

"Damn right, sister."

And, after deliberating a moment, Jules stepped forward and put an arm around Kitty's waist, drawing them into an embrace. She looked back at Mags, afraid she'd see jealousy, but instead Mags grinned from ear to ear and said, "Honey, this is amazing. I'm so happy for you."

By then, the others had made it up to them, a group of about fourteen individuals, more different kinds of people than Jules had ever seen all in one spot before. The sight of the group, in that way that she still couldn't describe but was becoming so familiar with, felt like home, and her smile stuck on her face as she, Mags, and Kitty followed them inside. The patrons gave them a wide berth as they made their way to a far corner and began dragging unused tables and chairs over. As they worked, Kelly looked their way and asked, "Anything I can get for you folks?"

"We don't wanna be a bother," Miri said. "A couple jugs of wine, and whatever's for dinner."

"Coming right up, Granny."

"Kelly, you are a saint."

"I know."

The group took seats in a circle as Kelly brought two jugs of wine and a few glasses over, stopping to wink at Mags, who blushed as red as her hair, and when all were seated Miri said, "Alright, I reckon this is everybody we could pressgang in at such short notice; don't worry, there'll be more when the arguing starts. Who wants to take stack?"

There was a tense silence that dragged on into awkwardness until one of them took out a notebook and pen and grumbled, "Alright, fine, I guess I'll fuckin do it."

"Uh, excuse me," Jules said, "but what the hell is stack?"

Miri nodded. "Everybody, Julia here is new and will probably have a lot of questions. That will not be a problem. A stack is a progressive queue; if you've got something to say, raise your hand and Tara will mark you down and call on you when your turn comes up. If you haven't spoken yet, you got to the top of the list, and if you've been speaking a lot you go to the bottom."

Jules nodded, impressed. Miri lit a cigarette and went on: "Speaking of, a lot of us don't know each other too good, so let's do a round of introductions before I lead us off. I'm Miriam Methotaske, political commissar, one of the New Lawrence regional voting delegates. She/her."

As they went around the circle, introducing themselves, lighting cigarettes, pouring glasses of wine, Jules paid rapt attention, trying to fix names and identities to faces while also mentally going over the pattern: Name, affiliation, office if any, and what to call you. She was last in the order, sitting to Miri's right, and when her turn came up she stammered, "Uh, Julia Binachi, she/her, and I'm not really, like, with anybody, I don't think."

"What do you want to be with?" Miri asked.

"Uh . . . I guess the agriculturalist syndicate."

"That'll do fine. I see fourteen voices and about eight votes sitting at these tables, and that's not even counting supporters and at-large folks who couldn't make it on short notice, so that's a hell of a good place to get started. Our purpose in coming together as a bloc is to address the serious problems plaguing the Ashland Confederated Republic and the Ashland Farmer-Worker Union. Too many people think that purging Kilroy and his supporters a few years ago was enough to put an end to the threat of stagnation and bureaucracy, but we all know that that was only treating a symptom while ignoring a disease. Our order is stagnating, and it's become unstable, because we're dangerously close to abandoning the principle of the permanent revolution. We've gotten complacent in our success, and we're growing too timid to take necessary risks, which means we're ignoring necessary next steps. Broadly speaking, our purpose here can be summed up in the maxim, 'But for ourselves, alone'; a lot of people in the Republic are clinging to archaic and unscientific ideas about what it means to build a society, and they think that democratizing the means of production has just magically fixed everything overnight, but really our revolution is a deed half-done. Things like race and gender aren't being deconstructed, and the issues we face are not being adequately addressed. Hell, I'm the goddamn war chief of the goddamn Shawnee nation and I gotta twist arms to get a word in around here. This can't stand, and we have to come together and advocate for own interests, because nobody else is gonna do it for us."

Fists began to pound the table in approval. Miri cleared her throat and spoke louder over the racket: "A more pressing business, and a perfect example of all this mess, is the matter of the Blacklanders and the ongoing war. We share a border with a fascist state that oppresses workers, murders people of color, does unspeakable things to women and queers, wages wars of extermination against our siblings in the northwest, and routinely sends raiding parties onto our land to burn our farms and kill our people while they sleep. That's untenable. That border is an irreconcilable contradiction; our order and theirs cannot exist together on the same piece of ground. Moreover, we know that they're planning a renewed offensive. We know that that offensive would've been launched weeks ago and probably would've destroyed us if it weren't for Comrade Blackadder's decisive action, and we may have slipped that noose, but they are still massing troops along the border for what can only be a hell-for-leather drive into either our agricultural or industrial base. The conservatives in the General Assembly and the army officer corps refuse to consider anything more ambitious than building more pillboxes along the Ohio Valley and sending more guns to the Oceti Sakawin, because they're convinced that the war can't be won under present conditions. I think that that's bullshit, on a couple of points. They're ignoring centuries of struggle and ignoring the lived experiences of Reyez and Bluecrow and thinking about war the way settlers think of war; they say we can't take a more aggressive stance because we have no hope of winning a force-on-force conflict or conquering territory, which is true, but either of those things is a dumbfuck way to win a war. Comrades, now is the time for action, and that action needs to be ambitious and it needs to be bold, because if we allow this war to play out on the enemy's terms, we very well may lose, and even in victory we would still lose because our revolution is stagnating. The revolution is everywhere, or it is nowhere; it is for everyone, or it is for no-one; and if it is said to have any ending, it can never truly begin. We go forward. We take the risks. The rising tide of history leaves us no other choice."

They were all banging their fists on the tables then, and even Jules—who had only understood about half of it—felt stirred to action, and many of the patrons had turned to stare at them, giving them approving looks. And Miri concluded: "I believe in this Republic and its institutions, and I believe in the good will of the people involved, even if a lot of them are dumb as fuck. What I want us to do here is hash out some concrete proposals to bring to the All Soviets Congress; everybody here is a citizen of some or other body of our commonwealth, and better than half of us are voting delegates, too. I'm especially interested in hearing from our out-of-towners; the lovely Miss Tara over there is part of the Musko delegation, and Kimimela there is part of the Oceti Sakawin delegation, and Kitty and Julia there came here from Ohio, right in the heart of the beast. But before we get going, does anybody have any questions?"

Jules took a long drink of wine and raised her hand. Tara, a serious-faced Black woman with an impressive cloud of rich, dark hair, gave her a nod, and she said, "I got a couple. First of all, I know I've heard that name before, but who the hell is Kilroy?"

The entire group groaned in unison, and Mags said, "He's the reason general secretary-treasurers aren't allowed to stand for consecutive terms anymore. Ken Kilroy was a shop steward from the transportation workers' syndicate who got voted in as general secretary a few years ago. Nobody really liked him—he was an asshole—but being general secretary is a shit job that nobody wants, and he turned out to be pretty good at it, so he stood for a second term and got in again. He pretty much led the drive to deescalate the war and harped on a lot about how we couldn't win in a direct conflict and needed to focus our efforts on internal development. Then, at the end of his second year, he announced that he was gonna stand in election for a third time, and nobody had ever done that before and it left a bad taste in a lot of our mouths, so a whole bunch of people voiced their displeasure, but it wasn't against the rules back then. So then Kilroy pulls some real bullshit: He called a meeting of the General Assembly in the middle of the night, so that the only people who showed up were his supporters, and all twelve of them unanimously voted to expel all the people who'd spoken up against him. That stood, because it wasn't technically against the rules yet—and this is how Professor J wound up in Freeside—but it didn't take no time at all to call a regular meeting to vote to recall the fucker. So Kilroy gets a real galaxy-brain idea and he calls up some of his friends in the officer corps and convinces some of them to send troops to occupy Liberty Hall ahead of the assembly."

"Holy shit. How'd that play out?"

"We—the Commissariat—did our jobs and maintained civilian control of the military. In the end, only like ten people actually showed up, and Miri over there told them to go home and they went home. So the General Assembly recalled Kilroy, rehabilitated all the people he'd purged, made the rules about parliamentary procedure more specific, and kicked out Kilroy and all his little sycophants. Last I heard, the sorry Stalinist weasels were working at a coffee co-op down in Florida, ten million miles away from me."

Tara cleared her throat and spoke up. "Well, that ain't the case anymore, I'm afraid. He, uh . . . he's back in town."

"He's fucking what?"

She shrugged. "The term of exile was four years, and it's been four years, and the rest of them said that they like Musko better than Tennessee—or maybe they just know what shame is and don't wanna show their faces—but Ken said he wanted to come back. We couldn't stop him—he's a free worker and he can do what he wants with hisself—but if I'm being honest, even if we coulda stopped him, wouldn't have tried real hard."

"Oh, motherfucker. He's gonna speak at the congress, isn't he?"

"Probably."

"Hell."

"Alright, I think I'm trackin now," Jules said, lighting a cigarette. "But what the hell is 'permanent revolution'?"

Mags' sour expression warmed at once, and she rubbed her hands together and said, "So, the way we see things, real progress happens when working people have got their hands on the levers of progress, directly and without any intermediaries; middlemen are just dead weight. We have that here in the Republic; all our industry is collectively owned, and it's managed through workers' assemblies. But if this thing we've started rolling is allowed to slow down, it'll stall out and degenerate into just another nation-state, and we came perilously close to that with Kilroy. The only way to safeguard the revolution is to continue the revolution, to keep moving on to the next stage of progress. And right now, we're not doing that. Our focus is turned inward, to our own safety and comfort, when we should be looking outward. Seizing state power in one country is supposed to be just a first step, not an end unto itself. In order to be successful, the revolution must be continuous."

Jules looked at her skeptically, but nodded and said, "Alright, I . . . I *think* I'm following everything now."

"Alright," Miri said, "let's get started."

A forest of hands shot up at once, and Tara rushed to write down names and call on speakers. The conversation was energetic, emotional, heated, and most of it was wholly esoteric, but Jules was reluctant to ask any more questions and spent most of the afternoon nursing her wine and leaning against Mags, trying to listen. As the afternoon dragged on, the talk started to grow more and more coherent, and Jules was able to follow a solid line beginning to form: When war came, the Republic might be able to hold the border, and that could be enough; victory, and the success they depended on on the other side of victory, depended on their co-belligerents. With the right kind of help, and enough of it, opposition from outside of and from within the BNR could tear it to pieces. Jules liked the sound of that just fine.

As the discussion began to wind down, Tara called on a speaker who said, "This all sounds really good from, like, a strategic perspective, but something doesn't sit right with me. It sounds like we're advocating for a proxy war. Is a proxy war really all that different from conquest? And if we're not willing to throw away Ashlander lives to win this, are we really willing to throw away other people's lives instead?"

Kitty's hand shot up at once, and they locked eyes with Tara and asked, "Can I jump stack to give a direct response?"

"Of course, baby."

"Well," they said, taking a long drink of wine, "I don't think that that's really any issue, because we're not proxies, we're co-belligerents. I think my Oceti Sakawin and Miami comrades will agree with me when I say that we don't wanna fight *for* the Republic, we wanna fight *alongside* the Republic, as equal partners."

Jules perked up, noting the use of *we*, rather than *they*.

One of the attendants, a person of indeterminate gender wearing a trad goth outfit with intricate bead and shell jewelry draped over it, their hair tied into two long black braids, slammed their fist onto the table and barked, "You're goddamn right we do."

"Thank you, Kim. See, Rain's order is built on sand. There's a rot at the heart of the BNR, there are cracks to be widened. In the western districts and in the big cities, huge parts of the underclass are already organized into support and communication networks that we depend on for survival. I'm not exactly sure what the situation on the ground is, that would be DIS business—it's possible, hell, might be probable that everybody in the underground I knew is dead by now—but the underground exists; it always does. If Ashland can help us out with things like leadership, technical training, and, most importantly, *guns*, then the BNR eats itself alive from the inside. Provide a spark, and the entire shit could go up like a hay barn. This isn't a proxy war any more than it's a war of conquest. This is a revolution."

Jules noted the pronoun choice again; us. Most of the group pounded their fists on the table in support, but no-one else spoke, and after a beat Tara shushed them and said, "Stack's open, y'all. Who's got two cents?"

No hands went up. After another beat, Miri said, "Y'know what, I think we did it. I think we've got a proposal. If nobody else wants to speak, I move to adjourn."

Kimimela, who'd spoken up in favor of Kitty a moment ago, poured themself another glass of wine and said, "As usual, I'm with Granny. We've done good here, and I second the motion to adjourn."

"We'll meet back up here right before the congress, along with whoever else we can pressgang. Sound good?"

There was a chorus of approval, and the meeting dissolved,

with most of the group disappearing to other parts of the bar. Mags pulled Jules closer and asked, "So what do you think, hon?"

"I like it. Most of this is above my pay grade—I know small unit tactics and that's about it—but I think we got a plan. I think this'll work."

Kitty moved into one of the empty seats near the two of them, and they took another drink of wine, swayed a bit, and said, "God, I know, right? I'm so excited; I might finally be going home."

"Home," Jules repeated, dubious. "I noticed that during the meeting; you talk about Ohio like it's home."

"That's 'cause it is, sweetheart. I . . . I think I can make some educated guesses about what you went through in order to get here, and I figured you wouldn't have anything to go back to, but that's not me. If I'm right, they tried to break you by ripping home away from you; me, though, I only survived as long as I did because I found home. You never got to see the underground scene in the big cities, did you?"

"Nah. I went right into the army when I left Somerset, and that was my life until . . . well, until it wasn't."

"Sweetheart, there's a whole other world that you never even saw the surface of. I left where we grew up and I went to the big city and—if you can believe it—I found other people like me. And the lives we carved out, it wasn't much of a way to live, but we kept each other alive, and we loved each other, and sometimes . . . sometimes, it could be so nice. That's what I think about when I think about home. The way I see it, Julia, I'm not a runaway, I'm an exile. Home is a riverside drag bar. Home is a gang of queers and junkies beating the shit out of a marshal. And, honestly? Home is my uncle's place outside of Somerset. Home is a red sunrise lighting up a grey sky over the prairie. You ever think about the prairie, Jules?"

Jules shrugged. "Sometimes. But like you said, I don't really got anything to go back to. My whole life, I been looking for home, and I found it here."

"And that's valid. But for me, better or worse, Ohio is home, and when I come back they ain't gonna be ready for me."

Jules nodded and took another long drink. Kitty's enthusiasm was infectious, but what it woke up in her wasn't the defiant hope of an exile determined to return, but something bitter, something melancholy. it brought up memories of things that had been taken from her, things she was sure she'd never see again even if she wanted to, which, for the most part, she did not. With a long sigh, she turned to Mags and asked, "Sugar, we're . . . we're going to Ohio, ain't we?"

Mags lit a cigarette and held her closer. "Honestly? The way things are playing out, that's probably right. I'm a political officer, and you're an asset."

"When I left, I swore I'd never go back, but . . ." She let the statement hang in the air.

Kitty leaned over and put an arm around the two of them. "We're gonna finish it. We're gonna put an end to this bullshit and we're gonna pay some people back for their dirty work."

"Kitty, I learned a while ago that I ain't in the paying people back business. But I think I'd like to take you up on that offer to sit down and swap war stories. And, Mags? Tomorrow, I wanna go find Peterson."

"Who's Peterson?"

"A friend. He was . . ." Jules sucked air through her teeth. "He was my squad leader, in my Arditi operating group. Before I . . . disappeared, he was my best friend. Then, after I ran away, I ran into him again 'cause he fragged our old group and he . . . he saved me and my girl from a guy who wanted to hurt us. Came here after that."

"Wow I . . . kinda can't believe there could be two of y'all."

"That's what Miri said. But ol' Peterson saved my ass, and more importantly he saved her ass, and when we parted ways again he called me his little sister. I hope he's making out okay, and anyways he's probably an asset too."

In the midst of the talk, the door swung open and two people with brown skin and indeterminate genders came walking in. One wore a leather jacket and a pleated skirt and walked with a bit of difficulty, leaning on the other's arm. The two of them noticed Jules in the corner as soon as they walked in, and Jules grinned, nudged Mags, and said, "Holy shit, check this out."

Mags looked up to see Millie and TJ walking toward them. TJ gave a jaunty wave and called out, "Wassup, red? Small fuckin world, huh?"

"Sure is," Mags said, raising her glass. "What are y'all doing here?"

"We're two of the voting delegates for Freeside," Millie replied, sitting down. "They sent along some adults to babysit y'all authoritarians."

"Well, hell, they couldn't have sent anybody better. How have you been?"

"Eh, same old. My back hurts, my brother-in-law ain't good for nuthin but I love him anyways, I'm living the good life free from the exploitation of illegitimate hierarchies. Wish I could say the same for you."

Mags chuckled. TJ took a seat and asked, "Say, speaking of babysitting, is this where that feminism thing is gonna be? I heard y'all were gonna tell some people about themselves."

"Sweetheart, we adjourned like half an hour ago."

"Aw, hell."

"We're meeting back up here before the congress, though, and I think most of the delegates are already here, so, hell, the congress might be tomorrow. And I can give you the short version."

"Please do. This sounds like some shit I wanna get into."

Mags launched into the spiel, and Jules relaxed against the wall, enjoying the sound of her voice and the warmth of her closeness. Kitty leaned over a bit further, and Jules, her head silly with wine, noticed how conspicuously close together the three of them were and thought about how Mags hadn't shown any of her usual jealousy. She felt something brush the back of her head and looked over to see that Mags had, idly, likely without thinking, put an arm across the both of them. Looking ahead, she locked eyes with Millie, who was watching them with a warm, wide smile.

During a lull in the conversation, Jules looked at TJ and asked, "Say, you live in Parson's Hollow, right?"

TJ nodded. "Yes, ma'am, I sure do."

"Have you seen Becky? What's she up to?"

"Eh, I wouldn't exactly see much of her. I've been out of town a lot; there's a lot less hunters around nowadays and it's been a whole new world for scavenging. Also, I sleep at night. But I know she's getting by; she's got the old man to take care of her, after all, and y'know he's got a soft spot for strays."

"Oh, I know. I used to be one."

"Yeah, I guess you did. By the way, sweetheart, how are *you* holding up?"

"I'm okay. Some days are better than others, but . . . it does get easier. It really does."

Kitty squeezed her shoulder, and she added, "Hell of a lot better since getting here. I'm with my girl, and I found a new home, and I really feel like I belong here."

"Aw, hell, girl, they're gonna ruin you! Make a red out of you!"

The group laughed together, and Jules yawned and asked, "Say, what time is it? I dunno how long we been here, but it feels like ages."

"It's about 7:00," Mags said.

"Sugar, where are we gonna sleep tonight?"

Kitty leaned closer so that they were almost sitting in Jules' lap and said, "I'm put up at the auxiliary barracks down the way. I've got a single room."

"Huh."

"Only one bed, though."

The three of them looked back and forth at each other, and Mags and Jules locked eyes and shared a solemn nod. Jules looked at Kitty and said, "You, uh . . . I think you understand why I might hesitate to do that."

"Oh, believe me, sweetheart, I get it. I'm the same. But I . . . I feel like I trust you."

Jules took their hand in both of hers. "I think I trust you, too, Kitty."

"And that is the sexiest thing anybody has ever said to me."

———

Jules couldn't sleep.

The bed wasn't particularly big or particularly comfortable, but the warmth and the cloying darkness and the closeness of the two other snoring, sleeping bodies made it feel safe and homey and downright decadent. The tiny room had been unoccupied a few days ago, and would be unoccupied again once their business was done, but it smelled of life and warmth and sex and, in that moment, it felt like home.

But Jules couldn't sleep.

As she lay in the darkness, listening to her lovers snore, her thoughts wandered, lingering on the past and on painful memories. Kitty's words from earlier in the evening echoed through her head, and reminded her of how different the two of them really were; any connection she still felt to her old home was a bitter one, and any fond memories she still held felt like they'd been violently ripped away.

Sighing, she rose up from the bed, threw on her jeans and shirt, and headed outside, where she sat down on the sidewalk and lit a cigarette. The compound at night was dark and empty, but not silent; the air was thick with the droning of insects and night birds in the trees, the grass, the hanging gardens on the walls, the starlight would've been bright enough to see by. She looked up at the bright silver moon and her melancholy started to fade.

After a beat, the door swung open again and Kitty stepped

outside, flopping onto the ground beside her with a yawn. They kissed her cheek and asked, "Mind if I steal one of those, sweetheart?"

Jules handed them a cigarette. "I didn't wake you up, did I?"

"Nah. Well, I mean, you did wake me up, but it's cool. I'm glad we've got a minute alone."

"Yeah. Say, Kitty . . . what are we?"

"Well, that's a hell of a question. We're human beings, I guess."

"You know what I mean, *stronzo.*"

They chuckled. "I dunno, Julia, but I do know that I really like you and I really like Mags and we don't have to figure out exactly what this is tonight. We could be lovers, partners, or we could just be friends. Just three friends sucking each other's dicks; it don't gotta be gay or nuthin."

Jules laughed and put an arm across their shoulders. "Y'know, I been wanting to ask you . . . How come you always call me Julia?"

"Because it's your name, dumbass."

"I meant, like . . . You always say the whole thing. Never just Jules."

"I've been calling you Jules ever since we were little kids. I wanna say the whole thing because now I have the honor and privilege of knowing the whole thing—the whole you. One whole entire Julia."

"Ah, you're too good to me. And I . . . I don't think I wanna just be buddies. Tonight was amazing, and I think there's something else here. Can I be just horribly sappy?"

"Of fucking course you can be horribly sappy."

"I think there was always something else there. I'm glad I found you again, 'cause, like . . . it feels like tonight confirmed something I sort of always knew."

Kitty grinned and kissed her cheek again. "Julia Binachi, are you saying you had a gay little crush on me?"

"I wouldn't have thought about it like that at the time, but . . .

yeah. But while we're on the subject, I . . . I kinda don't know what to think right now."

"What do you mean, sweetheart?"

"Well, you're not a girl."

"Uh-huh."

"I'm a lesbian. I'm a girl who likes girls. And until a few hours ago, I thought I *only* liked girls. I know the real world is a hell of a lot more complicated than just men or women, but . . . Kitty, a long time ago somebody told me that if I like girls then I can't be one, that if I'm not into men then I'm not a real woman, and it really fucked me up. So claiming that is kinda, like, really important to me. If I'm a girl and you're a not-a-girl, does being so into you mean I'm not a lesbian?"

"I think you answered your own question, sweetie. The world's a complicated place, and labels are complicated things, and at the end of the day you are whatever you feel like you are. Now, does anything about this strike you as even remotely heterosexual?"

"Well, no. Not at all."

"Then I can't believe that the guy I used to smoke with behind the church grew up to be my cool lesbian girlfriend. Life is *wild*."

She laughed. "Yeah, if that ain't the truth. A lot of this shit is still so new to me, like . . . I really like you, Kitty, I like you a whole hell of a lot, and tonight was incredible, but . . . I love Mags. I love Mags so much that it hurts. I know it's stupid, but a part of me can't shake the feeling that I'm doing something wrong."

"Like what do you mean?"

"Call it social conditioning or whatever, but I'm having a hard time shaking the feeling that I can't be with you if I'm already with her."

"Ah, I think I see where you're coming from now. Maybe we should've taken more time to sit and chat before our clothes magically fell off on their own. I'm already with someone, too; I'm married."

"No shit?"

"Yeah, for a couple of years now. He's great, I love him so much, and I can't wait to tell him about all this. I can't wait for him to meet you two. In this the land of hope and glory, nobody can tell you who to love or how to love, and around here, love is like friendship; it gets bigger when you spread it around."

"I like the sound of that. It's just like everything else in this place, I guess; it's beautiful, I love it, I'm so happy to be a part of it, but I've only been out of Ohio for a little over a year and I've only been here for a couple of weeks. Everything's new to me and I feel like a dumb little baby. I don't know what the rules are."

"Ah, I get what you mean. I can't even imagine how super weird this must be for you."

"Well, you went through the same shit, didn't you?"

And Kitty gave her a sad smile and said, "no, Julia, I didn't. Like I said earlier, you and me may have come from the same place, but we came from two different worlds."

"I'd like to hear about that, if you're willing."

"You sure? It ain't no fairytale."

"Y'know, that is exactly what I say to people."

Kitty took a long drag on their cigarette and said, "Let me as you a question, pretty lady. When did you first know?"

"I pretty much always knew. As soon as I was old enough to understand that girls and boys are different, I knew which team I was supposed to be on."

"Well, I didn't. I went through a lot of what I know you went through—I was confused, I was scared, I hated myself so much— but I didn't have words for it for years and years. I knew I wasn't a boy, but I knew I didn't want to be a girl, either, and as far as I knew that was all a person could be. Right after you left, I moved to Cincinnati because I needed a change, and it helped some, but, well, it wasn't the kind of change I really needed. I didn't know that, though, so mostly it made me feel worse, and I went into a really dark place. Couldn't find work. Started shooting up. Spent a lot of time wandering around the run-down parts of downtown, sleeping rough, looking for shit to steal. But, eventually, do you know what I found?"

"What did you find?"

"I found people like us, Julia. People like *me*. The big cities are chaotic enough that the marshals can't be bothered about it half the time. I found people like me living in squats, going to bars, forming networks, keeping each other alive; I found a community. It was hard as hell, and I went through a lot of shit I'd rather not have done to stay alive, and I've buried a lot of friends, but it was . . . it was something, and it could be beautiful. I learned which bars and shops were safe, which streets to walk down and which ones to avoid, where my friends were, and I found the space to figure out how and what I am and to live, to live as myself. It ain't pretty, but there is defiant and tenacious life clinging on underneath the heart of the beast."

"Holy shit."

"Uh-huh. But, see, living like that wears on a person, wears a person down no matter how things go, and a few years ago things went from bad to worse. One day, people started disappearing. And that wasn't, like, unheard of; we were all wanted in some kind of a way, and sometimes a person would go out and just not come back. But this was . . . different. The marshals knew exactly where to go, who to snatch, which bars and squats to raid and when. Some of us fought back, and sometimes we won, but the networks were just too fractured; no way we could keep up. Eventually, I was all alone; I knew there were others, but the networks were just too fractured. No way we could keep up. Eventually, I was all alone; I knew there were others, that the community was still there, but I didn't dare go to them. So I ran. And here I am."

They sat together in silence for a long moment before Kitty spoke up again, saying, "Y'know, my brother was a blackshirt."

"Frankie? No shit?"

"Uh-huh. Frankie Braddock, staff sergeant. He's dead. Hanging. They caught him in bed with another man, so they say."

"Fuck."

"But, see, a part of me always figured that that wasn't the whole story. I never heard of anybody else hanging that night, just him, and it was less than a year before my little life started going to shit. I always figured that the two were connected somehow."

Jules felt a goose walk over her grave. Somewhere deep in the back of her mind, a connection was being made, but she couldn't bring to mind quite what it was. Kitty saw it in her face and asked, "You feel it too, huh?"

"Yeah, I do. Don't know exactly what I'm feeling, but I feel it."

"And, y'know, it's not as if the Arditi were ever great paragons of virtue or whatever. A lot of us were sex workers, y'know, and we did a lot of business with a lot of soldiers. It ain't about morality or whatever, it's about control; the bigshots only gave a shit when they got caught."

"Yeah, if that ain't the fuckin truth."

"Sure is, sister, and I bet you know all about that. I bet you know all about that in ways that most people don't." And they lit another cigarette, thought for a moment, and said, "Y'know, funny story. I met a blackshirt once who came to one of the squats I was staying at, but she didn't come to solicit anybody, nah, she wanted to, like . . . hang out with us. Tried to be our friend."

And every muscle in Jules' body tensed, and her head snapped up like a bird dog, and she hissed, "*She?*"

"Yeah, she; a girl like you. Except not like you at all, because she was a real fucking creep, and--"

"What was her name?"

"Huh?"

"What was her name, Kitty?"

"Ah, this was a long time ago, but I think she called herself Natasha."

Jules said nothing, but her jaw slackened, and her breathing quickened, and her face began to twitch, and Kitty looked at her and muttered, "Oh, Hell. Oh, no. No fucking way."

"Kitty . . . Kitty, I think I know where some of your friends went."

"Fuck."

"I don't . . . I don't know how much I can relive right now. But, Kitty, I know that bitch. I know that bitch entirely too well."

And Kitty looked into her sad brown eyes and muttered, "Oh, baby . . . what did they *do* to you?"

And Jules collapsed into their arms and whispered, "Short answer? Everything."

[*That same evening; outside of Sunrise, Ohio*]

It was all coming together.

Moving so many divisions through the mountains was a tricky business, but Roy Farley, blackshirt, brigadier general, relished a tricky business. The sight of so many men and machines massed between the hills was beautiful, stirring something deep in his soul. And he knew that it was just a fancy, just a trick of his own eagerness, but as he stood on top of a high ridge and looked south through the moonlight, he almost thought he could see the Ohio Valley a few miles to the south, and the Huntington bluffs on the other side.

Near the eastern edges of the two republics, about halfway across Land's End, the Ohio River bent south and back up again like a hairpin, and the bend formed a salient, a bayonet pointed into the heart of the ACR's industrial base. It would be a hell of a thing, crossing the river under fire, storming the Huntington battery, scaling the bluffs, but if there was one thing Roy loved, it was a hell of a thing; it would be a beautiful struggle, a struggle that would break the enemy's back in one great blow, and a purgative that would rid his army of those who were unworthy, those who lacked the courage and strength for what came next, once they were over the river: Liquidation. Extermination. Siege.

"*Siege,*" he muttered aloud into the darkness.

Roy stood atop the ridge flanked by three other men, two black-shirts—his boys, his staff officers—and a brownshirt, a lieutenant general, one of his supposed commanding officers. For now.

The two other blackshirts nodded; that single word weighted with terrible meaning for them. The general, however, turned to him and asked, "Whatcha say, Farley?"

"Siege," Farley repeated. "Just thinking about the campaign. It's going to be a hell of a bloody business."

The general started to nod in agreement, then noticed that Farley was grinning from ear to ear, like a shark smelling blood in the water. He shook his head and said, "Don't lose your sense, Farley. We've only got one shot at making this work, and this is bad country to be launching an invasion into. The butcher's bill is already gonna be high enough without you playing cowboy."

"That is the general idea. War is where heroes are forged, boss. I dunno about you, but I can't wait to burn Ashland to the fucking ground. You can do what you want, but that's what I'm gonna do."

"You'll do what you're fucking told, brigadier general."

"It's cute that you think that."

The general spun around, his face twisted into a look of anger and bone-deep frustration, and growled, "You'll belay that kind of talk this instant, brigadier general."

Farley smirked, plucking at the silver eagles on his collar, and said, "Nah, don't think I will."

"Listen here, Farley: You people might think you're special, but we have a chain of command here, and--"

Farley moved with smooth and practiced speed, and the speech was cut short as the general felt a shoulder slam into his chest and found himself tumbling through the air, landing on his back with a thud. Before he could get his bearings, Farley's boot came crashing down onto his throat, pressing into his windpipe with the brigadier general's full weight. He struggled as best he could, but this was far from Farley's first.

When the general stopped twitching, one of the blackshirts asked, "You want we should get rid of that for you, boss?"

"Nah," Farley sneered. "Leave him there, let somebody find him. Tomorrow night, it won't matter."

"Tomorrow night, man? I thought the Oberkommando scheduled us for two weeks from now."

"Yeah, that they did, but here's a counterpoint: Fuck 'em."

The two blackshirts smiled at that, though the one who'd spoken up added, "Boss, didn't those orders come straight from the Commander?"

"Is Rain here?"

"Heh. You got me there, boss."

"Good man. I know Rain, and I know what he likes: Results. And he might throw one of his little tantrums or he might not, but I know how to get results. Tomorrow night, boys."

Yes, Farley thought, surveying the camp spread across the valley below him, this was *his* army. Farley was only a brigadier, was still not the highest-ranked officer presence, but amongst the field marshals he was the only blackshirt, and so he was something that the others were not: Worthy.

Looking down the hill at the closest camp, he could just see his advance scouts flitting around through the darkness, darker shadows made clear only by the bright moonlight overhead. He had a detachment of them, the creatures from the east, at his disposal, and dispose of them he would; the hunters thought so very highly of themselves, but they were unworthy, a pitiful remnant of a fallen order. They would be the first over the river, and might deal out a few deaths before they caught bullets to save better men.

And, looking south, he wondered what sort of garrison he might be facing. The Bolshevists must have figured out that this would be the point of incursion—the mustering of such a large force could not be concealed—and would be arraying their own forces accordingly. That pleased Roy very much. Better to have all of the rotten, degenerate freaks in one place. It would save time mopping them up later.

It had been rough work getting everything into place after the unfortunate delays, but now all was ready. Troops in the hundreds of thousands, and their vehicles, and their lines of supply, and the war clerics embedded in each unit to stir up the men with the righteousness of their cause. The Commander had ordered them to wait, to make more preparations and build more strength while they waited to see how the Bolshevists' little circle-jerk in Ashland played out, and allegedly the Commander embodied the nation's will, but Roy couldn't help but laugh at the thought of Roland Rain embodying the nation's will. Rain had always been too conciliatory, trying to serve the Falange's interests in the government by playing silly little political games instead of by taking action, and the disruption in their plan had been hard on him. Ever since Baltimore had gone quiet, Rain had seemed far more worried about locking himself in his office and doing God-knows-what with that court eunuch of his than he was worried about military matters, about proper Falange business; Roy had certainly seen *that* coming, all those years ago, and was beginning to wonder about his old friend. During the muster, he'd decided that Rain was far more useful as a symbol than as a leader, and now the muster was complete. Now he was ready to move, and as for what Columbus might have to say about that, well, time would tell.

Tomorrow, he told himself, grinning like a wolf at the thought of the slaughter ahead. *It'll be tomorrow*.

[28]

MANDALAY

[That night; Marion, Indiana]

PETER WASN'T SURE WHAT HE'D BEEN EXPECTING, BUT IT certainly wasn't this.

Marion was, to put it mildly, a Falange town. The church was sparsely attended, in terrible disrepair, and administrated by only two presbyters—less than half the appropriate number for a town with a population in the low thousands. The town's garrison had not had its own war cleric for several years; and though it was a small garrison when he'd arrived, Marion was an important frontier town along the perpetual hot border with the Dustwalker confederation, and prior to the redeployments in preparation for the coming invasion, the garrison had been nearly the same size as the town itself. He was already mentally drafting a rather negative report to send back to the Ecclesiarchy.

And the garrison had been, to put it mildly, unenthusiastic about their new war cleric. The hundred or so brownshirts, local conscripts for the most part, couldn't be bothered to acknowledge his presence at all, and the special detachment of fifty or so Arditi stormtroopers had *laughed* at him; they seemed, at best, to regard him more like a mascot than as their appointed spiritual leader. When he'd come by the garrison camp to introduce himself, the detachment commander, a scarred and hulking giant wearing a captain's bars, had ignored the offered handshake, looked him up and down, and asked, "Kid, how the hell old are you?"

"Ah, I am 25, sir," Peter replied, confused.

"How the fuck are you a war cleric already?"

That was when the laughter started. The other blackshirts sniggered at the question, and Peter gritted his teeth and said, "I only follow the Ecclesiarchy's mandate, sir."

"I'll bet. What did you say your name was?"

"Wenden, sir. Father Peter Wenden."

"You'd be Father Elias's boy, then."

"Yes, sir."

"Yeah. Yeah, that explains it."

At that, two of the other blackshirts shared a look between them and burst into peals of laughter. The captain glanced at them and cocked an eyebrow, and one of them said, "We'll, uh . . . we'll tell you later, boss."

And Peter walked away, grinding his teeth, his cheeks crimson red.

The district's Commandant was also less than helpful. He was friendly enough, but Peter could tell right away that he was a lazy, unambitious man who cared more about his own present position than he did his duties as an agent of the Oberkommando. Peter had to look for him; his office at the town hall was vacant save for a secretary and an old farmer waiting in front of her desk, and the secretary suggested trying the Prairie Fire, the tavern a few blocks down the street. And that was where Peter found the Commandant, a jug of wine in one hand, his other arm around a woman with a suspiciously brown complexion, surrounded by other revelers and singing at the top of his lungs:

"By the old Moulmein Pagoda, looking westward toward the sea

There's a Burma girl a-sitting, and I know she thinks of me
For the wind is in the palm trees, and the temple-bells they say,
  'Come ye back, you British soldier! Come ye back to
Mandalay!'"

To his credit, the Commandant stopped his revelry as soon as he noticed Peter, and at once came walking over with a congenial smile on his face and called out, "Ah, hello there, my boy! You must be my new shepherd."

"Ah, yes, sir," Peter stammered, only half paying attention. His eyes were locked on the Native girl the Commandant had been carousing with; she'd slipped something out of his back pocket, and now she was heading for a rear exit with her back ramrod-straight and a blank, flinty look on her face; Peter wasn't the most experienced at such things, but he could still recognize a soldier, an enemy, when he saw one.

Before he could say more, the Commandant clapped him on the shoulder and said, "Well, it's a pleasure. It's Peter, right? Peter Wenden?"

"Ah, yes, sir."

"Well, Peter, I'm late for an appointment back at my office. Would you care to join me and see how the sausage is made?"

"Um, I suppose so, sir."

"Splendid! It's just this way."

Without another word, the Commandant led Peter back through the darkening streets and past the decaying, pre-War buildings to the town hall and into his office, an expansive, carpeted affair with a massive oak desk on the far wall. The farmer followed them inside and stood waiting in the middle of the floor as the Commandant took a seat behind the desk, motioning for Peter to take another chair nearby. The farmer looked like he'd been plucked out of a pre-War magazine advertisement, with his flannel shirt and his bib overalls and the fat, reeking cigar dangling out of his wild mop of a beard. He stared ahead with a bored, insolent expression which Peter found infuriating.

"I'm terribly, terribly sorry for the wait, Mr. Ballard," the Commandant said. "I was indisposed."

The farmer grunted.

"Now, tell me exactly what happened."

The farmer spat on the floor. "They stole my goats."

"Who stole your goats, Mr. Ballard?"

"The injuns."

"And how do you know that?"

"I watched 'em do it."

"Uh-huh. How many did you lose?"

"Twenty-two head and some kids."

"Uh-huh. And when did this happen, Mr. Ballard?"

"Wednesday."

"Uh-huh."

At that, Peter spoke up, indignant, asking, "And why—and why did it take you a week to report this incident?"

The farmer shrugged. "I were busy."

"Busy with what?"

"Farmin'."

Peter looked as though he were about to jump up and strangle Bill Ballard there in the Commandant's office. The Commandant sighed, raised a hand, and said, "Mr. Ballard, I am deeply, deeply saddened by this unfortunate tragedy. I will make absolutely sure that foot patrols are sent out beyond your family's property, and I can offer you compensation of . . . let's see . . . five in brass per head."

The farmer shook his head. "Ten."

"Six."

"Deal."

Bill Ballard approached the desk, took a receipt from the Commandant, and said, "Thankee, sir. That's mighty Christian of ya."

When Bill was gone, Peter glared at the Commandant and growled, "What—what on Earth was that?"

The Commandant leaned back in his chair, kicked his feet up onto his desk, and lit a cigarette. "That was business, my boy," he said with a smile. "Routine business, nothing more."

"Commandant, I could tell from that man's words and his demeanor that he did not miss his livestock very much. I believe he gave them away."

"Well, obviously. Do you think I don't know that?"

Peter stared at him in enraged disbelief. The Commandant stroked his mustache in a fatherly sort of way and said, "My boy, I can tell that you don't have much experience with frontier life. My district is a peaceful district; here, farms are not burned, clergy and officers are not kidnapped, foot patrols are not ambushed. This peace is a delicate state of affairs, and I maintain it through very careful diplomacy."

"Is your idea of diplomacy giving food to our enemies and giving money to traitors?"

"A greased wheel doesn't squeak, my boy. Tell me, is Marion the first frontier town you've ever been to?"

"Well, yes, but I don't see how--"

"Then shut up and listen to your betters. If you've never seen a frontier town, then you've never seen a frontier war, and you don't know what kind of Hell I'm avoiding by allowing Bill Ballard to lose track of his goats. You are aware that our garrison is depleted, yes? You are aware that better than three quarters of the piddly little force of brownshirts and marshals I did have has been diverted to go fight communists in the mountains? This fact has not escaped your observation?"

"Well, yes, of course, but--"

"So if a Dustwalker war party were to ride down the street right now and firebomb my town hall and drive out the remaining garrison, who would stop them? You?"

Peter sprang up from his chair, then, and bellowed, "This is sedition! There is an ongoing war in these districts, a holy war of extermination, that we might reclaim our rightful place as this

continent's masters! And prosecuting that war here is your responsibility!"

"Oh, hell, you really are a big-city boy, aren't you?"

"I am a war cleric of the High Church of the Blackland New
Republic! Do not call me 'boy'!"

"Oh, pish posh with your high-minded Columbus idealism.
Listen, do you know what that war really is? It's a great big hole in
the ground into which the Oberkommando pours blood and brass
and receives nothing in return. Yes, I could muster up a foot patrol
and send it out to brutalize our western neighbors, and that patrol
might come back, but far more likely they'd either be exterminated
or they'd desert. And that accomplishes, what, exactly?"

Peter gulped. "What's this about desertion?"

"Oh, you're not in Columbus anymore, my boy. One fun thing
you'll learn if you spend any amount of time out here is that about
half the raiders in those Sioux war parties have white hides and
shoot AR-10s. Some of them even wear black shirts. But we don't
need to worry about that here, because we keep to ourselves and we
don't make trouble and we know how to be harmonious neighbors."

"This is sedition! The Ecclesiarchy will hear of this!"

"Why don't you ever use contractions? My boy, you've found
the one tiny island of peace in an ocean of bloody war; if you had
two brain cells to rub together, you would want to preserve that,
and you'd save all the blood-and-iron talk for when roamers come
out of Indianapolis." And the Commandant stood up, stretched,
and said, "I'm going back down to the Prairie Fire for a few drinks
before bed. You should join me."

"I do not partake, sir, and I must attend to my church."

"I knew you'd say that."

The two men parted ways under the silver moon outside of the
Marion town hall, the Commandant shoving his long, elegant
hands into his pockets and turning to saunter down the cracked and
crumbling street toward the tavern. As he went, he rolled his eyes
and thought that the new preacher probably would snitch on him

to the Ecclesiarchy, and that could potentially cause a problem . . . but that was a problem for the future, and it had nothing to do with his evening plate of home fries and his nightcap. He did wonder, though how such a young man who had apparently done nothing with his life could possibly be a war cleric, let alone a war cleric appointed to the garrison of a barely-guarded frontier in the middle of a war. He wondered if Peter Wenden was any relation to old Elias Wenden, one of the senior Ecclesiarchs in Columbus. Yes, perhaps that explained it; little Father Pete must be Daddy's special boy.

As he walked back toward his favorite hole in the wall, he drew in a deep breath and began to sing:

"Ship me somewheres east of Suez, where the best is like the worst,

Where there ain't no Ten Commandments and a man can raise a thirst!

For the temple-bells are calling, and it's there I'd like to be--

By the old Moulmein Pagoda, looking lazy at the sea,

On the road to Mandalay . . ."

And Peter stood on the steps of the town hall, fuming with rage as he watched the Commandant walk away. Yes, it was right and proper that he'd been sent here, because this town—this entire district—was a hotbed of sin and sedition and would need to be dealt with immediately; even having only been in town a few hours, the negative report he would send to the Ecclesiarchy in the morning was already getting quite long. Yes, even if he'd rather be in the Ohio Valley, this was where he belonged, where he was needed.

As he walked through the darkened streets of the rotting little town, back toward his new church, his sister's words echoed around between his ears: *Not the most prestigious of assignments, but very important. That will suit your substantial abilities.*

Had that been genuine? Surely not; the family black sheep had never paid anyone a genuine complement in her entire life. But,

even so, it seemed to ring true; preserving the High Church's hege-
mony in such a godless place may not be a prestigious task, but it
certainly wasn't an idle one. As he approached his pitiful little
church, he thought to himself: *I will make my father proud.*

And following that came another thought, accompanied by an
eyeroll and a sardonic sigh: *I suppose someone has to.*

[29]

A DISTANT THUNDER

Mags, Jules, and Kitty awoke late the next morning, easing into wakefulness as they lay entangled in each other's arms. After an eternity of luxuriating in each other's presence, they got up, threw the previous night's clothes back on, and head back towards the Hundred Rads, hoping to catch the tail end of breakfast.

As they walked, Mags, who stood in the middle, draped an arm across each of her lovers and asked, "So are we, like, dating?"

Kitty laughed. "God, you two are in such a big hurry about everything."

"Well, Jules is the first person I've been with for longer than a night since Kelly dumped me, and now I'm in like a triad . . . It's just very exciting is all."

"Oh, you are adorable. Yes, Mags, we're dating; I have two girl-friends!"

Jules kept silent, leaning against Mags as they walked, her eyes sparkling and a bright smile splitting her usually sour face. They were almost to the bar when Kimimela came around a corner, spotted the three of them, and called out, "Oh, there the hell y'all are!"

"Were we missing?" Mags asked.

"Yeah, Miss Frizzle, a little bit. We tried to find y'all, but nobody knew where you and Shortstack had checked in for the night."

"They were with me!" Kitty said, grinning.

"Of course they were. Listen: The last delegate checked in just before sunrise. The congress is starting this afternoon. Granny sent me to let everybody know."

Mags blinked. "Uh . . . alright. Shit."

"Uh-huh. Granny's in there talking to Jimmy right now; if you hurry, there might be some breakfast left."

And Kim dashed off down the street without another word. The three of them walked into the tavern to see Miriam and Jimmy seated at the far side of the bar, having a spirited discussion with a small white man wearing a wide brown hat and a stupid mustache. Jimmy was visibly agitated, using lulls in the conversation to pull hits from a marijuana pipe; it did not appear to be helping. Miri was furious.

"It's not that simple, man," Jimmy said as they walked up, pinching the bridge of his nose. "The command economy is just one part of it; tackling the base doesn't mean you can just ignore the superstructure. Building a democratic society isn't something you can sleep on. Gotta teach the American beasts, right?"

"Ugh, more identity politics," the stranger groaned. "Racism and sexism and whatnot are secondary; they're just reflections of the antagonism between classes."

"Between what fucking classes, Ken? Our economy is owned by everybody and managed by syndicates. We don't even have a party bureaucracy. Where are these classes?"

"Oh, whatever. The point is, social movements in Ohio aren't developed enough to take on this hairbrained scheme that Miriam and her cronies have dreamed up; we need to develop productive forces *here* before we can--"

Miri slammed her fist down on the bar and barked, "Ken, that's Stalinism. I know that that word gets used to mean 'a thing that's bad' a lot of the time, but no, this is what Stalinism is, you are literally describing a program of building socialism in one country. And that worked out *so well* when the Russians did it, right?"

"Well, I wouldn't expect *you* to understand."

And Miri slammed both of her fists down on the bar and boomed, "Oh, you did not fucking just!"

"Well, if you're going to get all emotional--"

"Ken, you do not fucking talk to me, or anybody, like that! I did *not* get my favorite leg and half my fucking face blown off in Huntington to sit here and take shit from some dumb little white boy. Get the fuck outta my face, Ken. We can finish this conversation at Liberty Hall."

And the little man shrank under the withering gaze of her one good eye, got up, and faded into another corner of the tavern without another word. Jimmy examined the bar for a moment before declaring, "I *hate* him."

Miri patted him on the shoulder. "I know you do, baby. We all hate him."

"He just . . . he won't stop *talking*."

"They never do."

Mags walked up with Jules and Kitty, then, and said, "So I see everybody's favorite class reductionist is back in town."

"Lord preserve us," Miri grumbled.

"I think he's the one who's gonna need preserving."

Miri laughed, and as they sat down, Kelly walked up and said, "Oh, hey there, Magnolia."

"Hey, Kelly," Mags replied with a wave. "Been a while."

"Uh-huh. Y'know, I've got a bone to pick with you."

"Oh?"

"You lot didn't move my tables back when y'all got done last night."

Mags, Miri, and Kitty all looked horrified, and Miri said, "Oh my God, Kelly, I am so sorry. That won't happen again."

"Better not. Y'all need anything?"

"Any breakfast left?"

"Yeah, we got some hot chow left over. Coming right up."

And, as Kelly walked off, Mags looked into Miri's eye and asked, "So today's the big day, huh?"

"Sure is, kid."

"So what's the move, Comrade Training Instructor?"

"We stick to the plan, we stick to our principles, and we stick together. Honestly, Kilroy coming back is probably the best thing that could've happened for us; nobody's gonna want to be seen agreeing with him."

"Well, thank Heaven for small blessings."

As they talked, Jules—who had taken a seat around to Jimmy's left, off of the side of the bar, so that she could watch the door—saw two men walk in. One was a grim, scarred man in his early 50s, wearing a fedora and a flannel shirt tucked into faded blue jeans; she didn't know him, but something about his hearing and the way he walked seemed sickeningly familiar. She did, however, know the man he was with.

"Hey, fuckface!" she called out, laughing and springing up from her feet. "So they just let anybody in this place nowadays, huh?"

"How the hell'd you even get in here, Shortstack?" Peterson laughed, pushing past the man he'd come in with. "Ain't they got a height requirement?"

Jules threw her arms around him, kissed his cheeks, and said, "God, it's good to see you, you ugly piece of shit. Didn't I tell you we'd meet up again?"

"Yeah, you sure did. Good to see my little sister again."

"Hey, come over here, have a seat. How they been treating you?"

"Okay. Lots of questions, but that's about it."

"Told you. You already know Mags, and this here is Miriam, and Jimmy, and Kitty. Y'all, this here's Stu Peterson, the guy who saved my ass."

Peterson gave them all a friendly nod. "So you finally found yourself some friends, Binachi? About time."

"Hey, looks like you found one, too."

And the man Peterson had walked in with came over, and he looked down at Jules with his frosty grey eyes and said, "So you're the girl. Peterson says you're a hell of a door-kicker."

"Sure, bud. And you are?"

"Oh, you're not gonna believe this," Peterson said with an eager grin.

"Robert O'Shea," the stranger grumbled. "Voting delegate for Ohio."

Jules and Kitty both stared up at him with amazement, and Jules asked, "You're the fucking what from fucking where now?"

"Ohio. You met Kimimela? Came here with them."

"Ol' Bobby here is a bandit chief," Peterson said. "Leads a flying column out of Indianapolis. Renegades and strays like us."

Jules laughed. "For real? No shit?"

"Yes, ma'am," Oshea grumbled. "I heard a little bit about you. Sounds like you done good for yourself."

"Uh, thanks, I guess." And nothing how terribly familiar his speech and bearing were, she tapped the inside of her left elbow and asked, "Say, are you . . ."

He nodded.

"Well, I'll be goddamned."

Kitty looked up at Robert like they were gazing into the face of God. They took the pipe from Jimmy, took a long hit, and asked, "You mean there's an organized column?"

"Sure is."

"I knew that attrition was especially high in the west, but I didn't think . . . Holy shit, that's wonderful. I'm speechless."

"You're from Ohio."

"Sure am. And someday I'd sure love to go back. God, I . . . I have so many questions. How big is this column? Are they all deserters? Where do you operate? I . . . I have to know."

"We should talk after the congress. Where are you from?"

"Somerset, same as Julia, but I was living in Cincinnati before I came here."

"That's a shithole on a good day. You must have some war stories."

"Oh, yeah, I got a couple."

―――――――――

The attendees, about a hundred in all, began to form groups and file toward the cathedral just after lunch. It was a mixed bunch, all imaginable sorts of people conversing amongst themselves in a dozen different languages as they walked. Jules cleaved close to Mags, feeling overwhelmed by it all. Mags faced straight ahead with that blank look that Jules had come to call her "business face." Miri bore an identical expression.

The four of them—Jules, Mags, Kitty, and Miri—stepped off to the side just before reaching the big double doors, and Mags' expression wavered just a bit as she met Miri's eye and asked, "So we're really doing this, huh?"

"We sure are. You're gonna be amazing, kid. Just remember what I told you: Be bold, stick to our line, stick to your principles."

"I will. I . . . I won't let you down, Granny."

"Aw, hell, kid, are you trying to make me cry?"

Mags took a few more steps away from the crowd and lit a cigarette, and her expression melted away completely; Jules saw that she was terrified. "No, I mean it," she said. "I . . . I owe you so much. I owe you everything."

"Jesus, kid, we're just going to a meeting, we're not going into battle."

"It sure feels like it. I talked to Jimmy before we left the bar; he's sympathetic, so that's good, but . . . he's gonna call on me to lead us off."

"Well of course he is; you're the one who went on the big mission. Relax. You'll do great. And, hey, whatever gets decided, I want you to know I'm proud of you."

"Aw, shit, now you're trying to make *me* cry."

"It's true. You've come a long way, sister."

"Sister," Mags repeated, her face breaking out into a hopeful smile. "Sister. Girls like us gotta stick together, right?"

"Yup. But for ourselves, alone."

And Mags snuffed out her cigarette on the heel of her boot, took a deep breath, and declared, "Alright. Let's go win some hearts and minds."

Liberty Hall was spacious, built to accommodate a congregation three times the size of the present assembly, and comfortably dim, though every word and footstep echoed as though they were in a cave. And though the open space and subdued lighting made things easier, the experience still set Jules' teeth on edge, and she clung tighter to Mags as they walked inside and took seats alongside the rest of the faction. At the front of the hall, behind the podium, hung a massive flag of the Republic: A rectangle of red cloth embroidered with the hammer and plough. To one side of the podium stood Jimmy, shaking with nerves, and to the other stood a soldier whom Jules recognized as Lynn.

When people stopped filing in, Jimmy shuffled to the podium, his footsteps generating an otherworldly sound through a decaying and reverberating sound system. He faced the crowd and muttered, "Okay . . . okay . . . I guess we're getting started. Uh, hi, everybody, and welcome to the fourth All Soviets Congress of our little workers' international. I'm, uh, Jimmy Mahon, machinists' and fabricators' syndicate, and, uh, for some reason that's beyond my understanding I guess I'm the general secretary-treasurer of the Ashland Farmer-Worker Union, and I'll be chairing this meeting. We've got a lot of groups represented here today, with delegations from the Musko Workers' Republic down south, the Dustwalker confederation out west, and even a special delegate from on the ground in Ohio. Since, uh, since Ashland has the honor of hosting the congress, we've asked Comrade Lynn Ramirez here to lead us in . . . well, I guess you'd call it our national anthem."

And Lynn stepped up to the podium as Jimmy stepped away, and she closed her eyes, took several deep, nervous breaths, and—after a few false starts—began to sing:

"John Brown's body lies a-moldering in the grave
While weep the sons of bondage whom he wagered all to save
But though he's gone to glory, still we struggle for the slave
And his soul is marching on!"

Some in the crowd had begun singing along with the first verse, and as Lynn launched into the chorus, the rest took it up as well, and the hall echoed with a hundred voices:

"Glory, glory, hallelujah
Glory, glory, hallelujah
Glory, glory, hallelujah
His soul is marching on!
"He captured Harper's Ferry with his nineteen men so true
He frightened Old Virginia 'till she trembled through and through
They hanged him for a traitor, they themselves the traitor-crew
And his soul is marching on!
"Glory, glory, hallelujah . . .
"Now the stars above in Heaven are a-looking kindly down
The stars above in Heaven are a-looking kindly down
The stars above in Heaven are a-looking kindly down
On the grave of old John Brown!
"Glory, glory, hallelujah . . ."

By the last verse, most of those seated had risen back up, and were stomping their feet in time:

"And we're gonna hang Jeff Davis from a sour apple tree
We're gonna hang Jeff Davis from a sour apple tree
We're gonna hang Jeff Davis from a sour apple tree
And his soul is marching on!
"Glory, glory, hallelujah . . ."

And, panting, Lynn stepped away to thunderous applause. When the applause died down, Jimmy resumed his place and said, "Oh jeez, Lynn, that was beautiful. Well, folks, uh, I guess we better get started in earnest. Now, the, uh, the purpose of this congress is to settle how our various sections should orient towards the Blackland New Republic. We here in Ashland have, excepting periodic skirmishing and reprisals, been locked in a cold war with the BNR for the entirety of its existence, some sixty-odd years, and we've struggled to maintain the stalemate due to our own difficulty fielding large enough troop numbers for an extended campaign; our forces are better trained, better led, better organized, and have better morale than theirs, but they have us soundly whipped in the population department. Our comrades in the Dustwalker Confederation, however, do not have the luxury of our sedentary infrastructure or our hard broder. The BNR has spent its entire existence waging a colonial war of extermination in its western districts. It isn't going very well for them, on account of they're dumb as bricks and keep trying to field conscript armies on unfavorable terrain, but over the past couple of decades they have pushed their border west from the 227 corridor up to the edge of the Indianapolis Exclusion Zone corridor, at a substantial human cost and with no apaprent intention of stopping; hell, knowing those boneheads, they'll probably keep banging their heads against that wall until they find the Pacific Ocean. But, also . . ."

And Jimmy studied the floor for a moment and took several deep breaths before continuing: "Also, they are planning to turn our cold war into a hot one. Last month, one of our field agents—

Comrade Magnolia Blackadder—went out on a reconnaissance mission into the coastal exclusion zone and uncovered a plot to use the pre-War tech within the zone as well as the creatures who live there to put together a military force and launch a joint strike, BNR forces from the north and all of that God-knows-what from the east. We had no prior knowledge of this, and we've never had to worry about that kind of defense on our eastern border before, so if it weren't for Comrade Blackadder's decisive action, it's almost a certainty that I would not be here to talk to you today, that this city would not be standing. Hell. But . . . but it looks like the plan is still on, because BNR forces are still mustering in massive numbers in the northeast, just north of Huntington in our Land's End canton. We don't know when, other than very soon, but a war like we haven't seen in seventy years is coming. It's only a matter of time.

"What I hope we can accomplish here today is to hash out a solid plan for what we, as nations and as sections of a common-wealth, plan to do about this situation, especially given how it's escalating. The first on stack will be the aforementioned Comrade Blackadder, to give more detail on what she found the enemy doing out there in the wasteland, and following her will be Comrade Kimimela Strongbow from the Oceti Sakawin delegation, to give us a more detailed picture of the situation on the ground. After that, the floor is open for discussion."

And Jimmy took a step back from the podium, trembling and clutching his chest. Lynn walked up to him and put an arm over his shoulders.

Miri squeezed Mags' shoulder and whispered, "You got this, kid. And remember: Be bold."

Mags stood up on her chair, took a deep breath, and, her words echoing through hall, said, "Comrades . . . Comrades, I'm Magnolia Jane Blackadder, political commissar, chief warrant officer 3, brevet major, here as a voting delegate for the New Lawrence Militia council of soldiers' deputies. First off, with apologies to our comrade general secretary, a point of order: As those of you who've been briefed on my report know, and as those of you who've heard the rumors already ought to know, I was just one small part of a team on that mission. Comrade Julia Binachi, who is in attendance, and Comrade TJ . . . uh . . ."

"It's just TJ!" TJ shouted.

". . . and Comrade TJ, one of the voting delegates for our Free-side Special Economic Zone, were also on that team, and played equally vital roles in saving all our asses. The lion's share of the credit definitely doesn't go to me. If it goes to anybody, it should go to the late Wolfgang von Lukash, who came up with the plan we needed to execute and who sacrificed his life to give us the time we needed to pull it off. It is depressingly, brutally typical for a Jewish man to take point like that in the fight against fascist violence, and the least we can do is remember his name, and may that memory be a blessing.

"But to get to the meat of it: I was sent east of the habitable zone on a reconnaissance mission, to find a means of ingress into the pre-War facility colloquially known as the Citadel, roughly five hundred miles north-northeast of Ashland. While en route, we acquired substantial updated intelligence about the facility's occupants, operations, and present purpose. The Citadel was under the command of a group of hunters, many of them pre-War, and many of those . . . many of those hunters were old-school fascists, veterans of the Second World War. The facility's commander had reached some sort of agreement with the Columbus Oberkommando, as Jimmy said, to launch a join strike against the Republic. To this end, Rain was sending picked groups of his Arditi stormtroopers to staff the facility. Those who passed—or survived—some sort of vetting process were turned into hunters and inducted into this fifth column, equipped with Old American munitions, including CBRN ordinance. We learned, also, that the offensive was scheduled to begin within a matter of days. I tried to notify Land's End, but we were outside of radio range. It was at this point that I made the decision to operate outside the parameters of my mission.

When we arrived at the Citadel, we infiltrated the facility via its service tunnels, confirmed all of the above intelligence, and leveled the facility using its own ordinance. Had we not done so, as Jimmy already said, we would very likely all be dead."

And Mags hesitate, with Miri's instructions to be bold echoing around in her head. After a beat, she concluded: "We came so fucking close, comrades. If it hadn't been for a combination of dumb luck and the desperate courage of one man, our revolution would've been crushed by an enemy we couldn't even conceive of. The fact that such an inconceivable enemy was able to amass so much power is proof that the Blackland New Republic will never stop trying to destroy us, will stoop to any low and abandon all humanity in order to destroy us, and will succeed in destroying us if we don't take decisive action. Sharing a border with a fascist state is an irreconcilable contradiction, and there are only three possible outcomes: They will destroy us, or we will destroy them, or, if we continue to do nothing, we will destroy ourselves. Our job here today is to pick which one of those three options we can stomach our grandchildren inheriting. With that, I give the floor to Comrade Kim, who has far more visceral experience with this evil than I do."

Mags collapsed back into her chair amidst a roomful of excited chattering. Miri squeezed her shoulder and whispered, "You did great, kid. Knew you would."

A few seats away, Kim stood up on their chair, waited for the chatter to die down, and said, "My esteemed colleague Miss Frizzle is correct. *Huw tanyan yahipi*; I'm Kimimela Strongbow, machinists' shop steward, Oceti Sakawin nation, Dustwalker Confederation, and like Blackadder said, the fascists are not exactly good neighbors. We have been at war with those boneheads for as long as their state has existed, just as we were at war with the generations of petty warlords that preceded it, just as we were at war with the United States that preceded them, may it rot in piss. Our territory encompasses many thousands of square miles of prairie, desert, and pre-War ruins, including some of the most abundant and best-preserved pre-War technology in the rotting carcass of Old America and a lot of important mineral interests; that means that Dustwalker blood is the only thing standing between the fascists and unlimited brass, just like how Ashlander blood is the only thing standing between the fascists and unlimited food. Our nation is strategically situated; with the Great Lakes in the north and the Indianapolis Exclusion Zone in the south, the fascists are only able to expand westward through a narrow corridor. However, the area is sparsely populated compared to its size, meaning we're dealing with the same manpower shortage as you guys. We've been fighting this war for five hundred years, we know what we're doing, and the Ashlanders' supply of munitions and other equipment has been invaluable, so we are able to meet the fascists on an equal footing, and hold our own, but like Jimmy said earlier . . . we're losing. It's down to a crawl, and they have to bleed for every inch, but they're sapping our strength and they're creeping westward.

"And it is a dirty war, comrades. These people are not just fighting a war of occupation; this is a war of extermination. To them, we're not enemies to be defeated, we're filth to be cleansed. When a BNR force captures one of our settlements, they don't occupy it; they kill every single child and man, do unspeakable things to the women and the normal people, and burn it to the ground. We resist, but at present that's the best we can do, because, as has been said, there are just too many thousands of the fuckers; no matter how many desert and no matter how many we kill, they just keep coming, and they kill our people and burn our towns and brutalize our women and steal our land, and every year there are fewer of us and that border creeps a little bit further west. And without Ashland's iron, we would struggle to manage even that much."

They looked over and made eye contact with Miri for a moment before continuing: "But, a couple of things. For one, I mentioned desertion. Attrition amongst brownshirts in the western theater is very high, something close to twenty percent. Most of them disappear into the wasteland, a few of them trickle down into Ashland, but some of them side with us. Enough of them have done so to have established their own flying column, hence Comrade Robert O'Shea, in attendance, who has the honor of being our commonwealth's first Ohio delegate. Due to its peculiar specialties, this column is one of our most effective fighting units; and it's gaining new recruits at a regular rate, and has the potential to grow exponentially if we can find a way to escalate the war.

"Which leads into the second thing: To be perfectly blunt, y'all ain't been paying the rent. I'm a machinist, a gunsmith by trade, and I have a rhetorical question for the Ashland Central Soviet General Assembly: Why can't we just turn our own barrels? You send us Kalashnikovs and Semtex by the truckload, and we are eternally grateful for that, but nothing is stopping you from sending me grinders, lathes, and machinists. I know you hate the fascists as much as we do; I'm sure that there are plenty of Ashlanders who would gladly volunteer for that detail. I sure do hope that all of us, as students of history, as political economists, as revolutionaries, understand that there's more to winning a war than guns. The Oceti-Sakawin elders sent me here, not to beg for more help from Ashland, but to *demand* that we receive our due as a section of this commonwealth, as your co-belligerents, as *equals* who share a common enemy. We don't just need iron, we need infrastructure, and if we have that then we can turn this war around. And paying the rent is not a big ask; I want the Ashlander delegates to ask themselves if they're serious about internationalism, if they're serious about their own revolution, and if they're serious about winning this war. *Wana woe gla ka yea*; I am finished speaking."

The chamber erupted into more excited chattering as Kim returned to their seat. Jimmy walked up to the podium, tapped the microphone, and muttered, "Okay . . . okay, everybody settle down. Thank you for that, comrades. With that, uh . . . the floor is open for discussion. Standard stack rules apply; if you've got something to contribute, raise your hand, and me and Lynn will keep track of everybody."

And almost a hundred hands went up. Jimmy and Lynn rolled their eyes and sighed in unison.

Ken Kilroy had been the quickest on the draw. When Jimmy called his name, he stood up on his chair, twirled his mustache, cleared his throat, and said, "First of all, I have to say that I find it highly irregular that the general secretary gave our discussion leadoff to not one, but two comrades who are both members of the same disloyal splinter group, and it's unacceptable that the two comrades then used the allotted time as a bully pulpit for their fractious agenda. But to get to the point, I think that both of the comrades are dead wrong in any case. Now, I don't expect either of these . . . of these libertine socialites to understand the finer points of revolutionary theory--"

"'Libertine socialites'?" Mags whispered. What does that even mean?"

And she glanced at Miri, and saw that the older woman's face was contorted in a look of murderous rage, and she hissed, *"Oh, he did not fucking just--"*

Jules looked at Kitty and cocked an eyebrow, and Kitty rolled their eyes and whispered, "He just called Mags and Kim men in dresses. But he did it in a roundabout way so that we'll look like jackasses if we call him on it."

Ken was still speaking: ". . . so this really is just rank, infantile ultraleftism. It's simply a fact that social forces in the Blackland New Republic are not sufficiently developed to sustain the kind of mass popular movement that these people seem to be advocating for. Barring an invasion and occupation by our forces, which we do not have the capability to do and which I hope we would not be willing to do even if we did, there is nothing we can gain from escalating the war. We will secure our station and secure the enemy's defeat by focusing on developing our own productive forces. Furthermore, let us suppose they do invade: What of it? We've held that border before, and we will do it again. And if by some calamity they do manage to overwhelm our border forces, well, what of that? This is the Ashland Confederated Republic. Ninety percent of our population has some capacity of military training; seventy percent of our *civilian* population is under arms; and every single one of our major cities is an impregnable mountain fastness. I say let them come. Let them try. If they do, this will be their Belfast, their Vietnam, their Stalingrad."

And Kilroy sat down with a smug smile on his face.

Miri's turn was next. Mags and Kitty helped her up to where everyone could see her, and in an even, motherly tone she said, "Comrade Kilroy, I'm very impressed, because literally every word of what you just said was wrong. To begin with, there is no disloyal splinter group within the Ashland Farmer-Worker Union or within this commonwealth. I'm one of the people who've caucused with Comrades Magnolia and Kimimela, and I fucking dare anyone to look at the state of me and accuse me of disloyalty. I had my favorite eye and my favorite leg blown off by a fascist machine gun in the defense of this Republic, its people, its ideals, and its institutions, and I would fucking do it again. Mind yourself, son.

"But to get to the stuff we're actually supposed to be discussing, I won't waste time going over all of this stages-of-development nonsense, since anybody who's read an economics textbook or read Lauri Bluecrow's war diaries will already know horseshit when they smell it. What I take issue with primarily is Comrade Kilroy's assessment of our national defense. Yes, we are in a position that makes defense in depth a sure thing, and an invasion by enemy forces that breached our border defenses would be bogged down and destroyed in detail, and any attempt to occupy our territory would be a bleeding ulcer that the Blacklanders could not afford to maintain. But before we start talking about defense in depth, I want us to consider the butcher's bill. Millions died defending Vietnam. Almost a million died defending Stalingrad. And Belfast remained a part of the United Kingdom for as long as there was such a place.

I take the radical position that all of the Ashlanders who don't live in the mountains or who live outside of the cities are human beings whose lives are worth protecting. Of course, the price of freedom is often blood, and if it came to such an emergency I don't doubt anyone's resolve or anyone's willingness to sacrifice, to do what is necessary, but it would be just that. An emergency. An unimaginable tragedy that we need to take every step to prevent.

"Comrades, my name is Miriam Methotaske, political commissar, chief warrant officer 5, brevet major general, ole of the regional delegates from the New Lawrence Soviet, war chief of the Shawnee nation. There's no such thing as a careerist here, but I have been involved in military matters since before most of you could walk and I think I know a thing or two about a thing or two. And my professional assessment is that, if that border suffers a sustained and dedicated assault from the kinds of forces we're seeing massed at the Huntington salient, that border will not hold. And if that border is breached, Ashland bleeds. So the question is the same now as it ever was: What is to be done?

"As Comrade Blackadder hinted to us, and as Comrade Strongbow correctly admonished us, we have to take decisive action, and we have to do it quickly. We have active co-belligerents on the western borders of the BNR, and we have allies inside of it, and they will escalate the fight alongside us if only they have the tools to do so. Our army isn't large enough to sustain a force-on-force campaign, but our strength has always been our flexibility. In our regular army and in our militias, every soldier is a sapper, every soldier is a designated marksman, every soldier is an organizer, and those are force multipliers. We have a pool of technical and organizational experts to draw from, and I would insist that the Ashland Confederated Republic follow Comrade Strongbow's admonition to make good on all our high-minded talk about internationalism. We have allies outside of the BNR, and we have allies within it, and with them we will win this war and the people of Ohio will liberate themselves, if only they had the tools to do so. Comrades, we here in Ashland have those tools, and we should be goddamn ashamed of ourselves if we just sit on them like a landlord sitting on a pile of grain. The war is here, whether we like it or not, and the choice we're faced with is whether to meet this challenge on the enemy's terms, or our own."

And they helped Miri back down, and she crossed her arms with a satisfied smile on her face. Mags stared at her old mentor with a combination of admiration and mischievous glee: She had managed to more-or-less deliver their proposal while destroying Kilroy and being seen destroying him.

Before Jimmy could call the next speaker, Kilroy lept up from his chair and shouted, "This is unacceptable! Miriam, I know this may be difficult for *the likes of you*, but in this chamber we respect parliamentary procedure and we have *real* discussions! Comrade general secretary, how on Earth can you allow this kind of talk, and all of this subversion?"

Miri's smile didn't waver as she reveled in her victory and in Kilroy making an ass of himself, but many people had risen to their feet and were simmering with outrage, including Mags, Jules, and Kitty. And Kim was already running.

As Kim ran towards the front of the chamber, they bellowed, *"Oh, you do not fucking talk to Granny like that!"*

Kilroy seemed shocked. Before he could speak, Kim came up to him with their face an inch from his and shouted, "That woman takes a shit and does more for our cause than you've ever done in your pitiful little life! You are going to respect her."

"Everyone," Jimmy mewled, "please . . ."

"Jimmy, you need to get your honkies under control!"

And Jimmy drew in a deep breath, stood up ramrod-straight, and—to everyone's shock—boomed, *"EVERYBODY SHUT THE FUCK UP!"*

They did.

"Ken, you are going to follow parliamentary procedure and you're going to show your comrades some goddamn respect. If you don't settle the fuck down, you're waving your right to speak at assembly and Lynn is going to drag you out of here by the hair, assuming somebody else doesn't beat her to it. Everyone else . . . everyone else, please continue on like you have been; excepting Ken's outburst, this is going very well. And thank you, Kim."

Amongst shocked silence—shock at the breach of decorum as well as shock at the new knowledge that Jimmy Mahon was capable of being angry—Ken sank back into his chair, Kim returned to theirs with a smug smile, and the discussion resumed. Mags and Kitty listened to the various bouts of soapboxing and back-and-forth and grew ever more pleased; the tone of the discussion had been set, and Kilory had done an excellent job of ratfucking himself and undermining his own supporters, and where the discussion would lead seemed a foregone conclusion.

And as the afternoon dragged on into evening, Jules grew ever more impressed by the razor-sharp efficiency that seemed to underlie the apparent chaos. She saw that the congress was, essentially, the previous day's faction meeting writ large; even as people traded rhetorical blows, went on seemingly irrelevant tangents, dithered over seemingly unimportant details, and even as the Freesiders opened all of their comments with razor barbs about authority and consensus, each speech was more pointed and more coherent than the last, and the discussion approached a single point, a coherent line.

After sunset, Mags tapped Jules on the shoulder and gestured to the door. Mags, Jules, and Kitty got up and tiptoed outside together, and Mags leaned against the wall, lit a cigarette, and said, "Okay, so this isn't nearly as painful as I thought it would be, but I need a fucking break."

"How much longer you think it'll be before we make a decision?" Jules asked.

"Honestly? I think we pretty much already have. The conservatives got shot all to pieces in the first volley, and we spent the afternoon hashing out the big stuff, and now we're really just kvetching.

We've hit the 'two old ladies in rocking chairs having an argument on the porch' stage. Hell, depending on how many words some of these windbags decide to chew on, we might be starting to wrap by the time I finish my smoke."

Jules wore a dark and sullen expression, and said, simply, "Yeah."

"Something wrong, honey?"

"Yeah, kinda."

Before Mags could ask anything more, Kilroy came walking out of the hall. He adjusted his hat, lit a cigarette, gave the three of them a jaunty wave, and said, "Pretty energetic in there, huh?"

The three of them glared daggers at him, and Mags took two long steps up to him and growled, "Don't you fucking howdy-do me like we're friends, you goddamn beefsteak."

"What? I was just being polite. No need to get all emotional."

"You think I'm stupid, man? I know what the fuck you said about me."

"I'm sure I don't know what you're talking about."

"I swear to God, beefsteak, if you say one more word to me, I'm going to stove your teeth in."

Kilroy looked up into Mags' eyes, a killer's eyes, and he shrank away from her, turned around, and walked away, not heading back into Liberty Hall, but walking off down the street and away from them.

The three of them tiptoed back into the chamber just as night drew on and Miri began speaking again, saying, "Comrades, it sounds like we're in broad agreement, and I think all that remains is for us to hash out the details and practicalities. I would like to put forward a provisional proposal for us to discuss and amend. We here in the Ashland Confederated Republic will increase our arms shipments to the Oceti Sakawin and Miami nations, adding to that tools and other equipment and volunteer detachments of technical experts and auxiliary troops. Our Department of Intelligence and Security will launch a similar program, albeit on a smaller scale, developing our contacts within the enemy's borders. And we will continue shoring up our own defensive capabilities for the looming campaign and preparing for a symmetrical campaign of reprisal insofar as we're able. I would request to their delegation that the Musko Workers' Republic similarly step up supplying Ashland with warm-weather commodities such as sugar, tobacco, salt, and coffee, and deploy auxiliary troops to shore up our defense, insofar as they're able, accounting for their own border disputes and the difficulties of transportation around the Atlanta Exclusion Zone. All of this should be done with the goals of preserving Ashland's border along the Ohio Valley, building up the offensive capabilities of our Oceti Sakawin and Miami sections, and assisting the people of Ohio in liberating themselves. I think that this is a solid plan that's well within the bounds of feasibility, can be implemented the second we adjourn, and that plays to our strengths without letting the war develop on the enemy's terms."

There were murmurs of approval, but no-one spoke. After a moment's silence, Tara raised her hand, stood up on her chair, and said, "I'm empowered to speak on behalf of the Musko Workers' Republic and its constituent nations, and I think that Miriam has come up with something we can all work with. As for us, we came here a bit worried about how much our section could actually contribute, given our relative isolation geographically, but Ashland's request sounds more than doable and I'd be glad to take it back to Mobile. Honestly, y'all . . . I think we're done here. Hashing out the particulars of how to make it happen is a job for individual sections, not for the international congress. I move for a vote."

"I second the motion to vote without amending," Kim said. "As usual, Granny is right. We have a plan; let's all do what Granny says, get some supper, get some sleep, and tomorrow we tear the fascists down."

"Anybody opposed?" Jimmy asked.

Silence.

"Alright then," he said, beaming with relief. "All voting delegates, please move to the front of the chamber."

The assembly began to shuffle places. Mags gave Jules and then Kitty a kiss as she and Miri got up to change seats. When the shuffling stopped, Jimmy cleared his throat and said, "Alright, all those in favor of implementing Comrade Methotaske's proposal as it stands, let's see some hands."

Hands began to go up, slowly at first, but gaining momentum as it moved through the crowd. There were no dissenting votes.

"Alright," Jimmy said, laughing. "Y'all . . . we did it. We did it in *one day*. It's done. Let's get the hell out of here, start spreading the word to our sections and departments, and tomorrow, we tear the fascists down. Our fourth All Soviets Congress is officially adjourned."

There followed a hushed silence and a hundred relieved, exhausted sighs. Those were still seated rose up, and, shaking each other's hands, clapping each other on the shoulders, the assembly broke up and began to head for the doors, tired but satisfied.

The calm was broken by the sound of boots clapping across pavement. An Ashlander soldier came running into the chamber, shouldered his way through the assembly, slid to a stop in front of Jimmy and Lynn, and whispered something to them. Both of them stepped back, looking horrified, and Jimmy, shaking and wrapping his arms around himself, shuffled back up to the podium and stammered, "Everybody . . . everybody . . . Fifteen minutes ago, they started shelling over the river. Everybody, Land's End is under attack."

Somewhere far off in the distance, a siren began to wail.

[30]
HAVOC

[Huntington, West Virginia]

IT WAS HAPPENING.

The crisp, late-summer mountain air and the stillness of night over the valley were split by an infernal symphony. From in front of Matt's position, from the hills north of the Ohio River, came the whistling of artillery shells flying toward him and over his head, and from his back came the endless whine of a tornado siren, and, in time with the whistling, the terrible, earth-shaking roars of the shells detonating within the city.

But Matt was over it. The shells seemed to be aimed at the city's heart, and the gunners would most likely not think that a ruined, derelict building on the riverfront was a worthwhile target, and certainly they couldn't see the little marksman's loophole in its upper floor. And the shelling wouldn't do all that much good anyways; for one, it was nighttime, and the crews would have to be judging their shots based on maps and known distances rather than observation, meaning that the destruction was random, and for two, they'd known that an attack was imminent, so the Huntington garrison had tucked themselves away in a thousand dugouts and hidey-holes as soon as the whistling began.

And there they would stay. When the shelling stopped, the infantry attack would begin, with blackshirts swimming across the river and brownshirts trying to set up floating bridges and the rest of the enemy force moving up for the main assault, and when that happened the red field artillery on the bluffs south of town—the infamous Huntington battery—would open up on the north bank of the river, and mortar and rocket crews would creep out of their foxholes to deliver a more precise hammering, and whatever was left of the fascist advance force would arrive on the free bank of the river haggard, tattered, and diminished, and then the fun would begin. As the fascists marched into the city, they would be met by riflemen and grenadiers popping out of holes in the ground every few hundred feet, and the artillery raining death onto the fascists queuing up on the north bank would not stop.

It all struck Matt as just so deliciously stupid. It was a bad business to cross a river under fire in the best of circumstances, and crossing a river under sustained artillery bombardment was nothing short of madness; they would've had a chance if they'd made the assault a few miles to the east or west, where things were less built up, but it looked like the entire Blackland New Republic was lining up to march right into an abattoir. And even that might be doable if their indirect fire support was anything close to precise, but the attack was coming *at night*; their artillerymen probably couldn't put eyes on a single target.

Matt would've felt some kind of a way about the impending destruction of thousands of people's lives, if fascists were people. As he watched the north bank and the ruins of the 527 bridge through the scope of his rifle—a Mosin-Nagant; archaic, but solid, and he liked it for this kind of work because it was much less fussy than a Dragunov, and anyway the Republic had untold thousands of them just lying around; it wouldn't do him much good in a real firefight, but he had an MP10 for that—he mused on why this extraordinary situation might be. If the army preparing to steamroll its way into the Republic was half as big as the spooks said, it would have to add up to some two thirds of the Blacklanders' entire military force; mayhap the fascists were walking right into a killbox in the hope of knocking out Huntington's guns in one fell swoop and moving southwest too quickly to get bogged down in the mountains. Fat chance of that. It would be a workable, maybe even clever idea, if it weren't for Land's End's helicopter gunships awaiting takeoff orders a few towns over, or the untold thousands of Ashlanders who would take old battle rifles and civilian pieces down from their mantles and put a marksman on top of every ridge and behind every tree the second they heard that Huntington had fallen.

As for why the attack was coming at night, well, that just strained credulity; fascists were not known for being clever under the best of circumstances, but this was some galaxy-brain shit and he could come up with no explanation for it. No matter; though he didn't have night optics, the moon and stars were bright enough that he'd be able to spot human figures moving on the north bank just as soon as they appeared.

The two-way radio next to him crackled to life, and a voice called out, "Hey, Big Iron, you got eyes on anybody yet? Over."

"Nah, boss," Matt replied, "don't see shit yet. But the night is young. Over."

"Word. You give me a holler as soon as you spot the fuckers and I'll play 'em a little tune on Stalin's organ, see if we can't flush 'em outta the trees for ya. Over."

"Believe me, boss, soon as I see a bonehead, you and everybody else will hear it; I got an instrument of my own, y'know. Over."

After a beat, a squad of human figures did appear on the far bank, not far from the fallen bridge, and Matt drew down on them and was about to merc one when he noticed that they'd stopped moving just as they'd reached the river. They seemed to be studying it, as if they didn't know quite what to make of it. One of them did move forward, and Matt was about to take him out when he noticed that it was only the one figure, and he wanted to see where this strange spectacle was going. The human-shape on the far side waded out into the Ohio River, stopped when the water was about knee-deep, turned around, and headed back, and the rest of the group faded back into the trees.

"Huh," Matt pontificated.

A moment later, a group of silhouettes appeared on the far side of the 527 bridge, and these did advance, though they walked calmly across the span and toward the fifty-foot gaping hole in its center as though they were taking a stroll through a model forest rather than assaulting a fixed position at night. Matt shrugged, took aim, fired, and one of the silhouettes dropped with its head snapping back at a delightful angle, accompanied by the nugget's deafening roar. Another marksman somewhere on the line did the same, and another silhouette dropped, and from his back Matt heard new, louder whistling, and heard and saw the infernal roar and red glare of a rocket barrage coming off of the bluffs.

But the figures on the bridge were still walking, unfazed by being under fire, and when they were about a hundred feet from the void in the middle of the bridge, they came to a dead stop, looked back and forth at each other, and sprinted forward at such blinding speed that they became lost in the shadows. They lept the fifty-foot gap in the broken bridge, landed in expert rolls on the other side, and kept running. Matt only managed one more shot before the whole group was out of sight, inside of the city.

And just as the shells began to light up the trees on the far bank, another group of shadowy figures appeared on the far side of the bridge, this one a platoon-sized element, making ready to pull the same trick.

And he couldn't see anything in the streets below his hide, but he could hear them, could hear the sound of running feet coming inexorably closer at chilling, inhuman speed.

"Hey, cap," Matt barked into the radio, "Big Iron here. You got your ears on? Over."

"Yeah, kid. What's the move? Over."

"Boss, we got a problem."

The assembly chamber was subdued and organized panic. People formed groups and began to file out as calmly as they could manage, but by their bearing and their faces it was clear that everyone was terrified. Mags, Kitty, and Jules stood rooted in place, looking at Miri and waiting for her to speak.

Miri suggested going back to the bar for coffee, as it would likely be a long night, and from there going to the Commissariat headquarters, but before they could move out, Jules noticed Lynn walking right toward them in long, determined strides, and when she came up to them she looked them over with an apologetic expression, pointed at Mags, Jules, and Kitty, and said, "Gee, I hate to do this, but . . . I need you three to come with me."

"What's the move?" Mags asked.

"We can talk outside. Just . . . there's no time."

The three of them followed Lynn out of Liberty Hall and around the side of the cathedral, away from the crowds, and when they were alone Lynn lit a cigarette, rubbed her temples, and said, "God, y'all, I'm sorry about this."

"About what?" Mags asked. "What's going on?"

"Well, I guess I'm not sorry it's happening 'cause it was always gonna happen, but, like, I was hoping we'd have time to be cool about it. Julia, sweetheart . . . Yesterday, didn't you think it was a little weird that the gate guard who waved you in was also the political officer who did your interview?"

Jules shrugged. "Lynn, everything here is a little weird."

"That's fair. Anyways . . . You know political commissars aren't, like, regular soldiers, right? You report to a special internal chain of command that reports directly to the General Assembly, and get embedded in a unit to maintain civilian control of that unit. So like . . . I'm one of that, and my unit is DIS."

"This?"

"DIS. The Department of Intelligence and Security."

"So you're a spook. I kinda gathered that much."

"I said yesterday that I wanted to do all of this gradually and gently, but it looks like we're out of time. Jules, I'm your handler. I already knew the answers to most of those questions I asked you yesterday; we were making sure you weren't gonna lie about it. If you'd been some kind of concentration camp guard or barn-burner, we would already know about it and you would already be in deep trouble."

"I guess . . . I guess I shouldn't be surprised."

"Uh-huh. But there are some gaps we want to fill and some things we think you know that we really need to know, so I need all of you to come with me—this concerns all three of you, and some-body's going to go track down Peterson and probably O'Shea too and send them along—and, Jules, I'm so fucking sorry we don't have time to handle this better, but I need to ask you some questions, a lot of questions, and some of them are going to be very personal and probably very painful questions."

And Jules sucked air through her teeth, chewed her bottom lip, and reached out and squeezed Mags' hand. After a tense moment, she said, "Alright. I . . . I think I can handle that."

"follow me. Don't worry, there'll be coffee. Just so much coffee."

They followed Lynn around to the back of the cathedral and down a narrow alley between two of the brutalist tower blocks, an alley that came to a dead end at a nondescript brown door bearing the same insignia Jules had spotted the previous day. Lynn opened the door with a flourish and gestured for the others to follow her in. It opened up into the foyer of a ground-floor office complex, a cramped room with filing cabinets lining the walls and several large secretary desks filling the floor. Each desk sported a map, a stack of notebooks, and a hotplate with a simmering pot of coffee. But the room had only one occupant, a middle-aged woman with hair dyed an electric neon purple, exhausted bags under her eyes, and several days of accumulated beard stubble. In addition to the maps and notebooks, her desk held several empty coffee cups and two full ashtrays. Her lapels sported a lieutenant colonel's palms.

"Oh, hey, Lynn!" she called out as they stepped inside. "You got 'em?"

"I got the officer and two of the assets, and somebody should be sending the other one down here anytime now. Say, Kate, are you . . . okay?"

"Never been better!"

"How long have you been awake?"

"About three days. So what all do you need?"

"Uh . . . just Binachi's file and the provisional orders. Which booths are open?"

"All of 'em. This place was dead until like 20 minutes ago."

"Okey dokey. Jules, if you'll follow me; the rest of you can wait here and hang out with Kate, she's a hoot."

"I'm not leaving her alone," Mags said.

"That's chill, assuming she's okay with it."

Jules nodded. "Mags and Kitty go where I go."

"Sure thing, sweetie. Whatever makes you more comfortable."

Lynn led them through the foyer and down a hallway to a room identical to the one she'd led Jules to the previous day, containing a desk, two chairs, and a filing cabinet. She ushered them inside, ducked back out, and returned a moment later juggling two more chairs and two pots of coffee, and asked everyone to take a seat across from her.

"Like I said," she began, "this is probably gonna be . . . difficult. We've got all night and we can take breaks as needed, and I can find you a mental health councilor or, like, some kittens to cuddle if you want me to."

Jules laughed in spite of herself. "A spook drags me into an interrogation booth and says she'll bring me a shrink and a kitty cat. I fuckin love this place."

"Oh, that's standard procedure, sweetie. We respect human needs and human dignity around here. And even if you were still our enemy, we'd do it the same way; to put it in cold and utilitarian terms, a shepherd is supposed to fleece the sheep, not skin it."

"Oh, that's clever. I like that."

"So, first question. And this is a real question; no more tricks; I wanna know if you know. did you ever wonder where the Blacklanders got all their sugar and coffee and tobacco?"

"Y'know, I don't believe I ever thought about that."

"Sugar and coffee and tobacco are warm-weather commodities; we grow some in our greenhouses and market gardens, but even we have to import most of it from our friends down in Alabama and Florida. All your drinkables and smokeables came into Ohio through Ashland's command economy."

"The fuck?"

"One of the annoying things about this war is the lack of good human intelligence. We've had . . . bad luck with agents and informants inside the BNR; the marshals and Blackshirts are a suspicious bunch, as you know, and people we send in or recruit have a bad habit of disappearing. We managed to keep one—one—agent active for a few decades before she went dark, but the average is about three months."

"Shit."

"Yeah. So we--" Lynn stopped mid-sentence, giving Jules a funny look as wheels turned in her head, and she muttered, "Oh, no way."

"What's up?"

"Julia Carlotta Binachi . . . Sweetie, what was your mother's maiden name?"

"Uh . . . Moreno?"

Lynn's eyes went wide, and she muttered, "We, ah . . . we don't have time to unpack all of that right now. As I was saying, we don't really, like, do human intelligence anymore. We've developed a lot of assets on the ground through Kitty's underground contacts, but those are a lot more useful as dissidents and organizers than they are as informants; drag queens and cutpurses are not exactly close to the halls of power. Our biggest intelligence source is intercepted radio transmissions, which we do very often and very well, but our second biggest is the blackmarket trade in coffee and cigarettes. Brown- and blackshirt garrison commanders along the river are eager to get their hands on it, and the barter good they bring to the table is information. People get powerful, powerful talkative when they're low on smokes."

"Holy hell . . . that's brilliant."

"It was Kate's idea, back when she first joined DIS a million years ago. But they aren't exactly what you'd call reliable, and we can't really fact-check their intelligence until after it's been collected and collated, so it's at least half bullshit. The half that isn't bullshit is still bought at a bargain, so it's a good system, but . . . I think you can understand why you and Peterson being here is such a great big screaming deal."

"Like I said yesterday, I'm happy to help. If I know anything you wanna know, just say the word."

"Yeah. Your service is deeply appreciated. And like I said . . . I'm so fucking sorry about having to do it like this, but we are out of time."

And Lynn took a pen out of her pocket, took a few sheets of paper out of her accordion folder, and continued: "What we're really focusing on right now is developing profiles on the Oberkommando; how the high command relate to one another their personal relationships, people they're close to, interpersonal tensions, tensions between the Falange and the High Church, stuff like that. We want to figure out who's really calling the shots up there, where there are cracks and contradictions within the command structure we might be able to exploit, and most of all we want to be able to profile how they're thinking so that we can plan our next moves a step ahead. You tracking?"

"Yeah. And I think I know here this is going."

"Mmhmm. Julia . . . tell me about Major Wenden."

———

Jules maintained her composure through the interview, speaking in a cool, even, all-business tone that gave her story an even more chilling impact; Lynn Ramirez reflected that this tiny, frightened woman who studied her boots wherever she walked was a soldier, a blooded killer, and could compartmentalize like a soldier.

·By the end of the interview, roundabouts midnight, Jules' resolve had begun to waver, and she sat scrunched up in her chair like a gargoyle, her arms wrapped tight around her knees, staring at the floor with wide eyes as Mags and Kitty massaged her shoulders. And Lynn gawked at her with a mixture of sympathy and deep moral, almost spiritual disgust, and after a long moment she said, simply, "*Holy fuck.*"

"Yeah," Jules replied.

"Sweetheart, do you . . . do you need anything?"

Jules glanced back and forth between Mags and Kitty and said, "Nah, I'll . . . I'll be okay. Listen, Lynn, was that at least helpful? Did this mean something?"

"Oh, fuck yeah. Our picture of how the Oberkommando functions and how its general officers interact just got a whole lot less fuzzy. Your service, as always, is invaluable." And Lynn stared off into the middle distance, and they could almost see the wheels turning in her head, and she muttered, "That's why the attack happened so soon; Rain is weak, and Farley knows he can be undermined. And, yikes, I wonder if Rain's *wife* knows anything about this."

"I don't know how she couldn't, honestly."

"Yeah. That's . . . that's it, that's where the schism is; he . . . he kept her alive as leverage, so that the Falange can control the High Church without a constitutional crisis."

"You've got a higher opinion of him than I ever did, then; I always figured he was just a creep who didn't wanna throw his favorite toy away."

"I . . . I gotta drop off this report on Kate's desk, assuming she didn't pass out smoking and set the place on fire yet, and then once Peterson gets here it'll be time for the rest of you."

"Speaking of," Mags said, "what exactly is it you need from us? I've been on our side of the river my whole life and I don't know shit about shit, and Kitty has been a citizen for years and Kate's basically written their autobiography."

"Oh, you're not here to be interviewed. You're here to be debriefed for a job."

"Aw, mother*fucker*."

When Lynn was gone, Mags stroked Jules' hair and cooed, "Honey, how are you holding up, really?"

"Oh, I've been better, sug."

"I'll bet. You wanna talk about it?"

Jules let out a deep sigh and said, "Sugar, they're gonna tell me to go back. I know they are."

"We always knew that that was a possibility."

"Sugar . . . I don't know if I can do that. I don't . . . I don't wanna fight anymore, and I guess I will if I have to—it's still the only thing I'm good at—but . . . I don't know if I can do *that*. Maybe I'd rather be hanged for a criminal than do that; it's a mercy compared to what the blackshirts would do to me if they caught me."

"Honey, you remember what Lynn said, about respecting human dignity? You're cleared now, which means you're a full-fledged citizen of the Republic, and being an asset means you can invoke the Soldiers' Bill of Rights, and all of that means that you get to say no. I'll fucking kill anybody who tries to violate the Soldiers' Bill of Rights—it's literally my job—and given your circumstances I don't think anyone in the world would think any less of you for invoking it."

"You're not gonna say no, though, are you?"

"No, honey, I'm not. I'm a soldier, and I do what soldiers do."

"Aw, fuck you."

"Huh?"

"You think I'm gonna let you go off alone, *stronza*? With no adult supervision? Not a chance."

And Kitty kissed the back of Jules' neck and said, "Y'know, seeing the way you two cleave to each other, it's something else. Makes me think the world might be worth saving after all. What is it about women in love?"

"Hey, bitch," Jules chuckled, "you know it ain't just us girls anymore, either. You're part of this three-ring shit circus, too, and you ain't getting off that easy."

"You sure do know how to sweet-talk a person, Jules Binachi."

"It's that hot Mediterranean blood, y'know. But while we're on the subject, I been wondering . . . what are you gonna, like, do? You're not a soldier."

"Well, I'm an intelligence asset, too, dummy. But I could be a soldier if I needed to; I'm a chemical technician."

"No shit?"

"No shit. Mostly I flip-flop between isolating pharmaceutical precursors in plants and wet-batching in manufacturing, but I could be a mad bomber if somebody asked real nice."

"Hot damn. I got real good taste in partners, looks like; shacked up with a sapper and a sniper."

"Designated marksman," Mags corrected.

From back down the hall, in the foyer, they heard Lynn scream in shock and outrage: *"It's fucking WHAT?"*

Someone else said something they couldn't make out, and Lynn shouted, "How in the whole goddamn . . . Oh, well, just *fuck me running!*"

And there were hurried footsteps coming down the hall, and

the door flew open to reveal Lynn, who looked as though she'd aged twenty years in the past few minutes, accompanied by Kate, and Peterson, and Robert O'Shea. Lynn, laughing without humor, said, "Okay, folks, so, uh . . . we were supposed to have a couple of days to get ready for this, but apparently it's possible to run out of time twice in the same night. We don't have days, comrades, we have hours."

"Lynn," Mags asked, "what the hell is going on?"

"I guess I'll give you the brief brief. High command wants to put you folks in with the auxiliary troops we're shipping out to Indiana where you'll attach yourselves to O'Shea's column and assist the war effort there in seizing settlements and pushing the border back east while the fascists are busy stomping the shit out of us down here. All of your various experience and expertise and records of service make us think you'll be perfect for this, yadda yadda yadda. It's an all-volunteer outfit, so if anybody would rather die in Tennessee then die in Indiana, just say so."

"We're all in," Jules said. "We figured on this and we talked it over while you were gone."

"Excellent. Awesome. Yrah. Right now, they're loading trucks over by the Academy and your estimated time of departure is in about an hour and a half."

"Lynn, what the fuck's going on?" Mags asked again. "Why's this happening so fast?"

Lynn pinched the bridge of her nose and said, "Mags . . . the Huntington battery has been overrun. We were expecting them to hold out for at least a week. They made it six hours. There are whole divisions mustering on our side of the river right now."

"What the fuck?"

"Apparently they had some kind of super-special high-speed forward operating group that knocked out the shore defenses' observation posts. Blackshirts forded the river with nobody shooting at them and were able to keep the artillerymen busy long enough for regular forces to start crossing. And that was all she wrote. We can delay them in the mountains for however long, but like Granny said . . . we're gonna bleed. We need to get the ball rolling on this operation and take some of this pressure off, fucking yesterday."

"How the fuck could that happen?" Kitty stammered.

And Mags, Jules, and Peterson all shared a knowing look, and Mags said, "Y'know, I might have a couple of guesses."

It was, by all accounts, a wonderful night.

Summons to the Commander's office were routine, but every once in a while, when Mrs. Samantha Rain and her lovely children were away, he would summon her to his bedroom. It was always blissful; for one, making love in the big, soft four-poster was much nicer than getting bent over a desk, and it allowed her to indulge in one of her favorite fantasies. She thought that, by now, Samantha must be aware of their little indiscretions, and that was a pleasant thought. She hoped that it was on her mind when they were in bed together. In this bed.

She lay there, wrapped around him, panting an endless stream of complements into his ear, running her hands across his scarred and tattooed body as he reclined on the bed with a cigar dangling from his lips. It felt like a scene from a movie, and when her hand brushed the wolf-hook inked into his collarbone, she kissed his cheek and whispered, "Darling, didn't I give you this one?"

"Mmhmm," he grumbled. "Back during the Maysville blitz, I think. Same campaign where you saved Eddie Stockdale."

"Yes, that's right. I'll always remember that campaign; we butchered the enemy and returned home bathed in glory, and that night . . . our first night. When you made me yours."

"Mmhmm. Thought I was gonna have to fight you, but you were into it."

"Oh, of course I was, darling. You were so brave, so wild, so strong, just as much as you are now; indeed, dear, that was when I knew--"

She'd been about to say "I love you" when, from the pile of clothes at the foot of the bed, a phone began to ring; the special, emergency phone that no-one was ever supposed to call. Rain shoved her aside, almost pushing her off of the bed, and dug around in his discarded fatigue trousers until he found it, accepted the call, and barked, "What?"

"Sir," came a voice down the line, "I'm so very sorry to disturb you at this hour, sir, but, uh . . . we need you in the war room."

"I am indisposed, Stockdale," he growled.

"Sir, at this point all of us are uncomfortably aware of your indisposition. But I'm afraid that this is an emergency. Well, half of an emergency. I have good news and bad news."

"The fuck does that mean?"

"Well, sir, the first thing that happened, the bad news, is that Roy Farley has gone rogue. He initiated contact with the enemy at around 8:30 last night, sir."

"He did fucking *what?*"

"He began the invasion, sir."

"I fucking told that cowboy we needed at least two more weeks! Oh, I'm gonna skin his ass."

"Well, that brings me to the good news, or I hope it's good news. It, uh . . . it worked, sir. Things are a bit, well, you might say they're confused, hence why this call is coming so late, but the reports we're getting from the field show that the Huntington battery fell after about six hours of fighting. I don't know if I trust Farley's reports, but it looks like our butcher's bill for crossing the river was only about three companies. Farley's moving his entire force across and plans to start a blitz into the mountains sometime tomorrow."

And, laughing, Rain replied, "Oh, I shoulda known that Roy would never let me down."

"Wait, so . . . you're approving the action, sir?"

"Damn right I am! It worked, didn't it?"

"Sir, Farley went behind your back, disobeyed a direct order, hell, disobeyed several direct orders, and put our entire war effort in jeopardy. With all due respect, sir, that kind of insubordination would be unconscionable coming from anyone, but this is a general who has put himself in charge of an army. You . . . you can't let that slide, sir."

"Farley didn't put himself in charge, Stockdale; *I* put him in charge."

"You . . . But, sir, Farley is only a brigadier; he's not even the highest ranked officer in his division."

"Roy Farley is a *blackshirt*, Stockdale. He's a made man. Worthy. Something *you* wouldn't understand. And, anyway, I only care about one thing: Results. And it sounds like Roy got me results."

There was a long, tense pause, and Stockdale asked, "So I am to take no punitive action against Brigadier General Farley, sir?"

"That's right, Stockdale. You're to give the man a fucking medal."

"Yes, sir. Will you be joining us in the war room, sir?"

Rain glanced over at Tasha, who was pouting and shaking her head, and said, "I am indisposed, Stockdale."

"Of course, sir. I'm sorry again for bothering you."

Rain hung up the phone. Tasha nuzzled his chest and cooed, "I love the way you handle those fools, darling. There's no sense in you sacrificing your evening with the situation so well in hand. You work very hard, and you need your rest."

"See, that's why I keep you around, Wenden," he yawned, taking another puff on his cigar. "You're the only one around here who ever tells me the truth."

"I only do my duty as God has ordained, darling. You are our Commander; you embody the collective will of our race and our nation. And such an important man who bears such a heavy burden deserves to be . . . looked after."

"That's what I like to hear."

"Of course, sir. You know, darling, lying here with you like this is . . . well, it is simply magical. I wonder, sometimes, about how life would be if this were *our* bed."

"Huh?"

"You are such a perfect specimen of masculinity, darling; truly, in you, the man and the hour have met. And I wonder, in another life, if . . . if things were different, perhaps I could've been Mrs. Natasha Rain, and you would not have to fret over sharing a bed with that other hag. Ah, isn't that a marvelous fantasy, darling?"

And Rain laughed, a long, hard reverberating laugh from deep in his chest, as though that were the funniest thing he'd ever heard. He gave her another shove, and this one did force her onto the floor, and, wiping his eyes, he said, "God, the things that pop into that head of yours."

A few blocks away, in the war room of the Oberkommando office, Major General James Stockdale stood staring at the phone in his hand for several minutes before he calmly, coolly set it down on the table in front of him, walked to the far side of the room, and pressed his forehead into the wall. One of the other staff officers approached him and asked, "So . . . is he just not coming?"

"No, he's not coming," Jimmy Stockdale grumbled. "He's indisposed."

"The hell does that mean?"

And Stockdale turned to face him, a look of rage and bone-deep frustration on his face, and growled, "It means he's shacked up with the creepy ladyboy pimp from the nuthouse down the street getting his rocks off doing God-knows-what, and that's too important for me to bother him with mundane matters like, oh I don't know, running the goddamn government during a goddamn national emergency."

"Wait, he's doing *what?* With who?"

"Ah, that's right, you're new here. You know Rain's secretary? Tall, blonde, always smiling?"

"What about her?"

"My boy, that is Father Elias's *son*. He calls himself Natasha. Rain keeps him around as a political token to keep the Ecclesiarchy from getting ambitious, and—according to my brother, at least—the arrangement comes with some fringe benefits."

"So our Commander's into traps?"

"Oh, were he *only* a pervert. Our Commander keeps an attendant eunuch at his court, like some kind of eastern potentate."

"Well, that's . . . disconcerting. But what did he say about Farley?"

"You want to know what he said about Roy fucking Farley? He said he approves of Farley going rogue and taking personal command of the entire fucking army against direct orders. He told me to give that goddamn cowboy a medal."

"Well, to be fair . . . Farley's plan kinda worked, didn't it?"

"My ass. He crossed the river, yeah, and that's not nothing, but the next leg of the plan is to blitz from Huntington straight to Ashland. To blitz through three hundred miles of mountains and forests with some kind of crossdressing, social-justice-crusading faggot kike hillbilly with a Kalashnikov waiting for him on top of every ridge and behind every tree. I'm sure that's going to work out *so well* for us; if you remember your military history, you might remember, oh I don't know, *Vietnam. Afghanistan.* And our illustrious Commander can't be fucking bothered about it. And do you know what else *der Fuhrer* said to me? He said it's okay for Farley to subvert the chain of command and commit high treason, stealing an entire army, because Farley's a blackshirt, which means he's *worthy*, and I could certainly never understand that." As he spoke, Stockdale plucked at the eagles on the collar of his own jet-black campaign shirt.

"What does that mean for us, Stockdale?"

"My boy, it means that our government is officially headless mere hours after we started a war. God help us."

"Jesus Christ. Jimmy, what are we gonna do?"

"Oh, I have some ideas about that."

[*West Virginia*]

Becky was lounging on the roof, watching the stars.

Her work detail as the clinic's night clerk never took more than a couple of hours to complete, between her innate speed and strength and the lackadaisical ordered chaos innate to the work in such a place, and by midnight most nights she would leave a spotless and well-ordered clinic to go for walks, or go visit with Millie and Connor (who seemed to have only a casual relationship with sleep), or leap cat-like onto the building's eaves and sit up chain-smoking and watching the stars. There wasn't fuck-all to do at ass o'clock at night in Parson's Hollow, which was primarily a farming and scavenging community, both of those being work that depended on daylight, and even the town's night owls were not quite used to her presence enough to make friends.

She felt like a pariah in a city of pariahs, an outcast amongst outcasts, and her heart still hurt, and she was exquisitely lonely and painfully, mind-bendingly bored.

So she felt something approaching relief when she heard a convoy of big diesel trucks lumbering through the darkness towards town, and felt relief approaching joy when she spotted the trucks and saw that they were painted olive drab green and flying red flags. Finally, something interesting.

The convoy rumbled to a stop in the center of town, a little ways in front of the clinic, and as people started filing out of their houses and grumbling about so much noise at such an ungodly hour, a political commissar hoped out of the cab of one of the trucks, climbed up onto its roof, cupped his hands around his mouth, and shouted, "Hey! *Hey! Hey, everybody!*"

"The hell are you hollerin about, red?" one of the townsfolk grumbled.

"Hey, everybody, listen up: *Boogaloo!*"

There was a moment of shocked silence, and then the assembling crowd began to cheer. Becky cocked her head to the side like a confused dog and muttered, "What in the whole hell . . ."

"War's back on, folks!" the commissar shouted. "The boneheads are on the move again! Land's end is under attack! We're here to take volunteers. Any scavver wants to be a wasteland ranger, we're putting some black brigades together!"

The cheering crowd, which was still growing, cheered louder and began to form queues around the trucks. Becky jumped down from the roof, put her sunglasses on, and shouldered her way to the front of one of the queues, where she looked up at a political officer and said, "I want in."

"Hell yeah. Say, lady, are you . . . okay? You look sick."

"I got a condition. Anyway, I want in."

[31]
THE BRIGADE

[West Virginia, near the Kentucky border]

THE COLUMN ASSEMBLED IN THE MOUNTAINS AND WAITED FOR dawn.

There were about a hundred of them, formed as a company with hastily-elected sergeants, lieutenants, and captain. As soon as the tornado sirens had gone off the night before, they'd thrown together what armaments they could at short notice, and the column included six technicals, farm trucks with tube mortars or chain guns mounted in their beds, but it was primarily, by both necessity and design, an infantry force. All hundred or so had been through some sort of scouting or civil defense program in their young adulthood, and many were militia reservists or regular army veterans, and all had their rifles. When the call came down, magazines and depots were opened to hand out Kalashnikov battle rifles and Dragunov marksman's rifles and, of course, the ancient Mosin-Nagants that the Republic had so many thousands of sitting in crates and gathering dust. Most of those were slick with cosmoline and bore East Asian or Eastern European maker's marks; elegant relics of a far less civilized age. But most of the rifles—the battle rifles, the marksman's rifles, the outdated war relics, the Remington and Winchester hunting rifles—had come down from over the Ashlanders' mantlepieces, the where they'd been sitting in wait for just such a day.

The column formed up on top of a ridge a few miles northeast of Centerville, under a double watch, awaiting dawn. It would've been better to move out through the dark, would've maximized their home field advantage and given them more chance of surprising the enemy, but by then they had all heard the rumors about who—or, rather, *what*—the fascists were using for advance scouts. And the fires all around them in the distance and smell of smoke on the wind stood in dark testament to that fact. So they would clean their weapons, count and recount their supplies, and wait for dawn.

The captain and lieutenants they'd elected stood on the highest point of the ridge, chattering into radios, establishing contact with other flying columns and with militia and regular army units and the remnants of the Huntington garrison, coordinating their maneuvers for the coming day. It was only coordination in the broadest since of the word, given that most of their radio communications were at this stage unencrypted and wide open to the enemy, but it wouldn't take much; every unit was an army unto itself, capable of planning, moving, and acting on its own, and anyway Roy Farley's plan was just as obvious: The fascists were going to steamroll down the 152 corridor, shift to the 37 corridor around Echo, cross the Big Sandy River at Louisa, and then hard-charge into Ashland canton and down to the city of Ashland itself. Given the difficult terrain, it was the only route on the table, unless Farley planned to split up his army by divisions and cover more ground, which didn't appear to be the case. And this was good for the Ashlanders; it was a long, tedious route that would give them endless opportunities to make the enemy bleed.

The fascists would reach Louisa and the river, at least, without serious resistance—the invading force numbered at least a quarter million, and the partisans had no illusions about offering them pitched battle—and on the way they would burn every town and shoot or hang every Ashlander they came across, but the beast was going to bleed for every inch, and it would be a diminished force hemorrhaging from a thousand cuts when it reached the canton line.

In any case, Lavalette had already been evacuated along with Huntington, and Ardel and Wayne would be evacuated by the time the dawn came. The children and elderly and those unable to fight were already over the river, or on their way, and the other residents were mustering into militia units or flying columns of their own. The loss of so many weapons foundries and machine shops and biomass plants, to say nothing of so many residences, would be a hard blow for the republic to take, but for the most part the fascists would be burning ghost towns, and they would bleed for the privilege.

The column had even managed to find themselves a political commissar amongst their stock of weekend warriors—protocol dictated that, if a unit elected a commissioned officer, even a partisan flying column had to have a political commissar in order to operate, lest that officer attempt any funny business—and as they awaited dawn she was engaged in a spirited discussion with some of the troops.

"Ah, it's all bullshit," said the commissar, a small Korean woman with a machete hanging from her belt and a Winchester rifle over her shoulder, waving a cigarette around for emphasis. "Defeatist settler bullshit. Don't even worry about it."

"Don't worry about it?" one of the partisans grumbled. "They got tanks! The hell are we gonna do about tanks? All we got is a few technicals."

"And what are they gonna do with tanks? Drive 'em up cliffs? All tanks are good for in this terrain is holding ground and forcing passes, neither of which we're worried about. Let the gunships worry about the tanks; we're worried about infantry. And, son, we are going to *slaughter* infantry."

"Suppose we do go head-to-head with one of them tanks?"

"Well, my advice to you is real simple: Fuckin don't. But if you can't help yourself, well, they ain't exactly top-of-the-line war machines. A well-placed grenade or nail bomb or satchel charge can knock the treads off. A Molotov cocktail can blind the driver for a few seconds and light it up nice and bright for our mortar teams. A case of Molotovs can cook the crew. We got options. But I wanna reiterate and make double-triple-quadrupe clear: If you don't see a good way to engage the enemy armor, then don't fuckin do it. When we hit their line, you take that rifle you got there and take a few shots at any exposed human body you see, and then we run away. If they don't follow us, which they probably won't on account of they're cowards, great. If they do follow us, which they just might on account of they're stupid, even better, 'cause then we can bushwhack 'em. It don't seem like much, but there are flying columns all up and down these mountains getting ready to do the same shit, and the beast is gonna bleed to death from a thousand cuts before it ever makes it much of anywhere."

"Alright, so what about the helicopters?"

"What about 'em. We got SAM sites all over these mountains— that's what the regular army is up to while we're having all the fun. And if that don't work, those chain guns will shred a helicopter to pieces, and you know in a pinch you can take out a helicopter with small arms fire. Listen, we've got the bastards soundly beat in the one department that matters." And she tapped the barrel of her Winchester and asked, "You know what that is?"

"A rifle?"

"A soldier and her rifle. We are better drilled and better motivated troops operating on favorable terrain, a whole nation of soldiers with rifles. No army in the world can beat us."

"Some rifle that is. Man, I wish we had more AKs."

"Me too, bud. But when it comes down to it, the gun you have is a better gun than the gun you don't. If you want an upgrade, go shoot a fascist and take his AR-10 off of him."

The partisan nodded, not quite satisfied, but sated, and after a beat the captain called out, "Alright, folks, sun will be up in one hour. Stand-to and let's get ready to roll out."

"What's the plan, boss?" one of them asked.

"Real sharp bend in the road just north of Lavalette, and their line of advance is gonna be all staggered while they're busy burning the town down. We're gonna stack up on the bluffs and bring the trucks up behind us. On my say-so, y'all start shooting, and we get the trucks in position and fire one volley. Once those shells go off, we make tracks for parts unknown, regroup in the hills down near Big Creek, and get ready to do it again. Sound good?"

"I dunno about 'good', but it sounds like a plan."

And the column mustered, and their muster was accompanied by the smell of smoke from far off, and by a rising *whop-whop-whop* of helicopter blades; their own or the enemy's, they supposed they'd find out soon enough.

The Academy was another jumble of hempcrete tower blocks, along with a parade field, a training ground, and a concrete Quonset hut where munitions were stored. A convoy of seven big diesel trucks, two technicals, and an Abrams tank were parked in front of the hut, with a detail of soldiers rushing to load boxes into the trucks, accompanied by the Dustwalker delegations. Miri was there directing the loading process, and Kimimela stood next to her, reviewing a shipping manifest.

"Looks like a fine place to start, Granny," they said with a nod of approval. "Seven whole trucks of vermilion and firewater, huh? We'll pay y'all back pound-for-pound in fascist dicks. Sound good?"

"Oh, is that a service we offer now?" Mags asked, walking up behind them.

Miri doubled over laughing. Kim looked Mags, Jules, Kitty, and Peterson over and said, "Well, I see that our vaunted allies in the Ashland Confederated Republic are sending us their best and brightest, to be sure. I even get Too-Tall and Shortstack as a package deal. Y'all gonna be with O'Shea's brigade?"

"So they say."

"Uh-huh. What is it you do, Kitty?"

"I'm an intelligence asset," Kitty replied, "and I'm a chemist."

"Cool. Pharmaceuticals? Manufacturing?"

"Yes."

"Awesome. Yeah, I'm sure we'll keep you nice and busy. And you said it's they/them, right?"

"Uh-huh, it sure is."

"Fucking thank God they're at least sending me another normal person. Alright, y'all, we're wanting to roll out in about half an hour, so get ready to load up. We went ahead and took the liberty of packing your stuff—it's in that truck right there—but if you want extra they told me we're free to raid the Girl Scout lodge over there. Don't forget to hit the little nonbinary's room, 'cause once we hit the road we ain't stopping except for fuel; the Indianapolis corridor is rough country and I'd like to be back in the land of the living by lunchtime."

Jules, who'd been observing everything in silence with a dissatisfied sneer on her face, looked up at them and asked, "My piece in there?"

"The Armalite? Yeah. But hey, as long as we're here a minute, you could head in and grab a '74 like an adult if you wanted to."

"Nah. The 10's special."

"What makes a hunk of Amerikanski plastic special?"

"I took it off a blackshirt after I killed him with my bare hands. It's special."

"Yeah, that does sound pretty special. I went ahead and threw a couple cans of .303 in there for you, too."

"Much obliged."

Kim turned away to help with mustering, and Miri walked up, squeezed Jules' shoulder, and said, "Hey, it's a hell of a thing that you agreed to do this. Thanks."

Jules stole a quick glance at Mags and said, "I'm not doing it for y'all."

"Oh, so you're telling me that you're only doing it for the best and most noble reason anyone possibly could? Cut out the antihero schtick, kid. You're among friends."

Jules' sneer curled up into a smile. "Yeah. Yeah, I guess you're right."

"I'm always right. And listen: That girl means a lot to me. She told you the story about how we met, right?"

"Yeah."

"So you know she's like a daughter to me. And I'll be able to sleep easy and not worry about her, knowing she's got you watching her back. And, hell, I guess that makes you sorta like a daughter to me, too."

"Goddamn, woman, you tryla make me cry?"

"Listen, kid, I'm not really in the business of giving people special pats on the back just for being basically decent, but . . . I can tell you've come a hell of a long way. I'm proud of you."

Jules examined her boots, feeling unworthy of the praise, and Miri laughed and clapped her on the back and said, "There you go being a fuckin antihero again. Listen, if I thought you were a shit, or if I thought you weren't good enough for the kid, wouldn't I say so?"

"Yeah, Miri, I reckon you would."

"Damn right I would. So don't insult me by acting like you're not the person I see in front of me. But, listen . . . For all our nice words, this is a hell of a thing however you slice it. What is it you're chasing after, kid? Vengeance?"

"Nah, that ain't me. I ain't in the revenge game. I'm just . . . I'm just trying to do right by my girl and keep on doing the next right thing, y'know?"

"Yeah, I know, and that's a noble pursuit. It would be right and proper for you to be after vengeance, but I'm glad you're not, on account of the kid's gonna be with you and vengeful soldiers die easy. Y'all just stick together, trust your instincts, listen to Kimimela and listen to the folks who've been out on the prairie a lot longer than you have, and you'll be fine. I know you will."

The gear and auxiliaries were loaded up in good order and the convoy started rolling out fifteen minutes ahead of schedule. In spite of Miri's words, Jules brooded, and the brooding was encouraged by how terribly familiar the whole exercise felt: Sitting on a wooden bench in the back of a deuce-and-half with a rucksack under her knees and an Armalite between them, packed in with a bunch of other reeking bodies, everyone too tired to sleep as they rumbled off into the night with vague orders to go God-knows-where and do God-knows what. It all felt like home in a grim and unwholesome sort of way, the way smelling hooch on Jack Binachi's breath would've felt like home.

Mags and Kitty let her have her space, and so she sat brooding in fellowship with Peterson, which made the whole exercise feel worse. After a while, she lit a cigarette, offered the pack to him, and grumbled, "This is fucking gubu."

"Ain't that bad, sister," Peterson said, lighting up. "We're just going out on a tickle. We go out, deliver the mail, we hit the rack, nice and easy. Just like old times."

"Yeah, that's the trouble: Just like old times. And this feels a lot more like a float than a tickle, if you ask me. This is the very definition of gubu."

Robert, who was sitting across from them, nodded in agreement, but Mags leaned over and asked, "So . . . question."

"Huh?" Jules inquired.

"What the fuck did you two just say?"

Jules and Peterson locked eyes, and their serious expressions melted into suppressed laughter. Peterson took a deep breath and said, "Shop talk. Sorry. Uh, Jules was saying that this feels weird, so I says that, no, we're just going out on an op, nothing special, but she says it feels more like an improvised op than a planned one."

"What was that word . . . gubu? What the fuck is a gubu?"

"It's means something that's weird and dangerous."

"It's an acronym," Robert said, speaking up. *"Grotesque, unbelievable, bizarre, and unprecedented."*

Mags was silent for a moment before she put a hand on Jules' shoulder and said, "Honey, I'm sorry for a lot of the things you've had to go through, but I think most of all I'm sorry you had to grow up around people who talk like that. Are you sure that's soldiers' slang? Because y'all just sound like nerds."

That broke the spell, and, laughing, Jules fell over into Mags' arms and said, "Ah, I'm just being a drama queen. I know we're gonna be okay. Y'know how I know?"

"How do you know, hon?"

"'Cause you two are here."

Mags held her closer, and Kitty slid off of their bench to sit between them on the floor. They all sat in silence for a while, trying and failing to get some sleep, until Jules turned toward Peterson and said, "Hey, brother, can I ask you something? It's been on my mind."

"Yeah, of course. Whatcha got?"

"Stop me if this is too real, but . . . what all did you walk away from?"

"What do you mean?"

"When you went renegade. Like, for me, it was the only thing I could do; I think about my one other friend and I think about my mom, but they didn't exactly gimme a choice. And you never really talked about yourself before."

"Hell, it sounds like you had more to walk away from than I did. You already saw all that there was to me. I was a barracks rat; just a washed-up old gun thug with no family, no girl, no real friends outside of the unit. I only ever had two things tying me down, and one of 'em was a bullshit idea about brotherhood that never stood up to scrutiny."

"What was the second thing?"

"Aw, you know that. The second thing was my little sister."

"Aw, hell, why is everybody trying to make me cry today?"

"No, it's true. You're my best friend; have been ever since you passed selection. You were 17, so that was, what, eight years ago now? And when I found out I couldn't even protect my best friend, and found out that the friend I lost was my only friend, well, it really ain't that hard to turn your back and walk away from a whole pile of nuthin."

"That's about the way of it," Robert said with another solemn nod. "The service is like a machine that runs on human lives and outputs human misery."

Peterson returned the nod. "Hell, I'll drink to that, boss."

"Y'know," Jules said, looking Robert up and down, "I never did get your story. Where exactly did you come from?"

"Greenville garrison. Third assault battalion, fourth infantry."

"And what kinda bigshot were you?"

"Major. Assault group leader."

Jules jumped, but maintained her composure as she locked eyes with him and asked, "You ever spend any time in Columbus? Around the Oberkommando?"

"Not a piece. Never liked the big city, and I always knew they was assholes."

She visibly relaxed. "Good. So what made you turn renegade?"

"You ever been out west, Julia?"

"Nah. I was first assault battalion, first infantry. Cincinnati."

"Lucky. Out west fuckin sucks. Take everything you ever hated about the Ohio Valley and double it. Logistics problems, leadership problems, the enemy's as smart as they are brutal and relentless, and the weather is somethin else. Desertion is pretty high; easily one in ten conscripts and maybe one out of every twenty of us will just walk off the job if given half a chance. So I was there, hating every minute of it, starting to feel some kind of a way about the horrible shit we were doing, and just like ol' Peterson I was a joyless dumbass and the unit and the cult were the only life I had, so I didn't exactly have a lot to walk away from. a day came when we went out on an op, and it broke bad, and I couldn't help but notice that some of the enemy moving in to slaughter us were a bit on the pale side and their guns looked a bit familiar. I figured they had the right idea, so I threw mine down and surrendered. And here we are."

"So if desertion is that high," Kitty said, "that brigade of yours must be huge."

"Not as such. Most of the conscripts just wanna go home, and will take a new home if they can't do that, so Kim and their friends run a little resettlement program. Most time, folks only really hang onto the gun and go renegade if they've got a score to settle." And he gave Jules a knowing look.

"That ain't me, man," she said, leaning back further into Mags' embrace. "I never got anywhere trying to settle scores. Right now, I'm a soldier and I'm here to do a job."

The first leg of the journey went quickly, following the over-sized major highways, and they passed the time alternating between talking and taking much-needed naps, so they didn't realize how much time had passed or how much ground they'd covered until the convoy slowed to a crawl and one of the soldiers peeked out of the truck's canvas cover and announced that they were crossing the Ohio River. After a long and tedious crossing of a decaying two-lane bridge, the convoy circled up at a crossroads on the far side to refuel their vehicles, and the passengers all hopped out to stretch their legs. Jules took a look around and asked, "So where the hell are we?"

"Right in the asshole of nowhere," Kim said, walking up. "This is nominally Ashlander territory, so I guess we're nominally still in New Lawrence, but it's unoccupied and uncontested and un-whatever because nobody wants it. Welcome to the Indianapolis Exclusion Zone, our home away from home for the nest 200 miles. Home to some of the best scrap in the wasteland, but some damned fool fucked up and put a bunch of radioactive debris and roamers on top of it."

"Well, hell."

"Ah, don't even worry about it, Shortstack. Most of the actual trade and traffic gets routed through the Mississippi Valley, but that would take an extra few days at least, and probably more depending on what the rivers have been like; this is still the most direct route between my rascally southern neighbors and the northwest front in the war, so we know where we're going and we know how to get there safe. Just make sure and take this opportunity to get all your necessaries outta the way, because once we get back on the road we are not fucking stopping until we get to Wawpecong. The locals around Indie tend to get a little bit bitey when we stop."

Most of the assembled looked back and forth at each other dubiously, but Kim and the other Natives along with O'Shea looked as casual as though they were discussing a Sunday drive to the corner store for a pack of smokes, and so the others tried to follow their lead, though it was still with an air of nerves and apprehension that they filed back into their transports and got back on the road.

They stayed under cover and saw little of the scenery, but what glimpses they did catch reminded Mags and Jules rather of the coastal exclusion zone east of Freeside, with its disconcerting mix of dense and verdant new flora in the shadows of ancient, mummified trees and the decaying husks of buildings and towns looming in the distance, made all the more surreal because the landscape was so flat and open. There were clusters of buildings forming towns, and lone buildings standing out amongst the scrub oaks and prairie grass, and around the buildings they could see human figures looming in the distance, and as they passed those figures would attempt to follow along behind, keening, and the soldiers would clutch their rifles tighter and examine their laps.

"I don't get it," one of them said after a while. "Other than the unfriendly locals, of course, what's wrong with this place? I figure it woulda been settled, or hell, become another front in the war. Reminds me of Freeside."

"Be glad we're moving," O'Shea grumbled. "The dirt around here is about as hot as a fire. We'll be passing most of it by, thank God, but a ways up north they rained some serious hellfire down on this area back during the War. Even without the roamers, cleaning up all this contamination would take some doing."

And as the road grew more rough under them, and the moaning louder and more dense around them, the soldiers kept their heads down and conversation ground to a halt. After a while, though the convoy's pace never slowed, the sounds of agonized keening and shambling feet seemed to come from all around them, and in a few places the moans were answered by the while of the chain guns behind them, or the roar of the tank's turret. And passengers hugged their weapons, and those who were of a mind to prayed.

After a nerve-wracking drive that lasted hours, well into the day and beyond Kim's projection of lunchtime, things began to quiet down and a few of the passengers snatched cautious glances outside of their canvas security blanket to see a landscape utterly changed. They saw a rolling green prairie broken up here and there by copses of oak and ash and hemlock, with animals grazing in the far distance under a gunmetal-grey sky. And the area was populated with no shortage of warm, living human beings; each copse of trees sported a cluster of new, post-War buildings, and though they could see that the buildings were made to be dismantled or otherwise moved at a moment's notice, each settlement looked well lived-in and was accompanied by fields of corn and beans and herds of horses or cattle or goats. And above each settlement flew flags of red and black.

"Looks like we're almost there," one of the soldiers commented.

"I fucking hope so," Jules grumbled. "How the hell long have we been in this goddamn can?"

"Judging by the sun, just a smidge under twelve hours."

There was a collective groan as the convoy rumbled on, ever northwards.

After a while, but not long, the convoy came to a more permanent structure, a rammed-earth star fort looming up at them out of the prairie, capped by concrete pillboxes and by the barrels of artillery pieces peeking out of dugouts. And there were more people around, seeming thousands; the star fort was well-manned, and the buildings they'd seen further south clustered tight around it to form an ever-mobile but elegant and lived-in city.

The imposed border and accompanying war were only a few short miles to the east, and many of the people looked care-worn and bone tired, but there was an even deeper defiance around the whole affair, as though these people were aware of how inconvenient for their enemies their existence was and relished the thought —which was in fact the case. It reminded Mags of the border towns along the river near Cincinatti, and reminded Kitty of the same.

The convoy rumbled to a stop at the edge of a parade field tucked between two of the star fort's points, where they were met by a large group of people under arms; most of them wore street clothes or simple uniforms, but a few—mostly at the front of the group—were dressed in extravagant and beautiful regalia.

Kim was already out ahead of the Ashlanders filing out of the troop transports, and they huddled everyone together and said, "Alright, we made it. You're in the lovely town of Wawpecong, Indiana, which in this here the foul year of our Lord 2261 is jointly held by the Pottawatomie, Miami, and Sioux nations of the Dustwalker Confederation; of those three, I, your humble travel agent, would be the latter. Them over there is your welcoming committee and in a minute they're gonna come over here and give y'all some pats on the back tell y'all what fine comrades y'all are for volunteering for this shit detail, which I guess is true. I know everybody's probably all worried about diplomatic protocols and niceties and whatnot, so here's some simple advice: Keep your mouths shut and don't fuckin say anything except for 'thank you'. Tomorrow y'all will be divvied up and get your marching orders while we sort out where these vehicles and all this ordinance goes; technical experts will mostly stay with us and everybody else will probably be attached to O'Shea's brigade. Say, speaking of: Other than Too-Tall with the big hair over there, are any of y'all political officers?"

No hands went up.

"Hell. Hey, O'Shea, what rank did you say you gave yourself?"

"Major," Robert grumbled.

"Alright. Well, congratulations, Miss Frizzle, you've just been promoted. How does it feel to be a brevet lieutenant colonel?"

Robert and Mags shared an uneasy look as Kim and the rest of the delegates went off to go chat with their countrymen.

Looking around, Jules noticed a group that looked quite out of place. Six white men stood a few steps apart from the rest, all of them wearing long pants and sleeves in spite of the summer warmth, all standing around with their legs apart and their arms crossed in a way that exuded an infuriating sort of arrogance, a look that Jules recognized at once. O'Shea loped over to them, exchanged a few handshakes, and told them something which Jules couldn't hear, but she saw that he'd pointed her out. And three of the men came walking over toward her, and the largest and most grim of them stood in front of her for a beat before giving her a nod and saying, "The boss says you might be a blackshirt. That true?"

"Nah," Jules said, meeting his eyes. "I ain't. But I reckon somebody was once."

The man's grim expression broke into a warm, friendly smile, and he extended a hand and said, "That there was a real good answer."

Jules took the offered hand, going for a shake, but instead the stranger grabbed her wrist and pulled her into a big, warm bear hug, lifting her feet off of the ground. She almost started to panic, until she realized the stranger was laughing. And, squeezing her tight, he said, "Y'know, I don't reckon we've ever had us a sister before."

[32]

DUALITY, PART 2

[The next morning; West Virginia]

THE ADVANCE WAS, BY FARLEY'S ESTIMATION, GOING WELL.

The advance scouts had stalked far and wide through the mountains during the night and reported that the enemy was very busy but appeared to be busy running away. The remnants of the routed Huntington garrison as well as the regular army units in the area had mustered around hilltop artillery and missile batteries closer to the Big Sandy River or closer to Freeside, apparently to stay, as if daring him to attempt the trick a second time, and the civilian populace was in full flight, giving him an empty corridor to march his army down. Once his vanguard dug in at Louisa, which might be underway by the end of the day, complements to the enemy's cowardice, he would be near to done with his initial goal of bisecting the enemy's industrial base and would split off a few detachments to secure his supply lines back to Ohio and begin mopping up the garrisons. Let the cowards run; the reckoning was here at last, and sooner or later the bloodletting would begin. As

Farley directed the column's southward advance, his eyes sparkled as visions of hangmen and firing squads and great stacks of burning bodies danced through his mind. The Ashlanders were not merely enemies, but filth, and he relished the thought of scouring the world clean of them.

Some of the civilians, his blackshirts reported, had taken up rifles and were forming guerilla bands, but that was nothing. The invasion force numbered almost a quarter million line infantry, along with a full complement of armor—tanks, bearcats, mobile artillery, and technicals—and enough Arditi operating groups to form a division. And, once dawn broke, he heard the approach of his pride and joy coming over the Ohio River, the beautiful *thwok-thwok-thwok* of his little complement of helicopter gunships. Roy Farley would not concern himself with a bunch of degenerate hill-billies carrying Pawpaw's squirrel guns; might as well have been wild injuns with bows and arrows. Soon they would be over the river, within Ashland canton itself, and none of that would matter.

Easily a third of the invasion force had managed to cross the river and muster in the ruins of Huntington during the night, and in the gloom of early dawn, as the special scouts went to ground for the day and his beloved blackshirts disappeared into the forest to the left, right, and front to take their places and the war clerics bellowed calls for courage and jumped for Jesus, they began their advance.

They encountered, as Roy had expected, no real resistance, but the Ashlanders made their presence known. The first sign came from the air, and did not bode well. Land's End had its own fleet of gunships, and a few of those appeared right away, but only a few. Rather than giving proper battle, the cowards would approach the marching column in twos and threes, offer a few bursts of machine gun fire, and then bank hard and turn around to flee back into the mountains. This perplexed the men on the ground almost as much as it did the Blacklander helicopter pilots, until one group broke off to pursue and, as soon as they were away from the main body, white plumes of rocket exhaust billowed up from a nearby hilltop, and the pursuing helicopters pursued no more.

The advance was accompanied from the beginning by a steady tattoo of gunfire from far off as the flying columns and the groups of Arditi bumped into each other, and an hour or so after sunrise the infantry attacks began in earnest. They were small things—a group of partisans would appear on a hilltop, offer a few volleys of rifle fire and throw a few bombs, and melt back into the countryside as soon as they came under counterfire—but they were incessant, slowing the advance, fraying the men's nerves, and, as the day went on, the rising butcher's bill became more noticeable. And the men —or at least the conscripts—began to talk. Farley's was, for the greater part, an army of one- or two-year levies, and the men already disliked their officers, and as the day drew on and the men marched between hills listening to the endless symphony of gunfire, listening to the screams of the dying as the flying columns made their periodic raids, listening closely for the tell-tale whistling of incoming mortar fire, many of them began to wonder if perhaps they had better places to be.

Just after lunchtime, as the brownshirt conscripts began to wonder about the prospect of fighting an invisible enemy in the mountains, with hundreds of miles of higher, rougher mountains still in front of them, and as even Farley began to grow concerned with the delays, a helicopter gunship came barreling toward the column, coming in low and at frightening speed. As soldiers took cover and rushed to man their chain guns, the gunship banked hard and zipped along the length of the column for a moment before turning again to disappear into the hills. As it flew over them, it dropped something far deadlier than explosives. Reams of paper, stacks of thousands of handbills, fell from between its skids and billowed about in its propwash before settling like snow or ash amongst the invaders. Each handbill bore the same message:

"SOLDIER! WHAT ARE YOU FIGHTING FOR?

This is our home, and we will put a rifle in every hand and a marksman behind every tree and we will defend our home to the last bullet, to the last drop of blood. You will have to march over the corpses of tens of thousands of your comrades-in-arms to reach Ashland, and this war will not be over so long as one of us is left to take up the gun. If you want to take our home from us, you will bleed for the privilege.

We fight to defend our home, but why do you fight? Most of you are not our enemies. You should be in your own home, safe with your families. Was it your idea to leave home and die in the mountains? Or are you here because you were told to be?

Any Blacklander who throws down is gun and surrenders will not be harmed and will be treated with dignity and courtesy. Any Blacklander who holds onto his gun and uses it to do something about the people who've sent you to die here, well, I'll buy you a goddamn chicken dinner.

Love and kisses,

Lieutenant Colonel Katelynn Barlow, Ashland Confederated Republic, Department of Intelligence and Security."

[*Marion, Indiana*]

On the morning after the invasion, Peter Wenden held the inaugural service in his new church. he was well pleased with himself; he'd managed to bully the presbyters and some of the less refractory members of the congregation into at least cleaning the place up, rehanging the crooked old door, polishing the icons, and though there was still a lot of work ahead of him, he was at least satisfied to call this a house of God.

Only a grand total of fifty people out of the town's population in the low thousands were in attendance for the service, but those who did attend were energetic, enthusiastic, hungry for what he had to offer; his fears about the town's recalcitrance were assuaged just a hair, and he dared to hope that seeds planted would take root now that the High Church's period of dormancy was over. The townsfolk were pig-ignorant, but they were white and they were angry and they seemed pleased as punch to hear about the impending war and the cleansing it would bring, and were eager to get on with some cleansing of their own, in the west. Yes, perhaps this town was not so fallen as he'd feared; the sheep only needed a shepherd.

Peter did note, however, that the Commandant was not in attendance.

After the service, Peter stood outside of the church, conversing with those of his new congregation who were eager to learn more about their new preacher, when the Commandant did arrive, and arrived accompanied by three men in black shirts. Two of those were men in their mid-20s who walked with the practiced swagger of the typical bully, but the third was much older, his blonde hair greying about the roots, and he walked tall, proud, and dignified in a way that commanded respect. The four of them walked up to Peter, and the Commandant gave him a jaunty wave and called out, "Hello, hello, my boy! I'm terribly sorry to have missed your performance, but I was indisposed."

The older blackshrit winced. Peter gave him a nod and said, "Of course your duties must come first, sir. I do hope you will join us next week, though."

"Of course, of course, wouldn't miss it for the world. What kept me so busy today, my boy, is that I have big news that I know is going to just tickle you. Have you heard that the war's on?"

"What? Already?"

"They kicked it off late last night, and from what I've heard it's going just swell."

"Oh, that's wonderful! Lord be praised for letting us live to see such times."

"Sure. And it seems that the Oberkommando have decided to

be gentlemen and replace a bit of my purloined garrison. A little company of the nice men in the black shirts arrived here this morning, and I've been making the rounds introducing the new boss. Petey, this is General Stockdale, my new garrison commander."

"A pleasure," Stockdale grumbled, rolling his eyes. Peter noticed that he seemed displeased with everything those eyes settled on, and got the distinct impression that Stockdale was not here by choice.

"The pleasure is all mine, sir," Peter said. "I am your war cleric and local man of God, Peter Wenden."

At that, Stockdale arched his eyebrows, and the three black-shirts looked back and forth at each other for a beat before he asked, "I'm sorry, son, what was that name again?"

"Peter Wenden, sir. Father Elias's son."

The two blackshirts with him burst into peals of laughter, as though that were the funniest joke they'd ever heard; Peter blushed crimson and ground his teeth. Stockdale, however, nodded and asked, "Son, could I talk to you in private for a moment?"

"Ah, certainly, sir. Shall we talk inside?"

"That will do nicely."

Peter led Stockdale into the now-empty church, and the two other blackshirts followed them, shutting the doors behind them. Stockdale nodded at his two attendants and said, "Don't worry about them, son. My men are trustworthy."

"As you say, sir. What did you want to speak to me about?"

"You've heard that the invasion was kicked off last night?"

"Yes, sir. It's very exciting, isn't it? Things are moving so quickly, and ahead of schedule."

"How do you know it's ahead of schedule?"

Peter gulped. "I've, ah, heard rumors, sir."

"I'm going to go out on a limb and guess that you have a source who's close to the Commander."

"I . . . I suppose I shouldn't try to lie to you, sir."

"Good man. Now, son, the reason I pulled you in here is that I want to gauge your opinions on recent events. You're newly attached to the Falange, so I don't suppose you know who I am."

"Ah, no, sir. I'm afraid not."

"Well, I'll tell you. I was given this commission only a few hours ago. Until just last night, I was an Oberkommando staff officer."

"Oh, my. This post must be of great strategic importance, then."

Stockdale rolled his eyes. "The invasion was scheduled to begin two weeks from now, but it began last night. It began last night because one of the brigade-level general officers took personal command of the invasion force and launched the attack, against explicit orders."

"Jesus! What did the Commander have to say about that?"

"That's the matter at hand, isn't it? The Commander doesn't take issue with General Farley's actions, but I wanted to see if you might, and to see what you think of the Commander, given his . . . peculiar relationship to your family."

Peter gave him a suspicious look. "Sir, what exactly are you implying?"

"Nothing, son. I wanted to gauge my new war cleric's patriotism and loyalty, and you've shown that satisfactorily; I should've expected nothing less from Father Elias's boy. You're dismissed, Wenden."

That seemed to mollify Peter, and he left the church with a satisfied look on his face. Stockdale let out a long, frustrated sigh, and one of the blackshirts grumbled, "Well, boss, that went about as poorly as it coulda gone."

"Quite. I suppose I should've expected as much from a cultist, but I'd hoped he'd at least have more animosity towards the man who's assfucking his brother."

"They're all a bunch of fuckin weirdos, Jimmy. Y'know, I met Father Elias once; that guy is a top-tier piece of work, a real Jim Jones motherfucker. Bein a freak must run in the family."

"Being irritating certainly does. And I'll bet that being a snitch runs in the family, too. Keep a close eye on that boy."

"You want us to take care of him, boss?"

"Not just yet. For now, we wait and see how things play out with Farley. But it won't be long, no, it won't be long at all."

[33]
THINGS FALL APART

[West Virginia]

THE MUSTERING IN FREESIDE WAS CHAOTIC, BUT A RUTHLESS efficiency lay under the chaos, along with an eagerness and fervor that bordered on bloodthirst. The red commissars not only had no shortage of volunteers, but in fact suffered from an acute lack of transportation. So many of the anarchists took rifles and knives down from their mantlepieces and kit bags out of their cupboards and explosives out of their root cellars and marched out to declare their willingness to kill fascists that the planned single black brigade became three: One would load onto trucks and head for Land's End with all speed, one would follow in their train to reinforce, and a third, smaller but made up entirely of blooded wasteland scavengers, was heading north.

The forward brigade swore oaths of fellowship with each other and loaded into the trucks and raised their black flags as they headed into the west. For the commissars who hadn't fought with wasteland rangers before, it was a fascinating experience; political officers, by nature, did not lead troops, but more advised them, their primary functions in a combat operation being to shore up morale and to keep officers in check. But the anarchists often didn't listen to the very officers they'd elected, and seemed eager to kill and even to die with a zeal that approached religious conviction.

The commissars did have some worries about the brigade's lack of discipline, fretted that sustained contact with an enemy that couldn't be overcome through mere critical mass would cause the force to break down into small and isolated active service units at best, or more likely degenerate into a frenzied mob. But this force was moving over rough country at least a day behind Farley's invasion force, maybe two, and would be a fifth column fighting a rear action against an already engaged enemy; most likely it would be the fascists who would run once the bullets started to fly.

And the forward black brigade did have one powerful asset that even their red cousins lacked: They need not fear the night.

To Becky, the war was welcome work. Her new comrades-in-arms were still leery of her, but that was nothing; she outpaced them in leaps and bounds, covering far more ground on foot than they could in motorized transports, and they would see little of each other. And as she moved through the trees and over the mountains, she thought about how Jules had certainly been right about one thing: Nothing soothed an aching heart quite like action. And it felt good, felt right, to do the thing that nature had created her to do. To hunt.

And hunting was welcome work indeed. Farley's blackshirts were concerned only with warm-blooded enemies, had seen no reason to take precautions against any other kind, so it was such a small matter to find the advance scouts by sound and smell, to take care of watchmen in ones or twos, and to take care of sleeping men. In Freeside, food had been awkward to come by, and when she went to war she was hungry, so very hungry . . .

But the prize catches were wandering around in the dark ahead of any others just as she was, in groups of twos and threes, wearing their stupid Party City uniforms and chittering in German or Italian. And an enemy in the night who could see and hear and smell and move just as they could was the last thing any of them expected.

As she went about her work, two trains of thought kept running through her head. One revolved around the stories Jules had shared with her, and formed the rudiments of a plan; a terrible plan, to be sure, but she thought to herself: *What would he do?*

Him . . .

Every time she crept up catlike behind one of those black-eyed dinosaurs, one of the bastards that time forgot, and gave him a retirement check through the back of the head, she imagined him watching her. She wasn't sure if she believed in an afterlife, beyond the one she was already living at least, but she hoped that he was watching. And she hoped that he was proud.

Though her German was a bit rusty, she remembered just enough from her high school L2 centuries ago to be getting on with, and sometimes as she stalked through the darkness she would half-hum, half-sing to herself:

"Auf, auf zum Kampf, zum Kampf!
Zum Kampf sind wir geboren
Auf, auf zum Kampf, zum Kampf!
Zum Kampf sind wir bereit
Dem Karl Liebknecht, dem haben wir's geschworen
Der Rosa Luxemburg reichen wir die Hand . . ."

[*Cincinnati, Ohio*]

It started off as a routine raid.

Keeping order in their city had been an easy enough task when the marshals could count on outnumbering any gathering of citizens, could count on responding to disturbances with over-whelming force; it was a simple matter of applying that force with precision, of knowing which squats to raid and which citizens to disappear. Easy enough, when they had the men and guns to pull it off, but for the past month the city's pool of law enforcement officers had been dwindling as more and more warm bodies were diverted to the campaign in the mountains, leaving only skeleton crews to maintain order in the BNR's teeming cities.

So the plan was to get out ahead of the problem. Two truck-loads of marshals bearing AR-10s and chips on their shoulders rolled across the Mill Creek bridge and into the teeming, riverside parts of the city where the more disposable and expendable segments of the city's population lived, stacked on top of each other in decaying apartment complexes, many of them pre-War relics, a ready supply of people who could be safely brutalized and whom no-one would miss. The plan was to raid one of the abandoned buildings where junkies and degenerates were known to congregate, get rid of the inhabitants, and cow the rest of the citizens into keeping their heads down.

They came expecting some level of resistance—the area's residents had major-league prospects when it came to rock-throwing—but met only silence, an eerie and threatening silence that reeked of potential, like the sky before a thunderstorm. The air around them reeked of smoke.

After they'd rumbled down the silent, empty street a ways, they turned a corner and found the source of the smoke: Where the road narrowed between two of the decaying tenements, just down the way from the squat they'd been planning to raid, a great confusion of old furniture and derelict vehicles and garbage had been piled high across the street, forming a barricade, and in front of the barricade was a line of barrels of burning trash.

The two trucks slowed down to take stock of the situation, and the residents at last showed themselves and broke their silence. People appeared on the rooftops, and bricks and rocks began to rain down ont othe marshals, many scoring good hits. The marshals retaliated, pointing their battle rifles at the rooftops and windows and popping off bursts of automatic fire. The residents started to melt away into the shadows, as they always did.

And the rifle fire was answered. Which was new.

The deafening crack of an archaic bolt-action rifle split the air, and one of the marshals pitched out of his truck and into the street, his head cocked back at a beautiful angle. Counterfire from the surrounding rooftops picked up in time with the bricks and stones, and the trucks backed up and attempted to egress to find that, during all the commotion, someone had stacked more burning barrels across the street behind them. One of the drivers attempted to ram the barricade, but a glass jug of kerosene and motor oil with a burning rag tied around it came hurtling down from one of the rooftops and shattered on the truck's cab in a lovely, viscous fireball. They did not get far.

The street was filled with a general mood of exuberance as the last marshal died and as the residents went about the work of collecting their Armalites and other kit and shoring up the barricades. The previous night, the shipments of coffee and tobacco came over the river with a few extra goodies, wooden crates that were monstrously heavy and reeked of cosmoline, and the plain-clothes DIS offers who always oversaw the trade stuck along for the ride, which was not unheard of. The Ohio Valley garrison had learned not to ask too many questions.

And one of those DIS officers stood on a field of victory surrounded by an expectant crowd of bums and criminals, lit a cigarette, and said, "So that went pretty fuckin well, if I do say so myself. How long y'all think we got 'till these assholes are missed."

"Maybe a half hour," one of the townsfolk ventured. "Maybe two hours, if we're real lucky. But, listen, what comes next? They're just gonna send more guys to come through and burn us out."

"Oh, they're gonna try, but they're gonna half-ass it. Our friends are a bit preoccupied; like I done told y'all, shit like this is gonna start popping off all along the border over the next couple days, and we got time to stack the deck. We build stronger barricades, spread the word, get these poodle-shooters handed out, and we'll really be onto something. If you wanna meditate on grand strategy, I recon we ought to seize some streets down towards the river; once that's did, we'll have access to infinite food and ammo, and better guns. In the meantime, though, just worry about trapping and killing these dickheads. You shatter the illusion that they have a monopoly on armed force, make it clear that we're the law around here now, it lifts the spell and the whole motherfucker comes tumbling down like a house of cards. Easy peasy. Well, I mean, it ain't easy, but it's a plan."

One of them kicked a dead marshal and asked, "So what should we, like, do with 'em?"

"Oh, I got a few ideas. Y'know, back where I come from, we like to give the fuckers a taste of their own medicine."

"What does that mean?"

And the DIS officer's face broke into a sadistic grin, and they asked, "Anybody got a rope?"

[*West Virginia*]

Farley's men advanced through the hills to the thunder of guns, making excellent time. Though the flying columns were always there, like background noise, the enemy still didn't offer any resistance that could slow them down. The men were already tired and frayed, but that was nothing; they were advancing ahead of schedule, and in any case it was the nature of things for war to weed out the weak and to purge all that is base. The weak and degenerate and cowardly would fall, and those who stood in triumph over the burning cities and reeking bodies of their foes would be the strong, would be those who were worthy.

And the scouts that Farley had sent out to crawl around the mountains and keep the flying columns busy and keep eyes on the enemy were reporting back with less and less frequency, but that also was nothing. Soon the first leg of their campaign would be complete, and the enemy would fall before their momentum.

The blackshirts still in contact reported that the ACR's regular army was mustering in the valley around Louisa, where he planned to cross the next river and begin the march into Ashland canton. But that, too, was nothing. The prudent course would be to divert, to force a river crossing to the north or south where fewer of the enemy were mustered, and use the unmatched speed of his advance to confuse and scatter them further. But this, Farley thought, was not the time for prudence. This was the time for action, and if the enemy were so determined to all die in one spot, well, that suited him just fine. He would crush the enemy in a single stroke, and expected the war to be over in a couple of weeks.

And word had come down from Columbus that Rain approved of Farley's initiative and daring, and that the only one who'd dared raise a fuss in the Oberkommando was Stockdale, a yellow coward who'd immediately been transferred to the western front. Capitulation had been expected, of course, but for it to come so quickly told Farley that perhaps dear old Roland was even weaker than he'd thought. So Roy Farley stoked his ambitions as the invasion force stormed southward; he would lead a successful crusade, exterminate their enemies, double the size of the New Republic, return home a hero, and then . . . and then, perhaps, he would take the opportunity to measure the worth of the sanctimonious old blowhard who called himself Commander.

The vanguard made contact with the Ashlanders' regular army in the hills around Louisa and the Big Sandy River just as the rear echelon radioed in that the last detachment of troops had crossed the Ohio River. Excepting those lost to the flying columns, Farley now had near to a quarter million men under arms inside of Ashlander territory. A hammer with which to crush the enemy.

As the two sides began exchanging mortar and sniper fire ahead of the main assault, word trickled in that the flying columns in the mountains were attacking more frequently and with more vigor.

Farley ignored these reports; a wolf shouldn't care about being bitten at by a few fleas.

In the vanguard, he met with his officers close enough to the assault corridor to hear bullets whipping through the air and to feel the ground shake under their feet as mortar shells detonated, and Farley asked one of his men, "They're dug in pretty deep over there, huh?"

"Yessir," the officer replied. "Artillery placements and SAM sites up on the hills, rifle pits in the town, all that. Looks like they're real determined to die here. Gonna be some work burning 'em out."

"We need to keep advancing to maintain our momentum. What's armor and air support look like?"

"Bad terrain for all that, boss. We gotta do somethin about those hilltops before we can really play with our toys."

"Alright. Send word to my forward commanders. I want a full infantry assault. We go over the top in ten minutes."

"... What?"

"Did I fucking stutter? Momentum is on our side. We drive those cowards out of their holes and we advance over their broken bodies. This is war, soldier, and by God I love it when war gets ugly."

"Uh ... yes, sir. Whatever you say, sir."

As the orders were sent down the line, a signalman came running toward the huddle of officers, shouting, "Yo! Is Farley here?"

"Right here, son," Farley said. "What have you got for me?"

"Sir! There's been an attack on our rear. They're saying it's too big and too sustained to be another flying column."

"Where the fuck did that come from?"

"East, sir. Reports say they're flying black flags. Sounds like the reds managed to whip up their pet bandits."

Roy Farley grimaced in determination. Turning back to the other officers, he growled, "Full advance. Momentum is over-whelming right now; we break the fuckers over our knees here and now before we turn around and worry about some hillbillies. This is where they've concentrated their strength, and here is where we're gonna break them."

The advance through the town and up to the bank of the river was expensive. The mangled bodies of men in brown shirts lay piled like cordwood amongst the smoldering ruins of the town, accompanied by the burned-out husks of tanks and trucks and APCs. The attackers advanced slowly, ponderously, with every second of exposure inviting fire from mortar teams and unseen marksmen, and behind them their officers and war clerics goaded them ever forward, into death. The inexorable weight of their numbers drove the advance, but it was slow, ponderous, and expensive, with the reds charging a steep price for every inch.

The men advancing to the riverbank balked at the prospect of crossing the river under fire and took it upon themselves to dig in and wait for fire support to come up from the rear, even as their officers urged them to keep advancing. Behind the ruin of one of the brown hempcrete tower blocks, a company of brownshirts had gone to ground to await support. Support was not forthcoming, and the company commander motioned for his men to form up and keep moving to the river, to overwhelm the enemy by the inexorable weight of their momentum.

Nobody moved.

A war cleric stood up, his black vestments billowing in the wind, and he raised his arms high over his head and boomed, "Get up, you damned cowards! There is fighting yet to do!"

A sea of red eyes and tired, dirty, bloody faces glowered up at him and said nothing.

"Is this what they give us to fight with? A rabble of degenerate yellow cowards? If you are men, get up and be men, and be heroes, and fight! Our cause is righteous and God is on our side! Do you doubt His will? Get up, you cowards, and for the race, for the faight, for the nation, get out there and butcher those godless muds! Are you men or not?"

In the days afterwards, nobody was ever quite sure who did it, but from somewhere in the rear of the company, a shot rang out—the distinct crack and whip of an Armalite—and the war cleric reeled and fell to the ground with a yawning, bloody hole in his throat.

On the other side of the river, a sniper and spotter marking the enemy's positions watched one white flag go up, and, a moment later, another. The sniper blinked a few times and muttered, "Huh."

"Huh," the spotter, a commissar, agreed. "Well, that's ahead of schedule. I thought they'd at least make it over the river."

From over the river, they could hear the tattoo of automatic rifle fire rising to a new crescendo, but no browhsirts emerged to bound towards the river, and none of the fire seemed to be directed at them.

"Huh," the sniper repeated.

The commissar put their binoculars away, reclined against the parapet, and lit a cigarette. "Mmhmm," they pontificated. "That's conscripts for ya."

[*The next evening; Columbus, Ohio*]

Two general officers and a war cleric stood outside of the door to the Oberkommando war room, steeling themselves to go inside. They looked back and forth at each other for a long moment, fear and determination in their eyes, before opening the door and striding into the meeting in progress.

Rain was pacing around the table, the picture of command in his immaculate black uniform, bellowing orders at those watching as he spoke on the unfolding situation in Cincinatti, his flinty eyes daring them to dissent, while in the back corner the tall, doll-eyed woman whom nobody ever seemed to acknowledge sat the note-taker's table, her typewriter rattling like a chain gun.

The tree men stopped at the edge of the table and the war cleric stepped forward. During a lull in all the hollering, he cleared his throat and barked, "Sir! We've, uh . . . we have news."

"Jesus Christ, what now?" the Commander grumbled.

"We've, ah, we've been in communication with Farley's staff officers, sir."

"And? What about it?"

The three men looked back and forth at each other with fear playing across their eyes. The war cleric sighed and said, "Farley encountered stiff resistance after completing the first leg of the plan, sir. He's, ah, still trying to make the second river crossing. And, ah, while he was engaged there, the enemy took advantage of the confusion to pull off a successful flank. He's been cut off from the rear, sir. He's been cut off from the rear several times; sending men to reopen supply and communication requires taking pressure off of the reds in Kentucky. Farley . . . Farley has allowed the Bolshevists to encircle him, like Hannibal at Cannae."

"Good Lord. Go ahead and send a detachment to reopen lines of supply. I'm authorizing it."

"Sir, um . . . we . . . We don't have any more detachments to send."

". . . What?"

"We threw everything we had into the invasion, sir. It's over a third of our strength; over a third of the manpower we can possibly muster is kettled in the mountains. Relieving Farley will mean either diverting troops from the western frontier or diverting troops from handling the growing civil unrest, neither of which is possible. We just have too many irons in the fire. On the ground, the officers report that our new conscripts are deserting in frightening numbers; attrition in the new units is something close to one in three. Sir, our . . . our greatest advantage over the Bolshevists was always our superiority in numbers, but Roy Farley has soundly thrown that away."

"What the hell are you trying to say, soldier?"

"It's . . . it's over, sir. Our man on the ground chose high drama over sound strategy, and it's cost us. Unless we're willing to just write off a quarter million men, you . . . you need to contact Ashland start discussing terms for a ceasefire."

A silence fell over the war room. Rain's face started to contort with rage, but he took a deep breath, calmed himself, and—faster than anyone could quite register—drew the Colt out of his jacket and shot the war cleric in the face.

Amidst all the jumping and gasping, he bellowed, "I won't tolerate treason in *my fucking war room.* This kind of talk right here is why great nations lose wars. Now, one of you go find a fucking detachment, I don't care where you get it from, and go reopen Farley's lines of supply. Now."

And, as a few people jumped up to carry out the order while the rest stood staring in shocked silence at the dying man on the floor, he pinched the bridge of his nose and grumbled, "I'll be in my office."

The sex was especially good that night, as was often the case when he was so angry. Afterwards, Tasha lay panting on the floor, trying to catch her breath as another aftershock washed over her, and he lay a bit off to the side, puffing one of his cigars and watching her in that odd way that he always did.

"If it puts you in this sort of mood, darling," she cooed, "I wish someone would speak seditiously to you every night."

He brooded and said nothing.

"And the way you handle those fools is always a wonderful sight to see."

"Do I handle them, Natasha?"

"Of course you do, dear. You are our Commander; you command, and the rabble obey."

"Sometimes . . . y'know, sometimes it feels like I'm slipping. First Stockdale, and now this."

She threw her arms around him. "They're nothing compared to you, darling. They're foolish and weak; they lack your strength and the courage of your convictions. You are the Commander for a reason, and you came to be where you are through iron and blood and the strength of your will; I was there to see it from the beginning. I watched you earn the right to command as we were forged in war. No-one can deny that."

He chuckled. "Yeah, that's why I keep you around. You may be a freak, but you're good for at least three things."

"I do my duty as God has ordained, darling." She sighed and kissed his cheek. "Indeed, going to war with you all those years ago . . . that, really, was when I fell in love with you."

He shrugged out of her arms. "When you what?"

"When I saw you for the man you truly are, my love. I love you, Roland, with my whole heart; I always have."

"God, you're a piece of work."

Her smile twitched around its edges. "But, darling, I thought that--"

"You thought what, Tasha? Tell me what."

"Well, all these years . . . all these nights . . ."

Rain stood up and stretched. "You really are something else, Doc. You think being a useful pawn and a good fuck makes you special? Hell. I keep you around because you're useful, Doc; if I were you, I'd cut this crap out and keep being useful."

"But . . . but our first, lovely night, after I saved Eddie--"

"You mean when I threw you against a wall and rammed my cock up your ass? I was happy you didn't start crying about it afterwards, but maybe that woulda been better. You're a piece of ass, Tasha, and that's all you'll ever be; a political token and a piece of ass."

Tasha sat up, heaving beneath the weight of her entire world-view as it came tumbling down on top of her, and she stammered, "But . . . but for all these years . . ."

"We were friends? Hell. Nick was my friend, but Nick's been dead for a long time now. I don't know you."

At that, she sprung to her feet, and her perpetual smile cracked into a sneer of murderous rage. Rain recognized that sneer, and in it he saw echoes of the old Doc, the combat medic, the snake-eater. He readied himself.

With murder in her voice and tears streaming down her cheeks, Tasha growled, "Oh, *how dare you!* How the fuck dare you say that, Roland? You would not be where you are were it not for me! I have been dutiful, I have been obedient and inoffensive and endlessly helpful, and you cannot treat me like a--"

Killer though she was, she was too put out, too distracted to quite notice the clenched fist flying towards her left eye. The instant it struck, he followed up with a kick to her stomach, dropping her to her knees, then a knee to her face, dropping her into a heap on the floor in front of him. Towering over her, he put a foot on her neck and growled, "You're forgetting your place, Doc."

"This can't be," she wheezed, her face a mess of blood and tears. "I . . . I did everything I was supposed to do . . . I was *good* . . ."

"Shut the fuck up. You're not my girlfriend, and you're not my friend, and you're only here because you're useful. If you want to keep being a sniveling bitch and quit being useful, don't forget that I still owe Roy Farley your neck. He'll love that, y'know."

"But I was good . . . I did everything I was supposed to do . . . I was *good* . . ."

"Get up and get the fuck out of my office."

Natasha took in a deep breath and collected herself as best she could. Sitting up, she looked up at him, smiled, and said, "Yes, sir. Right away, sir."

And she pulled her clothes back on, left the office, left the compound via the back entrance, and made her way across the street, desperately willing herself not to think, not to think about what had just happened, not to think at all. In her own room in her own little domain, she sat alone in the darkness, trying her very best not to brood, to avoid allowing Rain's words to pierce her defenses. She sat at her desk in silence, tears streaming down her face, trying to convince herself that the exchange had not happened, for several hours until, late in the night, there came a knock at the door.

"*I am indisposed!*" she snarled.

There was a long, pregnant pause before a once-familiar yet half-forgotten voice called out, "Hey, Doc, you, uh . . . you got a minute?"

Cocking an eyebrow, she got to her feet and walked over to the door, opening it to reveal a middle-aged man in a black shirt with a lieutenant colonel's palms on its lapels. They stood considering each other for a beat before she asked, "Eddie? Eddie Stockdale?"

The blackshirt nodded. "Been a while, ain't it, Doc?"

"Oh, come in, come in, dear! Come, please, have a seat. What can I do for you?"

"I'll just be a second. I don't have very long."

And, taking the offered seat, he stared at her for a long, awkward moment before sighing and saying, "I don't . . . I don't know what to think about, well, this whole situation--" He gestured to all of her. "--and I'm probably signing my own execution order by coming here to talk to the head snitch. But maybe you remember, a lot of years ago, I was a gunnery sergeant and you were a corpsman-lieutenant and one day you dug a bullet out of my ribs. You remember that day, Doc?"

"Of course, dear. But what are you saying?"

"I'm saying I owe you a debt, and I'm a man who pays his debts."

"I'm afraid I still don't follow, dear."

Eddie Stockdale looked down, pinched the bridge of his nose, and drew in a deep breath. Looking up again, he met her eyes and said, "Something . . . something really big is happening out there in the world right now, and something here is going to change in a big bad way pretty soon, and your dad quit protecting you a long time ago, and Rain isn't gonna be able to keep protecting you for much longer. Those two black eyes and that busted nose makes me guess that you might know that already. You . . . you need to get out of Columbus, Doc. And you need to do it soon. If you've got two brain cells to rub together, you'll do it tonight."

"Eddie, what the fuck are you saying?"

"Just what I said. I said what I came here to say, and as far as I'm concerned I've paid back whatever I owe you, even though I'm probably gonna hang for it if you can't keep your mouth shut, which I know you can't. Goodbye, Doc. If we're both real lucky, we'll never see each other again."

And, with the finality of a man walking to his own execution, Eddie Stockdale stood up, walked out, and left the corpsman alone to brood.

[34]
DOWNFALL

[Four months later; Marion, Indiana]

EVER SINCE ASSUMING HIS NEW COMMAND, THE WAR HAD been going about as well as Stockdale had expected. Roy Farley, who had always been a true believer and always been a cowboy, had remained true to his nature and followed mystical horseshit rather than good military sense, commandeering their invasion force and leading it on a great heroic campaign; the Bolshevists, as Bolshevists down through history were known to do, had collapsed back into the mountains to defend their territory in depth, and so Land's End had become a proper Vietnam, with the two forces playing an endless game of keep-away with Farley's rear lines of support as the butcher's bill grew ever steeper. The largest force they'd ever assembled, a force that would've been able to storm the mountain strongholds and burn Ashland to the ground if sensibly led, was bottled up in the hills and dwindling away.

It would've been a salvageable situation, if it weren't for Rain's infatuation with Farley's bravado—the Commander refused to listen to any criticism of his old war buddy, even as the situation fell apart in front of him—and the pressures of having so much manpower tied up. Cincinnati was on fire, and Dayton was catching, and the dregs of the New Republic—degenerates, criminals, women, the working poor—were taking up rifles and declaring so-called "liberated zones," which fell to any determined assault, if only they could muster enough assault groups to put out the fires faster than they spread. And most of those rifles were Ashlander rifles, and the unrest in Cincinnati created an open line of supply. Things in the east were not quite so bad as in the south, but the fire was spreading; bands of Freesider wasteland rangers moved freely between the exclusion zone and Zanesville, spreading sedition, raising their black flags and declaring more of their damned "liberated zones" in parallel with their red cousins. Stockdale pictured a map of Ohio in his mind, and thought that, eventually, these two conflagrations were going to spread towards each other, south of Columbus and the Falange's base of power, and meet somewhere around the Scioto Valley, and then Farley and his quarter million men—or however many he had left—would be on their own indeed. It was only a matter of time.

And things in the west managed to be worse. With so much manpower tied up elsewhere in theaters that the Oberkommando considered to be just so much more important, the savages had ascended to new heights of belligerence, managing to accomplish something that had eluded them for five hundred years: Pushing the border east. Flying columns of infantry and technicals and soldiers and horseback moved almost unopposed through what had been Blacklander territory mere weeks ago, and they had right away graduated from raiding to steal supplies and destroy detachments in detail to directly engaging the enemy. And the Blacklanders melted away like snow in the sun, and the enemy moved freely and seized one settlement after another. Fort Wayne in the north had fallen within weeks of the renewed offensive, and in the south they moved as far as Union City and the 127 corridor, and now little Marion—which, one short season ago, had been a little nowhere place where seditious generals were sent to fade away into irrelevance—was now at the very uncomfortable tip of a swiftly shrinking salient.

The collapse of those settlements along the St. Joseph River was due in large part, they'd learned, to the brigade of deserters operating out of the west. The enemy seemed to operate ten steps ahead, with perfect intelligence, able to anticipate their every move, and the existence of this brigade had become a whispered legend amongst the Blacklanders' conscripts and regular forces, and their detachments would abandon their posts and melt away into the prairie at least as often as they were defeated militarily. Stockdale had learned that the brigade was organized and commanded by an assault group leader who'd disappeared from the Greenville garrison a few years previous, and that he was being assisted by the very same gangly red-haired faggot who'd sabotaged their original plan, and Stockdale imagined that that information might be useful to somebody who gave a fuck. He had other, more pressing concerns, and figured that he'd been the field marshal of this district for about long enough.

He'd taken the measure of his men and determined who could be trusted. His brother, a battalion commander, had done the same back in Columbus. Everything was in place; they only awaited the grand arrival of their new Provisional Commander.

The biggest obstacle, at the moment, was the war cleric. Peter Wenden put Farley to shame as a true believer, and he took well to his task of riling up the people's bloodlust and stoking the fires in their hearts for the holy crusade, which was rich coming from a boy who'd likely never been in a bar fight before. Stockdale almost wished that the entire Dustwalker Confederation might turn its attention towards Marion, if only to give little Father Pete a measure of what he kept asking for.

The main issue with Wenden wasn't just that he was irritating, though he certainly was. Wenden was an obstacle because he was Daddy's boy and an enthusiastic snitch. The padre sent reports back to Columbus and the Ecclesiarchy almost daily, reports that would find their way to Rain's desk in due time. So the padre was a roadblock that would need to be cleared before things could proceed, and that was a shame; Stockdale hated the little ingrate, but he mused that Father Elias could've made a useful ally. *So-wie-so*; he supposed that snitching and stupidity must run in the family.

When James Stockdale received word from his brother in Columbus that it was time to act before the situation deteriorated any further, going through with his leg of the plan proved almost suspiciously simple, owing to the padre's bloodlust. Eddie's message came on the heels of reports of enemy troop movements down from Fort Wayne, and the instincts he'd honed over a lifetime of war told him that this would likely be it, the beginnings of a real push to annex the district east to the 127 corridor, a couple of days' hard riding from the Columbus suburbs. His available forces numbered about one hundred regulars and fifty blackshirts, which might be enough to meet the attack, but the enemy could count on reinforcements while he could not; the summer's campaigning had soundly turned the tables.

Stockdale picked twenty Arditi to take with him, out of the eighty he'd arrived with and the fifty who were left. The rest, along with the regulars in their hideous shit-brown uniforms and, he made sure, the war cleric, he ordered north to investigate those troop movements. The war cleric was so excited, so eager for his very first taste of the bloodshed he so idolized that Stockdale would've felt bad for the kid if he weren't so goddamned irritating. Must run in the family.

In late evening, once the detachment was on its way north, Stockdale and his picked men loaded into two of the unused trucks and, hopefully unnoticed, hit the road east, hoping to put an end to all of this before it was too late.

Stockdale, of course, was a stormtrooper and an old hand as much as was O'Shea, and he'd anticipated that a small detachment heading north into the gathering dark would be too tempting a target for the bandits to pass up. They hadn't made it very far into the prairie before a rifle's crack split the still night air and one of the brownshirts went down, his head snapping back at a sickening angle. As the group went to ground, more fire hammered into them from unseen attackers in the darkness, seeming to come from everywhere at once, and the blackshirts—blooded professionals—recognized an ambush when they saw one and, without a word to the others, split up into fire teams and disappeared into the night. Those would make trouble, but they were too few for the trouble to count for much, and as the others watched them go, the group's will to fight was already broken before they'd seen the enemy.

Peter Wenden lay still on the ground, keeping a white-knuckle grip on his battle rifle, willing himself to move, to get up, to fight, but his body would not obey. Every noise in the darkness deepened the terror that rooted him, and soon he ceased trying to stand, knowing that if he did, he would turn and run. He looked over and saw the man next to him rise up into a crouch and aim his rifle at something ahead of them, but he never fired. A shot whipped out of the darkness and caught the man just between the eyes, spraying Peter's face in red and grey chunks of gore as the back of his head ceased to exist. Peter threw his hands over his face and screamed, and he was still screaming when the shooting stopped. Recovering himself, he took a look around and saw that what was left of the group were kneeling on the ground while rough-looking men with righteous hatred in their eyes looked them over and relieved them of their rifles. The entire engagement had lasted perhaps twenty minutes.

So this, he thought, was war.

It had been a hot summer.

Mags had grown up fighting in the mountains, and the speed with which tthey moved across the prairies was almost too much to keep up with. The Dustwalker cavalry ate up miles like they had someplace to be, leaving the little infantry column to operate on its own, though they saw evidence of their allies' passage all around them in the burning buildings that lit up the night sky. They'd coordinated in a drive up the Wabash valley and into Fort Wayne, and that was hard fighting and bloody work, but the city had fallen after only a week of assaults; the fascists, mostly conscripts, had lost the stomach for war and were deciding en mass that they had better things to do with their time. As the Dustwalkers turned southeast and overran settlement after settlement, the eastern front was collapsing, with an open line of advance into Ohio presenting itself like a shank of raw meat in front of a hungry dog. If the reports of civil unrest in the south were even half correct, Mags figured that they'd be assaulting the Columbus suburbs within a couple of weeks.

Jules had become an instant celebrity in the brigade, who looked on her with reverence and referred to her only as "sister." They all knew better than to ask questions, but enough people had educated guesses about her that she gained an immediate reputation as someone too mean to die and not to be fucked with. She never got used to all the attention.

Mags was in her element, spending every free moment getting into spirited arguments with the partisans, going over the Soldiers' Bill of Rights—which all of them were very excited to learn existed—and bullying them into forming a shop committee. The partisans respected her for her reputation and came to respect her for her dead eye and steady hand, and she was listened to, even if they sometimes got lost in the politics. A few had taken to calling her "Mom."

The brigade had turned its attention south after the Fort Wayne campaign, and one night toward the end of summer they ambushed a Blacklander detachment in the trees just north of a medium-sized settlement which their maps called Marion. When the detachment surrendered, as they always did, and the partisans went about the work of disarming the enemy and explaining the score to them, one of them came up to Mags dragging a young man in a priest's robes by the scruff of his neck and barked, "Oi, Mom, we got a fuckin war cleric over here."

"Merc him," Mags said, without looking up. "We can't keep up with prisoners. Officers and war clerics get merc'd."

"Hold up," Jules said, looking over and giving the war cleric a funny look, like a dog being shown a card trick. She walked over to him, looked into his eyes for a long, uncomfortable moment, and asked, "Hey, padre, do I, uh . . . do I know you?"

"N . . . no, ma'am," he stammered.

"You look real fuckin familiar, and listen, looking familiar to me is real bad for your health. You got a name?"

"P-P-Peter," he stammered, too terrified to be defiant. "F-Father Peter Wenden."

Peter saw ice-cold hatred replace the confusion in her eyes. She turned away from him, looked up at the bandit holding him by the neck, and said, "Yeah. Get rid of him."

Over dinner that night, encamped in the prairies north of town, the brigade discussed strategy. As they hunkered around the cooking fire, O'Shea got a second helping of food and grumbled, "No way we can hold Marion. We can take it, easy, but no way we got the strength to hold it."

"Shit's been progressing a hell of a lot faster than anybody thought it would," Mags said. "We need to consolidate our gains and reinforce, or we'll be overextended."

"Word. Here's what I think: We go into Marion, liquidate what's left of the garrison, confiscate any war material, and then head back to Fort Wayne. About all we can do for the moment. I don't wanna ask for any more reinforcements from the Dustwalkers; they got their own shit to take care of."

"Hey, banditry is a perfectly valid revolutionary activity. But yeah, that sounds like a plan to me. Damn shame, though. What's the political situation in Marion look like, anyways?"

"Nah, Mom, that dog won't hunt," one of the partisans said. "I grew up in Marion. That place is fash as hell. I don't think they'd object to us passing through too much, but if we wanted to hold it, we'd definitely need a garrison."

"Hell. Well, I guess we knock it over and then head north to consolidate our base area. Only thing to do. You have any idea what the rest of the garrison looks like?"

Kitty, attached to the unit as an intelligence asset, spoke up then: "The last we heard was that it got reinforced by a company of blackshirts led by some guy named Stockdale. Major general, real bigshot, supposed to be very good."

"Can't be that good if he just marched half of his garrison into an ambush."

"About that," O'Shea said, "what we did here tonight felt too easy to me. I don't like it when things are too easy."

"Yeah, I felt that," Mags replied. "I almost got the feeling that we were the ones walking into the trap, but . . . ain't shit happened yet."

"Hmm. Maybe we were the trap."

"Wuzzat?"

"With the way this war's going, I reckon Rain ain't exactly the most popular guy anymore. I reckon there's all kinds of backstabbing going on over the lines. And this little ambush had four-dimensional chess written all over it."

"Yeah, that tracks. If there's one thing boneheads love, it's back-stabbig."

At that moment, the brigade signalman came up, tapped O'Shea's shoulder, and barked, "Hey, boss, we got somebody on the horn wants to talk to you."

"Alright. Who is it?"

"That purple-headed one from down south, ol' what's-her-name. Uh . . . Barlow."

He got up and disappeared into the darkness, but returned barely five minutes later with his usual sour expression replaced by a trickster's grin. "Hey," he said, "y'all remember what we was saying about things progressing ahead of schedule?"

The people around the fire nodded, and he went on: "So I just heard that the partisans operating out of Dayton have affected a breakout. There's fighting in the Columbus suburbs. Ashland is diverting troops from the whole Farley situation to come north and help deal with it. And Columbus is starting to evacuate, but most of the civilians ain't heading north. They're evacuating south, into the liberated zones. All this shit started happening about twelve hours ago."

They stared at him in disbelief, and his grin widened as he concluded: "So we got new marching orders. They want us to bypass Marion and head southeast. We're gonna be part of the final push."

At those words, Kitty began to laugh, and tears streamed down their face as the laughter turned into sobs. Jules put an arm across their shoulders and asked, "Hey, babe, you alright?"

"Jules," they gasped, catching their breath, "do you know what this means?"

"What's it mean, babe?"

"I'm going home. I'm going home!"

[*The next morning, a few hours before sunrise; Columbus, Ohio*]

She woke up in the small hours and knew she was being watched, but that was nothing new.

When she woke up in the dark, she felt the familiar sensation of not being alone, of a pair of eyes watching her out of the shadows.

And though she couldn't see the intruder, the room felt colder than it had when she'd gone to bed, and a distant part of her mind could almost sense an aura of malevolence radiating out of the darkness. She heard a footfall on the tile and focused in on it, and she saw a person-shaped shadow moving through the dark from the door to a far corner. She sighed loud enough for the intruder to hear, shrugged out of her blanket, and turned over to lay facedown on the bed, silent and still.

"Oh, Jesus," came a hissed whisper from out of the darkness, a woman's voice. "No, no, no, that's not—Oh, Jesus."

"Wait," Tabby muttered, her voice slurred with sleep. "So you're not here to . . ."

"Oh, good Lord, no."

"Wha--who the hell are you?"

"Alright, before we go any further, I wanna make sure I didn't just fuck everything up. Are you the esteemed Miss Tabitha Markhov?"

"Uh . . . yeah. How the hell do you know my name? Who are you?"

"Oh, thank fuck. Listen, you do not even know what I had to go through to find this place and get in here, and I was about to feel like a real jackass if I'd done all that and wound up in the wrong room. Listen, uh . . . I'm here to do a favor for a friend. A mutual friend. You remember Julia?"

At that, Tabby sat up, her eyes wide and her jaw dropping. "Wait, you . . . you know Jules? She's alive?"

And the intruder stepped out of the darkness, a short woman with long black hair and pale, sickly skin. "Hey, keep quiet," she hissed. "But yeah, she's out there. Well, I mean, she was out there as of a few months ago, last time I saw her. But yeah, she's fine. She has a girlfriend now and they're in lesbians together, it's adorable."

"Holy shit. She . . . she sent you here?"

"No, we're both busy doing war stuff and I haven't seen her in months. This is all my idea; that's what I do, I'm the big idea lady. Listen, I dunno how much you people can keep up with current events, but that whole 'war' thing has just gone completely buck wild and things are about to start getting really super weird here any day now. You need to get the hell outta here. I'm here to help."

"Help how? And how the hell did you even get in here?"

"Oh, I can do all kinds of cool shit. Moving around unseen in the dark is kinda my whole situation. Not to make it weird, but, uh, I'm like a dracula."

Across the street, in the war room, things were a bit tense. The cabinet had long since given up trying to suggest reasonable courses of action or to convince Rain of the realities of the situation at all, lest they be dismissed or—like the war cleric a few months previously—worse. Meetings of the war cabinet consisted mostly of the Commander bellowing orders to move around detachments of troops which no longer existed while his staff looked on in silence and waited for him to run out of words. Natasha sat at the note-taker's table for all of these meetings, every one, but had given up typing long ago and only stared straight ahead, the bruises on her face giving her already unsettling smile a ghastly look.

In the midst of the meeting, the door swung open and a soldier stepped inside and stood at rapt attention, waiting for a lull in the conversation. When one came, he barked, "Sir! Uh, James Stockdale is here. He says he needs to give a report."

"Stockdale?" Rain growled. "What the fuck is he doing here? He's supposed to be in fucking Indiana."

"He says he has a report to deliver on developments in the western front. He says it's good news, sir."

"Alright, send him in. And it had fucking better be good news, for his sake."

Overhearing this, Tasha felt a goose walk over her grave. She thought about what the younger Stockdale brother had told her, on that night when everything started to go wrong, and she wondered if she'd made the right choice in keeping that conversation a secret, and for half a moment she considered jumping up and warning the Commander that something wasn't right. Instead, while he and the others were looking elsewhere, she calmly, quietly got up and walked out of the room.

The summons was answered by the sound of running feet clapping across the tiles down the hall, coming closer. Soon the footfalls were accompanied by gunfire, and James Stockdale did not enter the war room, but ten of his men did. Ten Arditi ran into the chamber and, with the calm of blooded professionals, they faced the assembled war cabinet, raised their battle rifles, and opened fire.

On the other side of the building, the brothers Stockdale sat in the Oberkommando's comms station, waiting for the gunfire to cease. The encrypted UHF radio in front of them was tuned to a special, designated frequency, one that had only been used a handful of times over the past seventy years.

When the shooting moved outside, James put on the headset, took a deep breath, closed his eyes, and broadcast, "This is the Provisional Commander of the Blackland New Republic, transmitting on the diplomatic channel. Is anyone on this channel? Over."

Only a couple of seconds passed before a response came, a woman's voice growling, "What the fuck do you want, boot boy?"

"Uhh . . . May I ask who I'm speaking with? Over."

"Barlow, lieutenant colonel, ACR Department of Intelligence and Security. And which the hell one are you?"

"Major General James Stockdale. May I, um . . . may I speak with one of your superior officers? Over."

"Absolutely not. Christ, it's been seventy years and you boneheads still don't know how our chain of command works?"

"I, uh, I'm afraid I don't follow you."

"If I went and pulled Jimmy Mahon out of cold storage and put him on for you, he'd still have about as much authority to make decisions as I do; big stuff goes through the General Assembly. I'm the section chief of DIS, so I'm about as high up as you can expect to get right now at butthole o'clock in the morning. Either talk to me or quit wasting my time."

"Very well. As of roughly five minutes ago, Commander Roland Rain and his cabinet are dead. I'm here acting as Provisional Commander until we establish a new Oberkommando."

Barlow laughed long, hard, and loud. "Palace coup, eh? Well, it fuckin took y'all long enough, didn't it?"

"Indeed. I, uh . . . I . . ."

"Oh, come on, just say it. You know we love to hear it."

"I . . . I would . . ."

"Go ahead, you can say it. Be a big boy. I believe in you."

"I would like to discuss the terms of my surrender."

"There it is! Well, buddy, I'll tell you what the terms are: There fuckin ain't none. You will order all of your troops in the field to stand down, you will step down and cede control of the government to the partisans in revolt, and you and whatever's left of the Oberkommando will surrender yourselves bodily to us. You agree to that, we end the war tonight. You don't do that, and you've got maybe a couple weeks until our tanks roll down the streets of Columbus."

"That's . . . that's unacceptable!"

"Sure, dude. Say, you boneheads love Classics, right? Greece and Rome and whatnot?"

"Well, yes, but I don't see--"

"Try this one on for size: *The strong do what they will, and the weak suffer what they must.* Thucydides."

"Listen, I'm willing to order my men to stand down immediately, but I have terms that will need to be met. I want immunity for myself and my provisional cabinet, and--"

"Nah, buddy, that dog won't hunt. Maybe if you'd grown a backbone and done something about Rain a few months ago, we would have something to talk about. But now? You're done, man. If you can accept that, you can find a way out of this with your life. But if you can't accept that, well, I suggest you go find a Luger and go find a bunker and follow your leader. Now, I got a lot of shit to do; feel free to call me back when you wanna recognize realities. Over and out."

Stockdale took off the headset and sat staring into the middle distance for a long, tense moment before someone asked, "Well? What did they say?"

"We waited too long," he muttered. "They won't discuss terms at all. They will only accept unconditional surrender. Gentlemen . . . we may be fucked."

"Jimmy, what are we gonna do?"

"Finish . . . finish liquidating all of Rain's supporters. Figure out who we can count on. After that, I suppose we'll move operations to Cleveland. If we stay here and fight, we die, and if we surrender, we die."

The group nodded in solemn silence, and he added, "Speaking of Rain's supporters, did anybody find Wenden?"

"The Ecclesiarch?"

"No, the other one. The palace creature, the court eunuch. I want that thing found and I want it *removed*."

Natasha made it across the street just as the dark of night started to give way to the gloomy blue light of pre-dawn, intending to run up to her office and gather some things. She was almost there when Claire met her on the stairs, the younger woman's face twisted up in shock and confusion as she sputtered, "Ma'am, we . . . we have a problem. We have a *big* problem."

"I should certainly say so, dear."

"They're . . . they're gone."

"Who is gone?"

"Tasha, the girls are gone. The rooms are empty. They're not dead and they're not hiding, they're just . . . they're not here. I don't know how it happened and I don't know what's going and I don't know what to do, I don't know what to do. And did I hear shooting across the street a minute ago?"

As she asked the question, they heard three quick bursts of automatic fire from outside, and another answering volley.

Claire was expecting shock and rage, but instead the director only smiled and said, "Don't worry, darling. I'll take care of it. You just wait here."

And she walked into her room and ignored all of her treasures and finery as she hauled the dusty green foot locker out from under her desk, which contained the only things she'd ever really needed: A long steel combat knife, a Browning automatic, a green canvas messenger bag with a red cross embroidered on it, and a pair of tall, black boots. Hideous, she thought, but far more practical than heels. Her future, such as it was, would involve a lot of running. She stripped off her uniform and pulled another, less conspicuous outfit from her wardrobe.

As she left, she again told Claire to stay calm and wait for her to return. And she walked out of the front gate, and once she was out of sight, she began to run.

The city was exquisite chaos. She could hear gunfire all around her, and the air was thick with smoke. She ducked behind a building, down an alleyway, and found herself facing a throng of people, civilians, headed south with tired and desperate looks on their faces. She collected herself and joined the throng, trying to look as if she was supposed to be there.

After a few minutes of walking through a city consuming itself, one of the refugees looked at her, motioned to her messenger bag, and asked, "Ma'am, are you a doctor?"

"Ah, yes, I am, as a matter of fact."

"That's good. That'll probably come in handy."

"It often does. Ah . . . where are we going?"

"Bloomfield. There's an autonomous zone down there, across the lines, and the reds are giving people food and beds. We're getting the fuck outta here."

Natasha grimaced, feeling the weight of doom heavy on her shoulders, a noose tightening around her neck. She looked back and could see, just over the rooftops behind her, the top floor of the Oberkommando building, with flames billowing out of the windows.

"I hear they treat people good down there," the refugee said. "I don't know, but I've heard they treat people good."

"Yes," she sighed, "I've, ah, I've heard that as well. I suppose we can only hope."

MANY MEETINGS, PART 2

[Two weeks later]

The sea of refugees streaming south out of Columbus was easy to get lost in. Hostilities moved north as the enemy retreated, leaving behind a mire of confusion as the Ashlanders struggled to process so many masses of people. With the government's collapse, resistance had collapsed as well, with the enemy abandoning the city east of the river and south of the 104, and the refugees picking a slow and ponderous path into the south suddenly found themselves across the lines by default.

A group of soldiers encamped in the fields south of the 270, awaiting orders to move north, had set up a makeshift checkpoint where a long line of frightened, exhausted people queued up and waited to be told where to go. Over them, a hastily-erected speaker system played the same recorded message on repeat in a thick Kentucky accent:

"Everyone interested in resettlement within the liberated zones, please form an orderly line in front of the lady at the booth. Tell her

532 / NATALIE IRONSIDE

your name, occupation, where you're from, and how many people you're with, and she'll give you an ID card. That card entitles you to food, medical care, and a warm place to sleep. There's plenty for everybody, so the sooner this gets done the sooner we all get our three hots and a cot. Welcome home."

Maria rolled her eyes at the last sentence every time the message repeated. "Home" was a concept she'd left far behind her, and she found that she wasn't particularly excited about the promise of shelter and safety, that she was merely shuffling forward because that's what the people around her were doing. She didn't care. She'd found it harder and harder to care about things over the past few years.

The inprocessing booth was a tent containing a folding table and a box of cards. A young Ashlander woman in flecktarn fatigues sat behind the table with a notebook open in front of her, and when Maria walked up the Ashlander said, "G'morning, hon. What's your name?"

"Maria Moreno."

"Mmhmm. Where you from?"

"Somerset."

"Okey doke. Occupation?"

"Seamstress."

"Cool. Last question: You with anybody? Or is there anybody out there you're trying to meet up or reconnect with?"

She considered the question for a long, hard moment before saying, "No. No, it's just me."

"Aw, hell, I'm sorry. Well, hon, here's your card. If you go straight past me, there's food, and beds are to the left and medical to the right. Welcome home." And she handed her a square of red construction paper with a number and her name scrawled on it. Maria rolled her eyes.

The refugees intermingled with the encamped soldiers, Ashlanders in uniform and partisans in civilian clothes, but the camp didn't seem to have guards. Maria stepped off to the side, desperate to get out of the stifling crowd. Food sounded nice, she thought, but she'd been walking for days and felt tired deep down in her bones, and first she would find a quiet place away from all these people and sit for a while. As she walked, she tried to let herself feel relief at being in a new place, at being safe, but she felt nothing, only tired.

Away from the crowd, near an empty church, she passed by three soldiers sitting under a tree smoking and drinking coffee. One wore the Ashlanders' uniform without a blouse, and the other two were in civilian dress. One of those two, a small woman with long, dark hair wearing leather vest, caught her eye; she felt maddeningly familiar, in some way that Maria couldn't quite place.

The third, a person of indeterminate gender who looked quite out of place in the army camp, wearing a bright yellow sun dress and a straw hat, locked eyes with her, gasped, and nudged the small woman's shoulder. The small woman's eyes went big as plates, and her jaw dropped, and she threw her tin cup of coffee to the ground as she lept to her feet and came running over.

"Ma'am," she cried out, shaking, overflowing with excitement, "ma'am, I . . . I need to talk to you."

Maria stopped and squared up to her. "Do I know you? I'm sure I know you. Who are you?"

"Ma'am, are you . . . Is your name Maria Binachi?"

"No. My name is Maria Moreno. I haven't been a Binachi for a long time. Who are you, and how do you know that name?"

"Oh Christ, oh Jesus, ma'am, I . . . I . . . I have information about your son."

"You . . . you know my boy? Is he here? And who the fuck are you?"

"Maria, look at me in my eyes and tell me you don't know me."

And Maria's jaw dropped, and she threw her arms around Jules and held her tight, trying to speak, but only sobbing. Jules began to cry as well, and Maria gasped, "This . . . this isn't real. This isn't real."

"It's real, Mom. I swear to God, it's real."

"My baby . . . my little boy . . . Oh, baby, what the hell happened to you?"

"A lot of shit, Mom. A whole lot of shit. I . . . God, I wish I'd listened to you. You were right. You were right about everything. But I'm okay now."

"I didn't even recognize you, you're so . . . different."

Jules smirked. "You remember the last thing I said to you, the last time we saw each other?"

"'*I'm sorry I can never be the son you deserve.*' You're . . . you're not my son, are you?"

"I'm your kid, Mom, but I ain't your son. I was all torn up inside my whole life, but I'm not anymore, and my name is Julia."

"*Julia . . .*"

"I still go by Jules. I'm not your little boy, Mom, but I never really was. Can I be your little girl?"

Maria wiped the tears from her eyes and looked Jules up and down for a moment. And she looked her in the eyes and said, "I'm . . . I'm not sure what's going on, baby, but I do know one thing. I know that my son never smiled like that."

"He never had much to smile about. But your daughter smiles all the time."

"Is that right? Well, my daughter seems so much better off."

"I love you, Mom. God, I can't fucking believe you're here. Hey, listen, I . . . You see them two over there? The tall one is Magnolia, and she's my girlfriend and she's the prettiest, smartest woman in the whole world and I love her so much, and the other one is Kitty. You know Kitty, except for you used to know them by a different name, same as me."

All four of them grinned like kids at Christmas as Jules walked her over. Kitty gave her a wide grin and a friendly wave and said, "Hi there, Mrs. Binachi. Never thought I'd see you again."

Maria stayed with them through the day and long into the night, talking, laughing, crying, and catching up. After midnight, Maria and her daughter sat outside of the tent where they'd gone to ground for the night, exhausted but unwilling to part, as Mags and Kitty snored softly inside. Jules rested her head on her mother's shoulder, yawned, and said, "This still doesn't feel real, y'know?"

"I know, baby. I was so sure you were dead. I'd . . . kind of been coming to terms with the idea of never seeing you again."

"Oh, I feel that. I thought that the path I'd taken in life had cost me everything, but Kitty's here, and you're here, and Peterson's here—you haven't met him yet, but you'll love him, he's my best friend, I owe him everything—and it's nice. It's so nice. Maybe God does answer prayers after all."

"Your nana certainly thought so."

"She did. But what do you think, Mom?"

"I only ever had one prayer on my lips, and she's sitting right here next to me, but it sure did fucking take Him long enough."

"Heh. I feel that, too. Y'know, Mom, I kinda got a bad habit of asking questions I probably shouldn't, but I got one."

"What is it, baby?"

"Where's Dad at?"

Maria didn't answer, but her entire body tensed up and she drew in a quick, nervous breath. Jules read the truth written across her eyes, kissed her cheek, and said, "That's kinda what I figured. Maybe you and me ain't so different after all, huh?"

"Did anyone ever say we were?"

"Heh. I guess not."

"I'd hope not. You're definitely my daughter, and I'm proud of you. I just wish your nana was here; she would be so proud to meet the person you grew up to be."

"I like to think so. I wish she was here, too; there's lots of stuff I'd like to ask her about."

The two women sat together in silence for a while, watching the stars, until a soldier came walking out of the camp toward them. The soldier looked terrified, kept glancing back over his shoulder as he approached, and when he came up to them he asked, "Hey, uh . . . you're, uh, you're Jules Binachi, right?"

"Last time I checked," Jules replied.

"You've, uh . . . there's someone here asking to see you. She, ah, she says she's a friend of yours."

"Doesn't seem like she was too friendly to you, buddy."

"Well, she, ah . . . If you could come with me? Please?"

With a shrug, Jules got up and followed the soldier out into the darkness. He led her a few yards outside of the camp, where a lone figure stood in the shadows. As they drew close, Jules saw that she was a girl of about 20, wearing a pair of black jeans and a Mindless Self Indulgence t-shirt. Laughing, she pushed the terrified soldier aside and ran toward her, shouting, "You bitch! What the hell are you doing here?"

Becky put her hands on her hips, feigning shock, and said, "Well! Is that any way to greet your very best friend in the whole entire world? The nerve!"

They embraced, and Jules kissed her cheeks and asked, "No, really, what are you doing here? There's like a war happening."

"Oh, really? I didn't notice. I'm part of it, dumbass."

"Yeah? What they got you doing?"

"The hell do you think? Hunting."

"Wow, I'll bet. You must be giving 'em some serious Hell, huh?"

"I like to think so. But I also, well, I kinda did something special. I think it was a good idea. I hope it was a good idea."

"Watcha got?"

"Follow me."

Becky led her around the outside of the camp and back toward the north, toward the pool of refugees waiting to be processed, and Jules noticed a group of people standing off to the side. Leading her toward that group, Becky called out, "Oi! I got 'er!"

A figure broke away from the others and walked toward them, coming into view. She was a woman in her late 20s with long, curly hair, wearing an ill-fitting secondhand set of clothes, her head bowed low, her arms wrapped tight around herself. Looking up, she broke into a wide, delirious grin and ran forward, her arms outstretched.

Tabby almost tripped over Jules, who'd collapsed prostrate on the ground like a supplicant at the sight of her. She laughed and declared, "Oh my fucking God, it's true! You're alive! I can't fucking believe you're alive!"

Jules pressed her forehead into the ground and sobbed.

"Jules, hon, are you . . . are you okay?"

Jules started to look up, failed to meet Tabby's eyes, and wheezed, "T-Tabby . . . Tabby, I'm so fucking sorry . . . I'm so fucking sorry . . ."

"Huh?"

"Tabby, I'm so, so fucking sorry . . ."

Tabby knelt down and rested a hand on Jules' cheek. When Jules at last looked up, she smiled and asked, "Sweetheart, what the hell do you have to be sorry for?"

A ways up the road, within sight of the camp but far enough north to hear the sounds of battle raging, two Ashlanders walking along the line of refugees passed by a tall, blonde woman who looked just as exhausted and terrified as the others but stuck out in a much nicer set of clothes, wearing—incongruously—a long black spring tea dress, her face obscured by a wide black sun hat. The two soldiers gave her a funny look and started to walk on, but one of them froze in her tracks and grabbed her companion's arm, pointing the woman out again. They stepped forward in unison, and she barked, "Oi! Hey, lady!"

She let out a long, defeated sigh and slipped a hand into the green canvas trauma bag hanging from her shoulder. "Yes?"

"Take off the hat."

"I think that I would prefer not to."

"I ain't fucking asking."

Natasha looked over and found herself staring down the barrels of two Kalashnikovs. She froze for a moment, then sighed again, slipped an empty hand out of her bag, and removed her hat.

The Ashlander's face twisted into a sneer of hatred and malice, and she growled, "Holy shit, it is. It's . . . *you*."

"I gather that my reputation precedes me."

"Yeah, you could say that. Lady, what are you . . . what are you *doing* here?"

She shrugged. "I . . . I didn't know where else to go. Look at the state of me; I have nothing to go back to. I thought . . . I thought I would take my chances. I've heard that you Ashlanders are kind to people like me."

"Lady, I'm gonna need you to come with us."

"I think that I would prefer not to."

"Well, I ain't fucking asking."

The soldiers bound her hands behind her back and led her through the camp, into the old church at the edge of the field. They bound her to a chair in one of the backrooms, looked back and forth at each other for a beat, and one of them asked, "Okay, now what to do we do? I've never caught a VIP before."

The woman slung her rifle and lit a cigarette. "I'll keep an eye on her. You go out and find a political officer or one of those spooks from DIS. They'll know what to do."

"Alright. Anybody in particular?"

"Nah, don't matter. It's all to a standard."

As her companion started to leave, she grabbed his arm and said, "Hold up, I just got a real fuckin great idea."

"Yeah?"

"That unit that rolled in the other day. They've got Blackadder with them, right?"

"Oh, yeah. I'll go find Blackadder."

[36]

TRAPPED

When they were alone together, the Ashlander's demeanor changed as though a switch had been flipped. Leaning against the wall and yawning, she looked at Natasha and asked, "Hey, you want some food or water or something?"

Natasha blinked. "W--what?"

"You're like a Class B war criminal at minimum, so I can't free your hands, but we'll figure something out."

"Ah, no, thank you, I'm not hungry. But, ah . . . I would love a cigarette, if that's possible."

The Ashlander walked over, took the cigarette out of her own mouth, and placed it between Tasha's lips. She took a long, grateful drag and said, "Thank you, darling. I must ask, though . . . What the fuck is the point of all this?"

"Huh?"

"You're being quite hospitable."

"Well, yeah."

"And to what purpose?"

The Ashlander cocked an eyebrow and looked at her like a dog who'd just been shown a card trick for a moment, then nodded and said, "*Oooh,* you think that everybody in the world is fucked up like you are. Nah, lady; when you boneheads give us the luxury of taking prisoners, this is how we treat prisoners. The commissar should be here to process you any minute, but until then, just let me know if you need anything."

"If I'm to be shot, I wish you'd hurry the fuck up and get it over with."

"Well, that's entirely up to you, ain't it?"

Tasha rolled her eyes and said nothing, staring at the burning end of her cigarette. When it burned down to its butt, she spat it out and stared at her lap in silence, tears beginning to well up in her eyes.

After another few minutes, the door opened and a tall, red-haired woman who looked like she'd just been roused from sleep walked in holding a notebook and a tape recorder and said, "Thank you, comrade. I've got it from here."

"Right on, boss."

"Don't you dare cuss me like that."

The commissar smiled at the little joke, but Tasha recognized the look in her eyes: This woman was full of roiling hatred and malice. She pulled up a chair, took a seat, turned on the tape recorder, and with a long, frustrated yawn said, "Alright, this is political commissar Magnolia Blackadder, chief warrant officer 3, brevet lieutenant colonel, New Lawrence Militia I guess, conducting the initial and I'm gonna go out on a limb and guess the only interview with one Corpsman-Major Natasha Wenden."

Natasha examined her lap and said nothing.

"Now, Natasha, my chain of command has informed me in very clear and unambiguous terms that we don't believe in punitive justice and that summary execution without trial is not the way we do things, so here we are. However, full disclosure, the fact that they asked me of all people to take time out of my night to do this makes me think that they might not be quite as enthusiastic about that policy as my CO led me to believe when I was on the carpet the other day. You tracking?"

She looked up, then, and examined the commissar for a long moment, reading her clipped and business-like tone, her tense posture, and the gleam of murder in her eyes. "So I'm to understand that I'm not necessarily doomed, but that you would very much prefer it if I was. And that I should be on my best behavior because my life is in the hands of someone who has reason to hate me."

"Thereabouts. Our justice system works like this: The goal is to reduce the overall amount of suffering in the world and to make amends for past suffering. Removing you from the picture might accomplish that, or it might not; the choice is entirely up to you. And because we're in the middle of a war zone, and because your crimes are quite literally a matter of public record, mediating that choice is my job. You have two options, Natasha: Option one is that you disavow all of your previous actions and affiliations and cooperate enthusiastically, which might lead to clemency and rehabilitation. Maybe. Someday. You'll probably spend the rest of your life on some kind of house arrest, but I think you're used to being kept."

"And what, dare I ask, is option two?"

Mags drew her Nagant, pulled back the hammer, and laid it across her lap. "Option two is I spend my evening scrubbing your brains off of the inside of this booth. And if we're being up-front about everything, then sweetheart I really hope you pick option two."

"Ah, I think I understand now. You must be a friend of Julia's."

"Oh, we got Sherlock Holmes over here. So is that, like, your thing? Making simple, obvious deductions and acting like they're clever?"

"What exactly is it that you want from me?"

"You have one shot at convincing me that there's some scrap of good inside of you that's worth trying to salvage."

Tasha sighed and met Mags' eyes. "So you're here to play with your food, then. I gather that there's no sympathy for me here, and I suppose it's a waste of words to tell you about the bruises on my face, or my unhappy childhood. Indeed, I . . . I am tired, and I am spent, and I do not have the patience for the theatrics of lying any more than I would for begging. Perhaps this will save us both some time: I apologize for nothing."

"Figured you'd say that."

"Have I done terrible things? Perhaps I have. But I did what I had to do to survive."

"Did you really?"

"Yes! I did what I had to do. You have . . . you have no idea what I've been through. You have no idea what life in the New Republic is like for people like me."

"'People like you', eh?"

"If you know all about me, then you know what I am: A trans-sexual. I was always told that people like me were well-treated in Ashland. Is that not the case?"

"Oh, it is the case. It's so much the case that they even let us be political commissars and brevet lieutenant colonels."

"Oh! So you're . . . you're . . ."

"I am. I've known myself as a girl for as long as I can remember. I started my transition when I was 18. That was about six years ago."

"I never would've guessed."

"We have excellent medical services in Ashland, and anyways I've never really had to worry about that. About passing. When I accepted myself as a woman, my community already had; didn't matter what I looked like."

Natasha digested those words in silence for a long while. At last, she muttered, "I . . . I was nineteen when I couldn't take it anymore."

Mags nodded for her to continue.

"I always knew, but I didn't have words for it. I . . . I was a medical corpsman in the Arditi, but I never liked being a sawbones; my interest was always psychology. I found words for my condition in very old books, and I . . . I knew what I had to do. I talked my way into the criminal underground and I found someone to supply me with hormones. You . . . don't want to know what I had to do to pay for that. The effects were swift. My operating group noticed."

"Oof."

"Indeed. Many of my dalliances were consensual, to be sure, but I . . . I couldn't tell them no. They would've killed me, and after taking what they wanted anyway. I thought that the man I loved would protect me, and I suppose he did for a while, but, well, here we are."

"That's horrible. I'm sorry that that happened; nobody deserves that, not even you."

Natasha cocked an eyebrow. "Well, thank you, but that's . . . the last thing I expected to hear."

"And why's that?"

"A moment ago, you were talking about how eager you are to put a bullet in my head."

"Well, my eagerness to watch you die is a me thing, and I'll admit that it's reactionary. Suffering is pointless, and it definitely isn't justice. I can recognize that suffering is pointless and that what happened to you wasn't your fault while still recognizing that you're responsible for your other actions. More than one thing can be bad at a time."

"Your sympathy is appreciated, dear, but I don't accept that. I did what I had to do keep myself safe; I would be dead if I'd done anything different."

"Nah. Maybe that would hold water if it was only your own life you were playing with, but that's not what happened. No, I don't know what it was like up there, not personally, but I know people who know, and you've already named one of them. That dog won't hunt, honey."

"I don't accept that. I did nothing wrong. I did what I had to do to survive. And moreover, I am a scientist, a sexologist, and I leveraged my position to *help* women like us!"

"You have some funny ideas about what 'help' looks like. You supervised a prison labor camp. And I know we've established that suffering is pointless, but I gotta say: That's one of the most despicable things about you, that your idea of 'help' seems to be making sure that what happened to you also happens to as many more women as possible."

"I don't have to justify myself to you," she sneered.

"I'm not asking you to. In fact, I'm asking for pretty much the opposite."

"I will *not* sit here and justify myself to some self-righteous, Hebraic troon! You have no right to judge me, and I will face God's judgment knowing that I did the only thing I could've done."

Mags stifled a laugh. "I'm sorry, but . . . wow. Listen, I've had your name on my lips for months, and when they came and woke me up and told me they'd found you, I thought that I was gonna walk in here and come face-to-face with the embodiment of pure evil. But now that I've actually met you, you're so . . . boring. The embodiment of pure evil is a low-level government functionary with a rich daddy and no sense of personal responsibility. Or self-preservation, looks like."

"And what the fuck is that supposed to mean?"

"As much as I, as a person, would love to just merc you, I do report to a chain of command and I am responsible for my actions; I will have to justify whatever I choose to do tonight, one way or the other. That means that you could get out of this with your life if you could just look me in the eyes and tell me that you're vewy vewy sowwy for committing all those waw cwimes, Miss Magnolia. But you can't even do that, because of, what, pride?"

"What is it that you don't understand? *I did what I had to do!* Anyone would've done the same in my position! Anyone!"

"I can think of several people who were and who didn't. You've already named one of them."

"Oh, *her*," she growled, with an edge of hatred in her voice. "Oh, I think I know what's going on here; I think I've found the real root of your animosity, and why those other two knew to find you by name. That's it; she fled out of my care and into your arms."

"Oh, looks like Sherlock Holmes is back."

"And did she tell you about her past? All the terrible things she's done? All the men she's killed?"

"Naturally. You might say that she did exactly what you're refusing to do."

That gave Natasha pause, and her failure to rattle Mags rattled her in return, and after a moment she muttered, "Is . . . is she here?"

"Yup."

"Ah . . . Can I see her? I would, ah, I'd like to see her again."

"No, you may not. And that's not my call, either. Hell, I'll tell you a story: When they came and got me, I was with her, and we told her, 'Hey, if you wanna, like, take care of her, we won't say anything.' She thought about it for a minute, and then she said, 'Nah, that bitch ain't worth the trouble of cleaning my knife.' So here I am, alone, and here you are, breathing. And whether you take the offer or not, one thing's for sure: You're never going to hurt her again."

"Oh, that traitorous, ungrateful *bitch!* I gave her everything! I drew her up from perdition! I saved her, saved her from a fate worse than death! I gave her a new life! And you . . . How dare you? How the fuck dare you--"

"Yeah, I think we've gotten our answer. Fuck this; I'm going back to bed."

A moment later, Mags walked out of the church. The soldier she'd relieved was waiting outside; she offered Mags a cigarette and said, "Well, I guess that's done with."

"Yeah. Yeah, I guess it is."

"How are you feeling, sweetheart?"

"I'm okay. Like, I got what I wanted."

"I'd say that that went okay."

"Nah," Mags said, extracting the spent shell casing from her revolver and giving the chambers a spin, "I wouldn't say that. But it sure went."

EPILOGUE: SNOW AFTER FIRE

"The faggots and their friends live the best while empires are falling. Since the men are always building as many empires as they can, there are always one or two falling and so one or two places for the faggots and their friends to go."

- LARRY MITCHELL, ***THE FAGGOTS AND THEIR FRIENDS BETWEEN REVOLUTIONS***

"Roads go ever ever on
    Under cloud and under star,
    Yet feet that wandering have gone
    Turn at last to home afar.
    Eyes that fire and sword have seen
    And horror in the halls of stone
    Look at last on meadows green
    And trees and hills they long have known."

- —TOLKIEN

[AD 2263; Kentucky]

"The thing about roses," Jules said as she lifted up another spadeful of rotted manure and eggshells, "the thing about roses is that they're prissy little bitches. They develop issues if you look at 'em too hard, and your soil is always gonna be deficient in something, so the most important part of growing roses is soil health."

Iris sat on the ground nearby, watching her like an acolyte watching a spiritual master, and nodded along. Jules spread the contents of the shovel around the base of the rosebush and added, "And they're also real sensitive; you can't use hot manure to fertilize because it's too rich and they'll get overwhelmed. These here are brier roses, so they're a lot tougher than the ornamental varieties, but they still need their love and attention just like anybody."

"Sounds like a lot of work," Iris mused.

"Oh, it sure is, but it's all worth it in the end. See these flowers? Brier roses aren't even supposed to bloom this rich, but I can do it 'cause I know how to talk to 'em."

She wiped the dirt and sweat from her bare forearms, which were covered in swirls of stars and gnarls of black brier roses, and she plucked one of the flowers and handed it to Iris. Iris took it, grinned, and said, "I really like gardening with you, Julia."

"Call me Jules. And I really like having you here, kid; you're smart as fuck, and hey, you keep me young."

Iris laughed, and Jules said, "No, really, I mean it. You . . . Hell, maybe when you're older, I'll tell you all about why having you around is such a big deal to me. How old are you now, anyways?"

"I'm 14."

"Kid, let me ask you something: Do you even remember being a boy?"

She shrugged. "Not really. As soon as I got old enough to know

how boys and girls are different, I knew which one I was supposed
to be. I'm just Iris."

"You sure are. Y'know, kid, if I told you about how I grew up, I
bet you wouldn't even believe me."

"Probably not."

"Ha! 'Probably not,' she says. You really do give me life, kid."

"I'd like to hear about it, though; seems important. Will you be
back here tomorrow?"

"Nah. I'm taking Mags on a little trip to see Kitty and my mom.
We can hang when I get back, though."

"Y'all taking the Triumph?"

"Of course. Only way to travel."

"You gonna teach me how to drive it one of these days?"

"Later, kid. I don't think you're tall enough yet."

"I'm almost as tall as you are, Shortstack."

"Ah, *stronza!*"

A ways off, Mags and Lilly sat together in the grass, watching
them through the trees as bees buzzed around them. Lilly reclined
back onto her elbows and said, "Y'know what that is? That is one
whole ecologist. I'm glad you found her for me."

"Yeah," Mags said in a faraway voice, her face split in an easy
smile. "Yeah."

"God, you two are adorable. Y'all gonna make it to the show
tonight?"

"Nah. Soon as she's done playing in the dirt, we're heading to
Somerset to see her mom and our partner for a couple days."

"Oh, nice. How's that going, anyways?"

"Pretty good, I think. This long-distance thing sucks and I wish
they were here, but y'know what? It's nice to have an excuse to
travel."

"As if a massive dyke like you needs an excuse to go on a run
with her cool biker girlfriend."

They laughed together, and Lilly added, "Y'know, this is nice.
How long have we known each other, sweetheart?"

"Hell, my whole life."

"Your whole life. We were kids together. And we've never really, y'know, talked before."

"We talk all the time, though."

"Yeah, we talked about social ecology and soil toxicity levels and shit like that. You were Comrade Commissar and it was all work, work, work every waking minute. We never had, like, conversations until you two came home."

Mags shrugged. "I guess I had a couple of missing pieces."

"Hey, you probably shouldn't put that kinda weight on your partners."

"Nah, nah, that's not what I meant. I meant . . . I had a couple of missing pieces, and she's been there to help me find them."

"Hey, Mags?"

"Yeah?"

"That was exquisitely gay."

A minute later, Jules came up to them, leaned her shovel against a tree, and asked, "You ready to hit the road, sugar?"

"Hell yeah. Just one more thing I wanna do."

She took Jules by the hand and led her a few yards down a trail, deeper into the forest. Nestled in amongst the hawthorns and laurels was a little clearing, one of the few places in the Republic where the grass was kept short. An azalea bush grew in the center of the clearing, and to the left of it sat a block of marble about one foot square. The humble, unadorned block bore a simple inscription:

LAURELEI BLUECROW
B. 2158, B. 2173, D. 2222

MAXINE REYEZ
B. 2155, D. 2221

MARRIED 2188

FOUNDERS, ASHLAND CONFEDERATED REPUBLIC, 2191

"You may forget, but I will tell you this:
That someone in some future time will think of us."

The two women stood contemplating the memorial for a few eternities before Jules released Mags' hand and walked over to set a single black rose on the grass in front of it. Mags grabbed her, buried her face in her long, black hair, and said, "God, honey, I fucking love you."

"I fucking love you, too, sugar. God, I . . . It's hard to believe in the future sometimes, but when I look at you, and I think about us, y'know what I see? I see a future worth fighting for."

"Hey, Jules?"

"Yeah?"

"That was gay."

THE END

NATALIE IRONSIDE was born in Warren County, Mississippi in the early 1990s and still hasn't recovered. At various points throughout her eventful and poorly-thought-out life, she has been a soldier, a (former) member of the white nationalist movement, and a soil analyst in addition to being an award-winning author of speculative fiction. The award she's always boasting about was for a short story contest at the Warren County Public Library that she won when she was in 10th grade. Also, she met Laura Jane Grace one time and hasn't shut up about it since.

Natalie currently resides in Florida, where she divides her time between gardening, looking at dirt, and organizing with the Industrial Workers of the World. She blogs regularly at https://wodneswynn.tumblr.com, can be found on Facebook at https://www.facebook.com/manygodsnomasters, and is very, very sorry.

Printed in Great Britain
by Amazon